THE SCARLET THREAD

the SCARLET THREAD

FRANCINE RIVERS

Tyndale House Publishers, Inc.
Carol Stream, Illinois

Visit Tyndale online at www.tyndale.com.

Check out the latest about Francine Rivers at www.francinerivers.com.

TYNDALE and Tyndale's quill logo are registered trademarks of Tyndale House Publishers, Inc.

The Scarlet Thread

Discussion guide section written by Peggy Lynch

Designed by Jennifer Ghionzoli

The Scarlet Thread is a work of fiction. Where real people, events, establishments, organizations, or locales appear, they are used fictitiously. All other elements of the novel are drawn from the author's imagination.

Library of Congress Cataloging-in-Publication Data

Rivers, Francine, date

The scarlet thread / Francine Rivers.
        p. cm.
ISBN 978-0-8423-3568-3 (sc)
I. Title.
PS3568.I83165S28 1996
813 .54—dc20   96-3721

Second repackage published in 2012 under ISBN 978-1-4143-7063-7.

Printed in the United States of America

18   17   16   15   14   13   12
7   6   5   4   3   2

To Sue Hahn, Fran Kane, and Donzella Schlager . . .

my traveling companions

Acknowledgments

Three very special people helped bring this story into being: Sue Hahn, Fran Kane, and Donzella Schlager, adventurers all, who shared a dream with me of traveling the Oregon Trail. With the blessings of our husbands, we took off in a Suburban and drove from Sebastopol, California, to Independence, Missouri. From there we followed the Oregon Trail to The Dalles, Oregon. Over five thousand miles together. We saw the beauty and vastness of our country, stopped at every historical landmark (and rest stop) along the road, visited every museum we could find (small town and large), and collected enough information to keep us reading for years to come.

Thanks, gals. It was one of the best times of my life.

When do we do the Lewis and Clark Trail?

Many thanks as well to Ryan MacDonald, for sharing his expertise in computer games and trade shows.

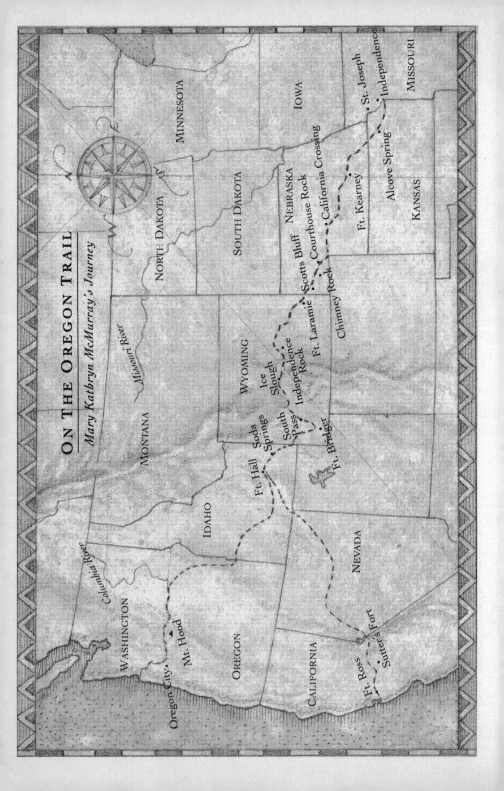

ON THE OREGON TRAIL

Mary Kathryn McMurray's Journey

PART I

THE CALL

CHAPTER I

SIERRA CLANTON MADRID couldn't stop shaking. Her stomach was quivering. Her head had begun throbbing with a tension headache the moment Alex had told her the news.

She hadn't had a headache like this since prom night during her senior year of high school. Alex had come to pick her up in his father's beat-up Chevy three minutes before her father turned in to the driveway. It was the first time in her life her father had come home *early* from work. She might have known it would be on that night. She could still remember the look on her father's face when he saw Alex—a drop-dead handsome, long-haired Hispanic boy dressed in a rented tuxedo—standing on the wide porch of her family's Mathesen Street Victorian. As if that wasn't bad enough, Alex was reaching forward to pin an orchid to the front of her fancy prom dress. When Sierra heard the slam of her father's car door, she almost fainted in fear.

The headache had started then and was only compounded by the inquiring look on Alex's face. "What's the matter?" he asked. What could she say? She had told her father about Alex; she just hadn't told him everything.

Words were exchanged, but, fortunately, her mother was there to intercede and calm her father down.

In the end, Alex escorted her to his borrowed car and helped her in while her father stood on the front steps glaring at him. Alex didn't so much as look at her as he put the Chevy in gear and pulled away from the curb. They were halfway to Santa Rosa before he said anything.

"You didn't tell him who was taking you to the prom, did you?"

"Yes, I did."

"Yeah, right. You just left out a few important details, didn't you, *chiquita*?" He had never called her that before, and it boded ill tidings for the night ahead. He didn't say anything more on the drive to the expensive restaurant in Santa Rosa. She ordered something cheap, which made him even madder.

"You think I can't afford to buy you anything more than a dinner salad?"

Her face aflame, she ordered the same prime rib dinner he did, but he didn't look any happier.

Things got worse as the evening wore on. By ten, Alex wasn't speaking at all, not to her, not to anyone. She ended up losing the nice dinner he bought her in the bathroom of the Villa de Chanticlair.

She'd been crazy in love with Alejandro Luís Madrid. *Crazy* being the operative word. Her father had warned her. She should have listened.

Sierra's eyes smarted with tears now as she drove along the Old Redwood Highway, which linked Windsor with

Healdsburg. For all of its turmoil, she preferred clinging to the now-romantic past rather than facing the uncertain, terrifying present and future.

Prom night had been such a disaster. When most of her friends were going to all-night parties in Santa Rosa, Alex took her home well before midnight. The front lights were turned on—and not discreetly. Her father had probably changed the 60-watt bulb to a 250 while she was gone. Even the inside lights were on that night.

There was plenty of light for her to see how angry Alex was. But his expression revealed something deeper than just anger. She could feel the hurt that lay hidden behind the cold, remote expression on his face. She thought he'd just walk away then. Unfortunately, he didn't intend to do so before he had his say.

"I knew it was a mistake to ever ask you out."

The words struck like a shotgun blast to her heart. He wasn't finished. "I'm not some character in a Shakespearean tragedy, Sierra. I'm not Romeo to your Juliet. And I didn't ask you out because I wanted to play around!" He turned away with that and almost reached the steps before she could speak past the tears choking her.

"I love you, Alex."

He turned around then and looked at her. "What'd you say?" His eyes were dark and hot, still filled with anger at her—with good cause. She hadn't considered what her silence would cost him. All she had thought about was avoiding a confrontation with her father.

Alex stood waiting.

"I—I said I love you."

"Say it in Spanish," he told her in the same tone he had used when tutoring her.

She swallowed, wondering if he only meant to humiliate

her more before he walked out of her life. *"Te amo,* Alejandro Luís Madrid. *Corazón y alma."* She started to cry then, hard wracking sobs. He caught hold of her and poured out his feelings in Spanish. Though she didn't fully understand the words, she saw in his eyes and felt in his touch that he loved her.

Infrequently over the years, he had fallen back into his first language during times of powerful emotions. He had spoken Spanish when he made love to her on their wedding night and again when she told him she was pregnant. He had wept and spoken Spanish in the wee hours of the morning when Clanton had pushed his way into the world and again when Carolyn was born. And he had spoken Spanish in tears on the night her father died.

But that night on the porch, they both forgot about the lights. In fact, they both forgot everything until the front door was jerked open and her father ordered him gone.

She was forbidden to see Alex. At the time, it didn't matter to her father that Alex was ranked number four in a class of two hundred students. What mattered was that Luís Madrid, Alex's father, was "one of those beaners" who worked as a laborer in the Sonoma County vineyards. Her father didn't care that Alex was working a forty-hour week at a local gas station to save money to put himself through college.

"I wish him luck," he said, and it was clear that luck was the last thing he wished Alex.

She reasoned, cajoled, whined, and begged. She appealed to her mother, who promptly refused to take her side. In desperation, she threatened to run away or commit suicide. She had gotten their attention with that.

"You so much as talk to that beaner on the phone and I'll call the police!" her father had yelled. "You're fifteen. He's eighteen. I could have him arrested!"

"You do and I'll tell the police you're abusing me!"

Her father called her aunt in Merced and made arrangements for her to spend a few weeks there "cooling off."

Alex was waiting when she returned, but he proved less malleable than her male parent. He had a few succinct Spanish words to say about her idea of meeting him in secret. Alex was a fighter who preferred facing wrath head-on. She had never expected that he would deal with the situation on his own. He just showed up at the house one day five minutes after her father had come home from work. She learned later from a neighbor that Alex had been waiting down the street for more than an hour. Her mother, sympathetic to their plight, invited Alex into the foyer before her father could get to the porch and order him off the property.

Clutching the steering wheel of her Honda Accord now, Sierra remembered how she had felt that day, seeing Alex standing in the front hallway between her mother and father. She had been so sure her father would kill him or at least beat him to within an inch of his life.

"What's *he* doing here?" She could still hear the anger in her father's voice as he dumped his briefcase on the floor. Sierra had been convinced he was only freeing his hands so he could get them around Alex's neck.

Alex stepped around her mother and faced him. "I came to ask permission to see your daughter."

"Permission! Like you asked permission to take her to the prom?"

"I thought Sierra cleared it with you. My mistake."

"You're right about that! A big mistake. Now get out of here!"

"Brian, give the young man the chance to—"

"Stay out of this, Marianna!"

Alex stood his ground. "All I ask is a fair hearing." He didn't even notice her standing above them on the stairs.

"I don't want to hear anything you have to say."

They were like two dogs with their hackles up. "Daddy, please . . . ," she said, coming down the stairs. "We love each other."

"*Love*. I doubt that's what he feels for you."

"You don't understand!" she wailed.

"I understand plenty! Get back to your room!"

"I'm not going anywhere but with Alex," she said, reaching the hallway and taking a position beside her boyfriend, and she knew in that instant that if her father came at him, she'd do whatever she had to do to stop him. She had never been so furious!

Alex clamped his hand on her wrist and firmly pulled her behind him. "This is between your father and me. Stay out of it." The whole time he spoke, he never took his eyes off her father.

"Get out of my house."

"All I want is a few minutes to speak to you, Mr. Clanton. If you tell me afterward to back off, I'll back off."

"All the way to Mexico?"

"Brian!"

As soon as her father uttered the words, his face turned beet red. Alex, with his own prejudices, had no intention of letting him off easily.

"I was *born* in Healdsburg, Mr. Clanton. Just like you. My father took his citizenship test ten years ago. Not that it makes much difference. He passed with flying colors. Red, white, and blue. He's never taken a dollar of welfare in his life, and he works hard for what he makes, probably harder than you do in that plush real estate office you have downtown. We don't live in a Victorian," he said with a swift, telling look around, "but we don't live in a shack either."

His little speech hadn't made anything better.

"You finished?" her father said, embarrassment burned away by anger.

"You might enjoy knowing that my father and mother disapprove of Sierra as much as you disapprove of me."

Her mouth fell open.

"Disapprove of Sierra?" her father said, insulted. "Why?"

"Why do you think, Mr. Clanton? She's white and she's Protestant."

"Maybe you ought to listen."

"I do listen. I've got a lot of respect for my parents, but I've got a mind of my own. The way I see it, a bigot is a bigot, no matter what color he is."

A long, hot silence filled the foyer.

"So," Alex said bleakly, "do we talk or do I walk?"

Her father looked at her for a moment and then back at Alex with resentful resignation. "We talk." He jerked his head toward a room off the hallway. "But I doubt you're going to like what I have to say."

They spent the next two hours in the small office at the front of the house while she sat in the kitchen with her mother, alternately crying and raging about what she'd do if her father wouldn't let her go out with Alex. Her mother hadn't said much of anything that day.

When her father came into the kitchen, he told her Alex was gone. Before she had time to scream recriminations, he informed her she could see him again, *after* she'd agreed to follow the *rules* the two of them had established. One phone conversation a night, no longer than thirty minutes and only *after* her schoolwork was finished. No dates Monday through Thursday. Friday night she was to be home by eleven. Saturday night by ten. Yes, *ten*. She had to be well rested for church on Sunday. If her grades dropped a smidgen, she was grounded from Alex completely. If she missed church, same consequences.

"And Alex agreed?"

"He agreed."

She hadn't liked any of it, but she had been so much in love she would have agreed to anything, and her father knew it.

"That boy's going to break your heart, Sierra."

Now, fourteen years later, he was doing just that.

Wiping tears from her eyes, Sierra drove across the Russian River bridge and turned right.

She knew her father had hoped things would cool off if he gave the relationship time to develop cracks. He hadn't known Alex then, nor did he see the determination and drive that burned in him. Alex graduated with honors from high school and entered the local junior college. Sierra had wanted to quit school and marry him, thinking it would be romantic to work and help put him through college. He squashed that idea. He told her in no uncertain terms that he intended to finish college *on his own*, and he sure didn't want a dropout for a wife. He completed two years of work at Santa Rosa Junior College in a year and a half and transferred to the University of California, Berkeley, where he majored in business, with an emphasis in computer technology. She finished high school and entered a local business college, counting the days to his graduation.

As soon as Alex returned to Healdsburg, he found a job with Hewlett-Packard in Santa Rosa, bought a used car, and rented a small bungalow in Windsor.

When they couldn't get their parents to agree on the kind of wedding they should have, they eloped to Reno. Nobody was very happy about it.

They had been married ten years. Ten wonderful years. All that time she'd thought Alex was as happy as she was. She never suspected what was going on beneath the surface. Why hadn't she realized? Why hadn't he told her straight out that he was dissatisfied?

Sierra pulled her Honda into the driveway of the Mathesen Street Victorian and prayed her mother was home. Mom had always been able to reason with Daddy. Maybe she could help Sierra figure out how to reason Alex out of his plans for their future.

Unlocking the front door, Sierra entered the polished wood foyer. "Mom?" She closed the door behind her and walked along the corridor toward the kitchen. She almost called for her father before she caught herself.

With a sharp pang, she remembered the call she and Alex had received at three in the morning two years ago. She had never heard her mother's voice sound that way before. Or since.

"Your father's had a heart attack, honey. The ambulance is here."

They had met her at Healdsburg District Hospital, but it was already too late.

"He complained of indigestion this morning," her mother had said, distracted, in shock. "And his shoulder was aching."

Now, Sierra paused at his office door and looked in, half-expecting to see him sitting at his desk reading the real estate section of the newspaper. She still missed him. Oddly, so did Alex. He and her father had become close after Clanton and Carolyn were born—amazing the way grandchildren seemed to break down walls between people. Prior to her pregnancy, she and Alex had seen little of her parents. Her father always found some excuse to turn down dinner invitations; Alex's parents were no better.

All that changed when she went into labor. Everyone was at Kaiser Hospital the night she gave birth. Alex had kissed her and said maybe they should name their son Makepeace.

They had settled on Clanton Luís Madrid, forging both families together. By the time Carolyn María arrived a year later, the Clantons and the Madrids had had plenty of opportunities to get to know one another and find out they had a lot more in common than they ever thought possible.

"Mom?" Sierra called again, not finding her in the kitchen. She looked out the window into the backyard garden, where her mother often worked. She wasn't there either. The Buick Regal was in the driveway, so she knew her mother wasn't off on one of her many charity projects or at the church.

Sierra went back along the corridor and up the stairs. "Mom?" Maybe she was taking a nap. She peered into the master bedroom. A bright granny-square afghan was folded neatly on the end of the bed. *"Mom?"*

"I'm in the attic, honey. Come on up."

Surprised, Sierra went down the hallway and climbed the narrow stairway. "What are you doing up here?" she said, entering the cluttered attic. The small dormer windows were open, allowing a faint sun-warmed breeze into the dusty, dimly lit room. Dust particles danced on the beam of sunlight. The place smelled musty with age and disuse.

The attic had always fascinated Sierra, and she momentarily put aside her worries as she looked around. Lawn chairs were stacked at the back. Just inside the door was a big milk can filled with old umbrellas, two canes, and a crooked walking stick. Wicker baskets in a dozen shapes and sizes sat on a high shelf. Boxes were stacked in odd piles, in no particular order, their contents a mystery.

How many times had she and her brother gone through their rooms, sorting and boxing and shoving discards into the attic? When Grandma and Grandpa Clanton had died, boxes from their estate had taken up residence in the quiet dimness. Old books, trunks, and boxes of dishes and silverware were scattered about. A hat tree stood in a back corner on an old braided rag rug that had been made by Sierra's great-grandmother. The box of old dress-up clothes she had donned as a child was still there. As was the large oval mirror where she had admired herself with each change.

Nearby, stacked in her brother's red Radio Flyer wagon, were a dozen or more framed pictures leaning one upon another against the wall. Some were original oils done by her grandfather during his retirement years. Others were family pictures that dated back several generations. Paint cans left over from restoration on the house were stacked on a shelf in case touch-ups were needed to the colorful trim. One bookshelf was filled with shoe boxes, each labeled in her father's neat printing and holding tax returns and business records going back twenty years.

A tattered, paint-chipped rocking horse stood in lonely exile in the far back corner.

Her mother had moved some of the old furniture around so that Grandpa Edgeworth's old couch with the lion-claw legs was sitting in the center of the attic. Opposite it was Daddy's old worn recliner. Two ratty needlepoint footstools served as stands for the things her mother had removed from an old trunk that stood open before her.

Marianna Clanton had a tea towel wrapped around her hair. "I thought I should go through some of these things and make some decisions."

"Decisions about what?" Sierra said, distracted.

"What to throw away, what to keep."

"Why now?"

"I should've started years ago," her mother said with a rueful smile. "I just kept putting it off." She looked around at the cluttered room. "It's a little overwhelming. Bits and pieces from so many lives."

Sierra ran her hand over an old stool that had been in the kitchenette before it was remodeled. She remembered coming home from kindergarten and climbing up on it at the breakfast bar so she could watch her mother make Toll House cookies. "Alex called me a little while ago and told me he's accepted a job in Los Angeles."

Her mother glanced up at her, a pained expression flickering across her face. "It was to be expected, I suppose."

"Expected? How?"

"Alex has always been ambitious."

"He has a good job. He got that big promotion last year, and he's making good money. They gave him a comprehensive health package and retirement plan. We have a wonderful new house. We like our neighbors. Clanton and Carolyn are happy in school. We're close to family. I didn't even know Alex had put out word he was looking for another position until he called me today—" Her voice broke. "He was so excited, Mom. You should've heard him. He said this new company made him a fantastic offer, and he accepted it without even talking to me about it."

"What sort of company?"

"Computers. *Games.* The sort of stuff Alex likes to play around with at home. He met these guys at a sales conference last spring in Las Vegas. He never even told me about them. He says he did, but I don't remember. Alex has been working on an idea he has for a role-playing game. Players could link up with others online and create armies and battle scenarios. He said it's right up their alley. And it doesn't even bother him that they haven't been in business four years yet or that they started business in a garage."

"So did Apple."

"That's different. These guys haven't been around long enough to prove they can *stay* in business. I don't see how Alex can throw away ten years' seniority at Hewlett-Packard when people are being laid off of other jobs left and right! I don't want to go to Los Angeles, Mom. Everything I love is here."

"You love Alex, honey."

"I'd like to *shoot* Alex! Where does he get off making a decision like this without even discussing it with me?"

"Would you have listened if he had?"

She couldn't believe her mother would ask such a thing. "Of course I'd listen! Doesn't he think it has anything to do with me?" She wiped angry tears from her cheeks. "You know what he said to me, Mom? He told me he'd already called a Realtor, and the woman's coming by tonight to list the house. Can you believe it? I just planted daffodils all along the back fence. If he has his way, I won't even be here to see them bloom!"

Her mother said nothing for a long moment. She folded her hands in her lap while Sierra rummaged through her shoulder bag for a Kleenex.

Sierra sniffled into the tissue. "It's not fair. He never even took my feelings into consideration, Mom. He just made the decision and told me it's a done deal. Just like that. Whether I like it or not, we're moving to Los Angeles. He doesn't even care how I feel about it because it's what *he* wants."

"I'm sure Alex didn't make the decision arbitrarily. He's always looked at everything from all sides."

"Not from *my* side." Restless and upset, she walked across the room and picked up an old stuffed bear her brother had cuddled when he was a boy. She hugged it against her. "Alex grew up here just like I did, Mom. I don't understand how he can turn his back on everything and be so *happy* about it."

"Maybe Alex wasn't treated as kindly as you were, Sierra."

Sierra glanced back at her mother in surprise. "His parents never abused him."

"I wasn't referring to Luís or María; they're wonderful people. I mean the assumptions too many people make about Hispanics."

"Well, he can add all that to the other things Los Angeles will have to offer. Smog. Traffic. Riots. Earthquakes."

Her mother smiled. "Disneyland. Movie stars. Beaches," she recited, clearly seeing a much more positive side to things. Daddy used to call it her Pollyanna attitude, especially when he was irritated and in no mood to see the good side of a situation. The way Sierra was feeling now.

"Everyone we love is here, Mom. Family, friends."

"You're not moving to Maine, honey. It's only a day's drive between Healdsburg and Los Angeles. And you can always call us."

"You talk as though it doesn't matter to you that we're leaving." Sierra bit her lip and looked away. "I thought you'd understand."

"If I could make the choice, of course, I'd rather you were here. And I do understand. Your grandparents were far from overjoyed when I moved from Fresno to San Francisco." She smiled. "It was a ten-hour drive in those days, but you'd have thought I'd moved to the far side of the moon."

Sierra smiled wanly. "It's hard for me to see you as some sort of beatnik living in San Francisco, Mom."

She laughed. "No less hard than it is for me to see you as a young woman with a wonderful husband and two children in school."

Sierra blew her nose. "Wonderful husband," she muttered. "He's a male chauvinist pig. Alex probably hasn't even bothered to mention this to his parents."

"Luís will understand. Just as your father would have. I think Alex has stayed here for ten years because of you. It's time you allow him to do what he needs to do to make full use of the talents he has."

It was the last thing Sierra wanted to hear. She didn't reply as she ran her hand along the books in an old shelf. She knew what her mother said had merit, but that didn't mean she wanted to listen. Alex had received other offers and turned each down after discussing them with her. She had thought the decisions mutual, but now she wondered. He had sounded so excited and happy when he talked to her about this job. . . .

She plucked *Winnie the Pooh* out and blew dust off the top. Stroking the front of the book, she remembered sitting in her mother's lap as the story was read to her. How many times had she heard it? The cover was worn from handling.

Just thinking about leaving and not being able to see her mother or talk with her every few days left Sierra feeling bereft. Tears blurred her vision.

"Alex gave notice this morning." She pushed the book back into its space. "It was the first thing he did after he got the call from Los Angeles. *Then* he called me with the *great* news." Covering her face, she wept.

Sierra felt some comfort when her mother's arms came around her.

"It'll be all right, honey. You'll see." Her mother stroked her back as though she were a child. "Things have a way of working out for the best. The Lord has plans for you and for Alex, plans for your good, not your destruction. Trust Him."

The Lord! Why did her mother always have to bring up *the Lord*? What sort of plan was it to tear people's lives apart?

She withdrew from her mother's arms. "All our friends are here. *You're* here. I don't want to move. It makes no sense. What does Alex think he'll find in Los Angeles that he doesn't already have here?"

"Maybe he wants the chance to prove himself."

"He *has* proven himself. He's succeeded at everything he's ever done."

"Maybe he doesn't feel he's done enough."

"He doesn't have to prove anything to me," Sierra said, her voice choked.

"Sometimes men have to prove things to themselves, Sierra." She took her daughter's hand. "Sit, honey." She drew her down onto the old faded couch. Patting her hand, she smiled wistfully. "I remember Alex talking with your father about all the frustrations he felt in his job."

"Daddy was the one who told Alex to settle in and stay put so he'd have all the benefits."

"Your father was worried Alex would do the same thing he did."

She blew her nose and glanced at her mother. "What do you mean?"

"Your father changed jobs half a dozen times before he settled into real estate."

"He did? I don't remember that."

"You were too young to notice." Her mother smiled wistfully. "Your father intended to be a high school biology teacher."

"Daddy? A teacher?" She couldn't imagine it. He wouldn't have put up with anything. The first student to shoot a spit wad would have found himself upside down in a garbage can outside the classroom door.

Her mother laughed. "Yes, Daddy. He spent five years in college preparing to do just that and after one year in a classroom decided he hated it. He said the girls were all airheads and the boys were running on testosterone."

Sierra smiled, amazed and amused. "I can't even imagine."

"Your dad went to work in a lab then. He hated that, too.

He said staring into microscopes all day bored him senseless. So he went to work for a men's clothing store."

"Daddy?" Sierra said again, astounded.

"Yes, *Daddy*. You and Mike were both in school when he quit. After that, he trained to become a police officer. I was as strongly against that as you are against moving to Los Angeles." She patted Sierra's hand again. "But good came out of it. I used to lie awake at night, worrying myself sick over him. I was so sure something would happen to him. Those years were the worst of my life, and our marriage suffered because of it. And yet the greatest blessing came from it, too. I became a Christian while your father was working the eleven-to-seven shift as a highway patrolman."

"I didn't know all this, Mom."

"Why would you? A mother hardly shares these kinds of struggles with her young children. You were four and Mike was seven. Neither of you were happy. You sensed the tension between us and didn't understand. You didn't see that much of your father when he was home because he had to sleep during the day. I spent most of my time telling you two to be quiet and trying to keep you busy with games and puzzles and long walks. The hours and stress were bad enough for Daddy, but I think it was missing you and Mike that finally made him quit. Before he did, he studied for his real estate license. He gave it a try and loved it. As God would have it, he started at the time when real estate was booming. It was a seller's market. Within two years of getting his license, your dad was one of the top Realtors in Sonoma County. He became so busy, he dropped residential and specialized in commercial properties."

She squeezed Sierra's hand. "The point I'm trying to make is this, honey: it took your father sixteen years to settle into a career he enjoyed." She smiled. "Alex knew what he wanted to do when he went to college. The trouble is, he's never had the opportunity to accomplish it. The greatest gift you can give him is the freedom to spread his wings."

Again, this wasn't what Sierra wanted to hear. "You talk as though I've put a ball and chain around his neck." She stood and began pacing again. "I'd like to have been consulted, Mom. Is that so hard to understand? Alex didn't even discuss the offer with me. He accepted it and then informed me of his decision. It's not fair."

"Who ever said life was fair?" her mother responded, hands folded.

Sierra felt defensive and angry. "Daddy didn't make you move."

"No, he didn't. I would have been delighted if he had."

Sierra turned and stared at her. "I thought you loved Healdsburg."

"Now I do. When I was younger, all I could think about was getting away from here. I thought how wonderful it would be to live in a big city like San Francisco where lots of things were going on. You know I grew up on Grandma's farm in Central Valley, and believe me, it was anything but exciting, honey. I wanted to go to the theater and attend concerts. I wanted to immerse myself in museums and culture. I wanted to walk through Golden Gate Park. And, despite warnings and pleadings from my parents, I did just that."

"And met Daddy."

"Yes. He rescued me from a mugging on the Pan Handle."

Sierra thought of the wedding photo on the mantel downstairs. Her father's hair had been long then, and his "tuxedo" consisted of worn Levi's and heavy boots; her mother, dressed in a black turtleneck and capri pants, had woven flowers in her waist-length auburn hair. The photo had always jarred with the image she had of her parents. They had been *young* once—and rebellious, too.

Her mother smiled, remembering. "If I'd had my way, we would have settled in San Francisco."

"You never told me that before."

"By the time you and your brother came along, my ideas about what I wanted had changed drastically. Just as your ideas will change. Life isn't static, Sierra. Thank God. It's constantly in motion. Sometimes we find ourselves caught up in currents and carried along where we don't want to go. Then we find out later that God's hand was in it all along."

"God didn't make the decision to move to Los Angeles. Alex made it. But then, I suppose he thinks he's God." Sierra could hear the resentment in her voice, but she hardened herself against any regret or guilt. Emotions raged and warred within her: resentment that Alex had made such a decision without talking to her beforehand; fear that if she fought him, she'd lose anyway; terror of leaving a life she loved and found so comfortable.

"What am I going to do, Mom?"

"That's up to you, honey," her mother said gently, tears of compassion in her eyes.

"I need your advice."

"The second greatest commandment is that we love one another as we love ourselves, Sierra. Forget yourself and think about what Alex needs. Love him accordingly."

"If I do that, he'll walk all over me. Next time, he'll jump at a job in New York City!" She knew she was being unfair even as she said it. Alex had given her two beautiful children, a nice three-bedroom home in Windsor, and a secure, happy life. Life had been so smooth, in fact, she had never once suspected the turmoil within him. Realizing that frightened her. It made her feel she didn't know Alex's heart or mind as well as she thought she did.

She couldn't see a way out. Part of her wanted to pick up the children from school and come back here to the Mathesen Street home and let Alex face the real estate woman alone; he couldn't sell the house if she didn't sign. But she knew if she did that, he'd be furious. The few times she had unintentionally hurt him, he had retreated into anger, putting up a cold front and withdrawing into silence. He didn't come from a family of yellers. She didn't even want to think about how he would respond if she hurt and angered him deliberately.

"It might help to take your mind off the matter for a few hours and then try to think about it later," her mother said.

Heart aching, Sierra sat down on the sofa again. She looked at the open trunk and piles of boxes. "Why are you doing all this now, Mom?"

Something flickered in her mother's eyes. "It's a good winter activity, don't you think?" She glanced around. "It's such a mess. Your father and I meant to go through all this stuff years ago, but then . . ." She looked sad. "Time has a way of getting away from us." She looked around the room at the odd assortment of treasures, some ratty and from long-forgotten sources. "I don't want to leave all this chaos for you and Mike to have to figure out."

She rose and walked around the attic, brushing her hand lightly over an old rocking chair, a bookshelf, a baby's pram.

"I'm going to sort and put all of Mike's and your things over there in the north corner. You two can decide what you want to keep and what you want to throw away. Special things from your father's family and mine, I'll repack. Most of your father's papers from the business can be burned. There's no point in keeping them. And Grandpa's paintings . . . some of them are disintegrating."

"Some of them are really bad," Sierra said, grinning.

"That, too," her mother agreed with a laugh. "It kept him occupied." She stopped near the window, glancing out at the front lawn, her expression pensive. "There are a lot of family papers. I'll have all winter to go through and organize them for you and Mike." She glanced back at Sierra and smiled. "It's a big job, but I think it'll be fun and interesting."

She came back and sat down on the old flowered sofa. "This trunk belonged to Mary Kathryn McMurray. She was one of your ancestors. She came across the plains in a wagon in 1847. I was just glancing through her journal when you came," she said, taking up a leather-bound volume from the trunk and brushing her hand over it. "I hadn't gotten very far. Apparently, this was an assignment book and then it became her diary."

She set the volume between them on the couch. Sierra picked it up and opened it, reading the childish scrawl on the first page.

Mama says livin in the wildurnes aint no resun to bee ignurant. Her papa wuz a larnud man and wud not want fuls in his famlee.

"The trunk was part of Grandpa Clanton's estate," her mother said. "I haven't gone through these things in years." She lifted out a small carved wooden box. "Oh, I remember this," she said, smiling. Inside was an embroidered silk handkerchief. She unfolded it carefully and showed Sierra the antique gold chain and amethyst cross.

"Oh, it's beautiful," Sierra said, taking it and admiring it.

"You may have it, if you'd like."

"I'd love it," Sierra said, opening the small clasp and putting it on.

Her mother took out an old tintype in an oval frame. The

couple were dressed in wedding clothes, their expressions solemn rather than joyful. The groom was handsome in his dark suit and starched shirt, his dark hair brushed back cleanly from chiseled features and intense pale eyes. Blue, Sierra decided. They would have had to be blue to be so pale in the picture. The bride was very young and lovely. She was wearing a gorgeous white lace Victorian wedding dress. She sat while her husband stood, his hand firmly planted upon her shoulder.

Sierra took out another box. Inside, wrapped in tissue paper, was a small woven Indian basket with designs. Around the top edge were quail plumes and beads. "I think this is a gift basket, Mom. It's worth a lot of money. They have them in the Indian Museum at Sutter's Fort."

"Is there anything inside the box to tell about it?"

Sierra removed everything and shook her head. "Nothing."

"Look at this old Bible," her mother said, distracted. As she opened it, a section slipped free and fell onto the floor. Her mother picked it up and placed it on the sofa beside her.

Sierra picked up the paper yellowed with age and read the pretty script.

Dearest Mary Kathryn,

I hope you have changed your mind about God. He loves you very much and He is watching over you. I do not know what hardships and losses you will face on the way to Oregon or what will happen once you reach the end of the trail. What I do know is God will never leave you nor forsake you.

You have my love and are in my morning and evening prayers. The ladies from the quilting club send their love as well, as do Betsy and Clovis. May the Lord bless your new home.

Aunt Martha

24

Sierra's mother thumbed through the black, cracked leather Bible and then picked up the portion that had fallen. "Look at how worn the pages are." She smiled. "Mary Kathryn favored the Gospels." She took the note from Sierra and read it. Folding it, she tucked it in the loosened pages and set the Bible carefully beside Mary Kathryn McMurray's journal.

Sierra took out a decaying flowered hatbox. She found a note on top saying simply, in beautiful black calligraphy, "Save for Joshua McMurray." The box was full of animals, carved of wood, each wrapped carefully in a scrap of flowered calico or checked gingham. She unwrapped a fierce-looking wolf, a majestic buffalo, a coiled rattlesnake, a prairie dog standing on its hind legs, a comical jackrabbit, a beautiful antelope, two mountain goats locked together in fierce battle, and a grizzly bear standing upright, ready to attack.

At the bottom of the trunk was a large package wrapped in butcher paper and tied with string.

"I don't remember this," her mother said and slipped the string off so she could remove the wrapping. *"Oh,"* she said in wonder and excitement. "I think it's a crazy quilt." She unfolded it enough so that Sierra could take one end of it and then stood, spreading the folds to reveal the full pattern.

It wasn't a crazy quilt, but a picture quilt with squares made of hundreds of different scraps of cloth, each with a different scene, each framed with an edging of brown, and all stitched together with vibrant scarlet thread. Each picture block was surrounded by a different stitch: blanket, crosses, herringbone, doves, fern, olive branches, feather, open cretan, fly, zigzag chain, wheatear and sheaf filling stitches, Portuguese border, and star eyelets.

"It's beautiful," Sierra said, wishing she could have it.

"If I'd known it was here, I would have had it cleaned and hung on the living room wall years ago," her mother said.

Sierra looked at the squares one by one. Along the top row was a homestead with a man, a woman, and three children. Two boys and a girl stood in the open space between the cabin and barn. The second square was bright with consuming flames. The third showed a baby in a manger, a young girl watching over him while darkness surrounded them both.

The telephone rang downstairs. A second later, the portable phone rang from nearby. Sierra's mother handed her the other end of the quilt and went to pick up the phone from the top of a box and answer it.

"Yes, she's here, Alex."

Sierra's heart lurched. Hands trembling again, she folded the quilt while listening to her mother's side of the conversation.

"Yes, she told me. Yes, but that's to be expected, Alex." Her mother's tone held no condemnation or disappointment. She was silent for a long moment, listening again. "I know that, Alex," she said very gently, her voice husky with emotion, "and I've always been thankful. You don't have to explain." Another silence. "So soon," her mother said, resigned. "How are your parents taking it? Oh. Well, I imagine it's going to be a shock to them as well." She smiled faintly. "Of course, Alex. You know I will. Let me know after you've spoken to them, and I'll call."

Marianna cupped her hand over the receiver. "Alex wants to talk to you."

Sierra wanted to say she didn't want to talk to him but knew that would put her mother between them. She laid the folded quilt back over the trunk and crossed the attic to take the phone from her mother's hand.

"I'll make us some coffee," her mother said with a gentle smile.

Sierra watched her go down the stairs, knowing her

mother was allowing her privacy to speak with Alex. She felt a tangle of emotions, from relief to despair. Her mother hadn't said one word to discourage Alex from his decision. Why not?

"Yes?" she said into the receiver, her voice coming out thin and choked. She wanted to scream at him and could barely draw breath past the pain in her chest. Her throat was tight and dry.

"I was worried about you."

"Were you?" Why should he worry about her just because he was ripping her life apart? Resentment filled her and hot tears welled again in her eyes.

"You're not saying much."

"What do you want me to say? That I'm *happy*?"

He sighed. "I suppose that would be expecting too much, especially considering this is the biggest opportunity of my career."

She heard the tinge of disappointment and anger in his voice. What right had he to be angry with her after making a life-changing decision without so much as hinting it to her?

"I'm sure the children will be thrilled to hear they're being uprooted and torn away from their friends and family."

"*We're* their family."

"What about Mom? What about your parents?"

"We're not moving to New York, Sierra."

"I guess you're saving that for next year's big surprise."

Silence followed. Her heart picked up speed; she could feel his growing anger.

Stop this now, an inner voice cautioned her. *Stop before you go too far. . . .*

She wasn't interested in stopping. "You might have hinted what was going on, Alex," she said, clutching the phone.

"I've done more than hint. I told you about this company

weeks ago. I've been telling you for the last four years what I want to do. The problem is you don't listen."

"I listen."

"And never *hear*."

"I do too hear!"

"Then hear *this*. You've had it your way for ten years. Maybe, just for a change, you could cut *me* a little slack."

Click.

"Alex?" Dead silence filled her ear. Sierra blinked, shocked. She stared at the phone in her hand as though it had turned to a venomous snake. Alex had never hung up on her before.

More distressed than when she had arrived, Sierra went downstairs. The tantalizing aroma of freshly ground caramel au lait decaf filled the kitchen. Her favorite. So, too, were the Toll House cookies her mother had put on a dessert plate in the sunny alcove overlooking the back garden. Clearly Mom wanted to cheer her up. Fat chance.

She plunked the phone down on the pretty flower-embroidered cloth covering the small table and sank down onto the chair. "He hung up on me." Her mother poured coffee for her. "He's never hung up on me before," Sierra continued, her voice breaking as she looked up at her mother. He'd made a decision he knew would tear her life to pieces, and then *he* hung up on *her*? "He said I don't listen."

Her mother set the carafe on a sunflower trivet and took the seat facing her. "Sometimes we only hear what we want to hear." She picked up her coffee cup and sipped, distracted.

"You look tired, Mom."

"I didn't sleep very well last night. I kept thinking about your father." Her mouth curved faintly, her expression softening. "Sometimes I imagine him sitting in his chair watching the news on television. The house creaks and I awaken, thinking he's coming along to bed." She smiled sadly and looked down into her coffee as she set the cup back in its porcelain saucer. "I miss him."

"I miss him, too." He might have been able to talk Alex out of going to Los Angeles.

Her mother lifted her head and looked across at her with gentle humor. "Your father wasn't an easy man either, Sierra, but he was worth it."

"If Alex insists, I'll go, but I don't have to smile and pretend to be happy about it."

"Maybe not, but it'd be better if you came to terms with his decision. Resentment and anger eat away at love as quickly as rust is corroding that metal lawn chair out there in the backyard. One of life's great tragedies is watching a relationship unravel over something that could've been resolved in one intelligent, adult conversation."

Her mother's words hurt. "One conversation isn't going to change Alex's mind."

"Then it depends on what you really want."

Sierra raised tear-soaked eyes to her mother's clear hazel ones. "What do you mean?"

Marianna reached out and took her daughter's hand. "It's simple, Sierra. Do you want your own way, or do you want Alex?"

CHAPTER 2

SIERRA LEFT HER MOTHER in time to drive to Windsor and pick up the children from school. They slammed into the car and immediately began vying for her undivided attention. She was often amused by their antics. Today their youthful exuberance and competitiveness irritated. As she drove along Brooks Road toward the foothills, she heard only bits and pieces of their day, distracted by her own turbulent thoughts. She longed for a quiet place to lick her wounds.

Her heart began beating a battle rhythm when she saw Alex's Honda in the driveway. He never came home before five thirty.

"Daddy's home!" Carolyn said, dashing out the car door toward the front steps, her backpack forgotten in the front seat.

Sierra pressed the garage door opener and watched the

door lift slowly. She drove in, shifted into park, put on the brake, and turned off the engine—each movement carefully measured and controlled. "Take Carolyn's things in, would you please, Clanton?"

"Let her come out and get 'em herself."

"It wouldn't hurt you to help—"

"I'm not her personal servant. Besides, she was just bragging about girls being better than boys. So let Little Miss Wonderful carry her own backpack!"

"Don't argue with me. I'm not in the mood for it."

Clanton grumbled, but one look at her face silenced further protests. Sierra gathered her own things and followed him into the kitchen. She could hear Carolyn chattering happily and Alex's deep laugh. A sharp pang shot through her, though whether it was pain or anger, she couldn't tell. Maybe both. How could he laugh at a time like this? Didn't he care at all how she felt?

"Why are you home early, Dad?" Clanton's excited voice carried easily, as did the thud of the two backpacks hitting the living room floor. Alex answered too quietly for her to hear what he was saying, and she clenched her teeth. As she opened a cabinet and took a can of coffee down from the shelf, she listened to the quiet murmur of voices, subdued now. Was he telling the children he had decided to uproot them and take them away from friends and family? How were they taking it? She knew she should be there, helping them understand . . . but how could she do that when she didn't understand herself? Her hand trembled as she measured grounds.

Her throat closed tightly when she heard Alex enter the kitchen. She didn't look at him. She couldn't and still maintain any semblance of control. She poured water into the coffeemaker and then turned her attention to the package of chicken she had left to thaw on the counter.

"I'm sorry I hung up on you." His deep voice was low and quiet.

Her eyes burned. She removed the plastic wrap from the chicken and turned on the water. "Did you tell them?"

"Yes."

She took a thigh from the open package and began washing it meticulously. "And?"

"Carolyn's going down to Karen's house. Clanton's riding his bike over to David's."

"I never let them go anywhere until they finish their homework."

"Well, I think this is a day for exceptions to the rule, don't you?" He sounded so in control. It grated on her nerves. "I told them to be home by five." He leaned against the doorframe and crossed his arms. "I thought it might be a good idea to have them both out of the house while we talk things over."

"Talk?" she said stiffly. "It's a little late, isn't it? I was under the impression you'd already decided everything."

"Fine," he said tightly. "We'll do this your way. We *won't* talk."

Glancing back, she saw him go back into the family room. Her heart pounded heavily, her stomach tightened. It was the second time today he had flung an unfair accusation at her! She pitched the last piece of rinsed chicken onto the cutting board, washed her hands with soap, and slapped off the tap. Snatching the towel from the oven door handle, she dried her hands quickly, then flung the towel in the direction of the counter before following him, trembling with anger.

"*My* way," she said. "You're the one who called and said we're moving. 'Oh, and by the way, Sierra, a Realtor's coming by tonight to list your home!'"

"*Our* home," he corrected, his dark eyes narrowing.

"That's what I thought until you dropped your bomb!"

"I made a judgment call."

"You just got a promotion *and* a raise. When most people are shaking in their boots about the possibility of being laid off, you have job security, pension, health coverage. We have a nice home. The children are happy—"

"Most people never get an opportunity like this, Sierra."

"An opportunity for what? To work for a new company that may go broke in a year?"

"I don't think that's likely."

"But you don't know for sure."

"No, I don't know for sure," he said, angry now. "I haven't got a crystal ball. But I have a strong feeling about where they're going, and I want to go along for the ride."

"A *feeling*? And you talk about me basing everything on emotions."

"This is different," he said through his teeth.

"What's different about it? You've worked so hard for security—"

"Security isn't everything."

She closed her ears to his remark. "And now you're throwing everything away on a whim."

"I'm not throwing anything away! You still don't get it, do you? Everything I've done up to now has been to prepare myself for an opportunity like *this*. I'm not going to spend the rest of my life building someone else's ideas. I have my own!"

"Why can't you do what you want on your own time *here*?"

"Because I don't have the equipment it takes."

"And what if it doesn't work out, Alex?"

"I'll cross that bridge *if* I come to it."

Shaking violently, she sank down onto the sofa, her hands clenched into fists as she fought her tears. "I don't want to move, Alex."

"Don't you think I know that?" he said, sounding torn between frustration and understanding. "You'd be happy if we stayed in this place for the rest of our lives."

She met his troubled gaze. "What's wrong with this place?"

"I want more out of life than a thirty-year mortgage on a tract house."

A tract house? Was that how he saw their home? He made it sound like a cardboard box. She thought of the time she had spent painting, hanging wallpaper, planting and tending the front and back yards so that it looked like an English garden. Hurt beyond words, she covered her face and wept.

Alex said a short, foul word under his breath and sat on the sofa beside her. "My little homebody," he said tenderly, touching her hair. She jerked away and started to get up. He caught her wrist and jerked her down again. "You're not going anywhere."

She cried harder, and he pulled her firmly into his arms, swearing softly under his breath again. "I know you're scared, Sierra. You've spent your whole life in Healdsburg. What do you know about anything else? You think this place is the end-all of creation."

"Most of the people in Los Angeles would probably think they'd died and gone to heaven if they could live where we do."

"People who aren't going anywhere, anyway. I should've taken you to Berkeley with me. Then maybe you'd understand how a place can hum with ideas and excitement. That's what I feel when I'm around these guys. *Energy*."

She didn't know what he was talking about, but she felt the excitement running through him.

"I graduated with honors, Sierra, and what am I doing with what I learned?" He gave a dismal laugh under his breath. "Nothing."

She struggled free. "How can you say that? You've been working only ten years, and you've already accomplished what most people spend their whole lives trying to do."

"Yeah," he said cynically. "A three-bedroom, two-bath tract house that looks like every other house on the block. Two children. Two cars. All we lack is the dog and cat to fit into the mold of middle-class America. Big deal!" His eyes burned with intensity.

She went cold inside at the way he described their life.

He searched her face. "Don't look at me like that, Sierra," he said, softening. He cupped her face. "I'm not criticizing you or what you've done to make this place a home. I didn't make this decision to hurt you. I *love* you." He kissed her. "You know I love you. I've done everything so far to make you happy."

"I am happy, Alex."

"I know," he said grimly, his hands sliding away. "The trouble is, I'm not."

His softly spoken words struck a stunning blow. Fear and confusion gripped her. He was telling her she wasn't enough; he wasn't satisfied.

"I want more, Sierra. I'm still hungry. I want to explore new frontiers in computer technology. I want a chance to do something meaningful." He smiled wryly. "And maybe even get rich while doing it."

When she remained silent, he spent the next hour telling her all the details of his new job. She couldn't remember ever seeing him so excited about anything. Depressed, she said she needed to start dinner.

"I'll fly down to Los Angeles on Saturday," Alex said, leaning against the doorframe and watching her work. "Steve Silverman made an appointment for me with a Realtor who handles rentals in North Hollywood. He knows everyone in that area."

Good for him, Sierra thought rebelliously. Her hands shook as she peeled potatoes. "How soon do we have to move?"

"I start on the first of the month."

"Three weeks?" She could feel the blood draining from her face. "But the house will never sell in three weeks," she said shakily, looking for any excuse to delay his plans.

"Probably not, but that's okay, too. One of the guys at work is going to rent it."

Sierra blinked. "Rent it?"

"His wife's expecting a baby, and they've been looking for a bigger place." The telephone rang. "Our house payments are less than what they're paying to rent a two-bedroom apartment," he said over his shoulder as he went to answer it in the family room.

She could hear Alex speaking in the other room. "We were just talking about it. No, but I didn't expect her to be. Don't worry about it." Silence for a long moment.

Sierra looked out the kitchen window at the daffodils she had just planted along the back fence. She'd never see them bloom.

"I land in Burbank at ten fifteen. No, but thanks for the offer, Steve. I'm going to rent a car. I want to drive around and get a feel for the area." He laughed. "I have a good sense of direction."

Tears ran down Sierra's cheeks as she finished preparing their dinner. Normally she enjoyed cooking; right now, even the sight of food made her stomach churn.

Alex was still talking on the telephone. Discussing terms. He sounded very cool, very much in control.

He was going through with this. Nothing she'd said had gotten through.

Oh, God, she prayed frantically. *If You're really there, don't let Alex do this to me. Put stumbling blocks in his way. Open his eyes to what he has here. Make him satisfied. Don't let the house sell. Change his mind. I don't want to move! Jesus, I want to stay right here where I am. Oh, God, please don't let this happen!*

Slamming the head of lettuce on the counter, she pulled out the core. She put the plug in the sink and ran cold water and then pulled the head of lettuce into pieces.

With each action, she whispered brokenly. "Oh, God. Oh, God, oh, God, oh, God." Her shoulders shook with her quiet weeping as she listened to Alex shattering her life with his plans.

PART 2

THE WILDERNESS

CHAPTER 3

EXHAUSTED, SIERRA PULLED her Honda in behind the big
U-Haul truck Alex had rented to move all their possessions
and to tow his car. Clanton got out the passenger side of the
truck and looked up at the big stark-white apartment complex. Sierra followed his gaze.

The place had all the charm of a fortress.

She rolled down her window, not eager to get out into the
cold, driving January rain. She could hear the roar of traffic
from two intersecting freeways half a block away. "Is this it?"

"It looks a lot better inside. Come on. I'll show you
around."

She leaned across the seat and kissed Carolyn, awakening
her. "We're here, sweetheart."

Carolyn looked out at the apartment house. "It's ugly," she said glumly. Sierra didn't disagree.

Clanton was already going through the iron gates into the complex. "Hey! There's a pool! Can I go swimming, Dad?"

"Sure, if we can find your suit," Alex said, laughing.

As Sierra climbed out of the car and came around for Carolyn, she was certain she could smell and taste the smog despite the rain pouring down on her head. She took her still-sleepy daughter by the hand and followed Alex through the gate. The inside courtyard was sterile: a gray cement patio, white stucco walls, and a black iron fence. Three stories of apartments were stacked together like crates in a warehouse. Geometric. Ultramodern. Cold and impersonal.

Sierra didn't see any signs of life until a woman peered out at her from a first-floor living room window. Sierra forced a smile. The woman drew back sharply and let the sheer drapes fall into place once more.

Welcome home, Sierra thought bitterly, following Alex.

"We're on the second floor, apartment D," he said. Clanton was first to the stairs, eager to see his new home.

The apartment was as white inside as the building was outside, except for the rug, which was a pale beige. The living room was roomy enough, but the kitchen was cramped and utterly utilitarian. The small dining area was barely large enough to accommodate a table and four chairs. Sierra wandered into the hallway. To the left was the bedroom Clanton and Carolyn would share. It was only big enough for twin beds and one dresser. The other dresser would have to go into the closet. Sierra's mouth thinned. Clanton and Carolyn were going to love this; they were fighting already.

A glance into the bathroom revealed walls, tiles, and a commode in antiseptic white. She continued down the short hallway into the master bedroom. Most of their furniture would fit, though Alex's armoire would probably have to go inside the closet. Sierra caught her reflection in the mirror on the closet doors; she did not look pleased. Turning away, she went to open the drapes covering a large window and discovered a view of the courtyard and pool below. Just like a hotel.

Depressed, she went back into the living room.

Alex hung up the telephone that Steve Silverman, his new boss, had been kind enough to have installed before their arrival. Steve had told Alex to call as soon as they arrived, and he and Matt would come with helpers to get them settled. "They'll be here in ten minutes," Alex said, grinning. Either oblivious to or ignoring her mood, he caught hold of her shoulders and kissed her before heading for the door.

❖

In less than two hours, all their furniture was in position and boxes stacked high against the living room wall. Steve had a couple of pizzas delivered. Matt had brought a six-pack of beer and another of soda. Clanton and Carolyn tucked away the food eagerly while Sierra pleaded no appetite and escaped into the bedrooms to hide her angst. She made the beds, hung pictures, laid out the bathroom rug and towels. Then she set to work on the master bedroom, the sound of the men's laughter irritating her more with each passing minute.

Clanton found his bathing suit. Her first *no* brought out his debating skills. Her mother always said Clanton would make a good lawyer. "I said no, Clanton. It's raining and . . ."

He followed her out into the living room and appealed to Alex. "Dad, can I go swimming? The rain isn't going to hurt me."

"Sure. Go ahead," Alex said, pausing in his conversation

with Steve and Matt long enough to gainsay her. He saw her expression after the fact. "What's the big deal?" he said as Clanton charged out the door before she could say anything. "He's going to get wet anyway, and the pool's heated."

"Fine. You stand out in the rain and keep an eye on him," she said, her fury far exceeding the incident. Swinging around, she went back into the master bedroom and plunked down on the bed.

Alex came in a moment later, tight-lipped. "We're going out for a while."

"Out?"

"For an hour or two. To talk business."

She clenched her hands, wanting to scream. "Is Clanton back from his swim?" she said with icy sweetness.

He stalked across the room. "You can sit nice and cozy where you are and keep an eye on him while you're sulking."

Raw and exhausted, she looked at him. "What about groceries, or will there be enough pizza left for breakfast?"

"If you look out the front gate, you'll see the back of one of the biggest supermarkets in North Hollywood. You've got a car, and you've got the checkbook. Get what you need." He went to the door and stopped. He uttered a soft curse and slammed the heel of his fist against the frame. "I'm sorry," he said bleakly.

Blinking back tears, she looked away.

"This is only temporary, Sierra."

Still she said nothing.

"I'll hook up the TV before we leave."

"Great. That'll be a real comfort," she muttered under her breath as he left the room. A few moments later she watched him walk by the bedroom window with Steve and Matt. They were so intent on their conversation that he didn't even spare a glance at her. She was already forgotten.

❖

Clanton and Carolyn were asleep in bed before he returned.

"An hour or two?" she said when he walked in the door.

He shrugged off his jacket and tossed it on the sofa. "We had a lot to talk about."

She snapped off the television. She hadn't even been paying attention to what she was watching, so intent was she on the time. "It's after midnight, Alex. I've been worried sick. You could've called."

"I would've if I could've remembered the number. We're unlisted."

An excuse, not an apology. "I'm going to bed," she said in a choked voice and left him standing in the living room.

She brushed her teeth and washed her face, then went into the bedroom to undress. Alex came in as she was pulling on her nightgown. "It's been a long day," he said.

"The longest of my life."

She got into bed and pulled the covers up to her chin, staring up at the dark ceiling. She heard the whisper of clothing as Alex undressed. The bed dipped slightly when he sat down on it. He didn't say anything more. What could he say? Swallowing hot tears, she turned her back to him while he set the alarm clock. When he lay back, he let his breath out slowly.

She felt his hand curve over her hip and squeeze slightly. "I'm sorry."

His apology brought a rush of feelings and a flood of tears. She dug her fingers into her pillow, trying to stifle her sobs. Alex turned to her. Curving his body around hers, he pulled her into him, holding her firmly when she resisted his comfort. He stroked her long hair back and kissed the curve of her neck. "I love you."

She cried harder.

He turned her to him gently. "Trust me," he said raggedly and kissed her, comforting her in the only way he knew how.

And for a while, Sierra was able to forget everything but the fact that she loved Alejandro Madrid above all else.

CHAPTER 4

ARMED WITH A MAP and an address, Sierra set off to enroll the children in school. She missed a turn and got lost. By the time she found what she was looking for, she and the children had seen North Hollywood, a portion of Studio City, eaten at a McDonald's, and toured most of Sherman Oaks and San Fernando Valley. They arrived and entered the school building just as the bell rang to end the day.

Children poured out of classrooms and filled the hallway. The cacophony of squeaking tennis shoes, friends calling to friends, and the general rush for the buses assaulted them. Carolyn clutched frantically at Sierra's hand as they went against the flow, while Clanton plowed ahead and led the way to the main office.

A secretary greeted them. She was polite, but cool, clearly tired and ready to go home. "Fill these out," she said briskly and went in to speak with the principal. Returning, she informed Sierra that Clanton would be in Mr. Cannon's fourth-grade class and Carolyn in Mrs. Lindstrom's third grade.

"Both teachers have after-school meetings today, so you'll have to wait to meet them until tomorrow morning. School starts at eight thirty." The secretary turned the forms around and looked them over. "Kling Street," she said. "That's only a few blocks from here." Sierra's face went hot with humiliation at the disclosure.

"We have a list of parents who take turns walking their children to school each day."

"I'll be driving mine," Sierra said, unwilling to entrust her children to anyone. Clanton groaned expressively, and she gave him a quelling look.

Back in the car, she sat studying the map before starting the engine. She didn't want to get lost again and end up in Watts this time.

Alex laughed when she told him about it. "I wondered where you were," he said. "I called twice today and got no answer. I was afraid you'd packed up and gone back to Windsor."

She didn't think his remark amusing.

"Don't worry about it," he said, leaning his hip against the counter. "My first trip down here, I had an appointment in Burbank. I got on the wrong freeway and ended up in Agoura. It's not hard to do."

His words were hardly comforting.

They went to Steven's house for dinner. Alex's new boss had even made arrangements for a professional babysitter to look after Clanton and Carolyn. She came complete with references and a list of classes in first aid that she had completed at Northridge.

Alex found his way to their Sherman Oaks home without

difficulty. Steven answered the door and ushered them into a spacious, elegantly decorated living room. His wife, Audra, was perfectly charming and courteous, but Sierra felt an undercurrent of disdain that nullified the show of warmth and hospitality. Audra wore a fine, lacquered veneer of friendliness, leaving Sierra to wonder at what lay beneath the flawless surface.

Alex seemed perfectly at ease with both of them, making Sierra wonder if she was imagining the crosscurrents and undertow. But within the course of the first ten minutes of conversation, she knew it was not her imagination. Somehow Sierra had been made fully aware that Audra was a graduate of USC who had studied—and mastered—liberal arts and who had been a member of one of the more prestigious sororities.

Then Audra turned her perfect, elegant gaze on Sierra and asked where she'd gone to college. It was the first time in Sierra's life that she was embarrassed to admit she had only graduated from high school and finished a year at a secretarial college.

"Oh," Audra said, looking utterly taken aback. There was a brief, mortifying lapse in conversation, until Steve jumped in.

"Do you like the theater, Sierra?"

"I haven't been to many plays."

"What have you seen?" Audra inquired, her eyes lighting with interest.

"*Joseph and the Amazing Technicolor Dreamcoat*," she said, not telling Audra it had been a high school production. "And a few concerts," she added, which was true—in just the last six months she'd gone to a country western concert and to hear a few Christian singers who had visited local Santa Rosa churches. Of course, she didn't think Audra needed to know the details.

And yet, even without the details, the other woman laughed. "Well, we'll have to correct that. Los Angeles has a great deal of culture to offer."

Sierra felt like a country bumpkin.

While the men talked business, Audra gave Sierra a rundown of the current cultural events. It seemed she had attended every major play and concert in the area and had a critique for each one. She quickly reviewed every theater company and artist currently performing, until Sierra wondered if she was dining with a normal woman or with some odd, sophisticated, upper-class incarnation of Siskel and Ebert.

Dinner proved spectacular. Any critic of fine cuisine would have given Audra a ten-star rating. She accepted all compliments with an air of casual amusement, skillfully turning the discussion to restaurants. Audra knew all the finest. She also knew where to shop for the highest quality meats, vegetables, and fruit. Prices never came up.

Sierra glanced at Alex and saw he was impressed with everything—especially with Audra. Was that the kind of wife he wanted now? Depressed, she ate the fluffy spinach soufflé. It melted in her mouth and made her heart sink into her stomach. What on earth was she going to serve these people for a reciprocal dinner? Her specialty was meat loaf and mashed potatoes. Oh, *that* would go over big! Or perhaps Clanton and Carolyn's favorite: tuna casserole. There was a meal custom-designed to impress high society!

❖

"You were pretty quiet tonight," Alex said on the drive home.

In her mind, she had been busily packing and moving back to Windsor. She didn't appreciate his interruption of her daydream.

He didn't seem to notice. "Audra was trying to make you feel welcome."

"Is that what she was trying to do?" she snapped, surprised herself at the coldness in her tone.

Mouth tightening, Alex stared straight ahead, the headlights from the oncoming traffic casting a glow over his handsome features. "She was offering to take you under her wing."

"I'm not a chicken."

"Give it a break, Sierra. She grew up down here. She could show you around."

"I'll remember to thank her properly next time, but I'll find my own way around, thank you very much. You gave me a map, remember?"

"A lot of good that did. At least try not to get lost again. I won't have the time to come find you in the middle of the day."

They didn't say another word to each other for the rest of the drive home. In fact, they said very little to one another over the next week. Alex left early, came home late, and always brought work with him. They shared a perfunctory "How'd your day go?" "Fine. And you?" "Fine"—and then he would settle in front of the television, studying the papers he spread out over the coffee table while she cleaned up the dinner dishes, saw to the children's baths, read them stories, and tucked them into bed.

It was a perfect life—for someone who adored misery.

Ten days and four telephone calls to her mother later, Sierra received a package in the mail.

"What's this?" Alex said, picking up a worn leather book from the coffee table before he spread his work across it.

"It's a journal. Mom sent it as a housewarming present."

He handed it to her.

"It looks old."

"It is," she said warmly. "It belonged to an ancestor of mine. Mary Kath—"

"Mm-hm," he replied absently, cutting her off as he turned to concentrate on the papers spread out in front of him. "That's nice."

Hurt swept over her at his casual dismissal. It shouldn't have surprised her that he wasn't listening. He seldom listened anymore. All that mattered to him was his precious work.

She left the room in bitter silence. She entered the bedroom, not even bothering to turn on the light. Enough light filtered through the window for her to see. Besides, the darkness fit her mood better. She prepared for bed, then slipped between the cool sheets. As she turned on her side, the journal, which she'd laid on the bed stand, caught her eye. She reached for it, fingering the soft leather wistfully.

At least Mary Kathryn wouldn't mind spending some time with her.

Mama says livin in the wildurnes aint no resun to bee ignurant.

Her papa wuz a larnud man and wud not want fuls in his famlee. The preechur brung buks and jurnals to rite in frum Ant Martha and now with snow up to the windows, we got time. Papa sits by the fire smokin and Mama reeds to us frum her Bible.

Matt dont like to rite much. He draws wulfs with big bludy dripin fangs that giv me nitmars. He drew me a hair once. I stil got it hung up over my bed. It iz nis. I wish he wud draw birds and flouerz stead of wulfs. He only seen one wulf his hol lif and it was ded. Magots wuz eting it.

Lucas does not draw nor rede nor rite. He says Papa dont no how an he dont need to neether. Papa tuk him to the wud shed fur sasing Mama, but he wernt no better wen he cum bak. So Papa giv him the gun and told him to go huntin. He wuz gon three daz. Mama wuz sure he got kilt by injuns or a bar, but he cum bak dragin a dear on a palot fixt up. Papa laft and gav him a cup of rum. Mama was mad as a wet hornet, but she dont tel Lucas to rede or rite no more.

> *Dearest Mary Kathryn,*
> *Please practice spelling the following words and*
> *then write an essay using them. I love you and have*
> *grand hopes for you.*
>
> *Mama*

> *living journal life whole read choice*
> *dead learned wolf/wolves come journal*
> *back flower*

If you want to be learned, you got no choice. You got to read and write your whole life until you are dead. You can not be a wolf or a flower who jest enjoys living. You got to come back to the table and werk in your journal until yer fingers is crampt and aking.

> *just cramped your are work aching*
> *just cramped your are work aching*
> *just cramped your are work aching*
> *just cramped your are work aching*

> *Stubbornness is unbecoming to a lady.*
> *Stubbornness is unbecoming to a lady.*
> *Stubbornness is unbecoming to a lady.*
> *Stubbornness is unbecoming to a lady.*
> *Stubbornness is unbecoming to a lady.*

"Spring"

Spring is the time when snow melts and flowers come up. Papa and Matthew plow them under and I have got to go to the wuds to pik some. I like to pik flowers in the wuds but Mama worrees I mit get took by injuns. One come to the house once askin fur food. Mama give him sum and I aint seen him since. I gues he didnot think much of her cookin.

Spring is also wen Matt turns the dirt in Mama's vechtable gardin. Every wurm he turns up I put in a kan fur fishin. I like catchin fish but I hate eatin em. Lucas told me he new a boy who chokt to deth on a fish bone. Mama said he wuz foolin me but I aint et fish since.

Papa says spring is a time for courtin. I askt him wat courtin wuz and he said it is when a yung mans blud comes up like sap in a tree. Wen I askt him what he ment, Mama giv him her look and he laft and wud not tell me. I askt Matt later but he turned red and wud not say. Lucas said courtin was wen Papa took the cow over to Graysons bull. Matt told him to shut his dirty mouth and Lucas hit him in his and Papa come runnin to stop them before they kilt each other. I am more and more interested in what courtin is.

Spring is wen the preecher comes and stands on a stump and screeems holy murder at us. He yells about GAWD and SALVATION and the BLOOD OF CHRIST. Peepull come from all rownd to see him. He gits so wurkt up his face turns red as fire. Frum up or down I aint sure witch. Mama says he is zelus for the Lord. Papa says he is plum crazy. But every tim he comes we go and watch with every one else. He is the best entertanmunt a rownd.

We always end up at the river with the preecher washin peepul clean of sin and buryin them and razing them up with Jesus. Mama says amen and creyes every time someone gets dunkt and Papa comes bak from the wuds smellin of whiskey and tobako.

Mama and I plant corn and squash and turnups and carots. Mama gave me a handful of seeds and askt me what I saw and I said seeds. She askt if they looked alive and I said they looked like stones. She said that is rit but when we bury them they will grow and bar frut. I said they will bar squash. She said when you plant a seed, God will soften it and water it and make it grow. She said people are like that.

Old Schmidt died last summer and they planted him but nothing come up that I can see cepting weeds. Lucas said worms ate him. So I reckon that is why.

"The Well"

The well is very deep and very dark. It is cool when you first go down but if you stay it is cold. The walls are wet and slimy and you can hear dripping. When you look up you can see a circle of blue sky unless Lucas puts the cover over. Then you dont see nothing. You just hear yourself screaming all around you. Lucas took the cover off and called down that I was a bludy coward. I hollared back up I wasnt. He said prove it and put the cover back. I sat in the bucket all day so he'd know.

Matt found me when he tried to get a bucket of water for Papa. He looked down and said what in hades are you doing down there. Mama is going crazy looking for you. Thinks injuns stole you. He hollared he had found me and Mama come running thinking I wuz drowned. My backside had no feeling and was stuck fast in the buckt. It hurt bad when Papa popped me out. Lucas was leaning against the house laffing. I yelled I aint no coward. No, you are a fool he said.

Papa took him to the wood shed and Mama cried and took me in the house. She made me sit in the tub of hot water and drink whiskey. I dont see what Papa likes about it. It burns all the way down and then comes right back up.

> Dearest Mary Kathryn,
>   Please practice these words on your slate until you are ready for me to test you. Use ten in an essay. And do not ask anyone else about courting.
>
>> I love you,
>> Mama

> Go witch/which people worry/worries
> zealous Indians woods garden
> choked liked laughed asked
> death pick when might
> from some/sum wood/would catching
> running washing raising cooking

God loves *zealous people* in the *woods*. He *might* love *some* Indians. Mama loves *washing, cooking,* and *raising* chikins.

> Mary Kathryn McMurray,
>   You will have no supper until you write chickens twenty-five times on your slate, and "A penitent heart is a humble heart" fifty times.
>
>> Mama

CHAPTER 5

"WHAT TIME do you think you'll be home?" Sierra said, trying to keep her voice neutral as she clutched the telephone receiver.

"Five thirty or six," Alex said, sounding distracted. She could hear him punching the keys of his computer.

Couldn't he stop working long enough to talk to her for two minutes? "What would you like for dinner?"

"Something light. I had a big lunch with Steve."

"Where'd you go?" she said, wanting to draw out their conversation.

"La Serre. It's a French place. Classy."

"Expensive?"

"Very." Alex chuckled. "It's nice when the boss picks up the tab."

Must be nice to have a fancy lunch and then ask for

something *light* for dinner. She looked at the breakfast dishes in the sink. She hadn't even had lunch yet. She opened the refrigerator while talking to him. Maybe she could open a can of peaches and finish off the carton of cottage cheese sitting on the top shelf.

"We were celebrating."

"What?" she asked, feeling left out.

"Vigilantes went into production today," he said, clearly proud of the game he had created. "Steve said they'll be sending out trial copies to game reviewers around the country by the middle of next week."

"What if they don't like it?"

"They will. Look, honey, I've got to go. I've got a call coming in, and I'm right in the middle of something important. We'll talk tonight."

He hung up before she could utter a word. She held the silent receiver and felt more bereft than when she'd called. Why had she bothered? He was always busy and it was always important. More important than she was, anyway.

Celebrating. He hadn't even bothered to share the news with her. *La Serre. Classy. Expensive.*

Angry, she took a package of frozen hamburger from the refrigerator freezer and tossed it on the counter. She'd fix spaghetti *again*. It was easy, and the children loved it.

Turning on the television, she set the basket of clean laundry in front of her. She had made a habit of doing the wash right after she dropped the children off for school, then saving the folding for now. At least then she could overcome her feelings of guilt for watching a soap opera. She plunked down on the sofa and began folding T-shirts, towels, and underwear while watching the episode unfolding before her. She used to scorn soap operas. Now she found solace in them. For an hour, she could forget how miserable she was and lose herself in the convoluted lives of television characters. Their problems were more tragic and complex than hers, their passions a lot more exciting. How many times had Erica Kane been married anyway?

The laundry was folded and set aside well before the third commercial promoting some new feminine hygiene product. She put the towels and clothing away. Sitting down again, she kicked her bare feet up on the coffee table and leaned back into the sofa. She *should* be doing *something*. But what?

They'd been living in this apartment house for three months, and she didn't even know the family next door. She knew they had children. The little boy ran along the corridor right outside the living room window a dozen times every day, even when it was raining. And there was that woman down on the first floor who peered out her curtains all the time and then ducked back in when someone chanced to notice her. What was her problem anyway?

Sierra didn't want to find out. There were twenty apartments in this complex, and she didn't know a single soul living in one of them. Everyone protected their privacy. They probably had guns in their side tables. She remembered having a phone conversation with her mother, in which her mother said, "Reach out, Sierra. You can never tell who God has just waiting for you to say hello." So she'd said hello to one woman who came into the laundry room, and the woman had barely acknowledged her attempt at friendliness. She just dumped diapers into one of the washing machines, poured in soap, twirled the controls, and left.

Rebuffed, Sierra didn't make the attempt again. If God had someone waiting for her, He'd have to tell them to make the first move.

She didn't leave the sofa until the credits were rolling, and then she clicked off the television. Collecting her things, she went out the door. She had it all perfectly timed. If she left immediately after the soap opera, she'd pull into Carolyn and Clanton's school just as the other children were boarding school buses.

The kids pleaded for McDonald's on the way home, and Sierra gave in. She didn't feel like making spaghetti anyway, and Alex had already said he wouldn't be hungry. Something light. Fine. She'd stop by the grocery store and pick up packaged salad fixings and dressing.

She straightened up the kitchen while the children settled at the table to do their homework and talk about their day at school. At least they were making new friends.

Clanton dug through his backpack and produced a fistful of school announcements, sign-up sheets, and graded homework. "Can I sign up for Little League, Mom?"

"You'll have to talk to your father about it," Sierra said, putting the last rinsed dish into the washer.

"You think Dad'll coach again this year?"

"I don't know, Clanton. You'll have to ask him."

Clanton did the minute Alex walked through the door. "Not this year, champ," Alex said, ruffling his hair. "I'm not going to have the time." He leaned down to kiss Carolyn hello.

Flipping the kitchen towel over her shoulder, she approached as he stood loosening his tie. "Did you have a good day?"

"Great." He gave her a firm kiss and pulled his tie free. Unbuttoning the collar of his shirt, he headed toward the bedroom. "I'm going to change and take a quick run."

Jogging was another new thing in Alex's life. Steve and Matt jogged; they claimed it was great as a stress reliever. So, of course, Alex had followed suit.

By the time Alex returned, Clanton and Carolyn had

taken their baths and were dressed for bed. She read to them while Alex showered and put on his worn Levi's and UCB sweatshirt. When she came out to straighten the living room, he went in to say good night to the children. She supposed she should be thankful he spent the next half hour talking with them.

"Jack called me just before I left the office," he said when he came out.

Jack and his pregnant wife had rented their Windsor home. "Problems?"

"On the contrary. He's got enough for a down payment on the house."

"They're buying it?" she said weakly. As long as they still owned the Windsor home, she held out the hope that they'd return. Alex's words tore the crumbling foundations right out from beneath her.

"That was their hope when they moved in. I told him what the house was worth before we left. He said today his parents decided to give him a portion of his inheritance early. He's contacting your father's old partner to take care of the paperwork. They shouldn't have any problem qualifying for a mortgage. We'll have the money in our hands by the end of May."

He cupped her face. "I know how much that little place meant to you."

That little place. He said it so casually, as though it had been a shack or a hole in the wall. He couldn't have any idea what it meant to her, or he wouldn't be so quick to sell it.

"Matt gave me the name of a good Realtor. I want you to start looking at houses. Four bedrooms, three baths, with a pool. Get together with Audra. She knows all the best areas. I want us in a *good* neighborhood."

"We were in a good neighborhood."

He let his hands slide away. "We'll be in a better one. Steve gave me a raise today. A *big* raise. He's that sure Vigilantes is going to be big."

She saw how bright his eyes were, aglow with ambition and plans. "Was all this the reason you spent a whole twenty minutes with your children?"

Alex didn't move, but Sierra could feel the cold front move in worse than an Illinois winter.

"The tongue is a restless evil, full of deadly poison . . . ," her mother's voice echoed in her mind, and Sierra felt a stab of shame. But before she could apologize, Alex spoke in a glacial tone.

"They like the idea of having their own pool."

"Do they also like the idea of changing schools again?" she shot back, trying to keep the edge of sarcasm out of her voice and failing.

"Audra suggested a private school. I have the name she gave me written down."

Naturally. "Has she offered to pay for it, too?"

Alex's temper came surging to the surface. "What have you got against her? You haven't liked her from day one, and she's done nothing but be nice to you."

"Is *that* what you call it? Remind me to kiss her feet the next time I see her!" Sierra moved away from him, filled with resentment and feelings of betrayal. She had tried to explain to Alex how Audra made her feel: uneducated, uncultured, and from the lower classes in a supposedly classless society. Alex insisted it was her imagination; she knew it was deliberate.

Every time she was with Audra, the woman made a point of mentioning this course or that course that she had taken at USC, any of which made her an expert on any given subject. Sierra might have an opinion, but it was an uneducated one.

"Oh?" Audra had said only two days ago in response to a comment Sierra had made. She arched her elegant brow. "And how did you come to *that* conclusion?"

They had been discussing the abortion issue, and Sierra had said she believed it was wrong to end the life of an unborn child. Clearly what her mother had taught her just didn't cut the mustard in Audra's eyes.

"Sounds like fundamentalist brainwashing to me," she said with a pitying glance that dismissed Sierra's lifetime of learning from her mother's knee. Then Audra launched into a dissertation complete with "facts" proving the nonentity of the human fetus.

"Why didn't you go to college, Sierra?" Audra finally said. "You learn how to think for yourself at college. If your parents couldn't afford it, you could've gone to a junior college and then finished at a four-year university." She said it so sweetly, it sounded as though she genuinely felt sorry that Sierra had lost out on the opportunities she herself had been given.

"Money was no problem. I just wasn't interested."

"Not interested?" Again the eyebrow arched. "Steve said Alex graduated with honors from UC Berkeley."

"Yes, he did."

"You might think about taking some night courses," she said seriously.

Sierra waited for more, but it wasn't forthcoming. Apparently, Audra felt she had said enough, and indeed she had. Even now, several days later, Audra's implication rankled: Alex would lose interest in her because of her lack of education. Just because she hadn't gone to college didn't mean she didn't keep up on what was happening in the world. She read the newspaper. She read magazines. She watched CNN!

Yet, even with all that, she was left feeling as though she were standing on sinking sand.

Shopping was even more excruciating. She had accepted three invitations from Audra because Alex insisted. Each time when Audra arrived, she tapped her long, coral-colored acrylic fingernails on the door and jangled the keys of her silver Mercedes when Sierra answered.

"Ready to go?" she said as though speaking to a recalcitrant child.

Chatting gaily, Audra drove to stores far beyond any ordinary citizen's budget.

"Aren't you going to buy anything, Sierra?" Audra said the last time while signing the slip for an eight-hundred-dollar dress. "That blue dress you were looking at would make you look wonderful."

"At six hundred and fifty dollars, even a chimp would look wonderful in it."

Audra had laughed at her remark, but Sierra felt the full force of an affronted glare from the elegantly attired saleslady. One just didn't say such things on Rodeo Drive.

Actually, Sierra had wanted to say more. She wanted to add for both women's benefit that if she had an extra six or seven hundred dollars lying around, she certainly wouldn't put it all on her back!

Audra offered to treat her to lunch at Lowry's. Sierra declined. She had been taught to reciprocate, and she doubted Audra would feel suitably recompensed at Denny's.

"I'm sorry, but I need to get home, Audra. The children will be getting out of school soon." She'd glanced at her watch to make her point. "I always pick them up."

"You should get involved in a car pool," Audra had commented, shooting the Mercedes in and out of traffic with the skill of an experienced Indianapolis 500 driver.

Sierra was tired of Audra "should"ing all over her. "Chauffeuring children to school is one of the delights of mother-hood."

"Delights?" Audra laughed. Weaving smoothly across three lanes of dense traffic, she glided down an off-ramp. "That doesn't say much for the quality of your life." Her eyes twinkled merrily. "We'll have to do something to give you a little excitement."

And now it seemed she had.

Was it really Alex's idea that they look for a house so soon? Or had Audra through Steve advised they do so? Once they were under the weight of a mortgage, it would be pretty hard to change their minds about working in Los Angeles.

She pushed thoughts of Audra away and tried to reason with Alex. "I think it's too soon to think about buying a house," she said.

"You like living in a cramped apartment?"

She bristled anew at his sarcasm but remained calm. "You haven't even been at your new job for four months, Alex. What if you decide you hate it?"

"I *love* it."

"I'm saying *if* you changed your mind. You're having a honeymoon at Beyond Tomorrow right now. The whole thing may come down around your head like a house of cards."

"Thanks for your vote of confidence."

"I'm confident in *you*, Alex, but I don't trust *them*. Everything's moving too fast. It's all too easy. We should wait at least a year, Alex. So much can change—"

"Get it through your head, Sierra. I'm not changing my mind about anything." Face rigid and pale with anger, he glared at her. "I'm getting pretty tired of you walking around with a black cloud over your head all the time." He went to his desk and turned on the computer. "Either you can look around for a house and help make the decision, or I'll just take care of it myself," he said, his back to her. "The choice is yours."

So much for priorities, she thought, tears brimming as she went into the kitchen.

She called the Realtor the next morning and made an appointment. Roberta Folse said she would be by at ten, which would give Sierra enough time to drop off the children at school and do her grocery shopping.

Roberta had penny-red hair, dark-brown eyes, and was slightly overweight. She was elegantly dressed in a green suit with a gold silk blouse and a string of pearls.

"Your husband said you moved recently and you were having a difficult time settling in," she said when they were on their way in her sleek black Jaguar. "He didn't mention where you lived before."

"We both grew up in Healdsburg," Sierra said, wondering how much else Alex had confided in this attractive stranger. "It's about seventy miles north of San Francisco, in the wine country."

"I'm familiar with the area," Roberta said and smiled with complete understanding. "God's country. No wonder you're having trouble. Culture shock. This area must seem like another planet to you."

Sierra warmed to her at once and felt herself relaxing. From that point on, they talked easily. Roberta had four children, all grown-up and in college or married. She had gotten her real estate license when the market was booming. "I've always loved looking at houses," she said, driving along pretty tree-shaded streets with charming ranch-style houses and some with a hint of Victorian. "You know, most people I know dream of retiring in the wine country or farther north in the redwoods. I like Garberville myself. It has an old-fashioned feel to it."

"My brother owns a place there. He has twenty acres out near Whitethorn on the way to Shelter Cove. He likes to go up on weekends and relax."

"Heaven." Roberta sighed. "Well, we'll see if we can't find you a house down here that'll have the country feel. Why don't we take a look at this one?"

Roberta showed her four homes, all with four bedrooms, three bathrooms, and a pool. The prices made Sierra's head spin and her stomach drop. They were four times what she and Alex had paid for their Windsor home! What was Alex thinking? Sierra confided her concerns to Roberta.

"It is a shock, I know. Your husband told me what you're going to make from the sale of your home and what he's currently making. It'll be tight, but I don't think you'll have problems qualifying. Especially with Steve Silverman cosigning."

Sierra could feel the blood running out of her face. "Cosigning?"

"It'll speed up the process of you and your husband having a new home. Steve simply guarantees the loan."

"So they would own part of our home?"

"Oh no, but should you fall into financial difficulties, which is very unlikely, Steve would have to assume responsibility for the mortgage. Alex told me his primary concern is location, which is wise. Should you decide to resell after a few years, any one of these homes would be snapped up quickly."

Warning bells were going off in Sierra's mind, but she couldn't pinpoint the cause. She tried to talk to Alex about it that night, but he thought she was suspicious of Steve's motives in offering to guarantee their loan and took offense.

"That's not what I said!" Sierra protested, upset.

"Pretty close."

"You don't *listen*."

"Then try making sense. Try thinking things through before you open your mouth."

"Forget it," she said, hurt. Did he think she was stupid just because she wanted all the facts? "Just forget it. We'll buy a house. After all, it's *your* money. Right? This marriage isn't a partnership. I'm just the stupid, uneducated little homebody who happens to be your wife!"

"I didn't say that!"

"You didn't have to."

Alex said barely a dozen words to her over the next week.

James Farr has come to live with us.

He talks to me sometimes when Matthew has other things to do. He is laid up with a broken leg and he is very sad because his mother and father was both dead from a terible Tragedy.

I herd him tell Matthew what happened.

James and his mother and his father was riding home from the camp meeting when his father says he sold out and they were moving West. James said his mother got crazy. She said she was tired of moving and had roots. She said if she was moving anywhere, it was back east to her family. His father said thar was better land West, and she said it werent land he was after. Her crying and his shouting made the horses start running. They wud not stop. A wheel brok off and the wagon turned over. God tuk mercy on James and threw him on soft ground. But his fathers head got cracked open like a melon and his mother got crushed when the wagon rolled over her.

I am sorry his mother and father are dead, but I am not sorry James is with us. I hope he stays forever.

When I grow up I am going to marry him.

James let me sit with him today. He did not say much to me and I did not know what to say to him. I read him two chapters from Exodus about Moses in the bullrushes and pharaoh's daugher finding him. James said thank you very much. He took my hand and kissed it.

I will never wash my hand again as long as I live.

God says we are to love one another, but it is very hard to love Lucas.

Lucas told Mama he wuz in the barn when I got locked in the henhouse. He's a liar. He always lies and Mama is so good she dont know the difference. I saw Lucas close the door. I heard him drop the bar. And I heard him laffing while I was screaming at him to let me out. He knows I am affeered of chickens.

Mama asked me why he wud do such a thing to his sweet little sister. I said he done it because he is mean. She said that was a very bad thing to say about my own brother.

Sometimes Mama dont want to hear the truth because then she will have to do something about it.

Matthew wud have done something. But Matthew was out in the fields with Papa.

Sometimes I wish I was a boy so I could grow big enuf to punch Lucas hard enuf to nock him down like Matthew does. Lucas needs nockin down.

Mama says that jest cause the devil nocks at your door dont mean you have to answer.

I think Lucas opened his door and invited the devil in a long time ago.

We went to camp meeting again. I did not like it much this time. Sally Mae Grayson and her yellow hair came. She has not been to a meeting in two years because she has bin living in Fever River with her grandmama and going to school. I wish she had stayed in Fever River with her grandmama.

Even Matthew who thinks girls are stupid and empty headed looked at Sally Mae like he was a sick calf. All the boys were following her around and wanting to talk to her. The only one she pad attention to was James. They sat together during meeting and ate together at supper. Sally Mae kept looking at me and saying little pitchers have big ears. James told me to go and get him another mug of cider and when I did and came back with it he was gone. So was Sally Mae.

I looked and looked until I found them.

Now I know what courting is.

I never want to talk about courting or hear about it again. No one is ever courting me like that.

Mama found me down by the crek washing my hand. She askt me why I wuz crying. I told her. I thot she wud go and make them stop what they wuz doing or at least tell Mister Grayson. All she did was hold me and rock me for a long, long time. She said idols always have feet of clay.

Sally Mae is not going bak to school in Fever River. James told Matthew that her grandmama wrote a letter to her father saying she was ailing and could not take her. She said Sally Mae wud be better off staying at the homestead with her papa. James said her schooling was lost on her anyway. He said Sally Mae knows more than she shud all ready.

I am going to die. My heart hurts so much I know I will be in the grave soon. James is goin. I'm never going to see him again. The only consolashun I have is Sally Mae wont get him either.

He thanked Mama and Papa over supper and said he cud never repay them for their kindnes to him. He said he is sixteen and old enuf to fend for himself. Papa said Fever River is a big place. James said he wants to be in a big place. He said maybe he will even go east. He said he wud like to see Boston and New York. He said he wud like to see England and maybe even China.

He and Matthew talked the hole nite before he left. I heard him tell Matthew he did not love Sally Mae and it wud be smart if Matthew did not love her either. You are not like me, James said. She will cut yor heart out and feast on it.

I walked with him to the crek bridge. I did not cry. I askt him strat out what he thot he wud find better in Fever River or China for that matter. He said he was not looking for better. He was looking for different.

Mama said he is lost.

I know I am.

CHAPTER 6

"BECAUSE IT'S THE WAY things are done down here," Alex said, irritated. "When are you going to stop worrying about money? I just got a bonus. We can afford to have a professional decorator."

"It isn't just a matter of if we can afford it," Sierra said, though that did concern her. Alex was spending money at an alarming rate, eating out at fancy restaurants every day for lunch, buying expensive suits. Why wouldn't he listen to anything she said anymore? "What's the matter with the way we've decorated? People are comfortable—"

"Nothing goes together. Look around you, Sierra. Does Steve's house look like this? Does Matt's? Most of what we have are hand-me-downs given to us by our parents when we first got married. That old armoire in the bedroom, the

73

hatch-cover table in the family room, those ridiculous brass lamps!"

"The armoire was the first piece of furniture your parents bought when they came to California."

"So what?"

"It has a family history to it! It meant something to them."

"It means poverty to me. I don't need reminding."

"That hatch-cover comes from an old merchant ship that sailed around the Horn and into San Francisco Bay in 1910. My uncle refinished it for us as a wedding present. Those brass lamps are almost a hundred years old."

"And look every day of it."

"I can get some new shades."

"New shades won't help. Don't you get it? Everything we've got is *junk*. If you buy something from a discount store today and save it for a hundred years, it's just hundred-year-old junk. That's what we've got. Old junk!"

Sierra stood there, stunned. Had he always felt this way? She remembered how nice everything had looked in their small Windsor house. Maybe he figured what they had just wasn't good enough in a five-thousand-square-foot, upscale, ranch-style house owned by an up-and-coming young executive.

"Look, Sierra," Alex said, his tone gentling, "there's a right way and a wrong way to decorate a house, and hiring a professional is the *right* way."

"Who told you that rubbish?" she said. But she knew without even asking.

His dark eyes flashed with anger. "*I'm* saying it. All right? Does that make it go down easier? I'm sick of living with other people's discards around me. I'm making good money. I bought this beautiful house for you."

Rolling her eyes, she turned away.

"I don't want it looking like it was decorated by someone running a flea market," he said through his teeth.

She wondered if he knew how much his words hurt. She had always done their decorating. People had always said she had a knack for it. Friends had asked her advice, and one even offered to pay her to decorate her house. She liked reupholstering old couches and chairs, tole painting, and making wreaths. She liked *country*!

Alex jotted some notes on her grocery list. "I'm giving you a couple of names of interior decorators. The one in Beverly Hills is the best. Call him first. If he's not available, call the second one." He tore the slip off the pad and handed it to her. Stepping past her, he picked up his briefcase. "Get it done today," he said, like he was giving a subordinate a command. It was all she could do to not salute him as he headed for the door.

It wasn't the first morning of late that he had neglected to kiss her good-bye. Sierra followed him, slip of paper in hand, and stood in the doorway to the three-car garage. Maybe he'd remember.

"I want it done as soon as possible," he said, opening the door of his new silver Mercedes. Tossing the briefcase onto the passenger seat, he slid in and slammed the door. Tapping the garage door opener, he turned away, slinging his arm over the passenger seat as he started backing out.

She looked at the white BMW sitting in the garage. Alex had bought it for her birthday last month. He'd been so proud when he drove it home.

"Where's my Honda?" she'd said weakly.

"I traded it in," he said, grinning and handing her the keys.

He'd fully expected her to weep with joy over having a new car. She'd wanted to weep, all right. The Honda was the car her mother and father had given them as a wedding present. Clanton and Carolyn had ridden around in it from the time they were babies. It was like an old family friend. The BMW was an unwelcome houseguest.

Alex had never spent much time keeping up the Honda. She'd vacuumed and washed it every few weeks. Now Alex spent every Saturday vacuuming, washing, and hand-drying both cars: first the Mercedes, then the BMW. He even rubbed the already-shiny dashboards with Armor All. He used a toothbrush to scrub the spoked hubcaps, for heaven's sake!

Three days ago, Alex had told her he didn't have time to make Clanton's Little League game—but he had two hours to spare for the cars. And she couldn't even remember the last time she'd received an eighth of that much time and attention from him.

A stab of pain ripped through her as she remembered the days, less than a year ago, when Alex couldn't wait to come home to her, to talk with her, to share and laugh and love. She remembered how it felt to sit together, sharing dreams and ideas. And the wonder of melting into each other's arms after a day apart. How could life change so dramatically in the space of six months? How could a man change so much?

She had always known Alex was ambitious and determined. What she hadn't realized was that his work could become the driving force and focus of his life. He was consumed with his career, impassioned by it, obsessed with it. It was as though the success of his first game, Vigilantes, merely whetted his appetite to do better on the next. Apparently success gave him an adrenaline rush she and the children couldn't.

Sierra readily acknowledged that Alex was making more than four times what he had made in his job in Santa Rosa. Two magazines had done articles on him in the past two months giving glowing forecasts of the future of Vigilantes. She had seen ads on television.

"Sick of what's happening in the world?" the announcer's smooth voice would ask. "Become the law!"

Industry columnists were predicting Vigilantes would be the most popular video game of the decade. In the interview for the second article, Alex said Beyond Tomorrow would be releasing a new gaming system called The Monolith by the new year. The system would come complete with a code breaker that would allow owners to play any game on the market. The Monolith was aimed at the older teens and adults and would come packaged with Vigilantes. Stores were already calling Beyond Tomorrow and placing orders before the system had even hit the market. And Alex was working day and night on a second game, The Chameleon, a role-playing game.

No doubt about it. Beyond Tomorrow was booming. "Changing the future of gaming!" their company motto, was becoming a catchphrase; Alex was determined to make it come true.

But Sierra felt little pleasure at what was happening. It was too much. Too fast.

Granted, Steve had proven himself a man of his word. He'd kept every promise he made to Alex. Bonuses, salary increases, benefits . . . He even hired a personal secretary for Alex and added several new employees to the marketing and distribution departments. Alex's place and position were guaranteed; he was a key in Beyond Tomorrow's incredible success. He was on top of the professional world.

And Sierra had never felt less secure in her life.

She and Alex barely talked anymore. He was constantly overworked and preoccupied. She tried to talk to him about it one night, but he wanted to know what she *needed* to talk about. The minute she said there wasn't anything specific, he returned his attention to his computer screen and immersed himself in work for the rest of the evening.

The next morning, she tried to bring it up again.

"So, go ahead," he said, sounding impatient. "What's on your mind?" He hadn't even bothered to lower his *Wall Street Journal*.

"Nothing in particular," she said. How did you start a good talk when you needed to talk about not talking?

"Pour me another cup of coffee, would you?" he said from behind the paper.

She wanted to pour the entire pot over him. "We used to talk about all kinds of things from the minute you walked in the door until we went to bed."

"We still talk."

"About business. About the games you're working on. About the kids."

At last he lowered the paper and looked at her. She could see him putting on his armor, getting his weapons ready. He had always been better equipped for fighting than she was. "What are you getting at, Sierra?"

God, what do I say? What do I do? she screamed inside her head. When Alex presented his cold front, she felt incapable of reaching him—and that seemed to be the case almost all the time now. Tears of frustration pricked at her eyes. He used to sense when she needed him. Now, he didn't seem to care what she was feeling or thinking. She wanted to say she missed him. She wanted to say she was lonely. She wanted to tell him she was afraid they were drifting apart, and that Audra was right: she was boring, uneducated . . . and losing him.

The very thought filled her with a bleak terror. But she was even more terrified to say those things aloud and find that he was indifferent.

Her eyes pleaded with him. *Just tell me you still love me, Alex. Don't make me ask you if you do.*

He just sat looking at her, eyes narrowed, posture defensive.

And so she leaned back in her chair, overwhelmed with a sense of defeat. "I'm not getting at anything," she finally responded, aching inside for the connection she had always felt with him.

How could you be with someone you loved so desperately and feel so alone?

He stared at her, as though he were studying a particularly curious insect on the window screen. He shrugged. "I guess we haven't been out for a while," he conceded, folding his newspaper and tossing it onto the coffee table. His gaze drifted from hers. Restless, he glanced at his wristwatch and got up. "I wanted to get into the office early this morning. I've got a lot to do." He downed his coffee and headed for the kitchen. "Why don't you figure out where you'd like to go and make the reservations?"

He sounded so offhand, so uninterested. . . . She closed her eyes against the pain swelling inside her. Alex had always been the one to suggest places they could go and things they could do. Several times, he'd surprised her with tickets to a show at the Luther Burbank Center. He used to take her and the children to pizza and a movie. Once, he'd even made arrangements for her mother to take care of the children so he could whisk her off for a romantic weekend at a bed-and-breakfast in Mendocino.

Now, he sounded as though the whole idea of taking her out was just one more responsibility he needed to handle.

She suggested a rib place.

"Too much fat and cholesterol."

Since when had he worried about fat and cholesterol?

They agreed on a movie, but that night Alex called and said he had some work to do. She asked him to reserve Friday night for dinner out with the children, but he called from the office at the last minute Friday and said he had an important meeting he couldn't miss.

She gave up making plans.

Now, it seemed, he didn't think she had the ability to decorate their home properly.

The whine of the garage door closing and the roar of Alex's Mercedes as he floored it toward work brought Sierra back from her dismal reverie. She needed to awaken the children soon so they'd have plenty of time to get ready for school.

Carolyn was invited to a birthday party this weekend. Her little friend, Pamela, lived somewhere in Studio City. Sierra went back into the kitchen and jotted down a note to buy a birthday present.

She glanced at the slip of paper Alex had given her: *Bruce Davies Interiors*. She tacked it to her noteboard beside the phone. She didn't make the call until later that afternoon, after Alex called and asked if she had done it yet.

The designer's receptionist had a rich, velvety voice with a heavy New England accent.

"I'm under orders from my husband to hire a decorator," Sierra said.

The woman was polite and efficient, making no promises and hinting that Bruce was in high demand and terribly busy. Too busy, Sierra hoped.

"Please hold." Yanni played softly in Sierra's ear. The receptionist came back on the line. "Is your husband employed by Beyond Tomorrow?"

"Yes, he is." Had Alex called ahead?

"One moment, please," the receptionist said, and Sierra heard Yanni playing again. Plucking a pencil from the kitchen drawer, she doodled flower and leaf patterns along the top edge of her grocery list. But she'd barely gotten started when the receptionist was back.

"I apologize for the wait, Mrs. Madrid. Mr. Davies will be pleased to speak to you."

Before she could protest, Bruce Davies was greeting her with the familiarity of a long-lost friend.

"Sierra, I'm *so* glad you finally called. I knew anyone with such a charming name wouldn't let me down. Of course, I expected your call several days ago, but this works out just as well. I've just finished a stunning home only a few blocks away from you, and I'm ready for something new and exciting! And believe me, the ideas I have for your home are definitely that!"

After a two-minute conversation with Bruce, Sierra felt she had been run over by a steamroller. He made the appointment for late Thursday afternoon and informed her he would bring an assistant with him. He knew who Alex was because Audra Silverman had faxed him an article from a well-known computer game magazine.

"Decorating for a game designer will be a challenge," he said, clearly eager.

"I'm not sure Alex will want to have much involvement, Mr. Davies."

"Oh, but he must. I *insist.*"

Surprisingly, Alex didn't quibble and assured her he would be home early Thursday.

Bruce Davies turned out to be an attractive man in his late forties, trim and elegantly dressed, who absolutely exuded energy. His assistant attended him in silence, writing notes as they walked through the house, Alex at Bruce's side.

It became apparent very quickly that Sierra was going to have little say in what was done to the house. Country,

Bruce informed her, was a definite "no-no," and anything even remotely Victorian "just wouldn't do, darling." Bruce was interested in the architecture, made suggestions for some changes, and poured forth with decorating ideas. Alex had his own, and Bruce listened as though every word was genius.

"A man who is going to change the future of gaming must have a house that reflects his creativity," Bruce said, his eyes sparkling as he surveyed the entryway.

By the time Bruce and his assistant left, Sierra was convinced the house would bear the stamp of Bruce Davies Interiors, a slight mark of Alejandro Madrid, and absolutely nothing of her.

"It's going to be expensive," Alex said, not noticeably worried about it, "but it'll be worth it. Bruce said he'll have sketches within a week, and decisions can be made."

She knew who would be making the decisions.

The next morning, after dropping the children off at private school, Sierra drove to the closest mall to look for a suitable present for Carolyn's new friend. Nothing looked right to her: The selection was too wide and the prices too high.

Depressed, she purchased a cappuccino and sat watching the hustle of people in the mall. Most were women. Some strolled at a leisurely pace, looking lonely and bored as they paused at window displays. Others moved with quick efficiency, looking for all the world as though they knew exactly where they were going and what they were doing.

Sierra longed for home. She wished her mother were sitting across from her so she could pour out her heart and ask her advice. But she'd done enough of that lately over the telephone. Her mother's parting words after their last conversation still echoed in her ears: "Remember, honey, God is in control."

If that was true, why did she feel so desperate?

Shaking her head, she turned her thoughts back to the matter at hand. What was she going to do about that blasted birthday present? When she was Carolyn's age, she had liked nothing better than taking her friends up into the attic so they could spend hours dressing up in her mother's and grandmother's old clothes, high-heeled shoes, hats, and jewelry—all perfect props for pretending to be Cinderella or Snow White or some other fairy-tale character.

Did children do that sort of thing anymore? All the dress-up Carolyn had ever done was back in preschool. The Windsor School had provided plenty of clothes to choose from: surgical gowns, nurses' uniforms, suit jackets and briefcases, a fireman's hat, a policeman's uniform. Nothing frivolous or fanciful. Everything geared to answer that all-important question: What are you going to be when you grow up? Sierra could still remember her frustration when she'd discovered the teacher was asking Carolyn and her classmates this. Was it really necessary to know at the age of four or five what one was going to do for the rest of one's life? It seemed so long ago. Now she wondered.

Wasn't being a wife and mother enough anymore?

Feeling defiant, Sierra finished her coffee and drove to Cost Plus, the area warehouse store. Wandering through, she found an intricately carved box imported from India. It was pretty and inexpensive. She bought it and drove to Kmart, where she purchased three beaded necklaces, a gold-tone charm bracelet with African animals on it, and two bright rhinestone pins, as well as a long, thin multicolored scarf. Pleased with her choices, she headed home.

While watching her soap opera, she used the scarf to wrap the gift. Twisting the tied ends, she curled them around until they looked like a plump flower on top of the box. During a commercial, she rummaged through her wrapping-paper box in the hall closet and found some gold ribbon. Cutting a long strip, she tucked it around the fabric flower and wrote on the ends: "Happy Birthday, Pamela. From Carolyn." She sat back and smiled, perfectly satisfied with the gift.

Then she drove Carolyn to the birthday party on Saturday.

Pamela's house was near the top of the hills with an iron gate in front. The gate was open, but a uniformed guard was on duty. He asked their names and checked his list before nodding them through. Other cars were already parked: two Cadillacs, three Mercedes, and a little red sports car the likes of which Sierra had never seen before. Everything reeked of money.

Sierra walked Carolyn to the front door, where a maid answered their ring. She was Spanish and dressed in a crisp black uniform with white collar and apron.

Carolyn's hand tightened. "Don't leave, Mommy. Please." Sierra forced a reassuring smile, but her daughter didn't loosen her grip until they entered a huge room with cathedral windows at the back and she spotted Pamela with several other little girls. Sierra spotted the mothers.

They were all standing near windows that provided a panoramic view of San Fernando Valley. Every one of the ladies looked as though she had just stepped out of a fashion magazine. Sierra cringed inwardly, wondering what they thought of her in her faded sweatshirt, black leggings, and scuffed tennis shoes. *Oh, God,* she thought, *please don't let Carolyn be embarrassed by me.* One of the women glanced toward Sierra and Carolyn. Smiling, she said a word to the others and left them.

"You must be Sierra and Carolyn Madrid," she said, her tone warm and welcoming. "I'm so glad you could come." She touched Carolyn's hair lightly. "Pamela has talked of little else since you came to school, Carolyn. She insists you're kindred spirits just like the girls in *Anne of Green Gables.*"

Marcia Burton had class and grace and dissolved every bit of Carolyn's shyness. Smiling, the little girl held the present out to Marcia. "Why, it's perfectly lovely," she said.

"My mother wrapped it," Carolyn told her proudly, and Sierra's face went hot. She could see the other gifts on the polished mahogany coffee table nearby, all obviously from expensive stores and professionally wrapped. She thought of the wooden box and cheap, gawdy jewelry inside it. She wished she could snatch it back and run.

As Carolyn joined the other children, Sierra thanked Marcia for inviting her and made her excuses to leave.

"Oh, please stay," Marcia said, sounding as though she actually meant it. "Pamela said your son plays on the school's baseball team, and I know they're practicing today."

She was right. Sierra had dropped Clanton off before bringing Carolyn to the party. The coach had invited all the boys back to his house for a barbecue and a movie.

Marcia smiled, her blue eyes amused as she confided her belief that Pamela had developed a crush on Clanton. "She says he's the most handsome boy in school."

Sierra wasn't surprised her son made female hearts flutter. Clanton had Alex's features and coloring, and her light-green eyes. It made for a startling combination that had always attracted attention from the time he was a baby.

"I really had better go," Sierra said.

"At least stay long enough to meet the other mothers."

As Marcia Burton put her hand lightly beneath her elbow, Sierra resigned herself to further humiliation.

All the ladies were polite. Only one looked her over as though she were convinced Sierra had just crawled out of a homeless shelter. Marcia, appearing not to notice, remained warm and friendly to all, while staying close to Sierra's side.

But the woman's efforts did little to ease Sierra's discomfiture. After what seemed a polite interval of stilted small talk, she made her excuses and left.

She breathed far easier after driving out the gate and heading down the winding road out of the rarefied air of the Studio City hills to the bank of smog in the flatlands of North Hollywood. One thing was certain: She wouldn't step foot over the threshold when she returned to pick up Carolyn.

Sighing, Sierra focused her thoughts on Alex. He actually had an afternoon free, and they were going to spend it together. When he had asked her if she'd like to do so, quick tears of gratitude had sprung to her eyes. It had been so long since they'd really been together, just the two of them. Maybe this would be a chance for them to bridge the chasm that had developed between them. Sierra wasn't sure if they could, but she wanted to. Oh, how she wanted to.

When she unlocked the door and went inside, she felt almost lighthearted. "Alex? I'm home," she called.

Silence met her.

"Alex?" she said again, going into the kitchen. The room was empty, but there was a note on the refrigerator. Cold fingers of disappointment closed around her heart as she moved forward and took it down.

Sierra,
   Steve called. A big client is in town unexpectedly, so we're taking him out to dinner. I'll probably be home late.

That was it. *I'm gone; I'll be home late.* No apology. No regret at not being able to spend time with her.

Angry, Sierra crumpled up the note and tossed it into the

garbage. She vacuumed, dusted, and made preparations for dinner for three. She considered changing her clothes before going back to pick up Carolyn, then rebelled against the idea. She was who she was. Besides, even dressed up she wouldn't fit in with that crowd.

Steeling herself, she headed back to Studio City. As she pulled up before the palatial house, she saw that all the cars were exactly where they were when she had left three hours before. Apparently, they had all stayed through the entire party, sharing the catered hors d'oeuvres and luncheon and the beautifully decorated cake, and enjoying the magician who had come to make sure the children were properly entertained. She got out of her car as several of the women and their little girls came out, each child holding a bag of party favors.

"Our girls are playing in the family room," Marcia said, greeting her at the front door.

"I'm sorry if I'm late."

"You're not late at all. Come in, please. Would you like some coffee?"

"Thank you, but I'd better not. I'm in something of a rush. I need to pick up Clanton soon."

Marcia's expression flickered with understanding and disappointment; it was an excuse, and both women knew it. "I'll show you the way," she said quietly. "Pamela loved the treasure box and scarf."

Polite to the end, Sierra thought sarcastically, then felt a twinge of shame for her critical attitude. *Shrew,* she chastised herself. *Marcia's shown you nothing but kindness. But then, maybe you don't know how to react to kindness anymore. . . .*

The girls were leaning close together and talking like little conspirators. To Sierra's surprise and pleasure, Pamela was bedecked in the scarf and jewelry. Carolyn laughed happily at what her friend was saying and then noticed her. "Oh,

Mommy," she said, obviously disappointed. "Couldn't I stay a while longer? Please?"

"We have to go, Carolyn."

"Clanton's staying at—"

"*Now*, Carolyn."

Carolyn rose obediently. Remembering her manners, she thanked Pamela and her mother for the lovely time and for the bag of party favors and treats.

"Why don't we get together sometime?" Marcia said as they walked back upstairs.

"That'd be nice," Sierra said, giving the proper innocuous response. She knew sometime meant never. The girls were talking again and going ahead of them out the front door, obviously trying to find another way to delay the inevitable.

"Are you free Monday?" Marcia said.

Startled, Sierra looked at her. "Monday?"

"For coffee," Marcia said and smiled. "Or tea. Or water. I don't care." She laughed at Sierra's look, then reached out and squeezed her wrist gently. "What I really want to do is get to know you better."

She spoke so sincerely, Sierra didn't doubt her. Quick tears burned her eyes, and she wondered that a casual invitation for coffee could affect her so deeply.

"Monday sounds perfect."

Mister Grayson cum over today, mad as a grizly.

He said Matthew is going to marry Sally Mae or he is going to shoot him dead. Papa said no son of his is going to marry a harlot. Matthew said Sally Mae is no harlot and they are already married in the eyes of God.

Lucas laughed and called Matthew a fool. Matthew hit him

in the mouth and nocked him down. He got on top of him and kept pounding until Papa pulled him off.

Mama has not stopped crying for two days.

Papa said Mister Grayson is sending a rider around to tell every one who comes to camp meeting that his daughter is getting married to Matthew Benjamin McMurray. Papa said he is actin proud about it.

Mama said some people have no sense of shame.

Matthew married Sally Mae today. She wore her dead mother's white wedding dress. I have never seen Matthew look as happy as he did when he put Mama's ring on her finger.

Sally Mae almost did not have a ring at all. Papa wud not let Matthew have Grandmama McMurray's ring. I heard Papa and Matthew yellin at each other in the barn. Matthew said he loves Sally Mae. Papa said no one like Sally Mae was ever going to wear his mother's ring. He said he wuz sorry he listened to Mama. He said he shud have taken Matthew to Fever River a long time ago to let him larn some facts of life about women and then maybe he wud not have fallen prey to one.

So Mama give Matthew her own wedding ring. Papa has not said a word to her since.

I wonder if James is still in Fever River and what he's doing there.

I got no time for writing in this journal, but it is the only place I can put down my feelings. And such feelings! Sometimes I think I will burst.

Mama is sick, bad sick. Sally Mae dont do nothing to help. She and Matt fight all the time. Or rather Sally Mae does all the fighting. He does all the taking. She says she is bored with her life and bored with him. All he does is work in the fields beside Papa and does nothing fun with her. Sometimes I hate her so much I wish her dead. Then she cries and tells me she loves Matthew and wants to be a good wife and I feel guilty. She just dont know how to be good cause she never had a mama like mine who wud not let her be anythin else.

Mama coughed up blood today. I dont know what to do. Papa dont spend much time with her because he cries every time he does. He said he can't bear to see her suffering. He told her he dont know what to do without her. He dont believe in God. He dont believe in nothing but what he can do for himself and he can't do nuthin for Mama.

Mama said today she is not afraid to die and I shud not be afraid to let her. She smiles when I sit with her. She says she is getting closer to God every minute. I tell her we need her more than God does, but she says maybe she is in the way. In the way of what I asked, but she coughed so long and hard she had no strength to tell me.

Mama died today. She said she could smell the lilacs through the window. She wanted to hold some. So I went outside and cut some for her. When I came back, she was dead.

I was with her three days knowing her time was near. Why did she send me away right then?

Papa and Matthew buried Mama yesterday morning. We could not wait another day for Lucas to cum home from hunting. Sometimes he is gone for a week.

The sun is going down again and Papa is still sitting by the grave with his jug.

I dont think much of Sally Mae being the woman of the house. She dont cook. She dont clean. She just tells me what to do. Matt says she is older and has the right because Sally Mae is his wife. I told him that dont make her my mother. He has never slapped me before. I told him he had better not do it again.

Papa spends all his time in the fields and dont know whats going on in this house. Only time he comes in is when the sun is going down. Then he just sits before the fire with his jug of whiskey drinkin until he dont know nothin anyway.

Matt went huntin with Lucas. I herd Lucas talking to Sally Mae before they went off. He said maybe he wud take his brother to Fever River and show him the sights. They have been gone five days. Sally Mae dont say much. Papa dont say nothing. Sometimes I feel like the old hoot owl and this journal is my only company.

Matt and Lucas came home today. They had no meat with them. Sally Mae did not say anything. So I asked Matt if they went to Fever River. He said yes. I asked him if he saw James. He said no. I asked him what it was like in Fever River and he said there were too many people. He did not say anything after that. Lucas wuz smirking at Sally Mae. He said they learned a lot while they was in Fever River, but he did not say what they learned. Sally Mae did not look well. She said she was going outside for air. Matt went out to help Papa in the fields.

When I went outside to do the wash I saw Lucas talking to Sally Mae. When he laffed at her, she slapped his face. He slapped her back and she ran off crying.

Papa sent Lucas to Fever River with the corn. Matt did not go with him this time because Sally Mae wanted him home. Papa said thar will be enuf money to pay the taxes, buy supplies, and put some by for hard times.

I gotta bad feelin, but Papa dont listen.

Lucas came bak from Fever River today wile I was workin in the garden. He and Papa had words. Lucas said the corn did not sell well this year, that he paid the taxes but thar was not much left for supplies. Papa said he is lying. He said Lucas must have spent the money gaming or on women. Lucas said it is a poor thing when a father dont trust his own blood.

Lucas is gone. He tuk Papas best horse and gun and left before sun up. I never herd such cussing as Papa did when he found out what he dun. Matt said he did not think Lucas wud come back this time. Papa said he wud kill him if he did. Papa said nothing after that. He did not eat breakfast or supper. All he does is wurk in the fields and drink.

I wud not grieve if I never saw Lucas again. As far back as I can remember, ther has been a mean streak in him Papa never cud beet out. Mama tried to talk it out of him. But I dont think Lucas ever herd a word she said. Mama believed we shud treat others the way we want to be treated. Lucas saz that is fools thinkin. He says take what you want or you dont get nothing.

So I guess Lucas tuk what he wanted. He tuk Papas money. He tuk Papas horse. He tuk Papas gun. The only things he did not take were Papas land and Papas house. And he wud have tuk them too if he cud have put them in a saddle bag.

Sally Mae is going to have a babee come winter. Matt is happy about it. It is nice to hear him laugh again.

Papa dont say much about it. Papa dont say much about anything these days.

Today is my birthday. I am fourteen. Not even Matt made mention of it. I guess he forgot jest like Papa.

CHAPTER 7

SIERRA SENT THE TENNIS BALL zinging across the net. It bounced far right of where Marcia was waiting for it, gaining her the winning point. "Yes!" she cried and jumped into the air, raising her racket in triumph.

"Devious," Marcia said in good humor. "Since you won, you have to jump the net."

"Not on your life," Sierra said, laughing. She walked over to the bench and picked up her towel. Dabbing the sweat from her face, she grinned at Marcia as she walked over to drink from a bottle of Calistoga water. "Maybe now I'll be some competition for you."

"You're getting better every time you play," Marcia said, her tone enigmatic.

"You're a good teacher." Sierra bent down to roll the

cotton overshirt she had left on the bench. She tucked it into her canvas bag and set the racket on top.

"Well, I'm not teaching you anymore," Marcia laughed.

Two men entered the court, one older than the other, both dressed in white tennis shorts and shirts, both reeking of affluence.

"First time I've ever seen you lose, Marcia," said the younger and more attractive of the two.

"She tossed the game," Sierra said with a laugh.

"Not likely," he said, a grin making him even more handsome. "Marcia puts her all into everything she does." He winked at Marcia and then looked pointedly at Sierra. "Aren't you going to introduce us?"

Marcia put her towel around her neck. "Sierra, this is Ronal Peirozo, a longtime family friend. Ron, this is Sierra Madrid. She's married to Alex Madrid, game designer for Beyond Tomorrow."

"My pleasure," he said, extending his hand.

"It's nice to meet you." Sierra felt cool strength in his fingers as they closed firmly around her hand. His eyes were an intense blue, and the way they rested on her was decidedly unsettling. He introduced her to the older gentleman with him, but, flustered, she failed to catch his name.

Marcia grinned at her as they walked along the pathway to the dining room. "Don't be embarrassed. Ron has that effect on most women."

"What effect?"

Marcia laughed. "Fine. We'll play it your way."

When Alex had been given the club membership as a Christmas bonus, Sierra had resisted coming to Lakeside Country Club. Not until Marcia invited her for lunch one afternoon had she even admitted being a member. "You're kidding. And you don't go?"

"No. I don't go."

"For heaven's sake, Sierra. What are you going to do? Sit home watching soap operas for the rest of your life? I've never known anyone to be so resistant to success and the benefits it brings."

Resigned, Sierra had accompanied her to the club. She had had so much fun meeting Marcia's friends, it had become a part of her daily routine. She met Marcia for tennis or golf or racquetball, depending on the weather, worked up a sweat, showered, and then relaxed for a few hours. Sometimes they sat in the salon and had a manicure or pedicure. More often than not, they joined others in the women's lounge for drinks and lunch.

As they reached the patio outside the dining room, Sierra saw that Nancy Berne and Edie Redmond were already sitting at the table they usually occupied. It was considered a primo spot, located as it was near the windows overlooking the golf course, but then, having the best was par for the course for these women. Both were married to high-powered executives. Beside them, Ashley Worrell—who was recently divorced from her well-known, extremely wealthy plastic surgeon husband—was sipping mineral water. Lorraine Sheedy, a close friend of Ashley's, sat next to her, looking grim. Lorraine's husband was an attorney who had made a fortune handling divorce cases for movie stars. The last of what Marcia jokingly called "The Rat Pack" was Meredith Schneider, an heiress who was four-times divorced, five-times married.

As Sierra took her usual seat near the tall ferns, she greeted the others with easy camaraderie. Wylie, the waiter who always took care of their orders, came to the table. He picked up Meredith's empty martini glass, replaced the napkin, and set a fresh martini before her.

"Thank you, Wylie," Meredith said, and Sierra could tell she had been drinking for some time. Meredith smiled benevolently around the table. "You girls going to have something? My treat."

Marcia glanced at her watch. "It's not even noon, Merry. Aren't you starting a little early today?"

"You're an hour too late with your warning, dear." She glanced at her Rolex. "Eleven forty-five. If you wish to be legalistic, wait fifteen minutes. Then you may order a drink."

Marcia ordered a gin and tonic with a twist of lime.

Nancy and Edie both ordered espresso. Ashley grimaced delicately. "How many times do I have to tell you girls what caffeine does to the skin?" she said and ordered a rum punch.

"And rum's good for it?" Nancy said, amused.

"Rum is made from sugarcane and molasses, both natural substances. Add a little fruit juice and you have a nutritious noontime libation."

"And a buzz," Edie said dryly.

Lorraine quietly ordered a double Scotch on the rocks. Everyone at the table looked at her in surprise. She never drank anything but white zinfandel. Meredith popped the green olive into her mouth, eyes amused.

Sierra ordered an iced tea. She had learned early on that she didn't like the taste of alcohol or its dizzying effects.

They talked of mundane things until the drinks were served. Lorraine finished the double Scotch with two swallows. Shuddering, she set the empty glass down before Wylie had taken three steps from the table.

"Feeling better?" Marcia said softly, astonished.

"Wylie," Lorraine said firmly, "bring me another, please."

"Yes, ma'am," he said, brows lifting in surprise.

"Doing some serious drinking today, are we?" Meredith cooed.

Lorraine gave a humorless laugh, her eyes glittering. "Frank's having an affair."

Ashley set her rum punch down hard and uttered a short, exceedingly foul word. "I swear. All men are pigs."

"Darling," Meredith said, too inebriated to be distressed by anything. "You're looking at it all wrong. Haven't you read *Men Are Just Desserts*?" She looked at Lorraine. "Did he fess up, sweetie, or did you have to pry the information out of him with a crowbar?"

"I asked him point-blank. He tried to worm his way around the issue with his usual legal jargon. He might be able to fool everybody in a courtroom, but I always know when he's lying."

"Are you filing for divorce?" Ashley said, her own having only recently been declared final.

"Actually, I was thinking about castration."

"Here," Meredith said, delighted. "Take the butter knife."

Ignoring Meredith, Marcia put her hand over Lorraine's. "Don't make any decision too quickly, Lorry. Try to work it out."

"Work it out!" Lorraine's dark eyes welled with tears. "I put the jerk through law school. Four years I worked two jobs just to get him through. You know who the woman is? That airheaded blonde bimbo I told you about, the one in the last divorce case he handled."

"Be thankful," Meredith said. "At least it wasn't the husband."

Nancy laughed before she could stifle it. Looking sheepish, she apologized quickly. "Stop making jokes, Meredith," she whispered. "It's not funny."

"Of *course* it's funny. It's hilarious!" Meredith said. She lifted her martini in salute. "To marriage, the biggest joke man ever played on womankind. I should know. I've been on the merry-go-round often enough." She downed the martini with a flick of her wrist.

"At least Eric's faithful," Lorraine said bitterly.

"Oh, of course, he is, darling. As long as I give him everything he wants, he performs like a trained dog, though I daresay a dog has more loyalty." Her mouth curved in a cynical smile. "That little sports car Eric is driving cost me one hundred and fifty-seven thousand dollars." She gave a bleak laugh. "Fidelity comes at a high price these days."

Sierra saw the sheen of tears in Meredith's eyes.

"I'd kill myself if John cheated on me," Edie said.

"Ah, now there are wise, comforting words," Meredith said, her tone hard-edged with derision. She flagged Wylie for another martini. "Far from an original idea. Attempt suicide, and your unfaithful husband will be wretched with guilt. I tried that with my second husband. Charles called an ambulance and had my stomach pumped. A completely disgusting experience, I can tell you. And did he beg forgiveness and tell me how much he loved me and what a mistake he'd made? Ha! He moved out while I was in the hospital." Pain flickered across her face as she revealed this old, obviously still unhealed, wound.

"I told Frank a long time ago that what's good for the gander is good for the goose," Lorraine said as the waiter moved away.

"Meaning what?" Edie said. "You're going to cheat on *him* now?"

"Why not?" Lorraine said fiercely, eyes brimming with tears. "Let him have a taste of what it feels like to be betrayed."

"That's the spirit!" Meredith said with an overbright laugh. "And I know just the lad to instill jealousy in any husband. James! Come over here this minute, dear."

Lorraine, fully aware of just how outrageous Meredith

could be when she'd been drinking, blushed as a handsome young waiter turned slightly to look over at them. "Don't you dare, Meredith!" she hissed.

"Isn't he a dish?" Meredith said, waggling her bejeweled fingers at him playfully. "Gorgeous, ambitious, and *half* Frank's age. In far better shape, too."

"If he takes one step in this direction, I'm leaving."

Meredith shrugged dramatically toward the young man. "Another time, dear. Lorraine's changed her mind."

"I swear, Meredith. You're completely incorrigible," Lorraine said.

"Comes with the territory," Meredith said, a bleakness seeping into her blue eyes. She quickly tried to hide it behind a bright, brittle smile.

Ashley glanced at her watch. "I'm going to have to get to the gym."

"She has to work off the rum," Meredith said dryly.

Ashley worked out an hour each morning at home and then spent another hour each afternoon at the club with a personal trainer who specialized in body shaping. She had a perfect body already but was convinced if she missed a day of exercise, she'd blow up like a balloon. Sometimes she ate nothing but salad without dressing, while at other times she gleefully devoured every dessert on the menu. Sierra had never known anyone so obsessed with her body and caloric intake.

"Can't you forgo it just this once?" Lorraine said, annoyed.

"Why don't you come with me? A good workout will do you a world of good."

Meredith smiled drolly. "Treadmills are wonderful things, aren't they? They reduce a normal human being right down to the mentality of a hamster in a wheel."

Ashley gave her a sharp glance. "A good workout would

be better for her than obsessing about Frank and getting drunk like *you.*"

Meredith arched an elegant brow. "The kitten has claws today."

Ignoring her, Ashley got up. "Are you coming with me, Lorry?"

"No. My heart already aches. I don't need my body aching, too."

"Fine." Swinging around, Ashley walked quickly across the room and out the exit into the lobby.

"That girl's so uptight she could turn coal to diamonds," Meredith said, shaking her head. "I say we spike her mineral water. Maybe she'll enjoy life a little more."

Sierra lifted her iced tea and sipped, wondering if any of these women enjoyed life at all. They had everything the world counted important, yet she couldn't see any evidence of *joy* in their lives. They were all hungry for something more. *Just like you . . . ,* a voice echoed in her head. She shifted uncomfortably, knowing it was true. The same hunger ate away at her and left her feeling restless and insecure.

Something was missing, but she didn't know what.

Marcia put her hand over Meredith's. "What's the matter with you today?"

Meredith gave a bleak laugh. "Nothing that isn't wrong with me every day of my life." She gave the waiter a radiant smile as he set another martini in front of her. "Thank you, Wylie." She lifted the drink to Marcia. "Cheers, sweetie."

"Did you ever see Dr. Worth?" Marcia said.

Meredith gave a derisive laugh. "I don't need a psychiatrist."

Sierra had been amazed to find out that the totally together Marcia had ever been to a psychiatrist, let alone that she'd been in ongoing therapy for ten years. Marcia claimed that was why she felt so at peace within herself. Dr. Worth had taken her on a journey into her past, where she had come face-to-face with the causes of problems in the present. Apparently, her parents had said and done things, seemingly unimportant at the time, that had had profound effects on her ability to function as an adult.

"Once I'd discovered what—and who—was responsible, I found I was free to move on," she'd told Sierra, that calm smile on her face.

Whenever difficulties arose in her marriage or life, Marcia simply returned to the refreshing, comforting counsel and couch of Dr. Worth. Once there, she received a booster shot of self-esteem, absolution, and direction.

"Don't you see, Meredith?" Marcia continued. "You'll never be truly happy until—"

"I don't think getting in touch with my 'inner child' would help much," Meredith said flatly, cutting her off.

"It would help. I guarantee it. It's helped me tremendously."

"Has it?" Meredith gave a mirthless laugh. "If it's so helpful, why are you back in therapy every other month?"

"Dr. Worth gives me a fresh view."

"Darling, I could give you a fresh view, and I wouldn't charge you two hundred and fifty an hour."

Marcia drew back with graceful calm. She gave a slow sigh, a sign she was striving for patience. "Why don't we order lunch?"

"Ah, ah, ah. I'm sure any self-respecting psychiatrist like Dr. Worth would tell you substituting food for a good fight is stuffing your feelings and counterproductive to your mental and emotional health."

"I'm hungry," Marcia said with a beatific smile.

"No, you're not. You're *mad*."

"No, I am not."

Though Marcia sat in her usual, elegantly relaxed pose,

Sierra could feel the tension radiating from her. She had seen the same thing happen before when Marcia was faced with a hard question.

Meredith gave her a bald grin. "You're getting angry."

"I'm sure you'd like me to be angry," Marcia said coolly, "but it's not constructive."

"Constructive?" Meredith smiled, her lovely, perfectly made-up face showing nothing of the inner turmoil that was clearly raging. "I'm always curious to see how deep your serenity goes, Marcia. I suspect not very."

Marcia arched her brow. "What do you mean?"

"You're not serene at all, despite appearances. I admire your control. Really I do. You're always so cool and so calm. Your husband never strays. Your children are a perfect little lady and gentleman. Not a single rapid in the river of your life, is there, sweetheart? Not so anyone can see, that is." Meredith twirled her beautiful, aristocratic, bejeweled hand gracefully in the air, adding sardonically, "And all because you've embraced the light, become one with the universe, and live on a higher plane of consciousness than the rest of us poor mortals." Her hand took rest beside the martini, her eyes shrewd. "Tell me, dear. Does the Valium help?"

Two spots of color appeared in Marcia's cheeks. "I face my problems head-on, Meredith."

"Oh yes, and wrestle them to the ground and choke them to death with the sheer strength of your will. I *know*," Meredith said. "I've seen the hunted look on Tom's face. I imagine if the poor man ever felt free enough to wear an open-necked shirt, we'd see the bite marks on his throat."

Marcia's face flushed beet red. She went rigid for a moment, then let out her breath very slowly and audibly, a yoga technique Sierra recognized. "I prefer your company when you're sober," she said with icy calm.

"And less honest, too, perhaps?" Meredith's blue eyes flashed with disdain. "Solve your own problems, dearie, before you try to fix mine."

Marcia rose regally and cast a stiff smile at the others seated around the table. "Why don't we all go in for lunch, ladies?"

Edie, who loathed conflict, rose quickly. "I think that's an excellent idea."

"We'd be delighted if you joined us, Merry," Marcia said as she gathered her white tennis sweater and canvas bag.

"Liar," Meredith said and raised her martini in mocking salute.

Sierra followed Marcia into the dining room. Nancy and Edie joined them; Lorraine, preferring the heiress's acerbic wit, ordered another bourbon and remained behind.

"I swear. Merry is turning herself into a drunk," Nancy said, taking her place at the table.

"What do you think Lorraine will do?" Edie said, accepting a menu from a waiter.

"Get sick and cry a lot," Nancy said with a pitying glance back toward the lounge. "Ending a marriage is bad enough, if it comes to that. If you happen to be married to one of the leading divorce attorneys in the country, you can expect to lose everything, including your children."

"If he wants them," Marcia said blandly. "You've heard Lorry say often enough that Frank hasn't shown any interest in the children since the day they were born."

Sierra thought of how little time Alex had for the children these days. When was the last time he'd played baseball with Clanton or talked with Carolyn? She had been shouldering the full responsibility of parenting since their move to Los Angeles. Then, when things didn't go right, such as Clanton's report card showing two Cs and a D, Alex always had her to blame.

"What about Ashley's situation?" Edie said. "Gerry demanded joint custody just to make her life miserable."

"I don't think that's true," Marcia said, closing the menu and setting it aside. "Gerry was concerned for the children, and rightfully so. Ashley is so obsessive about weight, and poor little Veronica is going through her plump stage. Can you imagine what it's like for a child of ten to be dragged to aerobics classes every afternoon after school? That's what was happening until Gerry stepped in."

"An hour of exercise each day won't hurt her, will it?" Edie said, looking at Marcia for answers. Her own children were enrolled in various sports programs and resisting attendance.

"It's not the exercise that's harmful, Edie," Marcia said, sounding as though she were explaining a basic equation to a slow-witted pupil. "It's the experience of being *forced* to do what she doesn't want to do. That will leave terrible scars on her psyche."

Sierra could imagine Veronica grown-up and spending an hour twice a week in Dr. Worth's office exploring her "inner child." Still, would any child do anything if not pressed? Didn't Marcia press her own children to excel? Where was the difference?

"Have you *seen* Veronica?" Nancy said, shaking her head sadly. "All that child does is sit around and eat snacks in front of the television. She doesn't talk; she whines."

Uncomfortable with the course of the conversation, Sierra stared at the menu. She couldn't help but wonder if the women talked about her and her children when she wasn't present.

She ordered lobster thermidor and let the current of conversation swirl around her without diving in.

"You've been very quiet," Marcia said at last.

Over the past half hour, Sierra had listened to her three

companions dissect Meredith's, Lorraine's, and Ashley's lives. They had laid bare every dysfunction, past sin, and private anguish, seeming to relish the action far more than they were enjoying their food.

She met Marcia's calm gaze. "My life is so full of problems, I don't feel I've any right to talk about theirs."

Silence fell around the table, and she felt the three women staring at her with a mingling of expressions.

Marcia blinked, her eyes widening in surprise. "You think we're *gossiping*," she said in quiet accusation.

Sierra glanced from Marcia to Nancy, whose eyes were hot with indignation. Edie, on the other hand, looked embarrassed.

Sierra felt surrounded. Sometimes her friends acted like a pack of hounds. They had the veneer of sophistication, but they'd proven many times just how savage they were beneath. They didn't use their teeth to rip a person apart—they didn't need to. Their soft-spoken words were sharp and barbed and effectively shredded one another with regularity. Didn't they realize what they were doing?

"I think you're concerned," Sierra said, wondering if that was only the guise beneath which they hid less altruistic motives.

"Of course we're concerned," Marcia said. "We *love* Meredith."

"And Ashley," Nancy said.

"And Lorraine," Edie added. "You know we do."

"Yes, I know," Sierra conceded, but she couldn't help hoping they wouldn't love her in the same way. "It's just that talking about their problems like this doesn't change anything."

"Then what will?" Nancy said.

"I wish I knew." She looked around at them, not knowing what else to say. Seeing their bleak eyes and defensive postures, she suddenly wished she were more like her mother.

She would have had something to offer, some wisdom or encouragement.

From the beginning, she had found the company of these women stimulating and challenging. They made her laugh. They made her think. They opened her eyes to the way the world was. She wasn't the innocent, small-town girl Alex had brought to Los Angeles over a year ago. And she was thankful for that. But sometimes, she felt that despite the sophistication, knowledge, and wisdom about life that these women seemed to have, they really didn't know anything at all. Nothing that mattered. Nothing that changed anything. If they did, wouldn't their lives reflect it?

"The fear of the Lord is the beginning of wisdom, Sierra."

She frowned at the remembered words; her mother had quoted them to her often. She looked at the women around the table again. It was bad enough that her words had brought an end to the conversation. There was no way she was going to try to bring God into this! That might work for her mother, but Sierra wasn't as confident as her mother that God had all the answers. If He did, He certainly didn't seem eager to share them.

Not with her, anyway.

She shifted again in her seat, wondering why she suddenly felt so depressed. Maybe it was because the discussion had revolved around the disintegrating lives of three women she liked and admired. Maybe it was because so many people all around her seemed to be hurting.

Maybe it was because her own life felt so empty and out of control.

"What's bothering you?" Marcia said, sensitive to her mood. Nancy and Edie were looking at her, too.

How honest could she be with these women? Was she

the only one struggling with a sense of hopelessness? "I don't know. A lot of things, I guess. I'm not even sure I can explain."

They sat waiting.

Sierra plunged in, taking the risk. "I'm so *busy* all the time. Yet, at the end of the day, I feel . . . empty, as though time has passed, but I didn't accomplish anything that mattered."

"What do you expect of yourself?" Nancy said. "To find the cure for cancer?"

"No. Just *something*."

"The best thing we can do is be happy," Edie said.

"Within ourselves," Marcia said in gentle admonition. "If we can't manage our own lives, how can we expect to manage those of our families?"

Manage. The word jarred. It was discordant. Sierra pictured a company president issuing memorandums to her employees. Meredith's words flashed back in her head; they had been harsh, but true. Sierra had seen the dynamics of Marcia's family. Watching her interaction with Tom and the children was like watching a master puppeteer working marionettes. Marcia always knew exactly what to say and do to get her family members to do what she expected of them. Both of her children were A students, active in sports, popular. Her husband worked hard, made good money, and came home from work every night at precisely five thirty. Marcia's life seemed to run so smoothly.

Was that the secret to having a happy family? A woman who could *manage* everything?

If that was the case, she was doomed to perpetual failure.

Manage Alex? What a laugh! She could hardly even get her husband to sit down long enough to talk anymore. When he did, they ended up fighting. He had a will of steel. Over the past year, that will had run over hers like a steamroller flattening macadam.

Edie changed the subject. She mentioned a play she'd seen, and Nancy chimed in to agree it was wonderful. Marcia talked about her plans to accompany Tom to a business convention in Detroit. When asked by Nancy, she admitted most of the other men from his company weren't taking their wives. Smiling, she said Tom had agreed it would be a nice time for them to get away by themselves.

"By yourselves?" Nancy said. "With Tom in meetings most of the day? What are *you* going to do?"

"I'll relax and read and have lunch and dinner with Tom. I imagine there'll be time to take in a museum or two between meetings."

"Are there museums in Detroit?" Nancy said.

"There's Henry Ford's Fair Lane museum," Marcia said with a bright laugh, but Sierra couldn't help wondering if her friend's real reason for going with Tom was to keep him under her ever-watchful eye.

Well, what if it is? she wondered, almost defiantly. *Is that such a bad idea in this day of disintegrating and broken marriages?*

Poking at her lobster thermidor, Sierra remembered Alex asking her to go with him to the Consumer Electronics Show in Las Vegas last year.

"What about my mother?" she had said.

"What's CES got to do with your mother?"

"She's coming down for a visit. You knew that! I told you weeks ago."

"You knew about CES, too!" He'd sworn in Spanish. "I gave you the dates."

"You did *not!*"

"Call your mom and ask her to hold off for a week."

"She's supposed to juggle her schedule just to please you?"

"She's *retired*. What sort of a schedule has she got to juggle?"

As it turned out, she didn't go to CES, though she did call her mother and change their plans. Instead of her mother coming south, Sierra drove north with the children and spent eight days in Healdsburg. Her mother had lost weight and looked tired, but otherwise she'd been in good spirits. They'd had long talks while sitting on Memorial Beach watching the children swim in the Russian River. Sierra had returned to North Hollywood remorseful, almost afraid of the greeting she would receive from Alex. Their telephone conversations had been stilted and uneasy while she was in Healdsburg. She apologized and things had been easier between them for a while.

Easier, but not the same.

Audra had mentioned CES just the other evening when she and Alex were all having dinner at Matt and Laura's house. Steve said several new members of the staff were going along this year. Alex didn't even look at her as he sipped his wine and said he was looking forward to a trip to Vegas.

Stabbing a piece of lobster, Sierra decided it might be to the best interests of her marriage if she went along this time.

"You wouldn't be interested," Alex said that evening when she brought up the subject.

"What makes you so sure?"

"It's all glitz and meetings, and a lot of people you don't know. Those you do, you can't stand."

"I suppose you mean Audra will be there."

"Yes, Audra will be there. She supports Steve whole-heartedly."

She heard what he didn't say: she didn't support him. Anger poured through her; it was always just beneath the surface these days. But whose fault was that? Alex was always cutting her down. She wasn't supportive. She wasn't a good mother or her children would be getting better grades. She wasn't doing anything other than spending his money at the club. Whose idea was it to go to the club in the first place?

"I'd like to go with you this year," she insisted.

He looked at her enigmatically. "You said you hate Vegas."

What she really hated was the way he remembered every word she ever said just so he could throw it back in her face. Breathing slowly, she clung to her self-restraint. "I've never been to Las Vegas, Alex. I'd like to see what it's like."

He didn't say anything. He just looked at her. She wondered why the decision was so hard for him to make. Hadn't he wanted her to accompany him last year? Didn't he want her along this time?

"Fine," he said, gaze flickering away, "but I don't want the kids coming. These shows are work, not play. You'd better keep that in mind, too. I won't be able to entertain you."

Gracious to the last. "I'll ask Marcia if she would mind having the children spend the weekend at her house."

"Don't expect to play tourist," he said. "We're going to be attending a lot of business dinners and company parties."

"Will I need some new clothes?"

"Ask Audra."

God, dont You listen when peepul pray?

Dont you care? Mama told me You did, but I dont see how with the Terrible Truble we got. I got doubts you are even there.

Sometimes I dont think things cud get worse. Then they do. First James leaving. Then Sally Mae coming here as Matts wife. Then Mama dying, then Papa turning to whiskey. If all that aint bad enuf, Lucas had to leave and take the best horse with him. God, what more you gonna take?

Mama used to say You had control of everything. So what
I wud like to ask is why you are giving us all this Sorrow and
Grief?

Sally Mae is sick most of the time. She is scared all the time.
Nothing makes her happy. She is either crying when Matt is
out working or screaming at him when he is not. She says she
wants to go home to her grandmama in Fever River. Matt will
not tak her and her pa washt his hands of her the day she wed.

Papa works all day and drinks all night til he sleeps. And even
with all his work it dont look like it will be a good year.

Weve had no meat in a month and since Lucas stole Papas
gun no way of getting any.

Things cant get wurs.

I wuz wrong.

I aint settin hope on god no more. There is no god. There is
only hell on earth. Mama is the lucky one. And Sally Mae too
now that she is dead. They have no worries. The rest of us have
got the wate of what they dun. Mama and her hopes of heaven.
And Sally Mae knowing she wuz on her way to hell.

I dont know what I am going to do now with this babee.

Matt burned Papas fields yesterday. He had good reason.
Sally Mae told him the babee werent his. She knew she was
dying and it made her crazy scared. So she told the awful
truth. *Do you think you are the father, Matthew? You had to go
off to Fever River with Lucas, didnt you? I knew what you wud
think of me when you come bak. I wanted to hurt you before
you hurt me and I did. O, I did. I wasnt goin to tell you but
I can't die with this sin on my head. I dont want to go to hell.
You hear me?* Matt said what are you talkin about? And Sally
Mae said *The babee aint yours. Your father put it in me.* Matt
called her a liar and she said to go and ask him. So he did.

Papa said he was drunk when she come in to him and lay

with him like a wife. He did not know what he was doing. Matt went crazy. He beat Papa until I thot he wud kill him. He nocked me down three times before I cud stop him. And Papa just lay in the dirt bleeding. Matt set the fields afire. I aint seen him since.

Sally Mae was screaming somethin awful. It raised the hair on the bak of my neck. The babee come with the flames. Thar was so much smoke it burned my eyes. The fire did not tuch the house. The wind changed and sent the flames across the fields to the woods and creek. If it had not, Papa, Sally Mae, the babee and me wud all be ded.

The babee come out of her at nightfall, and blood come too. I never seen so much. It soaked through the straw mattress and pooled on the floor underneath. She stopped screaming then. Papa cum inside the house when I called, but he jest stud in the doorway. I kept cryin for him to help me. He said leave that devil child to die with her. He said they cud both go to meet the devil together.

I cud not do it. I can't let this babee die. His mother was a wanton and his father a drunken fool. Does that mean he has to die for it?

Papa said he will not have Sally Maes devil spawn in his house. I said it was no devil, but his own son. He laid a curse on me. He said I am not his daughter no more. He said if I did not leave the house he wud kill me and the babee with me.

I can hear Papa digging her grave. Thar aint going to be a ceremony or a marker and he is burning all her things and the bed she and Matthew shared.

He ought to be burning with it.

I hav deecided to call the babee Joshua. It is not a famly name like Matthew or Lucas. But why would anybody want to be in this famly? I like the sound of Joshua. I read it in the Bible.

Mama wud sing about Joshua blowing his horn and the walls of Jericho came tumbling down.

Maybe Joshua's crying will make Papa's walls come tumbling down. And he will let us come back and live in the house before winter hits.

Maybe Joshua is not a good name for this babee. He has not come into this world to bring his famly to the Promused Land. He has stirred up nothing but trouble since the day he was born.

The preecher came today.

He said a lady acros the river wants a babee bad. I told him she shud talk to her husband about that and not send a preecher to me. Preecher said if I give the babee up, Papa might forgive me my sins and let me come back to the house. I asked the preecher what he knew about what happened and he said he knew all he needed to know and I told him he did not know much. He got all puffed up like a toad and turned red. He said an unwed girl with a babee shud not talk to her betters the way I was talking to him and it was no wonder Papa threw me out. He said Papa did rite. He said in the old days I wud hav ben stoned to deth for what I dun. So I did not say nothing else until he left.

Nobody is taking Joshua away from me.

I tried to talk to Papa today but he walked right by me like I was not thar. I followed him out into the blackened fields and begged, but he did not let on he herrd nothing until Joshua started cryin. Then he turned around and looked at me. I never seen such a look on his face. I never seen such a look on nobodys face like that. He said to git away from him or he wud kill us both.

I said winter is coming, Papa. You want us to die?

He said yes.

First snow came today. The goat is going dry. Seems like I did not save this babee from deth at all. Just made him suffer.

The right reverend came again today. He said if I do not send the babee to that lady across the river, Papa is going to send me and the babee to Mamas sister in Fever River with the Reinholtzes, the German family moving out. Preecher says they lost two children to fever a month ago and can not bear to stay another winter. It wud be Christian kindness to give them my babee. I said if they cud have two babees of their own, they could have more, but I was not giving my own blood away to strangers for any reason. He said I was unrepentant and arrogant. When I did not say nuthin he askt if I knew what arrogant meant. I said it is when someone already thinks he knows everything there is to know and dont know nothing at all.

He said I am hell bent. Maybe I am. All I know for certain is the right reverend wud find truth harder to swallow than the lies hes chewing on. The truth would choke him to death.

I aint going to tell him what happened. Better he thinks Joshua is mine than know where he cum from. It is bad enuf God knows without havin the hole county hear of it.

God dont care.

I did not think Aunt Martha wud let me in the door of her fine house. The Reinholtz told me to wait an hour before coming into Fever River. The town is called Galena now after the ore they mine hereabouts. Reinholtz did not want anyone knowin they had anythin to do with a girl who had a babee and no husband and did not even know where she was going. So I did what he askt and waited til nightfall before comin into town. I askt the first person I saw whar Martha Werner lived. The boy tuk me strat here. I almost died when I saw the house.

It is so grand and up on a hill street. Two stories of wood and block with steps up one side.

A black woman answered when I nocked. I askt for Martha Werner. She called for Clovis. A black man come runnin and started untying the rope around my wast. I got scared and said I wud not let him take my goat. My baby needs milk or he will die. He said he wud not take him far and he wud see the goat was fed and watered.

Aunt Martha is the prettiest woman I ever seen. She was wearing a yellow dress with white lace. She knew me rite off. She said I look like Mama. She tuk Joshua from me. A good thing she did because I cud not stand no more. It is a long walk from the home place to Fever River or Galena or whatever it is called. Worse when you are eatin wagon dust. I did not want to sit on her furniture in my dirty clothes but the black woman picked me up from where I sunk down and put me on the sofa anyway.

The black womans name is Betsy. She carried me into the kitchen and set me near the stove. Aunt Martha had Joshua. Clovis fetcht water from the town well and Betsy heeted it in big pots. I askt about the goat. He said the goat is fine and eatin supper and went out again for another bucket of water. Betsy tuk off my clothes and put me in the tub. I aint never felt anythin as good as that warm water comin over me. She washed me like a babee wile Aunt Martha washed and played with Joshua. Betsy said stop worrying about that goat. My man Clovis will take good care of her.

When Joshua started in fussin, Betsy went out bak and milked the goat. Aunt Martha sat in a rockin chair near the stov feeding Joshua and singing Mamas song. I cried. I cud not stop. I just sat in the warm water and the tears kept running.

Aunt Martha give me a real bed to sleep in and a room of my own. Joshua slept with me. He aint never ben in a bed before.

For that matter, I aint never seen one the likes of it. It is shiny brass like gold with a lacy tent over head. Aunt Martha said it belonged to Mama before she run off with Papa. She said her own Papa ordered it and had it shipped all the way from New York.

I wunder if James ever made it to New York like he wanted. He mit even be in China by now.

Aunt Martha dont ask me a lot of questions. And she dont look at me like most foks do. The Reinholtz were in church today and they wud not look at me at all. On the way home I told Aunt Martha Joshua is Sally Maes son. It is half-true. She cried and kist me. She said she loves me and I can liv with her forever if I want. She said *You are not to worry what people say. The truth always comes out in the end.*

I hope this truth dont.

Aunt Martha thinks as much of edukashun as Mama did. She says I got a good mind that needs fillin with good things. To that end, she is tutorin me in reding, riting, and numbers and teachin me the Bible. She says that the only way to do well in this life is to know the word of God. Mama knew the Bible front and back and it did not do her much good at all. I did not tell Aunt Martha this. I wud rather eat stones than hurt her feelings. Life does that easy enuf as it is.

CHAPTER 8

Sierra wandered down the crowded aisles of the Consumer Electronics Show by herself. The convention center was a beehive of activity. It reminded her of the state fair with its carnival atmosphere, but here few people were over the age of thirty and everyone dressed in suits.

Big booths lined both sides of the carpeted aisle. Videos of new games were going. Neon and vibrant-colored cartoon-like artwork was everywhere. It was dizzying to the eye and ear. She saw a short man wearing funky clothes and glitter-framed glasses talking with several taller men in suits. She could tell by the deference paid him that he was somebody important in the industry.

Sometimes she could tell who was important, sometimes not. Alex had introduced her to a man at a party the night before. He'd looked ordinary enough until he'd left them; then Alex informed her the man's company had built a two-million-dollar studio in his home just so he could work on sound for games.

Someone bumped her, glanced at her badge, mumbled an apology, and moved on. Everyone looked at badges. Alex could sniff out sales reps and reporters like a hound in the hunt. Not that he had to work very hard at it. Reporters from all the gaming magazines were fighting to make appointments with him.

Lost in the maze of booths and people, Sierra tried to get her bearings and figure out how to get back to the Beyond Tomorrow booth. It was almost five o'clock and Alex had told her to meet him there. They needed to go up to their room and change for a business dinner. The Beyond Tomorrow booth was near the center with huge screens displaying Alex's new game: Camouflage.

Everywhere she turned, she heard technical jargon; she didn't have the foggiest idea what anyone was talking about.

Over dinner, she had listened to Alex talk about his work and his new game. He exuded confidence as he answered questions and explained his theories and plans. He held his guests' rapt attention, fanning their interest. This was a side of her husband she'd never witnessed before. She was proud of him, of his obvious achievements and his ability to sway others. Yet she had felt set apart as well—like some kind of nice-looking but totally unnecessary adornment. After the introductions and pleasantries, she sat listening. The conversation went on around her, but hardly a word was directed her way.

"Do you play your husband's game, Sierra?" one of the young men asked her as their dinners were being served.

"No. I'm not much for video games. They're too quick and complex for me."

Alex laughed. "Sierra prefers physical pursuits, like tennis at the country club, manicures, and shopping."

The other men laughed with him. She laughed, too, pretending to share the joke while doing all she could to conceal the surprise and hurt she felt at his remark. He said it lightly, as though affectionately amused. Yet she felt belittled.

Was that how he saw her? As a shallow young woman with nothing important to do?

The thought had plagued her all night and most of the day. *God, I don't even know who I am anymore.*

Ahead of her now was a big screen with vividly colored warriors using medieval weapons to hack at one another. One split the other in half with an ax, sending splashes of neon-red blood in a shower. Repulsed, Sierra looked away and kept walking. At least she knew where she was now. Beyond Tomorrow was down two aisles to the right.

Alex was talking with two men in business suits, while Elizabeth Longford, Beyond Tomorrow's hotshot merchandising director, stood alongside him with a clipboard. The young woman was dressed in a designer suit of deep green. It fitted her slender body like a glove. No sign of a single wrinkle or crease, even after a full day of standing on the floor and talking to sales reps. Elizabeth's long blonde hair was permed into kinked tendrils that tumbled down her back.

Sierra had only met Elizabeth a few times and found her cool and remote. She was very attractive, professional, and ambitious. Sierra felt uneasy around her, even more so when she saw Alex talking with her so easily.

❖

"Yes, she's young," Audra said that evening at a party. Sierra stood beside her near the hors d'oeuvres, sipping champagne. "She just turned twenty-six a few weeks ago."

Alex and Steve stood not far away talking business to

several sales reps, who seemed more interested in admiring Elizabeth in her sleek low-cut black gown. The simple, elegant design bespoke money. Lots of it.

"She graduated from Wellesley," Audra said, setting her champagne down so she could put caviar on a small circle of melba toast. "She took her master's in marketing at Columbia." Sierra watched the younger woman move out onto the dance floor with one of the reps. Elizabeth's graceful undulations were in stark contrast to the enthusiastic gyrations of her partner.

"She's very lovely," Sierra said, noticing how Alex and Steve were both watching her.

"Indeed," Audra said enigmatically. "She knows how to present herself. She went to finishing school in Switzerland and was a debutante." She took up her glass of champagne again. "I asked her about it, but she disdains the whole thing. Family pressure. Understandable." She ate the cracker delicately. "Her father is a descendant of one of the crew of the *Mayflower*." She looked at Sierra. "She works very closely with Alex."

Somehow, Audra's words held warning. They planted doubt and fear.

❖

"Do you like Elizabeth?" Sierra asked Alex later in their hotel room.

"She's good at her job," he said, loosening his tie.

Hanging up his suit jacket, Sierra waited for him to say more. When he didn't, she looked back at him standing near the windows overlooking the lights of Las Vegas. He was so handsome, her heart ached. What woman wouldn't be attracted to him? He pulled his shirt free of his suit trousers and unbuttoned his collar.

Sierra's stomach fluttered. How long since they'd come together in passionate need for one another? How long since he'd held her and kissed her and said he loved her? She loved him so much. She needed him. Yet he seemed so distant, so distracted. Whatever thoughts were running through his mind clearly troubled him. Hadn't things gone as well as expected tonight? Or was it something else?

Her throat ached. She wanted to say something but couldn't trust her voice. They had been fighting so much lately, usually about the most trivial things. She wasn't sure what Alex would do if she reached out to him. She wanted to be close to him again, the way they used to be when they could talk about anything, when just being together and touching one another had been heaven. Now it took all her courage to cross the room.

Brushing his hands away, she unbuttoned his shirt for him. "I love you, Alex." He didn't say anything. He didn't touch her. But he didn't turn away either. When she finished, she looked up at him. "I'll never stop loving you."

Frowning, he searched her eyes.

She couldn't read his expression. Fear suddenly overwhelmed her, and she couldn't even say why.

His eyes softened. Sighing, he cupped her face. "You've always driven me crazy, Sierra," he said, his voice deep and rough as his fingers stroked her skin. He didn't look happy about it.

"*Te amo muchísimo,*" she whispered.

He loosened her French braid. Combing his fingers into her hair, he kissed her.

Sighing in relief, she let the passion sweep through her.

Nothing has changed, not really, she told herself, wanting desperately to believe it.

It has been a long time since I wrote in this journal.

I have had little time to do anything over the past months except complete the work Aunt Martha prepares for me. I am not complaining. She says she has Great Expectations for me. When I do well, she is more pleased than I. While everyone else in this town seems to look upon me as Mary Magdalene still possessed of demons, Aunt Martha sees me as Pure Delight. It is beyond me why. I question everything she teaches me. She listens and makes no condemnations while others would not even give me the time of day.

Aunt Martha tells me I was God's gift to her. She has never been married and therefore has never had children of her own. Now, she has two, me and Joshua.

Joshua is growing so quickly. Sometimes I am afraid. I can see Sally Mae in him. He has her blue eyes and gold hair. I see Papa, too. But it is the other things in him I see that disturb me. He has Papa's hot temper and Sally Mae's lust for life. I love Joshua so much. But I wonder what he will become.

Everyone in Galena thinks Joshua is my child. It is well they do. They think less of me, but treat him kindly. I think they do so for Aunt Martha's sake. She is a Strong Force in this community. Everyone loves and respects her. She is the Gentlest of Ladies and given to Good Works. They tolerate me for her sake. They love Joshua for his own. He is beautiful like Sally Mae and as charming as Papa used to be. Aunt Martha said it was Papa's charm and good looks that won Mama's heart.

I am restless tonight. I dont know why. I have the oddest feeling something is going to happen. Whether good or bad, I do not know.

Thomas Atwood Houghton is what was about to happen. He is an old and dear friend of Aunt Martha's who has come to visit. Everyone was a twitter when he came to church. He is very Well Known because he has Money and Land and Connections. Why he is here I am not certain. He told Aunt Martha he was in Galena on Business, but what kind of Business is Unclear.

I was a shock to him. He looked at me in the strangest way when first we met. Calf's eyes, Aunt Martha said. She believes he is taken with me. She is very pleased, but I am filled with Misgivings.

Thomas is as kind as Aunt Martha. Joshua adores him. Everyone in Galena is taken with Thomas. I like Thomas also, but he has made it clear he is thinking in terms of Matrimony. He spoke to Aunt Martha about it and she spoke to me. Why he wants to marry me I do not know. There is not a young unmarried woman in this town who would not be delighted with the prospect of being Thomas Atwood Houghton's wife. He is a contrary man to court a girl who aint interested.

I gathered my courage and asked him straight out what he was thinking. He said he did not want a simpering maid, but a girl who spoke her mind. I said Aunt Martha speaks her mind. He said Martha is his dearest and best friend. I said he would be wise to marry her. She is more suited to him and closer to his own age. He said it is a matter of love and not practicality.

It seems to me the harder I resist the more determined he is to make me his wife. So I am going to simper and sigh. Perhaps this will shake him loose.

The announcement of my betrothal to Thomas has changed my life completely. People speak to me now. They are even Polite. Some pretend to be friends. Elmira Standish *insisted* I come to her afternoon tea and visit with the ladies of the Women's

Society. Aunt Martha is a member. She has not gone to any meetings since I came to live with her, but she attended with me yesterday. I am thankful she did.

Several young ladies spoke with me now that I am considered *acceptable* company. Their mamas watched, but did not call them back. The girls were full of questions, not about Thomas, but about Joshua's father. I could feel my face go all hot. One girl said they heard my child's papa was a mountain man who spent the winter at our homestead. Another heard he was a drummer. One girl said her mama was very Upset because I had charmed Thomas the same way Sally Mae Grayson had charmed poor Noah Carnegie. I asked about that.

Sally Mae is remembered. Her poor grandmama died before I got here. One girl said old Missus Grayson passed on to heaven just so she would never go through hell with Sally Mae again. I asked her meaning, and another said Sally Mae was the sort of girl who bewitched men that were her betters. She was looking straight at me when she said it and I got her meaning clear enough. Another said Sally Mae's last beau was Noah, son of one of the elders in the church. He came confessing to Sally Mae's grandmama about what they was doing on their Sunday rides together. The other girl glaring at me said you know what a girl like that will do to get a man. The other said Noah was a foolish boy and wanted to marry Sally Mae and make things right. I thought of poor Matthew making things right. But Noah had poor Missus Grayson come to his rescue. She sent Sally Mae packing. After she did, Missus Grayson did not come out of her house again. The doctor went to see her, and people asked after her. But it was clear to everyone that the poor woman pined away out of pure shame over having Sally Mae for a granddaughter. As for poor Noah, he finally came to his senses and realized what sort of girl Sally Mae was. When he did, he was so overcome with shame and grief, he stood up in church and confessed his sins to the entire congregation. That is how everyone in town came to know about everything.

One of them said she wondered if Sally Mae would ever come back to Galena after the Great Scandal she had caused. I held my tongue. My feelings were over large right then. I almost said Sally Mae had destroyed my family. But had I said it, they would have descended on me like a flock of crows pecking and wanting to know the gory details of how and why. If I answered, they would have spread the Terrible Truth all over town like manure on a field.

It is better for Joshua if everyone goes on thinking he is mine than to know he came out of Sally Mae Grayson.

Poor Matthew. I cry every time I think of him. I miss him something fierce. Just like I miss Mama. I wonder where he went after he burned Papa's fields. I wonder if I will ever see him again. And if I did, what would he say to me about Joshua? Would he hate me the same way Papa does? I think he would. But that does not change my mind about what I did or why.

Aunt Martha says daily God is in control. If that is so, God has made a fine mess of things. Aunt Martha says there is a good reason for everything that happens. She says God has a Plan for everyone. I wanted to scream when she said it. Was it God's plan that Mama die alone choking on her own blood? Was it God's plan Papa turn into a drunk? Was it God's plan Matthew marry Sally Mae who brought grief to everyone? Was it God's plan Papa father a child on his son's wife? And what of kind, loving, faithful Matthew? What did he do to deserve what he got? What good reason is there for any of the Terrible things that happened?

Aunt Martha does not know everything. I would be the last to tell her so. She is happy in her Ignorance. I hope Aunt Martha stays blind. I would not like for her to know about the dirtiness and meanness of life. I would rather die than have her know about the shame Papa brought upon us all. Aunt Martha's Jesus heals the sick, raises the dead, and feeds the five thousand. Just like Mama's Jesus. Let her hold to that fine fairy tale.

The Jesus I know stands by and does nothing. He dont save nobody or put out fires. He starts them. Maybe he is like the gods on Olympus that I have been reading about. They enjoy playing with people too. When they get tired of someone, they throw him away. Maybe that is what God did. He got tired of Mama and Sally Mae and Matthew and Papa. Maybe our Father who art in heaven is like those other gods. I couldn't help thinking it would be better if Jesus just sat and watched the play unfold beneath him, but took no part in it, either good or bad.

And then sometimes I wonder if Jesus is just a man in a big black book.

I do not know anymore. I cannot bear to think about it much.

When I was a little girl and Mama and I picked flowers in the meadow, I thought God was there with us. I loved him and talked to him the way Mama taught me. I thought God was everywhere, even inside us. Mama always said it was so. And I believed her. I always believed everything Mama said.

I do not believe in anything now. It hurts less.

CHAPTER 9

"You're going to have to get a job." Alex's dark eyes were grim.

"A job?" Sierra said, astonished. She hadn't had a job since they got married. "Why?"

"Because the bills have been stacking up for the past six months, and I don't see any other way around it."

"You said we had more than enough money."

"That was before you started having lunch at the club every day of the week. The bill last month alone was fourteen hundred dollars!" He tossed it onto the desk, where he'd been working on their accounts.

"Fourteen hundred dollars?" she said weakly, feeling the blood drain from her face.

Alex swore in Spanish. "Don't you even bother to look at

the slips you sign or keep track of what you're spending?" he said in disgust.

Hand shaking, she picked up the bill and looked at it. Running her finger down the column, she saw she wasn't entirely at fault. "Green fees and dinners account for more than half of this bill."

"Those are business expenses!" he said hotly.

They still came out of their pocket until the end of the year and taxes. Last year, they'd ended up paying more. That had been a shock after ten years of getting refunds. "Alex, you were the one who encouraged me to go and meet—"

"Not *every* day of the week! I thought going to the club would give you something *constructive* to do with your time. You were sitting around every day watching soap operas, reading romances, and feeling sorry for yourself."

She dropped the bill from the country club back onto the desk. He was making her the cause of all their financial problems. How convenient. "I'm not the one who gave Bruce Davies carte blanche and ended up with eighty-six thousand dollars in decorating expenses. *That's* when the problems started."

A muscle jerked in his jaw and his eyes darkened. "The trouble started when you decided you needed a closet full of clothes so you could keep up with Marcia Burton and the rest of her bourgeois friends."

"If anyone's bourgeois, it's *us*."

Alex's face hardened.

"You're the one who told me to buy some clothes," she went on, lowering her voice.

"I want your credit cards."

"You're not being fair about any of this! You always blame everything on me! You go out to lunch in expensive restaurants every day of the week and pick up the tab for whoever comes along. You bought three tailored suits and half a dozen shirts just last week. And then you say *I'm* spending too much on clothes!"

"I *work* for a living."

She froze at the look of contempt on his face.

She worked, too, not that he ever noticed. She drove the children to and from school, sports activities, and doctor and dentist appointments. She attended parent-teacher meetings and open houses. She planned menus, shopped, and cooked dinner, though he was seldom ever home to enjoy it. Who did he think kept the house neat and clean during the week? A maid? Who did he think washed and ironed their clothes and saw that his expensive suits were cleaned and hanging neatly in the closet? She ran the hundred and one errands he gave her every day of her miserable life, and he never even bothered to say thank you!

Hot tears filled her eyes. "Fine." Anger and resentment filled her until she was shaking with it. She got her purse, took out her wallet, and extracted four credit cards. She tossed them on the desk.

"What're you going to do?" Alex said. "*Cry?* That'll solve a lot, won't it!"

"No. I'm going to get a job."

Alex raked a hand through his hair in frustration. "Keep the cards. Just don't use them for a while. And forget about getting a job. I don't want Steve getting wind of this mess." He gave a derisive laugh. "What would you find anyway? You've got a few months of business school. Big deal! Any job you'd get would pay a pittance." He swore. "Just back off on the club for a while until I can figure out how to juggle things around and pay some of these bills down."

Sierra stood in stony silence. When he left, she cut up the credit cards and tucked them into the bill box, where he was sure to find them. Then she called Marcia. "Do you know anyone who might have a job opening?"

"A job?" Marcia said in surprise.

"I'm sick of being made to feel like a parasite," she said, her voice wobbling.

"Did you and Alex have another fight?"

"Do bears live in the forest?"

"I'm sorry, Sierra."

"I'm tired of this, Marcia. Sick to death of it." She stopped, clutching the telephone so tightly, her hand ached.

"Ron Peirozo was over yesterday telling Tom he's in dire need of a secretary right now. Judy's baby is due at the end of the month. Do you have any secretarial training?"

"I went to business college before marrying Alex, but I didn't graduate."

"Well, charity organizations should be charitable."

"A charity? Didn't you introduce me to Ron Peirozo a few months ago at the club?" Sierra said. He didn't have the appearance of someone working for a charity.

"As a matter of fact, yes. I'd forgotten." Marcia laughed. "I can hear what you're thinking. No, he wasn't spending charity donations. He has his own money. His grandfather died and left him a lot of money, as well as a heart for philanthropy. The first thing Ron did was give several hundred thousand dollars to his alma mater for scholarships for minority students. Then he set up Outreach. As long as I've known Ron, he's been involved in community work of some sort. He's generous and brilliant. Besides that, his family connections bring him in contact with some of the most influential and wealthy people in the country. He could charm money out of the meanest miser and make them feel good about writing the check."

"I don't think he'd be interested in someone like me,"

Sierra said, positive she lacked the qualifications to work for a man like Ron Peirozo.

"Nonsense. He's looking for someone to handle office details. I'll call him. If the position's still open, I'll let you know, and you can see about making an appointment with him for an interview."

"I don't know, Marcia."

"Nothing ventured, nothing gained. You have to take control of your life."

Sierra did her grocery shopping and picked up two of Alex's suits at the cleaners. On the way home, she stopped by the post office for more stamps. She'd put the last one on a card to her mother this morning.

The telephone was ringing as she came into the kitchen from the garage. She laid the suits over the counter, deposited a bag of groceries beside it, and made a lunge for the telephone as it rang again. "Hello," she said breathlessly, dumping her purse and keys on the counter.

"Sierra? Sierra Madrid?"

"Yes," she said, frowning slightly. The man's voice was vaguely familiar, but she couldn't place it. "Speaking."

"This is Ron Peirozo. Marcia said you might be interested in a job."

She felt her face go hot. "Yes," she said simply, heart thumping nervously. "I thought I should do something more important than play tennis and drink iced tea at the club."

He laughed. "Still beating Marcia?"

She relaxed slightly. "Once in a while, when her guard's down."

"Would it be convenient for you to come in tomorrow morning for an interview?"

"That would be fine. What time?"

"Nine, unless that's too early at such short notice."

"Nine is perfect."

"I'll outline the position for you. Once I've done that, you may have second thoughts about working for me."

"I doubt that, Mr. Peirozo, but *you* may have second thoughts. How much did Marcia tell you?"

"Just that you were looking for a job."

"I went to business college but didn't finish. Basically, I've been a wife and mother. That's it."

He chuckled. "Seems to me that's a pretty big responsibility."

"I thought so," she said dryly. "Some people wouldn't agree."

"All right," he said slowly, mulling over her remark. "Are you willing to work hard?"

"Yes."

"Are you willing to learn?"

"Yes."

"Will you take directions?"

"Yes."

"Can you type?"

"Yes."

"Shorthand?"

"Some."

"You've got the qualifications. I'll see you at nine."

Alex called at six that evening. "I'm going to be late." Big surprise. Dinner was already on the table and the children were eating. "Steve and I are going over the new promo stuff," he went on when she didn't say anything.

"Do you want me to keep your dinner in the oven?" she said, proud of how calm she sounded.

"No, thanks. We'll order something in."

At ten thirty she gave up waiting for him and went to bed. She awakened at one in the morning when she heard the garage door open. She had left the bathroom light on so he could find his way around the room.

"Did you and Steve get everything done?" she said groggily, watching him go into the walk-in closet to take off his clothes.

"Sorry," he muttered. "I didn't mean to wake you."

Shrugging out of his suit jacket, he tossed it over a chair and headed into the master bathroom. She heard him turn on the shower. The glass door snapped closed. He let the water run so long, she fell asleep again and didn't awaken until the alarm went off at five thirty.

"Didn't you reset the alarm?" she said sleepily.

"I'm getting up."

She brushed some hair back from her face. "You worked until one o'clock in the morning, Alex. Is Steve turning into a slave driver?"

He sat up and raked his hands back through his hair. "Steve'll be in the office by six thirty," he said, his back to her.

She sensed something was wrong. Was it the fight they'd had yesterday? She'd had time to think things over and cool down. She reached out to touch him, but before she could, he got up and left the bedroom. Pushing the comforter back, she got out of bed, pulled on her robe, and followed. She found him in the kitchen, watching the stream of coffee filling the carafe. She knew he was aware of her standing there, but he didn't look at her. He pulled the carafe out and poured himself a cup of coffee.

"What's wrong, Alex?"

"Nothing," he said, a muscle clenching in his jaw.

"If it's the bills, I—"

"Look. I'm tired. I didn't get a lot of sleep last night."

"You're still angry with me. You still think it's my fault."

He winced. "I don't want to talk about it, Sierra."

She could feel him building the wall between them. "You don't want to talk about anything, do you?"

He looked at her, his eyes brooding. "Not now."

"Fine. Maybe this will please you. I have a job interview this morning. You could wish me luck." She turned around and headed for the bedroom before he could see the tears in her eyes.

Alex swore and slammed his cup of coffee down. "I told you *not* to get a job!"

She slammed the bedroom door. Dragging in her breath, she clenched her fists. She wanted to scream and cry at the same time. What was happening to them? They couldn't say two sentences to one another without getting into another fight.

Alex came into the bedroom, looking upset. "You don't have to go to work. We'll just cut back on spending until we catch up. I want you to stay home."

"Why? So you have a convenient scapegoat? You told me the bills are my fault, Alex. You said I spend too much on clothes. You told me when I'm not spending all your money at the club with my bourgeois friends, I'm sitting around watching soap operas, reading romances, and feeling sorry for myself!" She could hardly see through the sheen of hot tears.

"I was mad, Sierra. I said a lot of things. So did you!"

"I'm sick of being made to feel I'm on the dole! You think I don't do anything around here. Well, you're not around to see what I do! The only thing that matters to you anymore is how much money a person makes. And I don't make any, do I, Alex? So that makes me less than nothing in your eyes."

He grimaced. "I didn't say that."

"You say it every day in a hundred ways." Her voice cracked. When he took a step toward her, she took two back. "You were so worried about what Steve might think if your wife had to get a job. Well, if I am lucky enough to get this job, you can tell him I work for a charity organization. Maybe he'll think I'm volunteering." She went into the bathroom and locked the door.

Paradoxically, she hoped he'd knock and tell her to come out so they could talk. She hoped he'd say he was sorry for blaming her for their financial problems and admit that some of them were of his own making.

He did neither.

"We'll talk it over later," he said flatly. She heard the doors to the walk-in closet open and knew he was getting dressed to go to work.

Sierra sat down on the commode lid and wept silently.

"I'll call you later," Alex said.

It sounded like another empty promise.

When she had no more tears, she took a long shower and decided what to wear for her job interview with Ronal Peirozo. Suddenly, getting that job mattered more than anything.

Clanton and Carolyn said little over breakfast. Sierra knew they were aware something was wrong, and they didn't want to know what it was. She tried to be reassuring, but tears were too close to the surface, anger just beneath it.

She pulled into the gates of the private school, kissed each of them good-bye, and said she'd see them later.

Half an hour later, she walked through the front door of L.A. Outreach. It was precisely nine o'clock by her watch. A middle-aged lady in a flowered dress sat at the reception desk. Still speaking on the telephone, she glanced up and smiled warmly. As she put the phone back in its cradle, she said brightly, "Good morning! My, what a lovely suit."

"Thank you," Sierra said, put somewhat at ease by the lady's warmth. She had chosen an expensive golden-brown suit and cream silk blouse. On the lapel, she'd pinned a gold brooch of three children holding hands. "My name is Sierra Madrid. I have an appointment with Mr. Peirozo."

"Yes. We've been expecting you." She rose and extended her hand. "My name is Arlene Whiting. I'll show you the way, Mrs. Madrid." She led Sierra down a corridor and tapped on a door. As she opened it, Sierra saw a much-younger woman, obviously pregnant, rise from the chair in front of Ron Peirozo's desk. She smiled warmly.

Sierra immediately felt overdressed. Judy was in a simple cotton maternity dress.

Ron was wearing Levi's, a lightweight pale pullover sweater, and a navy-blue sport coat.

"Ron, this is Sierra Madrid," Arlene said, ushering her in. "Sierra, this is Ron Peirozo and his secretary, Judy Franklin." Brief pleasantries were exchanged, and the two women went out, leaving her alone with Ron.

"Right on time," he said, grinning. "I like that. Please sit down."

"Thank you," she said and took the seat Judy had just vacated. She crossed her legs carefully and folded her hands in her lap, hoping she didn't look as nervous as she felt.

"Let me tell you a little about Outreach to start off," Ron said. He spent the next half hour explaining the mission of the organization he had founded less than five years before. The primary goal of Outreach was to place homeless children in safe housing and encourage them to become responsible, productive citizens in the community. Ron raised money and dispensed it to shelters and foster families. Equally impor-tant, he maintained a list of professional counselors who volunteered a portion of their time as arbitrators between parents and runaways.

"We want to restore these children to their families whenever possible. Sometimes that takes time. Sometimes they need protection."

He also maintained an extensive list of agencies and services available to families in trouble. Many of the children who came in contact with L.A. Outreach were referred to drug rehabilitation programs, medical treatment, and counseling for incest, physical and emotional abuse, and any number of other serious problems.

Several major denominational churches were involved in the program, supplying volunteer tutors.

"We've had good luck. Twenty children passed high school equivalency exams last year. Four times that many have returned to grade schools and high schools throughout the county. Six started college in September. Twelve are in trade schools. Twenty-seven got jobs this year. The numbers aren't big, I know, but every case is important."

Each child who entered the Outreach program was required to spend two hours a day, Monday through Friday, in community service. "They groan about it in the beginning, but they cooperate. After a while, they learn that helping others makes them feel better about themselves. That's when the incentive changes and things get exciting."

His eyes glowed as he spoke. There was no doubt about his love for his work or for the children he hoped to help.

"The churches are instrumental in helping us with this part of the program. These kids aren't picking up trash along a road somewhere. They're mowing lawns for the elderly, helping at day care centers, serving meals to shut-ins, assisting at convalescent hospitals, any number of things that bring them into contact with people in the community." He grinned. "You'll hear people talking about 'going AWOL.' Don't let it throw you. It means they're going on 'a work of love.'"

"Do the children come here in order to get into the program?"

"Not very often. Unfortunately. Frankly, finding these kids was one of our main problems in the beginning. I used to go downtown with a friend of mine and talk to the kids we found living on the streets. Some of them didn't have any reason to trust an adult, let alone listen to one. It's getting easier the longer we're around. We've employed six kids who've come through the program to go back on the streets and spread the word we're here and ready to offer help to those who want it. Kids listen better to kids."

Ron leaned forward, his blue eyes filled with warm intensity and passion for what he was doing.

"The whole idea of the program is to get as broad a base of community people involved with these children as possible," he said. "At the same time, we try to keep a low profile. I want people sincere in their concern, not people out to get plaudits. It's one-on-one. Personal. We don't send out mass mailers asking for donations. We don't do radio or television spots. We don't have celebrities heading up committees or movie stars acting as spokesmen. We don't give out plaques or public congratulations. And we don't go door-to-door asking for donations."

"How do you raise money to fund all this?"

"Fund-raisers. Word of mouth mostly. Some of my friends helped me in the beginning. I speak to different congregations and community groups. People spread the word. We don't always meet our budget, but God always sees we have enough money to meet our needs."

Ron Peirozo mentioned God as easily as her mother did, as though the Almighty was personally involved in his life and work. She felt herself relaxing even more.

He leaned back slowly and smiled at her. "You finally unclenched your hands."

Sierra blushed. "I was hoping you wouldn't notice."

"I notice a lot of things," he said cryptically, studying her.

"You haven't said what the job I'm applying for would entail."

"Simple," he said, all business again. "You'd assist me in everything I do."

"I'm sure there's a lot more to it than that, Mr. Peirozo."

"Call me Ron. I intend to call you Sierra. We're not formal around here."

She could feel herself growing excited as he talked. He had important work to do, and he wanted her to help. She couldn't remember the last time she had felt so good. She knew she would like working for Ron Peirozo. If he hired her.

"I haven't much in the way of qualifications," she said frankly, wanting to get to the bottom line. Maybe it would hurt less if she got the whole thing over.

He smiled, his eyes warming. "I thought we already settled that. You can type."

"Ninety words a minute."

"And take shorthand."

"Yes, but it's been ten years since I used it."

"Don't worry about it. I dictate most of my letters while I'm trapped in five o'clock traffic. You'll find a recorder on your desk each morning."

He talked as though he'd already given her the job.

Ron picked up a pencil and tapped it lightly. He had strong, nicely shaped hands. Sierra noticed he wasn't wearing a wedding ring.

"The pay isn't great. You'll start at fourteen hundred a month."

Enough to pay last month's country club bill, she thought, though she doubted Alex would appreciate the gesture. "Then I have the job?"

"If you want it."

She laughed. "When can I start?"

He grinned. "How about tomorrow?"

"Tomorrow will be fine," she said, relieved and elated. "Nine?"

"Nine it is." Ron stood as she did.

"Thank you," she said, extending her hand as Ron came around his desk. He enclosed her hand firmly but didn't linger as he had the first time they'd met at the club. "I appreciate the opportunity you're giving me, Ron. I hope I won't disappoint you."

"You won't," he said with such certainty, she felt bolstered.

She spent a few minutes talking with Judy and Arlene. Both seemed genuinely delighted that she was coming to work for Outreach. "Ron is a terrific boss," Judy said.

As Sierra walked out to her BMW, she realized what it was she liked so much about Ron Peirozo. He made her feel like an attractive woman. Not only that, he made her feel worthwhile, intelligent, and capable.

She hadn't felt that way in a long, long time.

James Farr is in Galena.

I saw him in the mercantile today and almost fainted. Aunt Martha had sent me for some white ribbon. Thomas accompanied me and Joshua. He likes to stroll through town with me on his arm. Or so he says. We went into Coopers and he took Joshua to the counter to buy a stick of candy. I was looking at some new bolts of cloth.

And then there was James, standing in the doorway. My

heart beat so fast. He must have felt me staring at him, for he looked around and saw me. He smiled. He has never smiled at me like that before. He came to say hello. I could not draw breath when he did. Thomas saw him and came over to stand beside me. When he picked up Joshua and handed him to me, James tipped his hat to both of us and left the store.

I dont think he even knows who I was.

James came by the house today. Aunt Martha was not home. She had gone to market with Betsy. Clovis drove them. So it was I who opened the door to him. Joshua went right out to him as if James were an old friend of the family. James laughed and picked him up. I didn't know you the other day in the mercantile, he said. Little Mary Kathryn McMurray all grown up and pretty as a princess. I said I could not invite him in as no one was home and it would not look proper with me betrothed and all. He is too old for you, Mary Kathryn, he said. It is all decided, I said. Who decided, he wanted to know. I took Joshua back from him and said it would be better if he called when Aunt Martha was home. He said he would do that.

Thomas left for his homestead today. He must take care of his business. He kissed me before he left. It was a first kiss and chaste. I feel guilty for my lack of feeling. I care for Thomas, but wonder how we will fare together as man and wife. He told Aunt Martha to watch out for me. I told him not to worry. I can watch out for myself. It is a wonder why he wants me as a wife when he treats me like a child.

James came today. I introduced him to Aunt Martha. He stayed for a full hour talking about home and Matthew and Mama and Papa. He asked so many questions. I could not answer many. I gave him the facts. Mama died of consumption. Papa still grieves. Sally Mae and Matthew married. Sally Mae died in childbirth and Matthew went away. I have not seen my brother since. James did not ask a single question about how I came to have Joshua. I wonder what he thinks about that.

Aunt Martha was very quiet when James left. I asked her if something was wrong. She said I must be careful where James is concerned. I did not ask why. I know.

A mere look from James touches something deep inside me. When he is close, my heart pounds and I can scarse draw breath. Thomas Atwood Houghton loves me and I feel nothing at all.

I am in a terrible quandary. I dont know what to do.

This morning, I was feeling so restless. Perhaps it was a portent of what was going to happen. Joshua was fussing and Aunt Martha needed rest. So I took him out for a walk. Everything is in bloom. I think the scent of spring went straight to my head. I walked far from the road and let Joshua play in a small meadow.

James followed me. I thought I imagined him at first standing at the edge of the wood, watching me. He has been so much in my thoughts of late. I cannot get him out of my head no matter how much I try. I try to think about Thomas and our approaching wedding, but my heart betrays me and it is James who comes to mind. But James was not conjured by my imagination. He was real. All too real, as it turned out.

James came to me, and while Joshua played, sat with me in the soft grass amidst the flowers. He spoke of casual things at first. I did not stop to think why he came upon me as he did. I was so pleased to see him. Pleased and afraid. My stomach was trembling and my heart pounded so hard. I asked him about his travels to New York and the Carolinas and England. I delighted in his voice and the look in his eyes as he talked. It

made me sad in part, too. I kept wondering how long it would
be before he left again, breaking my heart as he did before.

James took my hand.

I said it was not proper for him to do so. He said he did
not care what was proper. He said I could not marry Thomas
Atwood Houghton. He will never make you happy, he said.
I told him Thomas was a good and kind man. James said that
may be, Mary Kathryn, but you are not in love with him. I said
love will come in time. James said it took us no time at all.
I knew I should leave right then, but instead, I said I did not
know what he meant. He told me not to lie. He said we both
knew the moment we saw each other in the mercantile. He
said Thomas knew it too. I said I did not know what he was
talking about and he said he would show me.

James kissed me. It was not a kiss like Thomas gave me. It
was not chaste or gentle. James shook me so badly inside I could
only think to get away before I was consumed by the fire he set
inside me. I pushed him away and got up. I told him he could
not court me like Sally Mae Grayson.

I ran to fetch Joshua, but James caught up with me. He said
he never wanted to marry Sally Mae and it was an awful pity
Matthew did. I told him to let go of me. He said he would hold
onto me as long as he lived. You belong to me, Mary Kathryn
McMurray. You have since you were a child and well you know
it. I told him he was a bad bargain. And he said not as bad a
bargain as it would be if you marry a man you do not love. I
shud of run then. But I didn't and he kissed me again. When
I could get my breath back, I told him to leave Galena. He
said he would leave when I was ready to go with him and not
before. I said he was crazy. He laughed and said he was. Crazy
in love.

And now, here I sit in the quiet of my room, trying to think
of a way out of this mess I am in.

Aunt Martha has been weeping all afternoon. Thomas came to call this morning and I told him I could not marry him. I told him why. He said he would give me time to come to my senses. I said I should have stuck with my senses in the first place and never agreed to marry him. I told him I never intended to hurt or anger him. I admire and respect him as a dear friend. I said I did not love him. He said it was not love I was feeling for James Farr. He said I should marry him and put away child-ish fantasies and passions. He said he would leave me alone to think about what I will be giving up.

I feel guilty for breaking my word to him. It would be worse if I married him and broke my heart and his and James in the bargain. But Thomas does not see things the way I do.

I went down on my knees before Aunt Martha and tried to explain. She said she knew very well what had happened. She said you are your mother's daughter, Mary Kathryn. She said some men are like strong wine that go straight to a girl's head and then they spend the rest of their lives paying for the plea-sure. If you do this thing, Mary Kathryn, your life will be a trial. James will take you into the wilderness. She said she had hoped and prayed for better to happen to me than happened to my mother.

James and I have been married for seventy-three days, nine hours, and fifteen minutes and I have not suffered one bit! He has made me so happy I have had no time to write. I have delighted in every minute with James.

We almost did not get married at all. It was Aunt Martha who insisted pastor perform the ceremony. He did not want to do it, but Aunt Martha said I must be joined to James before the Lord and if pastor refused, it would be on his head when we went off and lived in sin together. So he did the ceremony short as he knew how.

Aunt Martha, Betsy, and Clovis stood up with us. No one else came. I am a pariah once again, but I do not care. We are living in a small cabin on the edge of town near the mill and I see little of people anyway. James said we will go live in Chicago as soon as he has enough money to get us there.

This rented cabin is just fine. James makes me happy. When he holds me, I forget everything but how much I love him. I dont care what they all say.

James has taken work at the sawmill. He leaves early in the morning and does not come home until sunset.

There is little to do in this small cabin and only Joshua to keep me company. I spend most of the day thinking about James and waiting for him to come home. I have started a little garden.

James brought Aunt Martha. He is worried about me because I have been sick so much of late. Aunt Martha made me chamomile tea and we talked for a long time about many things. She asked me Questions. Some of them surprised me they were so personal. She kissed me like Mama used to and said I was not to worry. Everything is fine, she said. She called for James. When he came in, Aunt Martha told us what was wrong with me.

I am going to have a baby this winter.

Or die trying.

I am afraid. I never been so afraid before. Not when Mama died. Not even when Papa kicked me out of the house with winter coming. I was not this afraid when I tended Sally Mae during her last hours on this earth. But then what happened to her wasn't happening to me. Now I wonder if it will.

Sally Mae was a fine one for letting her passions rule her

and so it appears am I. James knows how to make me happy. He said that is the way it is supposed to be between a man and wife. He said it says so in the Bible. I asked him where. He could not show me but swears its true. I do not dare ask pastor. He thinks I am a Jezebel and treats me so. I will go to hell if he has anything to say about it and he talks to God all the time.

I cannot tell James about my fears. James knows something is wrong but he will only worry. I learned early worry changes nothing.

I spoke with Aunt Martha yesterday. I could not tell her either I was so ashamed. She agreed to take Joshua when my time comes. She said she would keep him until I was settled with my new baby. I know now even Aunt Martha thinks Joshua is mine. She mustve thot I wuz lying when I told her Sally Mae had him. I cried. I could not help it. She asked me why but I would not say. It hurts when people think the worst of you. I told her if I die I want Joshua to stay with her forever. She said I am strong and healthy and should have no prob-lems. It was on my tongue to tell her Sally Mae was strong and healthy, too. Aunt Martha says I must trust the Lord. She said God loves you, Mary Kathryn Farr.

I have no reason to trust God and little proof he loves me. I could not tell Aunt Martha that. She is so *convinced* and she would ask Questions. Even if I told her the whole truth, she probably would not believe it. She would probably think I was lying about the trouble like she thinks I lied about Joshua. Sometimes I have difficulty when I think on the matter. When I think of Papa, I remember the way he used to be when Mama was alive.

I wrote a letter to Thomas Atwood Houghton and asked him to forgive me. Maybe my mind will be at rest if he does.

Right now, I feel all manner of demons coming to rest upon my head.

It has been a month and Thomas has not responded to my letter. I went into Galena yesterday with James. I asked him to take me to church with Aunt Martha. So he did.

Only pastor spoke to us. Briefly. About the weather.

I reckon God feels the same.

The leaves are turning red and yellow. Joshua is my comfort all day while James is gone.

Aunt Martha came yesterday to visit. I did not feel up to talking much.

Aunt Martha came back this morning. She brought books with her. She said just because I am married does not mean I must let my mind go to waste. I am glad of her company. While I study and write lessons, she plays with Joshua.

Henry James Farr was born at sunup on December 11. He entered the world with a strong pair of lungs.

James fainted dead away before his son was born. He lay on the cabin floor, no use to me at all. I washed Henry and wrapped him in the cotton blanket. More came from me. It seemed it would not stop. I have never been so weak. By the time I washed myself, changed my nightgown, I had barely the strength to crawl back into bed. I fell asleep with my son. When I woke up next day, James was in bed with us, his arm around us both.

Joshua came home today. I have missed him terribly. He is my child. It dont matter how I came to have him. He may look like his father and mother, but that dont mean he will be like them. Henry is a week old and a fine, strong baby. Joshua tries to crawl into my lap when I nurse him.

I am joyful tonight. James is asleep on our bed. Our son is sleeping soundly in the cradle near the fire. Joshua is sleeping beside it bundled in his blankets. He scorns his bed because he wants to be close to his baby brother. Sometimes I think Joshua guards him the way Matthew guarded me. Everything is so peaceful. Especially me.

Aunt Martha brought me a package today labelled Master Henry James Farr care of Martha Werner. In it was a beautiful silver spoon and small cup. And this note.

My dearest Mary Kathryn, May God always bless you and your family. Always your friend, Tom.

I wept when I read it.

My heart is full to overflowing.

Henry James turned four months old today. He will have a sister or brother come late fall. James is pleased. Aunt Martha is mortified. She turned dark pink when I told her. She said it is too soon. What of your health? And think what people will say. I said I was stronger than most and she could tell everyone it must be God's will James and I be fruitful and multiply.

The truth is I have few pleasures in this world and no wish to shun James embrace. I told him what Aunt Martha said. He laughed. I said it was not funny. He said she is innocent and modest. As to the rest, they are jealous. He said everyone will get used to us having a baby every year and think nothing of it.

Martha Elizabeth was born midday November 20. She is healthy and beautiful. Aunt Martha was here at her coming into the world. She was first to hold her.

James says Beth has my blue eyes and red hair. Little Hank

had blue eyes too when he was born. Now they are dark brown. His blond hair all fell out when he was barely a month old. I was afraid he would be bald. Then it all grew back in black as Papas.

Betsy came to the cabin today. She said I look tuckered out. I felt better for her visit. A good talk can bolster spirits and renew strength. It gets lonely when the only people you have to talk to all day are a five year old boy and two babies. I love them dearly but they have not the makings yet for Stimulating Conversation. And Aunt Martha is often too occupied with Good Works to spend much time with me. When she does come, it is little Hank and Beth who have her attention. Betsy was like a breath of spring air even though she bossed me the whole hour she stayed.

I know I should not complain. Aunt Martha is ever kind to me and mine. I remind myself that I am more Fortunate than some.

I love James.

He loves me.

I have three beautiful children.

I am healthy.

I have a roof over my head with only a few leaks.

I have food on the table.

Yet there are times when I feel something is lacking. I despair. I *yearn*. I cannot put my finger on what I yearn for or why. It is just an ache inside that wont go away.

Maybe I am just tired. I weary of washing diapers. I think about the African women I read about in a book Aunt Martha brought me. They let their children grow up naked. Maybe their way is better. Seems to me it would save time better spent on other things.

CHAPTER 10

Arlene Whiting buzzed Sierra at her desk. "You have a call on line one. Michael Clanton?"

"My brother," she said in surprise and punched the button. Mike never called. He wasn't at ease on the telephone and left it to Melissa, his wife, to keep in touch. "How's everything down there in la-la land?" Melissa would always say and make her laugh.

Nothing short of an emergency would get him to lift a receiver to his ear. "What's wrong, Mike?"

"Mom's sick."

"Sick?" she said, alarmed.

"She's got cancer."

Sierra couldn't believe it. "She can't have cancer. I just saw her a few months ago." She had noticed at Christmas her mother had looked thin. She'd even asked about it. "She's lost some weight, but she said she was fine."

"She didn't want you to know."

Sierra clutched the phone more tightly. "You're sure?"

"She's known for quite a while," her brother said quietly. "She's just kept it to herself until recently."

"What do you mean she's known? When did she find out?"

Her brother was silent for a moment. "She was diagnosed with breast cancer just before you and Alex moved south."

"What?" Sierra felt her blood chilling with shock. "That was two years ago, Mike." In a blinding flash she remembered hints that something was wrong. She had wondered why her mother was so intent upon going through all the things in the attic. What was it she had said? She didn't want to leave the chaos to her and Mike. *Oh, God.* Sierra's eyes filled with hot tears. "Why didn't she say something?"

"You know how Mom is, Sierra. She doesn't want anyone worrying about her."

"What's being done for her?"

"She had a lumpectomy when the doctor first diagnosed her. They found out in the tests afterward that the cancer had already metastasized into her bones."

"Oh no," Sierra murmured. "And she didn't tell you?"

"She didn't tell anyone until a few days ago."

Alarm filled her. "What happened a few days ago?"

"Her right leg hurt so much she couldn't drive. She called Brady and asked if he could take her into the doctor's office." He was quiet for a few seconds. "They did another MRI. It looks bad."

Sierra closed her eyes, panic bubbling inside her. Her mother was her rock of strength. She couldn't lose her! She was only sixty-five. They'd always laughed and talked about how they'd celebrate her hundredth birthday when it came. "Is she going to have chemotherapy?"

"No."

"What do you mean *no*?"

"She said she didn't want it."

"But—"

"It wouldn't do any good at this point, Sierra."

"They have to do *something*. What about radiation? Couldn't they do that?"

"It'd already metastasized into her bones when she was diagnosed. It's spread to her liver."

Sierra lowered her head and covered her mouth for a moment until she could get control of her emotions.

Mike didn't say anything for a minute. "She's undergoing palliative treatments," he said hoarsely.

"What's that?"

"They're giving her radiation to ease the pain in her right leg."

Tears ran down Sierra's cheeks. She swallowed, trying to keep her voice steady. "Is she in a lot of pain, Mike?"

"Not that she talks about," he said with difficulty. "You know Mom." He was quiet for a minute. "I think she's been on pain medication for months. Melissa was putting dishes away in the cabinet the other day and found the prescription bottle tucked in the corner." He cursed softly, and she knew he was crying. "I'll call you back in a few minutes." He hung up abruptly.

Sierra put the receiver in its cradle and covered her face. She tried to fight down the rush of emotions: grief, fear, the desire to get in her car and start driving north right this instant. She was shaking and felt cold.

"Bad news?" Ron said, standing in the doorway that joined his large office to her smaller one.

"Yes," she said without looking up. She was afraid if she said anything more, she'd break down.

Her intercom buzzed. She snatched up the telephone and punched the line-one button. "Mike?"

"Sorry," he said hoarsely.

"It's okay," she said, clutching the phone tightly, keeping her other hand up to shield her face from Ron's perusal. Her throat was so hot and tight, she could hardly breathe. "How long do we have?"

"A month. Probably less."

She swallowed convulsively. Her vision blurred with tears as she stared at the calendar. If that was true, her mother wouldn't even make it to her sixty-sixth birthday. Her chest ached with the weight of fear. "Is she at home?"

"No. She's in the hospital. Just until she finishes the treatments. Five days, maybe six. Then she comes home."

"Which hospital?"

"Community." He gave her the number.

"I'll call you tonight, Mike." Her hand shook as she hung up the telephone. Ron was still standing in the doorway. He didn't say anything, but she sensed his deep concern. Over the past four months of working with him, she had learned he was a perceptive and caring man. "My mother has cancer."

He let out his breath slowly. "How bad?"

"It's in her liver," she said huskily, afraid if she said more, she'd start crying. She felt Ron's hand slide over her shoulder and squeeze gently in comfort.

"I'm sorry to hear that, Sierra."

She recalled how her mother had looked six months ago, thin, her hair graying. She had asked straight out if she was all right, and her mother had said everything was fine. Fine? How could she have kept such a secret? "She never said a word, Ron."

"What do you want to do?"

Her hands felt like ice. "I want to go home."

"Then go," he said simply.

She thought of the chaos she'd leave behind if she did. Her desk was piled with work. And what about the children? Who'd take care of Clanton and Carolyn? Who'd drop them off at school? Who'd take Clanton to his baseball practices or Carolyn to her piano lessons? Alex was gone by six thirty and never home before seven.

Maybe she should pull the children out of school and take them with her. But how could she do that when she didn't even know what she would be facing when she got home? What would they do while she was taking care of her mother?

"I don't know what to do," she said shakily. "I don't even know where to start." Her brother's words rang in her ears. A month. Maybe less.

Oh, God! God, where are You?

She wanted to be with her mother. She wanted that so desperately, she shook with fear that it wouldn't be possible.

Ron sat on the edge of her desk. "Call Alex."

She dialed Beyond Tomorrow. Alex's secretary told her he wasn't in the office. "He had an appointment at one."

"Can you page him?"

"He told me not to—"

"This is important! When you get in touch with him, tell him to call me here at work. Please." She hung up. Every time she called Alex lately, he was out.

Shaking, she began shuffling the papers around on her desk, wondering how she could get everything sorted out and finished by the end of the day. And what about tomorrow? She had the schedules to type up. She had calls to make. She had letters to write.

She couldn't concentrate.

Ron's hand stopped her agitated movements. "I'll call Judy. She said she and Max are saving for a down payment on a house. I'm sure she'll agree to stand in for you while you're gone."

"She can't, Ron. She's nursing Jason."

"She can bring her baby with her. I won't mind. And Arlene loves getting her hands on the little guy. If things get too hectic, I think we could track down a couple of responsible teenagers who'd pitch in."

"Miranda," Sierra said immediately, thinking of a fifteen-year-old runaway who'd entered the program about the same time she'd started working with Ron. "The day care center says she's wonderful with babies."

Ron smiled and brushed his knuckles lightly against her cheek. It was an oddly intimate and tender gesture that made her blush. "We'll take care of things around here. You go see your mother." He straightened from her desk.

When Alex didn't call back by one thirty, Sierra left him out of her arrangements. Marcia gave her the name of a professional nanny. Sierra called Dolores Huerta and explained the situation. Dolores agreed to meet her at the house that afternoon at four so they could go over the children's schedules and her household duties and fees.

Sierra was packing her bags when Alex came home. He stopped just inside the bedroom door and stared at the two open suitcases on the double bed. "What's going on?" he said, his face paling. "What're you doing? Where're you going?"

"If you'd bothered to return my call this morning, you'd know." She yanked open a drawer. "I'm going home."

He uttered a soft curse and came into the room. "Look. Let's talk about—"

"There's nothing to talk about," she cut him off. "My mother's in the hospital. She has cancer." She swallowed convulsively as she put a sweater on top of a pair of dark-gray slacks.

He let out his breath. "I thought . . ." He shook his head. "I'm sorry," he said heavily.

She spun to face him, pain etched in her features. "Sorry about what, Alex? That you're never around when I need you anymore? That my mother has cancer? That all this is going to complicate your precious work schedule?"

He didn't say anything.

She looked at him, hurt and embittered. "Where were you? Your secretary said she'd page you. Did she?"

"Yes."

"Why didn't you call me?"

"I was busy." He moved farther into their bedroom. "Look. I figured if it was really important, you'd call back."

She turned back to her suitcase in frustration. "It's nice to know where I stand on your priority list."

"You want a fight before you go? Is that what you really want?"

She went into the closet. When she came out with two more pairs of slacks, Alex was standing in the middle of the room, rubbing the back of his neck. Shaking, she dropped the clothing on the bed. "I needed you, Alex. Where were you?"

Turning, he looked at her. She saw something in his expression that made her sick. Guilt. Shame. And not just because he hadn't returned her call. It was something more, something deeper. His eyes flickered, stark and raw, and then the expression was gone, hidden.

"What can I do to help?" he said flatly.

She wanted to say he could hold her. He could tell her he loved her. He could promise to call her and talk with her each day. He could reassure her that everything would be fine with the children while she was gone.

"I don't know," she said bleakly. "Pray for a miracle, maybe?"

For whom, Sierra? an inner voice asked. *For your mother or you . . . and Alex?*

What had brought them to this impasse? They couldn't even talk to one another anymore. It was as though a wall stood between them, four feet thick and a hundred feet high. She was tired of trying to hack her way through it.

He shrugged out of his suit jacket and tossed it over a chair. "What are you going to do about the kids?"

Anger surged through her, twisting her stomach into a hard knot. Hadn't he just asked her what he could do to *help*? What a laugh. All he cared about was that he not suffer any inconvenience.

"Don't worry. I've already hired a nanny. You won't have to look for one. Her name is Dolores Huerta. She'll be here by seven each morning. I figured you wouldn't mind staying home an extra *thirty* minutes until she gets here. Dolores has agreed to cook and do the washing and take care of the house. She drives, so she'll drop the children off at school and pick them up. She'll also see that Clanton gets to base-ball practices and Carolyn gets to her piano lessons. I knew you wouldn't have the time or inclination to be there for the kids. I gave her some gas money and offered her a generous salary. You'll need to pay her on Friday." She looked at him, waiting for a response.

His face was rigid. "How long do you think you'll be gone?"

She bit her lip, fighting back the tears. "As long as it takes," she managed bleakly, turning away. She couldn't remember what she'd already packed and what more she needed.

"You can't take all of it on yourself, Sierra."

She wished she could believe he was concerned for her, but she couldn't. What was he really worried about?

"Mike said the doctor told Mom she has a month, maybe less. I want every minute with her I can have."

"You don't think I understand that? I love your mother, too."

Do you? she wanted to say. If he did, he never would have moved the family to Southern California. She wondered sometimes if he even loved his own father and mother. When was the last time he'd called them? He seemed to resent the time he took off to make two short visits home to family in the course of a whole year.

What he loved—apparently the only thing he really loved—was his work. Nothing else seemed to matter to him anymore, least of all her or the children. Her mother didn't even enter the equation.

"You don't believe me, do you?" he said, defensive.

"Should I? I hope you'll call and tell her while you have the chance." She glared up at him, hurt and anger spilling over into each other, flooding her with the desire to retaliate. "People *need* love when they're hurting."

His eyes cooled. "I'll leave you alone so you can pack." He walked out of the room.

The right reverend came by to talk to me today.

Seems he's in Galena preaching at the market place. First thing he did was look at my babies and my rounding belly and ask how long I had been married. Long enough I said. He told me Mister Grayson died last spring. He fell and cut himself on the plow blade and died two weeks later, jaws locked and body twisted like a pretzel. I asked him if that was what he had come to talk about. He said Papa is ailing and the homestead is going to seed and he thought I should know about it so I could do something to help. I said most likely Papa is not ailing but drunk. He said in Bible times Papa could have had me taken out to the gates and stoned. I said as near as I could tell the only people Jesus ever got mad at were church folk who were so busy looking for slivers in other peoples eyes they missed the logs in their own. He left none too happy.

Now I am left to wonder what to do. Even drunk, Papa never neglected the land.

I am staying with Aunt Martha while James is gone to the homestead to see how Papa is.

I had forgotten how nice it was to sleep in a big bed with a lace canopy and beneath a roof that does not leak. No wind blows through the windows and the walls are painted white with a framed picture of a Grecian girl pouring water from a jug. Beth sleeps with me in the feather bed while Joshua and little Hank sleep in the small room next door. I miss James.

People come and go quite often in Aunt Martha's house. She has her door open to all. She invited a drummer in yesterday to supper. He looked tired and worn down to bones. He looked better when he left. She gave him money to pay for a room at the hotel. Aunt Martha and three lady friends quilted all afternoon. She invited me to join them and I did. Betsy took charge of Joshua and my babies. They fared well beneath her wings. She made pound cake for Joshua and applesauce for Hank. The ladies were pleased to watch the children play. Their own are grown and gone off to who knows where.

I did not think it possible to enjoy womens company so much though I have always enjoyed Aunt Martha. But she is not like most I have met. These women were like her. They laugh about all manner of things, but not one unkind word did they utter about anyone.

Life is hard and cruel.

James said Papa is ailing and we have to go home and tend things for him. I did not dare ask if Papa's heart has changed toward me. I will know soon enough.

Truth is I am glad to be going home though I will miss Aunt Martha and Betsy and Clovis.

CHAPTER 11

A METAL TANK hummed in the upstairs master bedroom, the soft tick signaling an influx of oxygen that passed through a clear tube to Sierra's mother. Sierra checked the tube frequently, making sure it was in place beneath her mother's nose so that the pure oxygen would be infused into her mother's straining lungs. Edema was causing the difficulty with breathing. Over the past few days the edema had gone down. Her mother's breathing had eased and slowed. So, too, had the trickle of urine into the catch bag attached to the side of the bed. The hospice nurse had told her it would change color as death approached.

Sierra rose from the wing chair beside the bed and checked the tube again. She touched her mother's hair, once soft and dark auburn, now streaked white and oddly coarse. Her mother's skin felt dry, like fallen leaves. She was awake.

"Can I bring you some soup, Mom?" She was desperate

to do something, anything, to make her mother comfortable, to keep her alive.

"You can move me near the windows."

The rented hospital bed had wheels, but Sierra knew moving it would jar her mother and cause her more pain. She hesitated.

"Please," her mother whispered.

Sierra did as her mother asked, gritting her teeth each time the bed jiggled. Her mother didn't make a sound. "Is this all right, Mom?"

"Hmmm," her mother said, her thin fingers loosening their grip on the pillow. Her body slowly relaxed again. "Can you open the window?"

"It's cool today."

"Please."

As Sierra did so, she couldn't stop worrying. What if her mother caught cold? Even as she thought it, she knew it was irrational. The hospice nurse said yesterday that it wouldn't be long.

"Brady's mowing his back lawn," her mother said, and Sierra noticed her speech was faintly slurred. The morphine patches were doing their work. She noticed other things, too. Her mother's hazel eyes had lost their twinkle. Her skin was no longer tan from the long hours she'd spent tending her beautiful garden. "I always wanted skin as white as alabaster," her mother had teased a few days before. Sierra hadn't been able to laugh with her.

White. The color of purity.

The color of death.

"I've always loved the smell of cut grass," her mother said quietly. She reached out and took Sierra's hand. Sierra felt the tremor of weakness in her mother's grip. "This is my favorite time of year. The cherry trees bud, and the daffodils come up. Everything's so green and pretty." She sighed, and it was a sound of contentment, not sadness. "How can anyone fail to see God's hand in all of it?"

Sierra's throat closed. She stared out the window as the clouds moved slowly across the blue sky. Her mother wouldn't want her to cry. She had to be strong. She had to be *brave*. But inside, she could feel pieces of herself crumbling.

"Every year, Jesus shows us the Resurrection," her mother said and squeezed her hand lightly.

"It's a pretty day," Sierra said mechanically, thinking that was what her mother wanted to hear. She couldn't say what she was really feeling. How could her mother talk about Jesus now? She wanted to curse God, not praise Him! Her mother had served the Lord for as long as she could remember, and this was her reward? To die slowly, in pain? Her mother saw God's hand in everything. But where was God's hand in *this*?

"Can you raise the bed?"

"I think so," Sierra said and went to the controls. She pressed a button, and the bed came up. When it stopped, her mother had a good view down on the garden below.

"Oh, that's nice," she said, content.

Sierra checked her oxygen tube and readjusted the elastic straps looped behind her mother's ears. One had left a crease in her mother's cheek.

"Would you pick me some hyacinths?"

"Hyacinths?" Sierra said bleakly.

"I can see a few down by the walk, near the birdbath." Her hand trembled weakly as she tried to point. "The clippers are in the bucket under the steps."

Sierra hurried downstairs and out the back door to the porch. She found the clippers exactly where her mother said they'd be. She had always been one for believing a place for everything and everything in its place.

Walking quickly along the brick path, Sierra was dismayed at the state of the garden. Even during the winter, her mother had weeded and raked and kept everything neat. Now it was clearly neglected.

Sierra found a patch of the pretty blue flowers near the back of the garden. Hunkering down, she selected two stalks of perfect blooms and cut them for her mother. When she returned to the upstairs master bedroom, she saw her mother had the controls in her hand. She had raised the head of the bed a foot higher, giving her a better view.

What must her mother feel looking out at the sorry, deserted garden below?

"Thank you, sweetheart." She touched the flowers with her fingertips. She moved restlessly, pain flickering across her face. "It always amazes me to think how God made the garden and then placed man in it," she said, her words coming slowly, sluggishly. "Everything He made, from the bottom of the seas to the heavens, was for us to enjoy. Like hyacinths and blooming cherry trees and sunshine. Sweetness, hope, light."

Hope, Sierra thought. Where was hope when her mother's cancer advanced like an avenging army, ravaging her body, sapping her strength? Where was hope when death was imminent?

She readjusted the oxygen tube. "Is that better?" she said, touching her mother's face tenderly.

"It's fine, honey."

At night, when Sierra lay on the cot she'd set up near her mother's bed, she'd listen to her mother's breathing. And count seconds. One. Two. Three. Four. Five. Her own heart would stop after six and then beat faster at seven. Eight. Nine. Sometimes ten. And then her mother would take another precious breath, and Sierra would find herself relaxing for an instant before she started the count all over.

"Spring's coming," her mother said, gazing out the window. "The garden's always so beautiful."

All Sierra could see were the weeds that had come up and the suckers sprouting at the base of several unpruned rosebushes. The fall leaves from the birch trees had never been raked and lay like a heavy black blanket over the uncut lawn.

Over all the years the family had lived in this beautiful house, it had been her mother who had kept up the flower gardens and pruned the roses and trimmed the bushes and trees. It had been her mother who had been the gardener to loosen the soil, mulch in the compost, plant the seeds, and tend the young seedlings. Her mother had been the one to lay out the design so that flowers bloomed all throughout the year, filling the yard with a profusion of brilliant color.

Sierra remembered the hours she had spent with her mother outside in the sunshine, playing with her small tin bucket and little spade while her mom plucked weeds, thinned seedlings, and snipped dying blooms. She could remember the day her mother had planted the trumpet vine, gently tying green shoots to the lattice. The vine now covered the back wall.

Without her mother, everything would go wild.

Clouds moved across the sun, casting shadows over the yard below. "I hope it doesn't rain again," she said softly.

"It can't be sunshine all the time, or flowers wouldn't grow for lack of rain."

Even now, hurting, dying, her mother saw the brighter side of things. Sierra's eyes burned. Her throat ached with tears. She put her hand against her chest, wishing she could lift the weight of grief that grew heavier every day. She was choking on it. Suffocating. If it hurt this much seeing her mother slip hour by hour, what would life be like when she was gone?

"Sierra," her mother murmured softly.

Seeing her hand fumble weakly, Sierra took it. "What, Mom? Are you uncomfortable? Can I get you something?"

"Sit down, honey," she said.

Sierra did as she was asked and forced a smile as she enclosed her mother's hand in both of hers.

"I want you to do something for me," her mother said softly.

"What, Mom? What can I do?"

"Let me go."

Sierra's throat closed up. She had to press her lips together so she didn't cry out. She used every bit of willpower she had and still the hot tears bubbled into her eyes. "I love you," she said brokenly. Leaning down, she put her head against her mother's breast and wept.

Her mother stroked her hair once and then rested her hand weakly on her head. "I love you, too. You've always been God's blessing to me."

"I wish I could go back to when I was a child, sitting out on the patio in the sunshine while you worked in the garden."

Her hand trembled in weakness. "Each stage in our lives is precious, Sierra. Even now. The door isn't closing on me, honey. It's opening wider with each breath I take."

"But you're in so much pain."

Her mother stroked her hair again and spoke gently. "Shhhh. Don't cry anymore. I want you to remember that God causes all things to work together for good to those who love Him, to those who are called according to His purpose."

Sierra had learned those words as a child when she was in Sunday school. Her mother had helped her memorize them as they worked in the garden. But the words held no meaning. What good was there in suffering? She breathed in the scent of her mother and was afraid. Wasn't God supposed to heal those who had faith? Her mother had faith. She'd never doubted. So where was God now? She wanted to cling to her and beg her to fight harder, to hang on to life, but she knew she could not speak those words aloud and add to her mother's burden of pain. It was selfish to even think of asking her to endure more.

Anguish filled her. What would she do without her mother? Losing her father had been hard enough, but her mother had always been her counselor, her fountainhead. How many times had she run to her mother for help? How many times had her mother walked through troubles with her, gently guiding the way, showing her the higher road?

Sierra listened to the beat of her mother's heart. No one in the world knew her as well or loved her as much as her mother did. Not even Alex, her own husband, who should. Sierra's lips thinned. Especially not Alex, who hadn't even bothered to call in the past three days, the hardest of her life.

"Oh, Mom, I'll miss you so much," she murmured, wishing she could lie down beside her and die with her. Life was too painful, the future so bleak.

Her mother's hand moved slowly against her hair. "God has a plan for you, Sierra, a plan for your welfare and not for calamity, a plan to give you a future and a hope." Her voice was so weak, so tired. "Do you remember those words?"

"Yes," Sierra said obediently. Her mother had taught them to her as well, and like the others, they'd made no sense to her either. It had been her father and mother who took care of her. Then it was Alex. God had never come into the equation.

"Hold to them, honey. When you turn, you'll know I'm no farther away than your heart."

Sierra thought her mother had fallen asleep. She could still hear the slow, steady beat of her heart. She remained where she was, her head resting on her mother's breast, taking comfort in the closeness, the warmth. Exhausted, she stretched out beside her, arm around her, and slept.

She awakened when Mike came by after work. He stood beside the bed. "Her breathing sounds different." His expression was grim and controlled. "Her hand's cold."

Sierra noticed other things. The fluid level in the catch bag hadn't changed in hours. Her mother's skin color had changed.

She called the hospice, and a nurse was sent. Sierra recognized her, but she couldn't remember her name. Her mother would have remembered. Her mother always remembered everyone by name. She remembered things about them, too, asking after family members and job situations. Little things. Personal things.

"It won't be long," the nurse said, and Sierra knew the woman was saying her mother wouldn't be waking up again. The nurse adjusted the blankets and lightly stroked the hair back tenderly from her mother's temple. She straightened and looked at Sierra. "Would you like me to stay with you?"

Sierra couldn't make a sound. She shook her head. She just kept watching her mother's chest rise and fall slowly and counted seconds. One. Two. Three.

"I'm going to call Melissa," Mike said and left the room.

Soon after Melissa arrived, Luís and María Madrid came in. Alex's mother embraced Sierra and wept openly, while his father stood with tearless, grave dignity at the foot of the hospital bed.

"When is Alex coming?" he asked.

"I don't know that he is," Sierra said dully, standing by the window. "I haven't talked to him in a while." She listened to the click of the oxygen machine and counted.

She didn't want to think about Alex or anyone else just then. She didn't want to think about anything.

Seven. Eight.

Alex's father left the bedroom.

Melissa came in a few minutes later and stood beside Sierra. She didn't say anything. She just took her hand and held it in silence.

Eighteen. Nineteen. Twenty.

Melissa let go of her hand and moved to the bedside. She touched Marianna Clanton tenderly and checked her wrist pulse. Leaning down, she kissed her forehead. "Good-bye, Mama."

Straightening, she turned slowly to Sierra. "She's with the Lord," she whispered, tears running down her cheeks.

Sierra stopped counting. Her heart felt like a cold stone inside her chest. She didn't say anything. She couldn't. She just turned and looked down into the moonlit garden and felt the stillness closing in around her.

"She's not suffering anymore, Sierra."

Why did people always feel they had to say something? She knew Melissa meant to comfort her, but no words could. She heard another click as the oxygen machine was shut off.

Everything fell silent. Everything was still . . . so still she wondered if her own heart had stopped beating. She wished it would.

She couldn't think. She felt numb, so numb, she wondered if she was becoming exactly like the little statuette of the Virgin Mary her mother-in-law had brought and set on the windowsill. Bloodless. Hollow.

Mike came into the room again. He didn't utter a word. At least her brother understood. He just stood at the foot of the hospital bed, looking down at their mother. She looked peaceful, her body completely relaxed. When he turned away, he touched Sierra's arm. It was the merest brush of his hand, but enough to let her know she was there, alive.

Crossing the room, Mike sat down in the chair and leaned forward, hands loosely clasped between his knees. Was he praying? His head was down. If he wept, he did so silently. And he didn't leave the room or her, not until the men from the mortuary arrived.

Sierra followed the men downstairs as they took her mother away. She stood in the front doorway watching until the doors of the hearse closed. She'd still be standing upstairs if Melissa hadn't made the call.

Her mother had made all the arrangements two years ago, without anyone knowing. No fuss. No bother. Everything like clockwork. She would be cremated by tomorrow morning. Nothing but ashes left.

Sierra closed the front door and leaned her forehead against the cold wood. She was so tired, her mind whirring like an engine in neutral, going nowhere.

The telephone rang. She heard Luís answer. After the first word, he spoke in hot, hushed Spanish. The words might as well have been spoken in Greek for all the sense they made to her, but she knew he was speaking to his son.

He came into the parlor, where she was sitting. "It's Alex," he said and held out the phone. "He's been trying to reach you."

A lie, kindly offered, but unconvincing.

She took the phone and held it to her ear.

"Sierra? I'm sorry about your mother." He was silent, waiting. She shut her eyes tightly. What did he want her to say? Did he think one call and a little sympathy absolved him of days of neglect? She'd needed him. "I tried to call you yesterday, but the phone was busy." She couldn't speak, not with the weight of grief bearing down on her. "Sierra?" One word and she'd shatter. Worse, she'd say things she'd regret.

"I'll make reservations," he said at last. There was no

inflection in his voice to give away his own feelings. "The children and I will fly up to San Francisco tomorrow. I'll rent a car. We should be in Healdsburg by evening." He sounded as though he was making business arrangements. Silence again. It stretched. "Are you all right?" His voice was almost gentle. It filled her with infinite sadness and memories. "Sierra?"

Pressing the Off button, she put the phone down on the side table.

James works hard as Papa ever did.

He goes out at dawn and comes in for the midday meal. Then out again he goes until dusk. I am left alone to care for Papa.

Papa has changed much in the four years I have been gone. His hair has gone white and he is so thin and weak he can not get out of bed. I thought he was blind when first we came, but when Joshua came to stand in the doorway I knew he was not. His face got all red and awful. He started shouting loud enough for Aunt Martha to hear him all the way back in Galena.

He said—Keep that devil child away from me or I swear before God I will kill him.

Joshua ran out of the house. If I had not heard him crying, I would never have found him inside the hollow burned out tree. It was at the edge of the fields Matthew burned.

When I came back to the house, James asked why Papa would say such a terrible thing. I said he is crazy.

I know what's killing Papa. Hatred. It is eating him alive.

Sometimes I wish Papa would die and there would be an end to all his pain. And mine.

He is so weak and sick, he can do nothing for himself. And nothing I do for him helps. It makes things worse. He will not look at me or speak to me. He would not even take food from my hand until necessity and hunger made him. James does not ask for explanations. He thinks Joshua is my babee just like everyone else thinks it. I never told him otherwise.

James moved Papa into the little bedroom off the kitchen. We need the big bed for ourselves. Papa did not say anything, but I saw tears in his eyes.

I felt strange sleeping in the bed Papa shared with Mama. James wanted to love me the first night and I could not. All I did was cry. He said he understood, but I do not think he did. He thought I was tired and sad. What I feel is so much worse than that.

Papa and Mama made Lucas and Matthew and me in the bed James and I are sharing. Papa and Sally Mae made Joshua. That was on my mind too. I could see her sneaking in during the night while Papa lay drunk and unawares. She was just like Lots daughters. And look what come of that. My only comfort is remembering that Ruth was a Moabite.

I am all mixed up inside. Papa hurts me with his silence and meanness. But I am angry, too. And grieving. I wonder what Mama would think of all this. And me. I wonder where Matthew is and what he is doing. I hope he is well and happy wherever he is. But I doubt it. Matthew took everything to heart.

Seems to me Papa is the one who should answer for the pain he caused. Sally Mae did not do what she did without him helping. Being drunk is no excuse. I have not said so to Papa. It would do no good and he is Determined I done wrong by keeping Joshua alive. Papa does not think he is to blame for anything. It was all Sally Maes fault. And when she died, it was all Joshuas fault. When I took him up, it is all my fault.

So be it. I am stronger than Joshua and can take the heat of silent hell Papa pours down on me. Like God. I can feel it every time I walk through his door. Hatred is a powerful thing.

Joshua will not even come into the kitchen because he knows Papa is in that little back room. I am glad of it. I think Papa would kill him if he had the chance. And I do not intend to give him one. But at night I lay wondering what will come of all this.

When Joshua grows up he is going to want to know who his father is. What do I tell him if he asks?

I heard tell once that the sins of the father are visited on the sons. Does that mean Joshua must pay for what Papa did?

Life is not fair.

I put a marker on Sally Maes grave.

Papa is worse. His mind is going. Today when I went in to wash him and change the bedding again, he thought I was Mama. He said—Where have you been Katie love. I have missed you so much.

I took his hand and said I have been with Jesus these long years.

And Papa said real soft with tears in his eyes—Put in a good word for me.

I cannot stop crying. He was a good man once for all his drinking and wild ways. And he loved Mama more than life. Hearing him talk today made me remember what he was like when Mama was alive. And remembering made me miss her so much my body hurts with it. Everything inside me is clenched tight, aching and lonely.

It seems to me when God took Mama from us, Satan waltzed in the door and he has been living in this house ever since.

Papa is fading away. He does not eat. He sleeps most of the day.
When he is awake, he does not speak. He looks at the corner
of his room as though someone is there visiting with him.
Sometimes he smiles and mumbles something.

I am afraid. His curse still lays so heavy upon me.

Papa died this morning.

He was restless last night. He kept moving and moaning.
I did not know what to do to comfort him. He could not
breathe easy. He was better when I raised him up and sat
behind him and held him in my arms. I stroked his hair and
talked to him just like I do my babies when they are fretful.

And then near dawn a thought came into my head so powerful and clear it was like a real voice talking to me. I knew what
was wrong with Papa and what he needed. I struggled against
it but it was like a hand squeezing hard around my heart. I laid
him back and went down on my knees beside the bed.

I said—Papa I forgive you. Do you hear me Papa? I forgive
you.

His fingers moved. Just a little. So I took his hand and
kissed it. I said—I love you Papa. And I meant it. Just for
that minute after all the time before and between up to now.
I meant it. I forgot how much he hurt me and saw how much
he was hurting. Be at peace, Papa, I said. I couldn't say no more
than that.

And he seemed so. He did not say anything. Not one word.
He just gave one long sigh and was gone.

We buried Papa in the suit James wore when we were wed.
I sewed Papa inside the wedding quilt Mamas friends made for
them. With Mister Grayson dead, there was no one to come
see Papa laid to rest beside Mama and the babies they lost. It
was just me holding Beth and James holding Hank and Joshua

who stood beside the grave. I read words from the Bible. Mama would have liked that.

It has been raining ever since. Fitting weather for my feelings.

I cannot help wishing Papa had said something to me before he passed on to whatever was waiting for him. Even my name would have been enough. Or if he had looked at me before he died. Maybe then I would not feel this awful ache inside me.

Papa didn't say a word to me. Not from the day he cast me out to the day he died. But at the end, when he had no strength left, I think he wanted to. I hope so anyway.

Oh, what foolish creatures we are. Cursed with our pride! Cursed with our stubbornness!

No wonder God has forsaken us.

CHAPTER 12

SIERRA SAT IN THE FRONT PEW of the church with Alex on one side and Carolyn and Clanton on the other. Mike sat on the aisle, Melissa at his side, his three children next to her. The sanctuary was packed with people. As the pastor offered the eulogy, Alex took her hand. He had hardly touched her since arriving three days ago. She'd saved her tears for privacy, unwilling to share them with him or anyone else.

She couldn't stop thinking about the small polished wooden box placed on her father's stone at the cemetery. Was that all there was to a human being? One small box of ashes that weighed less than a newborn baby? The pastor had met them there and led the solemn but brief ceremony. Only family members had been present: she and Alex, their children, Mike and Melissa and their children, and Luís and María Madrid. So few. Too many.

Her mother's ashes would be mixed with her father's, and

in a few days a stone carver would come and add the date of her death to the slab that would cover them both.

Now, half-listening to the pastor's homily, she wondered if the forget-me-not seeds the children planted around the marble would come up.

"Marianna Clanton walked in the Spirit," the pastor said, using the opportunity to proclaim the gospel. Tearful, he rejoiced for his friend and parishioner. "Marianna will be sorely missed, but we can take comfort in knowing she's in the arms of her beloved Savior. And those of us who share her belief have the comfort of knowing she isn't lost to us. We will see her again."

One of the church ladies sang, "'Take my life and let it be consecrated, Lord, to Thee. . . .'"

Numb with grief, Sierra stared at her mother's picture on the linen-covered table at the front of the sanctuary. She would have chosen a different photo. On each side were vases filled with bright-yellow daffodils. In fact, the sanctuary was full of flowers—not funeral wreaths, but spring arrangements bursting with color and a mood of celebration.

"It was your mother's wish," the pastor had explained upon their arrival and her question. "She brought me this picture several months ago."

Far from the usual formal portrait used in solemn services, her mother had chosen one when she was years younger, laughing, with a bucket of yard trimmings in one gloved hand and her clippers in the other. She'd left a note as well. "Rejoice with me."

Finishing his homily, the pastor opened the service for sharing. One by one, friends stood and talked about Marianna Clanton and what she had meant in their lives. Some of the stories were funny, making people laugh. Others brought a hush and quiet tears. When all who wished to had spoken, Melissa went forward and spoke briefly on behalf of the family. More hymns were sung by all. Her mother's favorites. "Amazing Grace." "Ave Maria." "Standing on the Promises." And last, drawing tearful laughter, "Father Abraham." Everybody was on their feet, waving their arms and turning around. Even Sierra pretended to join in the spirit of rejoicing.

"Rejoice in the Lord always," the pastor said in benediction. "Again I will say, *rejoice.* Let your forbearing spirit be known to all men. The Lord is near." Sierra felt him looking down at her as his voice softened. "Be anxious for nothing, beloved, but in everything by prayer and supplication with thanksgiving let your requests be made known to God. And the peace of God, which surpasses all comprehension, shall guard your hearts and your minds in Christ Jesus."

A reception followed in the social hall.

Steeling herself against her inner turmoil, Sierra smiled and thanked everyone who came through the receiving line. The kind words slipped like water off a duck's back. She couldn't afford to let them sink in. Not now. Not here in front of everyone. Later, when she was alone, she'd bathe in the pool of tears.

Alex stood beside her, close but not touching. He was like a handsome stranger in his dark suit—polite, distant, but not indifferent. Everyone was impressed with his obvious success. They didn't know the cost.

Clanton and Carolyn sat with their three cousins across the room. They talked among themselves, sharing refreshments.

Sierra was ready to leave before the others. She asked Melissa if she'd mind watching Clanton and Carolyn. She knew the children wanted to visit as long as possible. "Why don't you let them spend the night?" Melissa said.

"I didn't mean—"

She cut her off with a gentle touch on her arm. "We'd love it. We see so little of them since you and Alex moved south." As soon as she said it, Sierra could tell she wished she hadn't. "Just don't worry about them. You need to rest."

Alex had driven his rented Cadillac to the cemetery and church. She debated asking him to take her home and decided against it. He appeared to be deep in conversation with his father.

She spoke briefly with the pastor and slipped unnoticed out the side door of the social hall. It was beautiful outside, everything in bloom. Her mother would have loved a day like this.

Three blocks away Alex pulled up beside her. "Why didn't you tell me you were leaving?"

It wasn't concern that tinged his tone, but impatience, anger. He didn't ask if she was all right. "You were busy." He was always too busy.

Alex got out of the car. When he touched her, he did so with gentleness. Then he put his hand beneath her elbow, his expression shadowed with sadness. "Get in the car, Sierra. Please."

She did as he said. Putting her head back against the black leather seat, she closed her eyes, feeling utterly bereft.

"What do you think people are saying about us when you just walk out the door without so much as a word to me?"

She looked at him. Was that it? Was that why he'd come after her? "Since when did you ever worry about what *other* people say?"

"You ought to care. Those people are family and friends."

"Don't worry, Alex. I didn't tell anyone you only called me three times in the past month." Ron had called more often than her own husband.

"The phone works two ways."

"It does, doesn't it? But then, every time I called you, you weren't home."

A muscle jerked in his cheek and he didn't say anything more. When he pulled into the drive alongside the Mathesen Street house, he turned to her. "I'm sorry. Sierra, I—"

"Forget the excuses, Alex." She got out of the car and walked along the cobblestone pathway to the front steps. Fumbling for her key, she shoved it into the lock and opened the door.

Shaking, she walked along the corridor toward the kitchen. Maybe a cup of coffee would brace her against whatever came.

The kitchen smelled of lasagna. The Pyrex dish still sat on the butcher block where she'd placed and forgotten it this morning. Sally Endecott had dropped the lasagna off along with a cellophane-covered bowl of tossed salad and a chocolate cake. Every day someone from the church came with food—spaghetti one day, the next a turkey dinner complete with dressing and cranberry sauce. Another brought roast beef and mashed potatoes, creamed carrots, and peas. Other friends brought home-baked apple pies and Toll House cookies.

No one wanted her to worry about having to cook. No one wanted her to worry about anything.

Not the least hungry, she measured coffee into the filter-lined holder and slid it in place. As she poured water into the top of the coffeemaker, she heard Alex come into the kitchen. He stood for a moment, saying nothing. When she kept her back to him, he went to the windows. She knew he was looking out at the back porch and garden.

"The house doesn't feel the same without her, does it?" he said quietly.

Sierra swallowed hard. She couldn't shake the feeling that

her mother was still upstairs or down the hall. If she called aloud, her mother would answer.

But it wasn't true. She had to remind herself her mother was dead. The ceremony in the cemetery this morning should have driven that fact home. Ashes to ashes, dust to dust. A few pounds of it equaled a human life.

One moment she felt numb inside. The next she felt a debilitating anguish and fear.

Pressing the heels of her hands against her eyes, she tried not to think about it. "How long can you stay?" she said, hoping Alex would say as long as she needed him.

"I made reservations for tomorrow."

She lowered her hands slowly, despair filling her. Alex had given her three days of his precious time. She supposed she should be thankful.

"The kids said they want to stay with you."

"That's fine," she said in a brittle voice. She took down a cup and saucer from the cupboard. "Do you want some coffee?"

"*Sí.*"

She glanced back at him and saw he was still staring into the backyard. Maybe her mother had meant something to him after all. She filled another cup and brought both to the table near the windows.

"Mom and I sat here together only a few weeks ago, before she was too weak to leave her bed." The cups rattled slightly as Sierra set them down and took a seat. "Roy Lubbeck is coming over at five to go over Mom's will."

Alex sat down across from her. "I'll stay another day or two if you want me to, Sierra."

Sure, she thought bitterly, he'd stay and resent every minute of it. She shook her head.

"What are you going to do about the house?"

"Do?" she said blankly, glancing up at him.

"You're going to have to rent it out or sell it. You can't leave it vacant. The place will fall apart. The garden's already going to seed."

She could feel the blood flowing out of her face. "I grew up in this house."

"I know how much the place means to you, Sierra, but you have no idea what it costs to keep up a place like this. Your mother was working on it all the time."

"I buried my mother this morning, and now you want me to give up this house?"

"Don't make it sound like it's my fault your mother died of cancer," he said, his eyes glittering.

"I didn't, but it would've been nice of you to wait a few days before telling me I should get on with disposing of my mother's property!"

"*Está bien, chiquita.* Take all the time you need. Stay for another month! Keep the place if you want. I don't care what you do!" He scraped his chair back and grated out the rest. "Just don't expect me to foot the bill for maintenance costs and taxes!" He left her sitting at the table.

A moment later, Sierra heard the roar of the Cadillac's engine. He revved it loudly and then sent gravel flying as he backed out of the driveway.

Pushing the cup and saucer back, Sierra put her head in her arms and wept.

❧

Mike pulled his van into the driveway an hour later. Carolyn and Clanton piled out with their three cousins. After a quick kiss hello, they went into the family room to watch a movie with their cousins. Melissa put her hand lightly on Sierra's shoulder and then took the lasagna out of the refrigerator and put it into the oven to warm up.

"Alex drove his mom and dad home," Mike said, pouring himself a mug of coffee. "He said he was going to stay and visit for a while, but to tell you he'd be back here before five. You told him Roy's coming by?"

"Yes." Sierra kept her gaze on her cold coffee. "I'm sorry I left the way I did."

"Don't worry about it. Everybody understood."

Except Alex.

Melissa came back and took the seat Alex had left vacant. "You look tired, Sierra. Why don't you rest for a while? I'll wake you when dinner's ready."

Sierra nodded and rose. She felt her brother looking at her and wondered if he'd guessed how bad things were between her and Alex. If he did, he was sensitive enough not to say anything.

As she climbed the stairs and walked along the upper hallway, she glanced at the narrow passageway to the attic. She remembered finding her mother there on the day Alex had turned life upside down. It hadn't turned right side up since.

She went up the steps and opened the door. Standing there, she looked in, amazed at the change.

The attic was swept and dusted, new Nottingham lace curtains hung over the four small windows. The old sofa had a new forest-green slipcover and four bright throw pillows, two of a deep golden yellow, two white with embroidered sunflowers and green ruffles. The coffee table had been refinished. On it were several old picture albums. The old brass lamp, now polished, stood between the sofa and her father's old worn leather recliner.

The walls had been painted pale yellow, the open-beamed ceiling white. On the south wall hung a dozen paintings and pictures. Sierra took one down. Not recognizing the face, she turned it over and saw that her mother had written the pertinent historical information on a card and glued it to the newly papered back. She smiled. Her mother had always been a stickler for detail.

The bookcase where her father's old files had been stored was now full of old books. The top three rows were designated for Mike, among them *Robinson Crusoe*, *Treasure Island*, *The Works of H. G. Wells*, *Earth Abides*. The bottom three were for her. She pulled out a worn copy of *Little Women* and leafed through it. Tucking it back in the shelf, she ran her fingers over *Anne of Avonlea*, *Daddy-Long-Legs*, *Captain from Castile*, *The Black Rose* and looked away.

In the far east corner of the attic, standing in a beam of sunlight, was the ornate wood-framed oval mirror. The old braided rug had been cleaned, the trunk of dress-up clothing repainted white with tole-painted flowers and leaves. She opened it and saw everything had been washed, ironed, and neatly folded away. Nearby was a small bookcase with children's games and books.

When she turned around, she saw two distinct stacks against the west wall, one for Mike, one for her. Her brother's red Radio Flyer wagon was neatly packed with other mementos, favorite books, an old worn teddy bear, a baseball bat and glove. Next to it were boxes neatly labeled: "College Texts," "Trophies," "Comic books," "High School Mementos/Block sweater."

Her own things were sorted, consolidated, and labeled as well, "Clothing/Prom dress," "Dolls," "Scrapbooks/Albums," "Stuffed Animals." In one container was clothing she'd tired of but had been unwilling to give away. Mary Kathryn McMurray's trunk sat next to the new white boxes, a white envelope taped to the top. *Sierra* was written in her mother's familiar handwriting.

Sierra removed it and opened it carefully, extracting the note.

> *My dearest Sierra,*
>   *This trunk and all its contents were meant for you. I read the journal before I sent it and couldn't help but feel you and Mary Kathryn McMurray share a great deal in common. The quilt has a message for you. You may not see or understand it now, but one day it will come to you like a star bursting in the heavens. And what a day that will be!*
>
>   *I love you.*
>   *Mom*

Kneeling down, Sierra ran her hands over the clean wood and metal braces of the trunk. She could smell the linseed oil her mother had used. Unlatching the top, she opened the trunk. The scent of mulberry sachets rose and surrounded her. The beautiful antique quilt lay on top, cleaned and carefully refolded. Sierra lifted it out and saw the gift wrap–covered boxes beneath. In one was the Indian gift basket. In another were the carved wooden animals with the note saying they were for Joshua. A blue velvet box held half a dozen wedding rings, each tagged with a name of the relative who had worn it. Her throat closed when she found two tied together with a small tag reading, "Brian Philip Clanton, Marianna Lovell Edgeworth, married December 21, 1958, in San Francisco."

Sierra put everything back the way she had found it. She folded the note and put it on top of the quilt. Closing the lid, she ran her fingertips over the wood- and metal-braced surface. She walked to the small attic window and pushed it open. A bracing spring breeze fluttered the lace curtains.

"I'm no farther away than your heart."

Grief tore at her, and Sierra went back to the sofa and sat down. She opened the top album. On the first page were two pictures of her father as a young man. One showed him with shoulder-length hair and dressed in worn Levi's and boots. Right next to it was another picture of him clean-shaven, hair shorn, and wearing a policeman's uniform. She smiled at the contrast. On the next page were pictures of her mother. In one, she appeared to be dancing in a meadow. Her arms were outstretched, her head back, her waist-length hair swirling. In another, she sat on a beach gazing pensively out at the surf. There were pictures of Mike, a bundled baby asleep on his father's shoulder, a baby playing in his crib, a toddler playing in the sandbox in the backyard. On the next page were pictures of her, wrapped in a blanket in her mother's arms, another of her sitting in a high chair with her face covered with spaghetti, yet another of her toddling along the cobblestone pathway in the backyard garden.

Each year was chronicled in pictures. Stretching out on the sofa, Sierra paged through the albums, seeing her mother and father in the early years of marriage. She smiled over pictures of Mike from infancy to his wedding. She went through her album, reliving memories as she saw herself in the garden with her mother, playing dress-up with friends in the attic, swimming at Memorial Beach, playing baseball, wearing her cheerleader's uniform. She came across a picture of Alex in cap and gown. She was standing with him, and they looked at one another with open adoration. Young love in full bloom. She had forgotten her mother came to the high school graduation ceremony. Her father had ignored the invitation. On the next page, she saw herself in the full bloom of her first pregnancy. The next picture showed her in a hospital bed, looking tired and happy, Clanton in her arms. María and Luís were on one side of the bed, her mother and father on the other. Beneath the picture was written, *Reconciliation*.

Outside the attic window, a nest of baby birds chirped excitedly. Sierra laid the album against her breast and listened. She knew when the mother bird was close and when it flew away by the sounds of the chicks. Closing her eyes, she drifted.

"You can't let it go." Her mother smiled at her as they both worked on their knees in the garden. "You need to take notice each day. See how they've come up already. If you give these weeds a day or two, they'll begin choking the flowers." She sat back on her heels and brushed strands of dark hair back from her temples. She looked young again, healthy and happy. "It's like that with life, too, honey."

Sierra awakened abruptly when the album was lifted from her chest. Alex stood over her. "Roy Lubbeck is downstairs."

"Oh," she said sleepily.

Alex closed the album and put it back on the coffee table. He moved away slightly as she pushed herself up and raked her hands back through her hair. She felt unkempt. Her church dress was rumpled and creased. "I need to freshen up before I come down." She was so tired. She wished she could lie down again and sleep here in the attic, where she was surrounded by happy memories. Maybe she'd dream of her mother again. Meeting with Roy Lubbeck would merely drive home the fact that she was gone.

Staring out the window, Alex shoved his hands into his pockets. "I'm sorry about what I said earlier."

Sierra didn't want to talk about it. "I can't make any decisions yet, Alex."

"I can understand that."

"I grew up here."

"I know."

His response was clipped, neutral. The wall was still firmly in place between them. The first brick had been laid when he took the job in Los Angeles. More had been added since, day by day, month by month, over the past two years. She didn't even know anymore who was inside the wall and who was outside.

"I miss you," she said softly, brokenly. "I miss the way things used to be."

He looked at her then, his eyes bleak. She knew he was deeply troubled, that he wanted to say something of import. Maybe he was as worried about their marriage as she was.

"I'm going to leave tomorrow. I think it'd be better that way. It'll give you the chance to think things over."

What things? she wondered. The house? Or was there something he wasn't saying?

He left the window. "I'll go down and tell the others you'll be with us shortly."

"Alex?"

When he turned, she stood. Gathering her nerve, she took the risk and let her feelings show. "Would you hold me? Just for a minute." He came to her and did as she asked, but she felt no comfort. His arms were around her, but it was as though he withheld himself, his heart.

How could he be standing there, holding her, and yet seem so very far away?

When she joined the others in the parlor, she sat in the wing chair near the cold fireplace. Alex took his proper place beside her. He didn't so much as put a comforting hand on her shoulder. Mike and Melissa sat on the couch, holding hands.

She tried to listen as Roy Lubbeck talked. He was explaining that after her father's death, her mother had put all the family assets into a living trust so that, in the event of her death, their inheritance wouldn't be tied up in probate.

Her mother had put the house in Mike's and her name two years before. The taxes, which amounted to a considerable sum, were paid through the year. She had also set up an account intended to take care of any minor problems that might arise, such as plumbing, appliance repair, and the like.

Sierra remembered that shortly after her father had passed away, her mother had hired a contractor to reshingle the entire roof. She'd spent a great deal to have the southern eaves and back porch torn out and rebuilt after termites were discovered. Roy went on to explain that the rest of her mother's assets were in certificates of deposit and treasury bills, including fifteen thousand earmarked for each grandchild, the money to be held in trust until their eighteenth birthdays.

Closing his briefcase, Roy cleared his throat. He looked at Mike and then at her. "Your mother was a remarkable woman. It was my good fortune to call her and your father friends." He started to say more and couldn't. As he rose, he took an envelope from his suit jacket and held it out to Alex. "Marianna asked that I give this to you."

Disturbed, Alex took the letter, folded it in half, and pushed it into the front pocket of his slacks. "I'll walk you out," he said.

Sierra heard the murmur of their voices. After a few moments the front door closed, but Alex didn't return. Glancing at Mike and Melissa, she rose and went into the foyer. She could see through the leaded window on each side of the door. Alex stood outside on the front steps, his hands shoved into his pockets. As Roy Lubbeck's sedan pulled away from the curb, Alex went down the steps. Her heart began to beat heavily in dread, but he didn't head for his car, which was parked in the drive alongside the house. He went out to the sidewalk and headed for the Plaza, where they used to sit and listen to the summer concerts in the bandstand. Relieved, she rested her forehead against the door for a moment and then went back into the parlor.

"We've already eaten," Melissa told her. "Do you want something?"

Sierra closed her eyes, shaking her head. The thought of food was enough to make her stomach lurch.

❈

"Try to get some sleep," Melissa said when the mantel clock chimed eleven.

Sierra went upstairs to bed. Lying in her canopy bed, she tried to think of happier times. Her mind was consumed with what-if scenarios. When she awakened in the morning, Alex wasn't beside her.

Donning her robe, she came downstairs to the kitchen and found Melissa making waffles for the children. "Have you seen Alex?" she said.

"Daddy left for the airport," Carolyn said, pouring syrup on her waffle.

"When?" Sierra said, heart sinking. Had he really left without even saying good-bye to her?

"About an hour ago, I guess. He came in and talked to Clanton and me while we were watching television."

Turning away, she blinked back tears.

Melissa poured batter into the waffle iron. "He said he didn't want to awaken you," she said quietly. "He felt you needed sleep."

When Melissa looked at her, Sierra knew Alex hadn't fooled anyone with his excuses. Sierra gave her sister-in-law a cynical smile, poured herself a cup of coffee, and sat down with the children.

If this baby is not born soon, I will burst like an overripe melon.

James is worried sick. He makes me nervous. There is no midwife and I am too far gone to go back to Galena by wagon or any other way. So we will have to manage by ourselves. I cannot even bend over to pick up the babies I have and there is no lap left for them to sit on. Some days this baby kicks so much I wonder if there are not two inside me. Maybe they are contending with one another just like Esau and Jacob.

Matthew Lucas Farr was born mid-morning May 5 or there-abouts. He is as strong and loud as his older brother ever was. Deborah Anne followed her brother into the world straight away. They do not look at all alike, but sound pretty near the same.

James is back at work in the fields. He is much relieved to have me up and around again. He has not the patience for tending toddling and crawling babies, though he had charge of his offspring for three whole days. I could not help but laugh at his Frustration. Joshua had to show him how to change a diaper, but washing soiled ones is a chore James would sooner die than do. Does he think I like it?

I am beginning to feel like our poor milk cow.

It has been two years since I wrote a word in this journal. Where has all the time gone? Back on the homestead, by the time the day is done, I am too tired to put two thoughts together in my head let alone put anything sensible on paper.

Now, I am visiting Aunt Martha and my Burdens are lifted. She is enthralled with the twins and Delighted to have Joshua, Hank, and Beth back under her roof. Betsy and Clovis are pleased, too. Joshua is Clovis's shadow. Hank and Beth spend most of their time in the kitchen with Betsy. They have discovered her fine cooking. The only time Aunt Martha gives up the twins is when they need nursing.

Galena is so much bigger than it was three years ago. Aunt Martha said there are more than ten thousand souls living here now. I think it more likely that four thousand of them have no souls at all from what I've seen. The river is busy with ships from the Mississippi. Irishmen and Germans swarm the docks and negras as well. Betsy said there is a new African Methodist Episcopal Church. She and Clovis go there to worship Jesus. There's so much noise now you can't hear yourself think.

Aunt Martha has a new cistern. She said too many people use the town well and it is too long a wait for water.

James and I saw a man haul a box out onto the sidewalk near the marketplace today. He stood on it and talked about Oregon. He talked about the Preemption Act of 1841 saying every person head of a family can have 160 acres of prime free land in Oregon. James insisted we stay and hear what the man had to say. The man claimed Oregon is a land flowing with milk and honey on the shores of the Pacific. He said there are great crops of wheat there that grow as high as a man's head. He said pigs run about under great acorn trees, round and fat, and already cooked with knives and forks sticking in them so you can saw off a slice anytime you have a mind to do so. Some believed his hogwash and were ready to sign up and go right off with him in their farm wagons. I am glad James had more sense.

James sold our corn crop today. Prices are down. He has worked hard the past few years paying off Papas debts and making improvements on the homestead. If Papa could see the land now, he would be proud of James.

We will go home soon. I will miss Aunt Martha and Betsy and Clovis. I will miss the good cooking, the feather bed, the piano, and the ladies from the quilting club.

For all that, I can hardly wait to be home again.

James has westering fever. He talks of nothing but Oregon.

What is it about men that they always think the grass is greener on the other side of a mountain? The grass is green enough right here. I told James we have land all paid for, a sturdy house, a barn, two horses, a milk cow, some goats, and a flock of chickens. We have our health and our babies and we are happy.

He said—You are happy, Mary Kathryn. The way I see it we will be living hand to mouth all our lives as long as we stay in Illinois. In Oregon there is a chance. A chance for what I wanted to know. To build something that will last he said. And the winters are milder.

I told him when something sounds too good to be true, it most likely is.

But all he said to that was—Free land, Mary Kathryn. Think of it.

I said—Free land two thousand miles away. Free land we have not seen and know nothing about. We have land right here already.

He said—Poor land full of rocks and roots and heartache.

Sometimes James sounds just like he did when he was talking about going off to New York and England and China.

I am sick of hearing about Oregon.

PART 3

THE SURRENDER

CHAPTER 13

THE HOUSE FELT VACANT when Sierra unlocked the side door from the garage. Carolyn and Clanton followed her in, lugging their suitcases through the kitchen and down the hallway to their bedrooms. Sierra set her own down in the living room and wandered through the house.

Something didn't feel right. Sierra couldn't put her finger on it, but a strange foreboding filled her. At first, she wondered if the house had been burglarized, but nothing was missing. She opened the drapes in the living room and let the spring sunshine in, but that didn't help dispel the dark atmosphere.

Picking up her suitcases, Sierra went down the hallway to the master bedroom. Her brows lifted slightly when she found the bed made. In thirteen years of marriage, Alex had never made a bed. The rugs had been vacuumed. Clean towels hung in the bathroom. She put her hand on the doorknob to the walk-in closet and then hesitated, irrational fear gripping her. Taking a deep breath, she opened it and breathed in relief when she saw Alex's suits hanging to the right. The shelves at the back were neatly stacked with shirts.

She went back into the bedroom, where she had put her suitcases. Hefting one onto the bed, she unlatched it and began unpacking. As she tucked her clothing back into the dresser and put her toiletries into the bathroom, she couldn't shake the doubts and fears that had been building since Alex had left Healdsburg.

The children had raised them.

Over the past two weeks while she'd remained in Healdsburg to make some decisions with her brother, little things had come out in conversations with the children. During the time Sierra was in Healdsburg by herself, Dolores had spent the night babysitting four times, and Clanton and Carolyn had spent one weekend at Marcia Burton's.

"Daddy!" Carolyn cried out in the other room, and Sierra heard Clanton chattering away as their father returned early from work. Sierra's pulse skyrocketed. She looked around the bedroom again and bit her lip. Had he hired a maid service? If so, why now when he never had before? Closing the empty suitcases, she lifted them off the bed and set them near the door. She would put them away in the garage later.

Her stomach knotted with tension. Trying to calm down, she sat in the chair by the window. Resting her hands on the arms, she waited.

It seemed an hour before Alex stood in the doorway. "I'm glad you made it back safely." His tone and expression were enigmatic.

"Thanks." Her heart drummed harder, not in the way it used to when she looked at him, but with something deeper, something primeval. "Where are Carolyn and Clanton?" she said, keeping her tone neutral.

"Carolyn's on the phone with Pamela, and Clanton's down the street playing soccer with some friends. He'll be in before dark." His eyes narrowed slightly. "What's the matter?"

"You tell me, Alex," she said without inflection. When he said nothing, she drew in her breath slowly to keep herself from shaking. "I heard Dolores had to spend four nights with the children while I was gone." His expression flickered slightly. "And they spent a weekend with Marcia." A pink hue seeped up from his collar and filled his face.

Sierra closed her eyes.

She heard Alex come into the bedroom and close the door quietly behind him. When he spoke, his voice was low and heavy. "I didn't want to talk about this. Not the first day you got home." He sat down on the bed. "Things aren't working between us anymore."

She opened her eyes and looked at him. His eyes grazed hers and shifted away.

"You don't understand what's important to me," he said.

"What is important, Alex?"

He looked at her then, coolly. "My work. You've resented what I do from the beginning."

"Can you tell me truthfully it's *work* that kept you away for six nights while I was gone?"

The small lines around his mouth deepened. "We've got nothing in common anymore. Our marriage started disintegrating a long time ago."

"We have two children in common," she said quietly. "We're married to one another. We have that in common."

"Then let me put it to you straight. I'm not in love with you anymore."

Sierra hadn't realized how much it would hurt to have Alex

say those words straight out. She remembered listening to Meredith talk about her ex-husbands. *"They always say you never understood them, that you don't have anything in common anymore. But it usually boils down to one thing. Another woman."*

Her heart sank into the pit of her stomach.

"I'm sorry, Sierra. I—"

"Who is she, Alex?"

He looked away from her and sighed. Standing, he moved restlessly, finally stopping near her dresser. "What difference does it make?"

"I'd like to hear the news from you before I hear it from someone else."

Alex pushed his hands in his pockets, reminding her of the night Roy Lubbeck had given him a letter from her mother. Had he ever bothered to read it?

"Elizabeth."

"Elizabeth?" Her heart plummeted. "Elizabeth Longford?" she said weakly, cold clarity washing over her like a tidal wave. "The woman from Connecticut?"

"Yes."

"The one who graduated from Wellesley?"

"Yes."

Alex said she didn't understand him. Oh, but he was wrong, so wrong. She knew him better than he knew himself. She saw him so clearly in that instant. It was as though all the veiling had been ripped away, leaving his soul bare for her to see.

"You finally made the grade, didn't you?" she said softly, hurt beyond anything she could ever have thought possible.

Alex turned slowly and looked at her. Sierra watched her husband's face change. Shock. Pain. Rage. She knew her words had struck true, right to the very heart of the matter. He knew exactly what she meant. The poor farm laborer's son who had never felt good enough had finally bagged himself a worthy trophy. Beautiful, well-educated, accomplished Elizabeth Longford, daughter of the American Revolution. Maybe he didn't fully realize she had always understood his insecurities and loved him despite them. Certainly she had never expected to throw them in his face. But then, she had never expected him to betray her with another woman.

"*Bruja,*" he said through his teeth.

"And what are you, Alex? A cheat and a liar."

Had Alex been another kind of man, he would have struck her. She saw how much he wanted to. She almost wished he would. Maybe then she wouldn't feel this sick anguish. She'd be glad to see him leave. She wouldn't care. It wouldn't feel like he was ripping her heart out. Looking into his eyes, she saw no hint of tenderness or regret. She saw a man determined to be free, eager to be gone.

"This farce of a marriage is *over!*" he said, enraged.

Pain gripped Sierra until she could hardly breathe. She knew Alejandro Luís Madrid so well. If she apologized, it would make no difference. She had done the unthinkable by putting light on his secret pain. If she begged, it wouldn't change anything. He would never forgive her. His very blood would cry out against it.

"It's not over for me, Alex. It never will be."

Crossing the room, he opened the door. "That's your problem," he said and walked out.

<hr />

Lucas came back today.

If I could wish a man dead, it would be him. He was a bad seed as far back as I can remember and he has grown up tangled and full of treachery.

He rode right up to the house on a good animal and dressed in fine clothes, claiming the homestead belongs to him. I told him he was a thief and a liar. He laughed and said it dont matter. What is important is he is Papas firstborn and I am disinherited. He has a letter from Hiram Reinholtz to prove it.

And then he said bold as brass—But since James has done such a fine job working the place, I will be generous and allow you to stay on as sharecroppers. And if you don't like that arrangement, Mary Kathryn, you can pack up and go straight to hades.

James said he will not fight Lucas over the land. No matter what I say, he will not listen. This land is my home. I was born in this house. James has done more work in the fields than Lucas ever did. And now my no-good brother shows up after all these years and says the homestead all belongs to him. Not without a fight, I say.

James says no. He says we are going to Oregon.

Lucas came to the house today and he brought a man and woman with him. They all were in a wagon. I stood on the front porch with a rifle, but James took it from me before I could shoot my brother dead. Lucas brought Elder right into my house. The man had his hat in his hand and would not look at me. It did not help knowing he is ashamed for taking my home from me. Lucas said he has a contract with Elder. Elder will work the land and share profits.

I am writing this in the barn by candlelight as I am pushed out of my own home and my own husband helped. I am sleeping in the hay with my babies. Where James is sleeping I don't know and I don't care.

Aunt Martha welcomed us with open arms. So did Betsy and Clovis. I had not cried a tear until I saw them and now I cannot stop.

It was a long ride here by farm wagon from the homestead. Not in miles. The children fretted and kept asking how long it would take to get to Galena. James was short-tempered. If it's like this for two days travel, what does he think it will be like on a two-thousand mile journey through Indian infested wilderness?

He said—You will see I am right when we get to Oregon, Mary Kathryn.

I did not answer or even look at him.

I hoped in vain that by the time we got here, he would change his mind. I hoped he would see I am right and he would turn this wagon around and go back and fight for what belongs to us.

He didn't change his mind about nothing. He's dug in his heels deep as Papa ever did. He went right down to the market place and sold our wagon and used part of the money to buy passage on a steamboat. He says we're going down the Mississippi the end of this week and getting off at Independence Landing.

I said—Good bye, James Farr. It was nice knowing you.

He said—You are going with me if I have to hog-tie and carry you! I told him he would have to do just that. So he went out and got so drunk Clovis had to fetch him home. Poor old Clovis had to carry James home slung over his shoulder like a sack of grain. I told Clovis he could dump James in the potato cellar and leave him there until he grows eyes and rots. He is not welcome in my bed.

I reckon that is what Clovis did with him.

I can barely see this page for the tears. How is it possible to hate a man I love so much?

Aunt Martha says God's hand is in this. If that is so, then I have a bone to pick with God. Not that he will listen. Not that he ever did.

Aunt Martha and I sat all day today talking and crying. I asked her if I and my children could stay and live with her when James goes to Oregon. She said no. She said she cannot come between a man and his wife. She said God joined us together and she will not help me split the sheets. So I am stuck with James Addison Farr and his dreams of Oregon.

I should have married Thomas Atwood Houghton.

Aunt Martha bought me a trunk. James is outfitting us in Independence. So for now, all I have is a medicine box with Quinine, bluemass, opium, laudanum, whiskey, hartshorn for snakebites and citric acid to treat scurvy, books, slates, chalk, and ink aplenty. I do not want my children growing up ignorant like their father. The ladies from the quilting circle packed pieces of fabric in every color and pattern imaginable so I can make my own quilt someday. I have packed stout linen thread, large needles, beeswax, buttons, paper of pins and 2 thimbles and packed in a pretty candy box Thomas gave me a long time ago.

If I had married Thomas I would not be going to Oregon.

Pack three sets
1 linsey-woolsey dress
1 wool dress
unmentionables
4 pairs of woolen socks
2 pairs of walking shoes
1 good shawl
1 bonnet
comb, brush and 2 toothbrushes

Pack two sets
2 flannel overshirts
2 woolen undershirts
2 pairs thick cotton drawers
4 pairs of woolen socks
4 color handkerchiefs
2 pairs of walking shoes
1 pair of boots
1 gutta percha poncho
1 coat
comb, brush, 2 toothbrushes each

frying pan
kettle
coffee pot
pie tin
butter churn

2 saws
2 shovels
2 axes
3 belt knives
1 whetstone
1 rifle
1 pistol
ammunition

James says he has the money to buy the rest of what we need when we get to Independence. I think it would be cheaper to buy supplies here, but he said it would cost too dear to freight it down the river. So we will go with what little we have, which is not much.

Aunt Martha offered money to James, but he would have none of it. I was not so proud.

I said Good Bye to Aunt Martha this morning. It near broke my heart. It is breaking still as I sit on this miserable shallow draft steamboat taking me down the Mississippi away from her and Betsy and Clovis and my home. Aunt Martha kissed me and took off her cross necklace and put it on me. It is the pretty one with amethyst stones I admired when I first come to Galena after my father cast me out. She has worn it every day of her life since her papa give it to her on her fourteenth birthday. She said—I want you to have it in memory of me. Let it remind you I am praying for you every day. She said—God is with you, Mary Kathryn Farr, and don't you ever forget it.

I was not comforted.

I will never see them again. She says I will, but she means heaven and I am not going there. I am not going anywhere God is.

I got God and James Addison Farr to blame for all this heartache.

Joshua asked me today why I will not speak to Papa. I said it was nothing for him to worry his mind over, but he is worried all the same. I said I was busy making sure Beth and Hank and the twins do not fall overboard into the river. But he said that is not so because Papa has Matthew and Hank with him and Deborah was asleep and Beth is too scared of water to get close to the edge of the boat.

He said—You will see Papa is right when we get to Oregon. I told him if I heard those words again, his papa will find himself in the muddy Mississippi. And he can't swim!

We got off the boat at Independence Landing two days ago. It has been cloudy and cold. James found a holding place for our possessions until we have a wagon to store them. It is a good thing it is not raining because we are camped without so much as a tent over our heads.

Independence is the wildest place I have ever seen. It is full of people from every walk of life, most I would not want to venture down. I have never seen so many people. Everyone is buying and selling something. Everyone is in a hurry to get ready to go to Oregon or California or Santa Fe.

It is dusk and I can still hear hammers pounding as wagons are being built and oxen bellowing and horses neighing. It is impossible to get a wink of sleep in this jumping off place.

James left me with the children so he can go walking around the town square and—get a feel for what is happening—as he put it. I am getting feeling enough from sitting by and watching. Most people hereabouts are as crazy as he is. The men at least. I have not seen a happy woman since we landed.

James talked all day to men camped near us with their wives and children about whether it is wise to buy oxen or mules. He came back and laid out all he had learned and then said—What do you think, Mary Kathryn?

He would not want to know what I think.

He said—You gotta talk to me sometime.

Not in this lifetime I don't.

James bought 4 teams of oxen today at $25 an ox! They are good sturdy animals and gentle, but not worth that much. He should have bargained harder. James said he will send me next time. He said if things get bad on the trail, we can eat them. I would like to know how he thinks he could do that with Beth taking these beasts of burden to her heart already.

I met Nellie Doane today. She and her husband Wells are
camped near us. She was washing clothes in the creek same
time I was. I am not the only one weeping about going to
Oregon. We cried together and laughed some too. We both had
some fine ideas about what to do with our husbands. She said
she supposed we would have to make the best of what comes.
She has three children all eager to go westering. Joshua and
her son Harlan are already fast friends.

Other people are gathering near us. Virgil Boon for one. He
is a cooper from Pennsylvania and up in years. He is at least
forty if he is a day. There is also Judge Skinner and his wife.
He is older still. Forty-three, he said. He figures they will
need Law and Order in Oregon. His wife is not friendly so I
do not know her name. Ruckel Buckeye is from Kentucky and
only fifteen. I asked him what his mother thinks about him
going off to Oregon by himself and he said she told him to go
and make a better life for himself out west. I cannot imagine a
mother telling her son to leave her knowing she will never see
him again. She must be a hard woman.

It has been raining near every day. Our clothes are as damp as
my spirits. I must trek through mud to get to the mercantile.
James said he needs me to do an accounting or we will not have
money enough to make the journey.

He said—You're going to have to help me unless you
want to live in this wild place for the rest of your days, Mary
Kathryn. He cant write or read and there are men in this
town that skin you for the pure pleasure of it. He said we have
$854.22 to our names and it took him all the years we worked
the homestead to save that. Aunt Martha gave me $120 that I
have hidden in the trunk for safe keeping and Dire Straits.
I did not tell him about it.

James brought Mister Kavanaugh to our campfire today. I saw this man two days ago in the mercantile. Or rather he saw me. He was standing at the counter and buying powder, lead, and shot when I come in with the children. He is a big man and hard to miss. He looks wild as an Indian in his buckskins. His hair is long and dark and held back by a piece of rawhide. He was carrying a Sharp's buffalo rifle and had bluer eyes than I have ever seen before and staring right at me from the minute I walked in the door.

Joshua wanted to talk to him but I told him to stay put by me and watch that Hank and Beth did not stray. I turned my back for one minute and next thing I knew Joshua took Hank and Beth right up to him. I should have been paying better attention, but I had the twins and was bargaining with MacDonald who is a thief and must be watched. When I turned around again, there was Joshua asking this rough stranger all manner of questions and him looking at me with those blue eyes of his. I shooed the children away from him, apologized, and left quick as I could.

I knew I would see him again. I did not know how or when. I just knew. How James met him I don't know and will not ask. I offered Mister Kavanaugh supper and he accepted. James did most of the talking while they ate. I did not say anything. I listened and learned Mister Kavanaugh has had commerce with the Kansa, Pawnee, Cheyenne, and Sioux. He lived with the Cheyenne two years. He has great respect for the Indians and not much for those he has seen getting ready to head west. He said most are ill-prepared for what awaits them.

I said—Do you mean us, Mister Kavanaugh?

And he said—Depends.

On what I asked to know. He just looked at me and did not say.

James and Wells and half a dozen other men are meeting
with John MacLeod tonight. A contract will be drawn up
and signed and fees set for his hire. James said he Highly
Recommends Kavanaugh as a scout but doubts the man will
agree. Kavanaugh has an affinity for Indians and little use for
his own kind.

James said Kavanaugh has agreed to go with us to Oregon.
He said John MacLeod was surprised and pleased. He said—
Kavanaugh knows this country like the back of his own
hand.

All the ladies are Impressed with him. They think he is
Very Handsome and Mysterious. The men ply him with constant questions. I wonder sometimes if James and the others are
not having second thoughts about this madness of going west.

It is raining again today and making mess of our camp. Last
night, the wind blew rain right into the wagon. It is too wet
for a cookfire. I wish I was at home at Aunt Martha's with my
children cuddled into that big brass bed.

I asked James what we would do if the children get sick.
He says we got Doc Murphy. What if the wagon breaks down?
He says we have spare parts and the wheels are made of osage
orangewood. What about Indians? He says Kavanaugh knows
what to do about Indians. James says I worry too much, and I
say he doesn't worry enough.

We ate cold beans and hard biscuits tonight. I kept thinking
about Betsy's fine cooking and that warm kitchen. I wonder if
I will ever know those Comforts again. By the time we get to
Oregon, it will most likely be too late to plant Crops. We will
all starve by springtime.

I wonder if any of us will be alive in a year.

EXPENDITURES

Concord spring wagon of white oak $85.00
Cotton duck covers 100.00
4 teams of oxen 200.00
Harnesses 25.00
6 barrels of flour 25.00
600 pounds bacon 30.00
50 pounds chipped beef 8.00
50 pounds lard 2.50
100 pounds dried fruit 6.00
50 pounds salt and pepper 3.00
100 pounds coffee 9.00
200 pounds beans 8.00
75 pounds rice 3.75
10 pounds of saleratus 1.00
5 pounds mustard 1.00
150 pounds sugar 7.00
powder, lead, shot 20.00
30 pounds tenting 5.00
matches 1.00
50 pounds candles 3.30
3 pounds castile soap 2.00
100 feet heavy rope 4.00
45 pounds bedding 22.50
Total $572.05
Savings 854.22
                                                              -572.05
                                                               282.17

Share for captain/scout
MacLeod and Kavanaugh . . . . *-44.00*
Savings 282.17
                                                              -44.00
                                                               238.17

MEMBERS

John MacLeod Wagon Company to Oregon Territory
Scout—Mister Kavanaugh
James and Mary Kathryn Farr—Illinois/farmer
    children: Joshua, Henry, Beth, Matt, and Deborah
Virgil Boon—Pennsylvania/cooper
Judge Skinner and wife Mary—Carolina/lawyer
Reese Murphy—New York/doctor
    sister: Susan
Cal Chaffey—Maine/farmer
Mary and Marcus Sweeney—Ohio/blacksmith
Mittie Catlow—Illinois/farmer
    son: Calhoun
Franklin and Paralee Sinnott—Missouri/merchant
    children: Frank and Patricia
Werner Hoffman—New York/farmer
    son: Herbert
Kaiser Vandervert—Massachusetts/tailor
Ernest and Winifred Holtz—New York/wheelwright
    children: Ernst, Louisa, Alicia, Gottlieb
Melzena and Arbozena Pratt—Alabama/seamstresses
    nigra servant: Homer
Wells and Nellie Doane—Missouri/baker
    children: Robert, Harlan, LeRoy
Lot Whimcomby—Massachusetts/clerk
Paul Colvigne—Delaware/teacher
Binger Siddons—Indiana/farmer
Oren and Aphie McKenzie—Virginia/farmer
Dunham and Celia Banks—Connecticut/shoemaker
    children: baby Hortense
A. J. Wright—Tennessee/harnessmaker
Wyatt Collins—Vermont/farmer
Cage Baker—Kentucky/farmer

Ruckel Buckeye—Ohio/hunter
Artemesia and Athena Hendershott—Georgia/drayage
    brother: Apollo
Stern Janssen—Sweden/sailor
Matthew Odell—Illinois/gunsmith
Less Moore—South Carolina/gambler

Payment rendered in advance to John MacLeod—$800.00
Payment rendered in advance to Bogan Kavanaugh—300.00

The sun has finally come out. We were busy all day repacking
to John MacLeod's instructions. Our flour is now stored in canvas sacks instead of barrels, 100 pounds per sack. Our bacon
supply is repacked in boxes, 100 pounds each. We surrounded
the bacon with bran. JM says this will prevent the fat from
melting and keep the bacon from spoiling.

    I am too tired to write more.

It is raining again. We have moved to higher ground. Everyone
is Wet and Cold and Agitated. JM says we will not move out
until the grass is four inches high. Right now, our stock is feeding on what grass there is which is not much.

    No one is happy, not even James who had this fool idea of
going to Oregon.

    I long for home. I cannot think about Aunt Martha, Betsy
and Clovis without crying.

James bought a milk cow for $20. Beth will have charge of it.
Joshua will help herd the stock the company has bought from
the common fund.

We have been on the trail three days. We left Courthouse
Square at sunup May 12. There are twenty-eight wagons

in our company and fifty-eight souls counted among them. We crossed the Missouri border and left the United States of America. The only law and order we got now is what we have agreed to among ourselves. We have traveled over muddy roads past a great big blue mound and then crossed Bull Creek. Heading due west, we saw a sign saying The Road to Oregon. We had a hard crossing at the Vermillion. A. J. Wright lost a wheel coming down the steep bank.

Crossing creeks is always trouble. Near the mission the Shawnee Indians helped me while James helped A. J. The children and I had a smooth crossing though my heart was in my throat the whole way.

Franklin Sinnott has two wagons, one for family and supplies and another loaded with goods he intends to sell in Oregon. He is driving it himself and leaving his wife Paralee to drive the other. She is scared of driving and with good reason. She is not much good at it and Very Fragile. When we were at the Wakarusa, she pulled out of line and waited. Franklin yelled at her something fierce, but she would not get back behind and follow him across. She would not budge. He had to come back and drive the wagon across himself. He was so mad, he made her get off and walk. Little Patricia screamed for her mama all the way across the river. Paralee came across in a bull boat with a Shawnee.

We crossed the Kansas and have followed the Little Blue for three days. James is letting Joshua drive the wagon. I am thankful. It is easier on a body to walk.

Someone pushing a wheelbarrow followed us all day yesterday and today. MacLeod said it was probably a Mormon and went out to see. I can see the glow of a campfire in the distance.

Artemesia and Athena Hendershott have asked Kavanaugh

to share their supper. They are very nice ladies. Perhaps he will take a liking to one. Apollo would be delighted to see one of his sisters wed.

John MacLeod just returned and told James it is a woman out there. He told her she is a fool and should go back, but she said it is a free country and she can go where she pleases.

It is beyond my thinking why any woman would choose to go to Oregon let alone work so hard to get there.

I wonder who she is and why she is so Determined to leave Civilization behind.

James said the woman following us is French and from New Orleans and I am to have no discourse with her. I asked him why and he would not tell me. I said I would talk to whom I please and he said I would not. I asked how he come to know so much about her and he said Kavanaugh told him. I told him it was his rotation on guard duty and he should go. Ruckel Buckeye and Apollo Hendershott are also on duty tonight. Kavanaugh told us from the start the Indians have a fondness for stock and the men must keep their Eyes Open. James was mad enough when he left the fire that he will have no trouble staying awake.

We have reached Alcove Springs. There were so many wagons, we felt we were right back in Independence. We will move on tomorrow for better forage for the animals. I spent the afternoon washing clothes.

I can hear fiddles playing on the night air. James wants to dance. He has not said so, but I can tell because his foot is tapping. He keeps looking at me and waiting for me to say something.

I would like to say something, but he would not like to hear it.

CHAPTER 14

THE INTERCOM on Sierra's desk buzzed. She pressed the button. "Yes, Arlene?"

"You have a call on line two."

"Thank you." Sierra pressed the line two button, thinking it was the counselor she'd been trying to reach. "Sierra Madrid speaking."

"It's Alex."

Her heart leaped, then crashed when he got straight to the point. "The house is yours. My attorney says I'm making a mistake, but I want you to have it. I've already had the deed changed over into your name. Same for your BMW. You'll get the papers certified mail in a day or two."

His voice was so cold, her fingers felt icy around the telephone receiver. "Do you feel absolved now? Do you think giving me a house and car makes everything *right*?"

"I think I'm being more than fair."

"Fair?" Her throat closed. "I never realized you thought adultery and desertion were fair."

"As soon as you get an attorney, we can get all the details of the divorce settled. The quicker it's done, the easier it'll be on all of us."

She had no intention of making it easy for him. Trembling, she put her hand over her eyes. "I won't give you a divorce, Alex. I already told you that."

He swore in Spanish. "I'm not coming back, Sierra. You'd better understand that here and now. I want *out!*"

"You're already out. You just don't have the legal documents to prove it. And you never will." She slammed the phone down.

She was shaking violently, her heart hammering. Clenching her fists, she pressed the heels against her eyes and tried to push the emotions down deep inside her.

"Are you all right?" Ron said from the doorway.

She didn't answer. Breathing slowly, she stuffed the feelings deeper and deeper, until she felt cold and still inside. She couldn't even feel her heart beating. "Yes," she said and turned away, finding her place on the schedule she'd been typing for the next week.

Ron came over to her desk and pressed the intercom button. "Hold all calls until I tell you otherwise, Arlene. Sierra and I need to have a conference." Releasing the button, he put his hands on the back of Sierra's chair and rolled it two feet away from her desk. "Let's talk about what's going on."

She didn't move; it was better if she kept her back to him. "I'd rather not."

"If you keep any more stuffed inside you, you're going to explode."

"I talk about it."

"With Marcia," he said simply. "I don't think she's helping much."

"And a few others."

"Meredith?"

"I've talked the situation over with her attorney," Sierra admitted. "Alex can't get a divorce, not without my help, and I'm not going to give it to him."

"You've lost weight in the last month, Sierra. You look like you aren't sleeping."

"Thanks, Ron. I needed to hear that," she said and looked away. Carolyn had come into her bedroom again last night. It seemed she came in every night, crying over another nightmare.

She felt his hand on her shoulder. "I care about you, Sierra. I hate to see you hurting like this."

The gentleness in his voice was almost her undoing. "I don't think there's any way around it."

"I want to help."

Maybe she did need to talk to someone other than Marcia. She was always so full of ideas on how to force Alex into coming home and taking up his proper responsibilities as husband and father—ideas that Sierra knew would be a waste of time. Manipulation wouldn't work with Alex.

It wasn't the first time Ron had offered his shoulder to cry on. She had hesitated to take up the offer, not wanting to bring her problems into work. But wasn't she doing that already? Ron cared about her. God knew, she needed someone to care. Alex certainly didn't.

"Come on," Ron said.

Letting out her breath, she rose and followed him into his office. He closed the door behind her.

"Didn't someone from the school call you this morning?" Ron poured a mug of coffee and held it out to her.

"Clanton was in another fight," she said, taking it. She sat in the wing chair in front of his desk.

Ron poured himself a mug of coffee and leaned on the desk in front of her. "That's two fights this week, isn't it?"

"The school counselor knows what's been going on. She says he's 'acting out his anger.'"

"Has Alex spoken to him?"

She gave a bleak laugh. "Even if Alex tried, Clanton wouldn't talk to him."

"Why not?"

She shook her head. "I told the children why Alex left. The first time he called, Clanton answered and said he hated him and never wanted to see him again. Alex asked to speak with Carolyn, but she was crying too hard to even talk to him." She held the coffee cup between both hands, wishing the warmth would seep through enough to stop her shaking. "Alex blamed me, of course." She took a slow breath, trying to control her voice. "He said I'd turned his children against him."

"What'd you say?"

"He didn't give me a chance to say anything. After he said his piece, he hung up." Alex had cursed her in Spanish before doing so. "All I did was tell them the truth. What else could I say when they asked why their father hadn't come home for three days? I told them their father had decided to live with another woman. Those are the facts. I told them it wasn't because he didn't love *them* anymore. It's because he doesn't love *me*. I'd like to know how else I could've broken the news."

"Take it easy," Ron said with a sympathetic smile. "I'm not criticizing you."

"I'm sorry, but I'm just sick and tired of having Alex blame me for everything. He says all the problems the children are having now are my fault. *He's* the one having the affair. *He's* the one who deserted his family. And yet everything is my fault."

"It's human nature to want to blame someone else."

Just as she was blaming Alex for everything? Was that what he was saying? She pressed her lips together. Well, wasn't it Alex's fault? If he hadn't left her and the children and moved in with his mistress, everything would be fine.

"Speak the truth, Sierra."

Her face burned at the remembered admonition. Whenever she or Mike had tried to justify something they'd done as children, Mom would always look them right in the eye and say those quiet words.

Speak the truth. . . .

The truth. Things hadn't been right between her and Alex in a long, long time. She knew it, but she also knew she wasn't ready to face it. She quickly averted her thoughts from that path and focused on the children instead. "I'm not sure what to do about Clanton. He's been in the principal's office four times over the last two weeks, and his report card is a disaster. He quit baseball without even telling me. When I asked him why, he said he didn't care about it anymore. He used to love it, Ron. Now, all he does is sit in his room and play video games."

"What about Carolyn?"

"She's the exact opposite. Clanton tells me every afternoon that he has no homework, whereas she works on assignments for hours. She was devastated the other day when she missed one word on a spelling test."

"Is she still having the nightmares?"

Sierra nodded. "She had another last night. She came into my room at one in the morning, crying and saying she'd dreamed I'd died in a car accident."

"Poor kid."

"Marcia says it's fear of losing both parents. With Alex gone, she's afraid something will happen to me, too."

"Marcia's spent enough time in counseling to be an expert," Ron said with a faint smile. "Listen, I think you all need a break. Why don't you and the kids go with me to Catalina on Saturday?"

Startled by the invitation, she looked up at him. "Catalina?"

"We're having great sailing weather."

"Sailing?"

"Yes, sailing. Don't look so doubtful. I'm good at it. I sailed to Fiji by myself when I was twenty-three."

"I had no idea," she said for the sake of conversation. Her mind was whirring. She felt vaguely uncomfortable, but she couldn't pinpoint why. Her cheeks grew warm as he continued to study her.

"I wasn't suggesting anything inappropriate," he said, his tone sincere.

Her face went hot. "Oh, I know that!" she said quickly. "But . . ."

"But what?"

"You're my boss."

His mouth tipped. "I'm also your friend." He straightened and went around his desk, sitting in his swivel chair. She wondered if he sensed she needed distance between them to feel at ease with him again. "I'll ask Marcia and Tom and their children to come along," he said. "They've been to Catalina with me several times. Pamela and Reed are good little sailors. They can teach Clanton and Carolyn how to man the ropes."

Sierra smiled bleakly. "It'd be a relief not to sit around the house all weekend obsessing about Alex and Elizabeth

Longford." As soon as she said it, she wished she hadn't. Somehow, pairing their names aloud brought up all the pain and humiliation. Feeling the warning prick of oncoming tears, she looked away briefly. "I think the children would enjoy it, too," she said when she'd regained her self-control.

"Good. I'll pick you up at five on Saturday."

"Isn't that sort of late?" she said, rising and taking his empty coffee cup. She'd rinse them out in the kitchenette down the hall. "It'll only give us a couple of hours before dark."

He laughed. "Five in the *morning*, Sierra."

"You've got to be kidding!"

"I'm being kind to you. I usually like to get an earlier start. I'll tell Marcia to give you a call. She can tell you what to wear."

It rained all day.

Aphie McKenzie had a baby boy as we were traveling. The road was mud and hard pulling. The jouncing made it even harder on poor Aphie. She is not a strong girl, and it was a Difficult Birth and she is in a Very Bad Way. Rain was blowing in on us as we helped her. Doc Murphy did what he could to make her comfortable. Oren gave the baby to Winifred Holtz to nurse.

Nellie is praying hard for Aphie but I don't think it will do much good.

We have had a week of good weather. I never imagined the prairie to be so boundless and beautiful. It stretches as far as I can see and not a tree in sight. Green grass waves and flows and wild flowers are growing everywhere and making splashes

of every color of the rainbow clear to the horizon. The great
distance scares me. There seems no end to it.

The Platte River is before us. I have heard much of this great
river that runs like a line from east to west. It looks to be running bottom side up it is so brown. The islands in the middle
have willows and cottonwoods. We are in need of firewood.
James and some of the other men have gone across to get some.
Others are making do with what they have. Werner Hoffman
burned his wife's Gothic bookcase yesterday. She is still grieving over it. It did not comfort her that Cal Chaffey broke up
a mahogany secretary that has been in his family for over a
hundred years. His grandfather brought it over by ship from
England.

Binger Siddons found a piano that had been dumped along
the trail. Athena Hendershott asked to play it before the men
put axes to it. She made it sound pure heaven. Cal Chaffey
joined in on his mouth organ. I sang The Orphan Girl and
Sweet Charlotte. James asked if she could play Are You Still
Mad at Me, Darling, and she did. I did not think it funny.
Athena played until the sunset and then left the men to break
it up. Kaiser Vandervert cried when he put his ax to it.

We are camped at new Fort Childs. It is named in honor of
Colonel Thomas Childs. Some think the fort should be named
Fort Kearny to honor General Stephen Watts Kearny and after
the other fort that was on Table Creek. I do not much care
who it is named after or where it was before. I am glad the old
Fort Kearny was moved here from Table Creek and we have
some sight of Civilization before we head out over the Great
American Desert to face God knows what.

There are Grand Islands in the center of the Platte and
more than 170 military men Working Diligently on the fort.

A few sod shelters are finished. Prices at the trading post are High. The soldiers are making adobe bricks and there is much cutting and sawing going on.

Indians are here in large number. Kavanaugh said they have come to trade. They have conical houses of poles and hides. Kavanaugh said they can take down the "tipis" and be on the move quicker than James can harness the teams of oxen. He said the Indians live this way because they follow the buffalo. I said there are no buffalo here and he said there will be plenty soon enough.

Joshua was very interested in the Indians. Kavanaugh said we are crossing their land and eating their game and leaving nothing in return. A day will come when they will not be so hospitable.

James found a carved bed and chopped it up for fuel. I could not help but wonder who slept in it. It was such a grand head-board with leaves and vines. What a shame to burn such a costly thing, but we have to eat and need a fire to cook over.

Beth and my sweet little Deborah just brought an armload of flowers to camp. They both have Mama's love of flowers. Beth is busy weaving garlands for our hair. The children seem to think we are on a long picnic! I am so tired by the time the sun goes down that I can hardly put two words together. James said we made 18 miles today. It feels more like 100 by the time we make camp, but he is pleased. He says if we keep the pace, we will reach Oregon in plenty of time before winter sets in.

I long for a bath. A week ago I was soaked to the skin with rain and my skirt was caked with mud. Now my skin is raw and itching from the dust that seeps under my dress. My shoes are already wearing out. I long for Sunday when we will have a day of rest. Virgil Boon preached last time. I did not agree with a word he said, but he was entertaining.

Poor little Aphie McKenzie died last night. Oren is Heart Broken.

The men dug her grave right in the trail so the wagons could go over it. Kavanaugh said no wolves would catch the scent nor Indians see the signs of a grave that way. It makes me sad that not even a marker bearing her name will be left, but it would make me feel worse to think wolves dug her up and ate her or Indians stripped her clean of the pretty wedding dress Oren insisted she wear to meet her Maker.

Oren is just nineteen. James says he will mend, but I am afraid for him. He has no interest in his son. I asked James to keep close watch over Oren. James said he would be pleased to do so as long as I keep talking to him. I said I would talk to the devil himself if he agreed to make sure that boy does not hang himself to whatever tree he can find.

The baby seems to be faring well in Winifred's care. She has milk aplenty and a good heart. Perhaps she will give him a name.

I have not seen the French woman's fire burning the last two nights. I asked MacLeod what become of her. He said he did not know. I hope Indians did not take her.

I never thought I would see the day that I would be cooking over a fire of animal dung. We have not seen a single buffalo yet, but are burning their leavings and thankful to have them. Kavanaugh said buffalo "chips" are good fuel and he is right. The cook fire is hot and there is no smell. Joshua shot two rabbits. I spitted and roasted them. The sparks that shot up made them taste lightly of pepper.

Harlan Doane was killed today. It happened just before our usual nooning. It was hot and he was dozing. He fell off the high wagon seat and broke his neck. No one knew anything happened until Nellie started screaming.

All I could do was hold Nellie and cry with her. I did not know what to say to comfort her. If I had a word of wisdom I could not have gotten it out. Joshua is just sitting against the wagon wheel not saying anything. Harlan was his best friend.

Death comes sudden and awful on the trail.

I am so afraid of losing one of my own.

We reached the South Platte this morning. Kavanaugh went across ahead of the wagons and drove long poles to mark the way. Ruckel thought he knew a better place to cross and almost lost his wagon in quicksand. MacLeod shouted loud enough to be heard back in Galena he was so mad. He said next time they would leave Ruckel in the river rather than risk life and limb for a fool who could not listen to those more experienced.

Kavanaugh came back to ride with us on the way across. He had James water the animals before starting out. He said not to let them stop or the wagon would sink into the sand. The Platte may be shallow, but it is treacherous.

We all made the crossing with no Disasters. Nellie gave thanks to God on the other side.

Beth and I doctored one of our oxen during the nooning. The poor animal was chaffed from being in harness. The wound was crawling with blow fly eggs and worms. I cleaned it out and put bacon rind over the chaffing. MacLeod said it will soothe the wound and keep the harness from rubbing more. Beth walked beside the animal until we made camp. The poor beast seems better this evening.

We had a terrible lightning and thunder storm last night. The
children were all crying and carrying on. It struck so close you
could smell Hades breath.

And then we heard a sound like rolling thunder only it did
not stop. The ground began to shake. Kavanaugh rode in fast
and shouted for the men to get their guns quick. A stampede
of buffalo were coming straight for us.

I have never seen so many animals. They are as numerous
as the stars in the heavens. Kavanaugh rode out with James
and six others and fired their guns to turn the stampede. That
was hours ago and the buffalo have been running by us all that
time. Dawn broke an hour ago. The sound of those hooves is
Deafening. I cannot keep my hand steady for the pounding and
my own trembling heart.

Joshua wants to ride with the men and I will not let him.
He is angry with me. I said he had to stay. He asked why and I
said we needed him to keep watch over us. He is not appeased.
MacLeod is here.

The truth is I am afraid he would get himself killed. It
is bad enough to be worrying about James without wondering
what is happening to my son.

The men have been busy all day butchering the buffalo that
were shot during the stampede. They did not shoot many as
they shot in the air most times to turn them. I told Joshua he
could go help the men do that but he has stomped off to pout.
Kavanaugh brought back a hump and tongue and some marrow
bones for us. The meat was very tasteful and tender. He told
me to roast the bones which I did and found the marrow was
delicious. Kavanaugh has been good to us. He seems to watch
over my family more carefully than the others. James likes him.
Joshua thinks he is next to God Almighty. He is always inviting

Kavanaugh to sup with us and then asks him a hundred questions.

Kavanaugh said the Indians do not waste anything. They use buffalo hides to build their homes. They eat the meat. He cut squares of hide and showed James how to wrap the hooves of the oxen. Beth is delighted. Our animals now have shoes to wear! I could use a new pair myself but will wait until we reach Fort Laramie.

Before leaving our campsite, Kavanaugh spoke to James away from the fire. They did not want me to hear. I know enough from watching that they have doubled the guard. James saddled one of the horses and tethered it to the end of the wagon a few minutes ago.

Kavanaugh expects trouble.

Sioux Indians came today. Two of them were wearing magnificent warbonnets. I near died of fright when I saw them riding toward us. MacLeod called the alarm and we circled the wagons. The men took up defensive positions while Kavanaugh rode out to talk to them. I was sure they were going to kill him, but he showed no fear of them and spoke to them at length. Joshua said young braves are dangerous because they have to engage and defeat an enemy in order to take their place on the tribal counsel. I asked him how he knew so much about it and he said Kavanaugh told him. He quotes Kavanaugh like Scripture about everything. Joshua said Kavanaugh told him prairie Indians are seldom at peace with their neighbors. That did not set my mind at rest.

Kavanaugh brought the Indians to camp. I have never seen such fierce faces. Kavanaugh said we are crossing their land and eating their buffalo.

Joshua pays no heed to my fears and warnings. He ignored me and went off with Kavanaugh. If that was not bad enough, while he was about it, he invited the Sioux to eat vittals at our fire! I was afraid they would not like my cooking. They did not care much about food. It was my red hair that impressed them. Joshua told me to take off my bonnet and let my hair down so they could see it. What for I wanted to know. To see if it would make a fine scalp? James laughed and said I have a temper to match my hair. Kavanaugh explained so the Indians would not think James was laughing at them. I was so mad, I let down my hair. They seemed to admire the color. So I cut six curls off and gave one to each of the braves. Kavanaugh told them it is strong medicine. I hope they are satisfied with what I gave them and will not come back for the rest of it! MacLeod gave them gifts of blankets, sugar, and tobacco from stores the company bought for such purposes. The Sioux seemed satisfied with the tariff and left.

Joshua just told me the Indians earn each feather in their warbonnets by killing an enemy. I am glad he did not tell me earlier!

MacLeod has posted extra guards around the stock. I am keeping close watch on my children. I want every one of them within sight and reach. I have heard Indians will steal children quicker than they will steal a horse or mule and Beth and Deborah both have hair the same color as mine.

Kavanaugh said a most alarming thing to me tonight. He said one of the Indians asked how many horses James would take for me. I asked him how many he said. Enough that he will be making no offers, he told me. He also said not to wander too far away from camp.

I am not certain he was serious, but I will take no chances. James will be surprised when I sleep beside him tonight. It will be the first time I have done so since we left home.

Two wagons were lost today.

We made a slow climb up a California hill to the top of the plateau. Kavanaugh and MacLeod had warned us of the Hard Descent to come, but no one was expecting a drop past perpendicular. Flocks of birds were rising and dipping in the wind. When I saw that hill, I wished we could sprout wings and fly down. As it was, the men rigged a windlass to lower the wagons one by one.

Paul Colvigne was snakebit before the first one made it down. That Event was a sign of other catastrophies to come. The ropes pulled free of Matthew Odell's wagon and the whole lot went crashing down the hill and made a sorry mess at the bottom. The noise startled the horses. As our luck would have it, Less Moore was in charge of the watch over them. He is better with cards than animals. Joshua and four others are still out rounding them up.

It is near dusk and the men are lowering Stern Janssen's wagon. It is the last one. The rest of us are camped in a hollow with many ash trees and good water. I have supper cooking and have hung wash on the wagon to dry. There is little wind here which is a relief from the last few days up on the prairie. I am tired of dust in my eyes and mouth and under my clothes.

This was one hill and we have yet to face the Rocky Mountains.

Joshua has returned. He said they found all but three horses. The Best Ones. Sinnott's Arabian was not recovered. He will be fierce about its loss. The other two were company bought prime stock. Kavanaugh said the Arapahoe are a little richer for our foolishness.

The hartshorn Doc gave Paul did no good. So Kavanaugh made an indigo poultice for him. He said the Indians use it to draw serpent bites. It may be too late. Paul is addled and doing poorly. I gave him whiskey to ease his pain.

We buried Paul Colvigne at sunup. The company voted to give his outfit to Matthew Odell.

CHAPTER 15

Sierra sat with her bare legs dangling over the side of Ron's sailboat as she watched Clanton and Carolyn swim in the cove with Pamela and Reed. It was a perfect early summer day, the sun high overhead, not a cloud in the blue sky. Looking back toward the mainland, she could see the haze of smog that lay over the metropolitan area of Los Angeles. Here, she could fill her lungs with clean, sea air.

"It's heaven, isn't it?" Marcia said with a contented sigh as she lay basking on a deck chair.

"Hmmmm," Sierra said dreamily. How long had it been since she had heard Clanton and Carolyn laugh or seen them having so much fun? Clanton was trying to catch Ron. Each time he came close, Ron disappeared beneath the surface and came up well out of reach. The four children tried working together and still failed to tag him.

"All I need is something to eat," Marcia said.

Sierra turned her head. Reaching up for the railing, she started to pull herself up. "If you'll watch the children, I'll—"

"No, no," Marcia said, adjusting her dark glasses as she got up. "I'll see about getting lunch. Stay where you are. There's not enough room in the galley for two people. Besides, Ron didn't leave much to do this time. He called a caterer. All I have to do is take off the plastic wrap. Stay and enjoy the sun." She shrugged into a lightweight hip-length terry-cloth robe that covered her bikini. "Tom can help keep an eye on the children." She flicked the hat off his face. Grunting from the shock of sunlight, he awakened abruptly. "I said you can help keep an eye on the children," Marcia repeated. "I'm going below."

"Yeah, yeah," he said.

"Go back to sleep, Tom," Sierra laughed. "I'll watch them."

"Thanks," he said and sagged back, picking up the hat and putting it over his face again.

Ron came up next to the ladder he had put over the side after dropping anchor. Shaking his blond hair back, he started to climb. Sierra couldn't help noticing he had a perfect body. Looking away, she kept her eyes on the children.

"You're getting burned," Ron said, toweling himself off a few feet from her.

"I put sunscreen on."

"It probably washed off when you took that two-minute swim," he said, grinning.

Two minutes in the cold Pacific had been all she needed to know she preferred toasting on the deck.

"You need another basting." Ron uncapped a bottle of lotion Marcia had left next to her deck chair. Squirting some into his palm, he rubbed his hands together and hunkered down behind her. The scent of coconut and tropics filled her senses as he rubbed the lotion into her skin. "Where's your hat?" he said, his strong fingers kneading her shoulders.

"I think I left it below."

"Deliberate disobedience." Unlooping the towel he'd put around his neck, he covered her head with it. "I don't want you getting sunstroke the first time you sail with me."

Laughing, she folded it up so she could see. "You're worse than a mother, Ron."

He flipped her French braid over her right shoulder and finished rubbing the lotion into her back and shoulders. "You're enjoying yourself, aren't you?"

"Very much."

His hands slowed. She felt his thumbs moving up her spine. He gripped her shoulders. "It's good to see you smile and mean it," he said. Releasing her, he straightened.

Marcia called for Tom and began handing up the food. There was a large platter of cut vegetables and dip, another of sandwiches, bowls of potato and fruit salad, and bags of chips. "How are we doing with the drinks?" she called from below.

Tom opened the ice chest that had been set on the deck when they got under way. "We could use some more wine coolers. We've plenty of everything else."

Ron gave a piercing whistle, drawing the attention of the four children, who were still splashing around in the cove. "Anybody out there hungry?"

Four voices gave a short *yes!* and started swimming for the boat.

"You'd better get what you want before they get here," Marcia said. "There's something about swimming and salt air that seems to triple the appetite."

Laughing, Sierra rose from her post. The only one who

hadn't served himself was Ron. He nodded for her to go ahead while he kept an eye on the children, who approached like hungry barracuda.

Clanton clambered onto the deck first. Shivering, he threw a towel around himself. Taking a plate, he heaped it with two sandwiches and two scoops of potato salad. Tucking a soda under his arm, he grabbed a bag of chips and headed for the bow. Reed, Carolyn, and Pamela poured onto the deck and raced for the food.

Ron laughed. "It's like watching sharks in a feeding frenzy."

"Take some vegetables, Reed."

"Aw, Mom."

"You heard me."

Glowering, Reed took a couple of carrot and celery sticks and put them on his plate before heading for the bow.

Shaking her head, Marcia glanced at her daughter and noticed she was about to take a handful of potato chips. "Pamela," she said, sounding weary. "You know very well what grease does to your complexion. No, take some of the fruit salad instead."

Cheeks stained red with humiliation, Pamela put her plate down and fled below.

"Oh, for heaven's sake!" Marcia said, annoyed. "I don't know what's gotten into her lately."

"I wonder." Tight-lipped, Tom leaned down and took another wine cooler from the ice chest.

Marcia raised her brow. "You've had four, Tom."

"Then I guess this one makes five." He headed for his deck chair.

Marcia stared after him in consternation. Clearing her throat softly, she glanced back at Ron and Sierra. "Well, I guess I'd better go below and see what's upset Pamela *this* time." She gave Ron a beseeching smile and whispered, "Would you please keep an eye on Tom?"

"He's a grown man, Marcia."

"Yes, but I think he's had enough to drink, don't you?"

Sierra noticed that as soon as Marcia went below, Reed pitched the vegetable sticks into the water and dug into the bag of chips Clanton had commandeered.

She and Ron shared a quiet lunch together, talking about Outreach and some of the children they were helping. Tom fell asleep in his deck chair while the boys rummaged through a waterproof case on the deck where Ron had laid in a supply of games. Carolyn sat with her legs dangling, waiting for Pamela to come up from below. When she did, her face was splotchy from crying.

"Mother says she has a splitting headache," she said as though delivering a rehearsed message. She picked up her plate and dutifully added a small scoop of fruit salad before she went to sit on the bow with Carolyn.

Sierra went below and found Marcia rummaging through her tote bag. "I know I brought them," she said in frustration. Upending everything onto the couch built into the bulkhead, she spread things out, searching again. Letting out her breath in relief, she picked up a small prescription bottle and uncapped it. Shaking out two capsules, she recapped the bottle and dropped it on the couch. Tossing the pills into her mouth, she headed for the galley. Sierra heard the hiss of tonic being shot into a glass.

"I don't know what to do about that girl," Marcia said from the galley. Sierra heard the thunk of a glass on the counter. "All I'm trying to do is protect her. Children can be so merciless to someone who's fat and has pimples." She came back into the chamber and sat down on the couch built into the bulkhead. She began to collect and toss the things back into her tote bag. "She misunderstands everything I say to her. Sometimes I think she does it deliberately in an effort to make me feel bad. Either that, or she's stupid."

Dropping the tote bag onto the floor, she leaned forward, her elbows resting on her knees as she kneaded her temples. "And now this headache. . . ."

"Can I get you a cold compress?" Sierra said, feeling sorry for her.

"Please," she said and stretched out on the couch.

Sierra went into the galley and dampened a cloth for her. "Thank you," Marcia said and pressed it against her eyes and forehead. "Would you please tell Tom I'm not feeling well? I must have a touch of sunstroke."

"Tell her to take a nap," Tom said when Sierra delivered the message. Yawning, he pulled the hat down over his eyes again. Clearly, he had no intention of going below and speaking with his wife.

Ron went in his stead and talked with Marcia while the children went swimming again. Sierra leaned on the railing near the bow and watched them.

When Ron came up again, he gave her a rueful smile and shook his head. "Sorry to desert you."

Sierra had enjoyed the solitude. She felt guilty that Marcia's problems made her feel less a failure for her own. She had always thought Marcia's family was perfect. She knew there were times of tension, of course. What family didn't have them? But what she'd seen today was clear evidence that all was not well in Camelot.

"Is she feeling better?"

"She's going to stay below and rest on the way back." Ron gave a loud whistle to catch the children's attention. "Wrap it up, mates. We're hauling anchor in half an hour."

Four children groaned expressively and went back to their game of water tag.

Under his tutelage, the children, with Tom's assistance, manned the sails. When the wind caught the sheets, the boat sped across the water toward the Long Beach pier. Closer in, they battened down the sails, and Ron used the engine to bring them to dock.

"We had a wonderful time, Ron," Marcia said, kissing his cheek while the children gathered their things. While Tom shook hands with him, Marcia turned to Sierra and gave her a hug. "Sorry I made a scene below," she said, kissing her cheek. "I'll call you tomorrow." Sierra saw her take the car keys from Tom's hand as they headed for the parking lot.

Ron took Sierra and the children to an expensive seafood restaurant. He laughed when Clanton and Carolyn both ordered hamburgers. Over dinner, he talked about sailing to the South Seas and spending two years exploring islands that were barely a spot on a map. Clanton was enthralled; Carolyn, quiet.

It was late when Ron finally pulled up in front of Sierra's house. She was sorry the day was over. The children had fallen asleep in the backseat of his Mercedes. They'd only lasted fifteen minutes from the restaurant before dozing off and leaving her and Ron to talk alone. And talk they did, about everything from his travels to her growing up in a quiet country town to racial prejudice, social climbing, education, and the importance of family. He'd grown up the only son of a Greek businessman and a Swedish actress. His mother died in a car accident when he was only fourteen. "My father never got over her death," he said quietly. "Now he's gone, too. I'm the only family I've got left. And I find myself craving the connection of family all the time." He smiled at her in the darkness. "All in God's timing," he said.

Sierra couldn't help feeling a twinge of jealousy. The woman he married would be lucky indeed. She didn't know anyone as caring and sensitive to others as Ron Peirozo.

He turned off the ignition, then glanced into the backseat. He chuckled. "If you have a wheelbarrow in the garage, I'll unload your children for you."

Sierra laughed. "I may have to take you up on that offer." She reached over the seat and tapped each of them. "Come on, sleepyheads. We're home."

As she unlocked the front door, she heard the children thanking Ron for taking them sailing. Clanton asked if they could go again. "Sure," Ron said, a hand on his shoulder. "I'm out as often as I can be when the weather's like this."

As the children shouldered their tote bags and headed down the hallway to their rooms, Ron turned to her again. His mouth tipped slightly as he reached out and lightly brushed her cheek with the back of his knuckles. "You got a little color today."

Ron always knew what to say to make her feel better about herself. "Maybe I'll actually look like a Southern Californian one of these days." She smiled, drawn to him.

"You look just fine the way you are, Sierra."

He couldn't have said anything kinder. Bruised and battered by Alex's desertion, she believed herself a complete failure as a wife, as a mother, and as a woman. Looking into Ron's eyes, she saw he valued her. She wanted to thank him for everything—for taking them sailing, for sharing so much of himself with her, for listening, for caring. She felt closer to him than she had felt to anyone in a long, long time.

An inexplicable shiver of alarm raced along her nerve endings at the realization.

His eyes flickered, and the warmth that stirred within her had little to do with sunburn.

He took a slow step back. "I'll see you Monday morning," he said, his smile both casual and tender. He closed the door behind him as he went out.

Disturbed, Sierra frowned, perplexed by her feelings. What had just happened? Was she so desperate to feel like a woman again that she could imagine a man like Ronal Peirozo was attracted to her? Ridiculous! The poor man had only been acting out of kindness and friendship. There was no reason to read anything more into it.

Stepping to the door, she opened it. "Ron!"

He paused halfway down the pathway.

"Thank you," she said, smiling.

"Any time."

Feeling a little better, she stood in the doorway until he got into his Mercedes. He gave her a wave as he pulled away from the curb.

Closing the door, she set the dead bolt. Gathering her things, she headed down the hallway to say good night to the children before she took a shower and went to bed.

Deborah is feverish and complaining of stomach pain.

I asked if she had eaten anything along the way and she says no. She has suffered often of stomach aches when she eats too many berries. The pain seems worse on her right side. I have bedded her down in the wagon where it is less dusty and am sitting with her until the fever lets up. Reese Murphy is looking in on her again in a little while.

I am so afraid and I do not know what I fear most. In the beginning, I thought it was just anger plaguing me. I was wrong. It was fear underneath. I knew what I had back home. I knew the face of my enemy. Out here, I do not know from one day to the next where the danger lies. It could be a fall from a wagon seat or a snake. It could be Indians or sickness. Or being tired unto death.

As tired as I am I know the men have the worst of it. They are the ones hauling the wagons across the rivers. They were the ones lowering the wagons down that dreadful hill. They are the ones digging the graves. But it is the men too who dream of Oregon. It is as though Heaven itself beckons them and we must all cross hell to get to it.

Aphie McKenzie. Harlan Doane. Paul Colvigne. Three gone already. I think of the hard trail and how many wagons will pass over these fine people and never know of their existence. How many more will we bury before we reach our destination?

I am afraid for my baby.

I dreamed of Aunt Martha last night. She seemed so close. We talked as we used to do. I wept when I awakened. Has she died? Is that why I dreamed about her? Is that why she seemed so near to me? Oh, that she were here with me now. The thought of never seeing her again makes my heart ache and my throat close up. When my father turned me out, she took me in and loved me. When I jilted Thomas, she loved me still. Even when I said I did not believe in God anymore, she did not forsake me. She cried but she did not turn me out. She said she loved me no matter what. I have never known anyone so good and kind and constant.

She said she would pray for me every day. I know she is a woman of her word. I think of her every day and feel perhaps in thoughts at least we are still connected.

I wish I could ask her right now to send up prayers to heaven on behalf of my little Deborah. God would listen to her.

Our precious little Deborah is gone from this life. Doc Murphy did no good at all. Neither could Kavanaugh with his Indian medicines. I hope the next life is better. She passed away last night as the sun was setting on the bluffs above us. They look like the ancient ruins of a once wondrous city. I will think of her playing up there with the angels.

I cannot cry. I cannot let myself. If I do, I will never stop.

CHAPTER 16

THE TELEPHONE RANG on Sierra's desk. Flipping over the page on her notebook, she picked it up. "Good afternoon, Los Angeles Outreach," she said pleasantly, hoping Arlene would return from her dentist appointment soon. The telephone hadn't stopped ringing since she left, and Ron was champing at the bit to get some dictation done.

"Sierra, it's Audra."

Startled, she stammered an innocuous hello, irritation quickly following. What did *she* want?

"How are you?"

How *was* she? "About as well as can be expected."

"Can we have lunch?"

"I don't think so," Sierra said stiffly, surprised that the woman would even ask. What were they going to talk about? Shopping? Audra's charities or the plays she'd seen? Beyond Tomorrow? Alex and Elizabeth Longford?

"Are you really going to throw in the towel?" Audra said.

Sierra's body went hot. "I beg your pardon?" Of all the nerve!

"Your marriage. Are you just going to quit?"

"I don't think it's any of your business."

"Steve asked me to call you."

"Should I care?"

"So much for having any kind of reasonable conversation with you!" There was enough anger in Audra's tone to keep Sierra from hanging up. "Do you think any of us are happy with this situation? It makes me sick! It makes Steve and Matt sick. It's the worst thing that can happen in an office."

So that was it! "What's the matter? Is the work suffering?"

"You could say that. Everyone's suffering."

"Maybe you should talk to Elizabeth about that."

"Elizabeth isn't the problem!"

"Good-bye." Sierra slammed the telephone down, shaking with fury. It rang again in less than ten seconds. Taking a deep breath, she forced herself to be calm and businesslike. "Good afternoon, Los Angeles Outreach."

"Well, that was childish," Audra said. "But then, that's where you excel, isn't it, Sierra?"

Sierra's heart pounded like a war drum. She wanted to hang up on her again, but that was what Audra was expecting. The last thing Sierra intended to do was what Audra expected or wanted. Picking up her pencil, she tapped it on the notepad, trying to calm down, determined to wait her out.

Audra let out her breath. "I should've known you wouldn't listen. I told Steve there was no use in trying to talk to you. You've been hostile from the first second I met you. Every overture I ever made to be your friend was met with a cold shoulder. You always acted as though I was beneath contempt. You've done nothing but criticize me and everyone else at Beyond Tomorrow from the day you arrived. And why? Because you were so determined to stay in your narrow little comfort zone!

"Three years I've watched you wallow in self-pity and keep up your temper tantrum. And it's been something to watch, Sierra. A real show! I can't even count the number of times I've wanted to shake you until your teeth rattled!

"You've made Alex feel guilty over everything, especially the crime of using his talents. God forbid that he should be happy in his work! Not once did you ever think to congratulate him for what he's accomplished. He buys you a house. He buys you a car. Were you ever grateful for anything he did? Did you ever *once* notice how desperate he was to make you happy? You resented anything he did that didn't put you in the center spotlight. You even resent who he *is*. And you're surprised the man turns to another woman!"

Sierra felt cold with shock over Audra's diatribe. She couldn't even think of one word to say in her own defense.

Audra let out a deep breath. "I swore I wasn't going to lose my temper, and now I have. Well, so be it. I called to give you some advice, Sierra. Here's a piece of it. *Grow up!*" Sierra heard the click as Audra hung up. Stunned, she put the receiver quietly back in the cradle. Ron was standing in the doorway. He looked as upset as she felt.

"Why do you keep holding on?" he said softly.

She started to tell him the call wasn't from Alex, but he came over to the desk. "You're not in love with him anymore, Sierra."

Wasn't she? Had she stopped loving Alex? She couldn't fathom the idea. She'd loved him for as long as she could remember.

Ron leaned down and put one hand firmly over hers. "Give him a divorce, Sierra. You don't need him." His eyes were intense, his feelings raw and clear, so clear she couldn't misunderstand what he was telling her.

"I'm back," Arlene said from the doorway to the corridor. Her bright smile died when she saw Ron's hand over Sierra's. Arlene's expression registered shock and embarrassment as she looked between the two of them. "Excuse me," she said, the disturbing question clear in her eyes. "I didn't mean to interrupt. . . ."

"You didn't," Sierra said, snatching her hand from beneath Ron's. She fumbled, banging the file drawer open. "I just had a disturbing call," she said, grabbing her purse.

"Sierra," Ron said, a wealth of feeling in his tone. "Wait a minute. Let's talk—"

"I've got to go," she said, stepping around him. She couldn't look into his eyes. Arlene stepped back so she could go into the hallway.

"Can I do anything to help?" Arlene said, following her. "I don't think you should drive when you're this upset."

"I'll be fine. Really." She pushed open the front glass door with the words *Los Angeles Outreach* printed in bold black letters. Fumbling for her keys, she ran across the parking lot to her car. Alex's birthday present to her. Audra's words still rang in her ears as she opened the car door. Sliding in, she slammed it, turned the ignition, threw the car into reverse and then back into drive. She gulped for air, not even bothering to stop to look before she pulled out of the parking lot. Someone blasted their horn just behind her.

Running the yellow light, she turned onto the main thoroughfare and headed for the freeway entrance. The BMW revved loudly as she sailed up the ramp. Another horn blasted, but she was crying too hard by then to notice. She darted between two cars into the second lane, then moved into the third and pressed down even harder on the gas, shooting into the fast lane.

"Oh, God," she said, gripping the wheel. "Oh, God, *God*! I didn't mean to make such a mess of things!" Choking on a sob, she slammed on her brakes so she wouldn't plow into the Mercedes in front of her. She whipped around to the right, passed it, and shot back into the fast lane.

Where was she going?

What did it matter?

She felt like driving straight off a cliff. Where was the closest one? Mulholland Drive? Maybe the canyons on the road to Malibu would be better.

She wanted her mother, but then she remembered with a sharp pain that her mother was dead. She needed Alex. No, not Alex. He was gone, too.

"Jesus, oh, Jesus," she cried, dashing tears out of her eyes. She wanted to dump everything at His feet and give up the fight. But how could she do that? What right did she have to ask God's help *now*? "Oh, Jesus, what can I do?"

She could hear a siren but paid no attention, not until a black-and-white highway patrol car pulled up alongside her, lights flashing. Her heart stopped when the officer jerked his thumb for her to pull over.

"Great! Just what I need!"

He slowed, moving in behind her. Traffic gave way as she moved over, lane by lane, until she was driving slowly along the shoulder. She rolled to a stop, put the car in park, and shut off her engine. Then, gripping the steering wheel, she rested her forehead against it and sobbed.

The officer tapped at her window. She had to turn the key before she could lower it. The roar of freeway traffic was deafening. Only the lane closest to them had slowed at all.

Just enough so everybody could get a good look at her as they drove by.

Could a person die of humiliation?

Leaning down slightly, the officer looked at her face.

"I'm sorry I was speeding," she said, tears running down her face. She hiccuped, making matters worse. He probably thought she was a drunk on a crying jag.

"Your driver's license and registration please."

Fumbling through her purse, she found her license. The registration was in her glove compartment. As soon as she handed them over, he stepped back, his hand resting almost casually over the handle of his gun. Did he think she was dangerous?

"Get out of the car, please, Mrs. Madrid."

"I haven't been drinking. I swear. I'm not smuggling drugs or firearms—"

"Get out of the car, Mrs. Madrid."

She obeyed, trying to get hold of herself as she did so. She couldn't stop crying. When the officer put his hand firmly beneath her elbow as he closed her car door, she wondered what he thought she was going to do. Try to run away? Where could she go? Into the ice plant? Or was it ivy growing alongside the freeway? She couldn't tell through her tears. It was *green* whatever it was.

Sierra could just see the headlines: "Woman Has Nervous Breakdown on Hollywood Freeway."

She could see herself being hauled away in cuffs.

She cried harder.

Opening the back door of the squad car, the patrolman told her to get in. She had thought things couldn't get worse, but now, on top of everything, she was getting arrested and hauled off to jail for reckless driving! She did think of running into traffic then and putting an end to everything.

The officer's fingers tightened slightly as though he read her thoughts and had no intention of letting her get off that easily. "Get in the car, ma'am."

Her thoughts went ballistic as soon as she was in the backseat. Who'd bail her out? She couldn't call Ron. Who'd take care of the children while she was moldering in jail? Alex? Oh, not Elizabeth Longford!

Hunching over, she covered her face and hiccuped more sobs as the officer got into the front seat and reached for his radio. He said her name and several numbers and then put the speaker back. While he waited for a response, he had her take an alcohol breath test.

"I clocked you at ninety-five," he said, making a note of the test results on his clipboard.

"I'm sorry," she whimpered. "I've had a *very* bad day."

The officer pushed his sunglasses down and looked at her over the rims.

"I know," she moaned. "You've probably heard that excuse a million times, but it's true." She let everything pour out. She told him about nursing her mother through her last weeks of cancer and how much she missed her. She told him about Alex leaving her for another woman the day she got back from northern California. She told him about Clanton getting into fights at school and Carolyn turning into a basket case over her grades. She told him about Audra calling to say it was all her fault.

"Ron was the last straw," she said, sniffling.

He didn't ask who Ron was. In fact, he didn't say anything at all. He just looked at her and listened with that frown on his face.

What was the use? The highway patrolman knew she wasn't drunk, but she'd convinced him she was crazy.

Would he call an ambulance and have her taken away in

a straitjacket? Where would they take her? Bellevue? Where *was* Bellevue? His radio crackled. He picked up the speaker. She felt some relief hearing the information given. At least he knew now she had no prior tickets or outstanding warrants for her arrest. She wasn't armed or dangerous, unless flooding his patrol car could be held against her.

Rummaging through her purse, she tried to find a Kleenex, muttering under her breath when she couldn't find one. Her nose was running. Her eyes were running. Her face was a watery mess. Desperate, she took her notepad out, tore out a page, and blew her nose into it.

Grimacing, the patrolman pulled a clean handkerchief out of his pocket and handed it over the seat to her.

"Thanks," she muttered, dabbed her eyes, and blew her nose. She started to hand the handkerchief back.

His mouth tipped up on one side. "You can keep it."

She blushed. "I'll wash it and return it to you." Maybe she'd be working in the laundry section of the jail. Or would she be making license plates? She felt better for having purged herself of everything that'd happened over the past few months, but she doubted that was going to change the consequences of barreling down the highway like a bat out of Hades. She could've killed somebody, not to mention herself. "You can take me in now."

He tipped his sunglasses down again. "Take you in?"

"To the slammer."

His mouth twitched. "I'm not taking you in to the slammer, Mrs. Madrid. I just thought it'd be wise to calm you down before turning you loose on the freeway again."

"But you *are* giving me a ticket."

"Yes, ma'am. I am giving you a ticket." He handed the pad to her and gave her a pen. Sighing heavily, she signed her name at the bottom and handed it back. He tore off the yellow copy and gave it to her. "Sorry to add to your grief."

She sighed. "My first ticket," she said, looking at it dismally. And it was going to cost her plenty. Folding it, she tucked it into her purse.

"Feeling any better?"

She gave a shuddering sigh and smiled. "Yes, but that's not saying much. I'll keep it under the speed limit. I promise."

"Good." He studied her for a moment longer and then got out of the patrol car. Opening the back door for her, he offered his hand to help her out.

Shouldering her purse, she looked up at him. He was young, probably no more than thirty or thirty-five. He had kind eyes. "You know what I was doing when you pulled up beside me, Officer? *Praying.* So much for divine intervention." Shaking her head, she started back toward her car.

She had just put the key into her ignition when the patrolman walked up to her car window again. He handed her a small slip of white paper folded in half. "My wife and I'll meet you on the front steps at quarter to ten. Bring your kids. Oh, and pull into traffic easy, Mrs. Madrid. I'll put my lights on and clear the way for you."

"Thanks," she said, confused. She watched him in the side mirror as he walked back to his patrol car.

Opening the slip of paper, she read the name and address of a church.

~

The trail is clearly marked ahead by the great rock formations.

We passed one a day back that looked like a courthouse with a jail beside it. The one ahead is like a giant funnel set upside down on the prairie.

We ate dust all day. It was our turn to be at the back.
Tomorrow we will be at the head.

Water and grass are plentiful. So are the mosquitoes.

I had words with Oren McKenzie today. He was talking about
Aphie again and crying with every word he uttered. I lost
patience with him and told him he was not the only one who
had lost a loved one. I said Aphie would be ashamed of him for
his endless carrying on. She was a good and sensible girl and
would not think kindly of him if she knew he had not even
bothered to give her son a name! He said I do not understand
how bad he feels and I said understanding was not what he
needed. What he needs is a good hard kick in the backside.

When Oren left our fire, James looked at me and said—It
is amazing, Mary Kathryn, how you can see the sins of others
so well, and your own not at all. I asked him what he meant.
He said Oren has been grieving over the loss of a wife and has
only been crying a few weeks while I have been grieving over
not having my own way for months. He said—You only know
in part, not the whole of his pain. He said I close my ears to
anything that does not suit me. I said he was wrong. He said—
You closed your ears to me before the first word was out of my
mouth about Oregon and why we had to go. He said—It never
even occurred to you that this journey is for your own good!

I said what good was there in Deborah dying. I said we
should have stayed in Illinois. He said he wished he had left me
there. He said he would sooner listen to Oren's weeping than
my endless carping.

David Alexander McKenzie was christened by his father last
evening and I am sore ashamed. James is right. I told Oren I
had no right to speak to him as I did. He said he was glad of it.

He had never held his son before today and doing so eased the pain of losing Aphie. He said David looks like her.

It never occurred to me that I could lose James as easy as I lost my daughter or Oren lost his sweet wife. Life is so uncertain. I do not know where James went to spend the night.

When he came back this morning, I told him I was sorry. It has done no good. The wall I built up still stands between us.

Kavanaugh sighted buffalo across the Platte to the north. Joshua insisted on going hunting with the men. He would give no ear at all to my fears. He came back a short while ago. Without so much as a word, he slid off his horse, took a couple of steps and fell face down on his bedding. He was covered with so much blood I thought he had been shot and stripped him like a baby to see if he was wounded. He will not thank me when he finds out. Kavanaugh rode up as I was doing it and laughed. I did not think it funny and told him so. He said Joshua is unharmed. I asked him what he had done to my son that he would have so much blood on him. He said he made Joshua dress what he killed. He said the boy needed to learn hunting is not all glory. It is hard work.

I could soak his clothes for a month of Sundays and not get all the stains out.

We are nooning longer today than usual because of the terrible heat. The land we are passing through is fertile for rocks and sagebrush and not much else. Some of the animals are sick from the heat.

MacLeod said we will move on in another hour and keep going until dusk. We will be lucky to make 15 miles today.

Joshua shot two rabbits. I will stew them for supper.

Kaiser Vandervert gave whiskey to his oxen. It seems to perk them up. Had we whiskey left I would try some myself.

We crossed the Laramie River this morning and made camp at
the fort. There are Indians camped near by. Kavanaugh said
they are Cheyenne. They are a fine looking people dressed in
buckskins like Kavanaugh and wearing bear claw necklaces
and eagle feathers. The chief is a handsome fellow. Joshua is
impressed with them. Kavanaugh knows them well and speaks
their language. He took Joshua with him when he spoke with
them. When he came back he said they are at the fort to trade
buffalo hides and furs for tobacco, sugar, and blankets. We
have no sugar or blankets to spare.

The soldiers have invited us to a dance in the fort this
evening. The men drew lots to see who would stay behind with
the wagons and keep watch. Ruckel Buckeye, Wells Doane,
Oren McKenzie, Ernest Holtz, and Werner Hoffman lost.
Artemesia is feeling poorly and is remaining behind as well.
Nellie said nothing will keep her away.

James said he will not go. He knows how much I love
to dance. This is just his way of punishing me.

James is speaking to me again. I did not expect him to forgive
me for another five hundred miles considering how many it
took me to come to my senses. When he said he did not want
to go to the dance last night, I knew what he meant was he
did not want to go to the dance with me. I said that was fine
by me and went anyway. There is little enough fun on the trail
without giving up what Opportunity comes along because a
man is pouting. James came later. Of course, he did not dance
with me because he was still mad. I had partners aplenty with
soldiers and MacLeod and some of the other men traveling
with us. I even danced with Oren McKenzie. I have not had
so much fun since I was engaged to Thomas Atwood Houghton
and considered Acceptable Company in Galena. James cut in
when Lieutenant Heywood danced with me a third time. He

said it was not proper for me to dance with that soldier again. I said it was as proper as him dancing four times with Nellie. He said Nellie is good and married. I said I am good and married too though my husband appears not to notice. He hauled me outside.

I said—What do you think you are doing, James Farr? I don't want to leave. I was having fun.

He said to shut up and kissed me the way he used to do. We went down to the trees along the river. I am glad the fire has not died in him or me. I was feeling soft inside and said—I am glad you have forgiven me, James Farr.

On the walk back, James said—You do not long for home anymore, do you, Mary Kathryn? I said I would be lying if I said I did not miss Aunt Martha and all the rest. I would be lying too if I said I was pleased with the way things turned out at the homestead. I told him I accept his decision and will not CARP anymore. We will wait and see what there is in store for us in Oregon.

James said Oregon will speak for itself when we get there. And then he said in a quiet voice—Or maybe California. I said what do you mean about California? He said he had been thinking Oregon might be too crowded in a few years with the numbers going and we ought to think about California instead. I could not get air to say anything but he went on real fast telling me that others are talking about it. I said like who? He said Ernst Holtz, Wells Doane, Binger Siddons and Stern Janssen have been mulling it over. I wonder if Nellie knows what is on Wells mind.

James said Kavanaugh has never seen the Pacific Ocean and has a desire to do so. Oh Grand I said. That is good reason for going someplace. Just because you have never been. Just to keep on to the ends of the earth until you have seen it all! Next he will want to see China!

James said—Stop talking, Mary Kathryn—but I had a lot more to say. So he kissed me again. He kissed me hard and for so long I forgot what my upset was about until now that I am writing my thoughts into this journal. When we all went back to the wagons after the dance, we bedded the children down in the tent so James and I could sleep under the wagon together. We slept last night like two spoons in a drawer the way we used to.

I don't have a house or land. But I have my James back and my children. They are home enough.

We all went down to the chalk cliffs. James does not know how to write. So I carved his name next to my own, and then carved Henry, Beth, and Matthew underneath. I carved Deborah last and a cross next to it. She will not be forgotten.

Joshua ignored my call and climbed up high to carve his name. I was sure he would fall but he would not listen and come down. Kavanaugh said the boy is sure footed as a mountain goat.

Joshua has become so difficult of late. I feel him pulling away from me and James and drawn to Kavanaugh. Kavanaugh encourages him. He told me just the other day that he was not much older than Joshua when he left home and headed west for the first time. I asked him why he left so young. All he said was he had reasons.

I am not ready to let my son go.

James did not leave my side all day today. We walked together while Joshua drove the wagon. I have missed talking with James. He is so full of dreams. I never thought any of them would come to anything but this one of going west has. We will see about the others.

As long as I have James I am safe and happy.

It is so terrible hot. The dust coats all of us. The ground is sandy and makes hard pulling for the oxen. Beth is sick. We made a bed for her in the wagon and she is sleeping. I asked Nellie to pray for her.

Dunham Banks was bad hurt today. A rattlesnake frightened the horses. His own pitched him off and he hit his head on a rock. Doc Reese said his chances are not good. Celia rigged a cradle and had two men help her rig a big sling inside her wagon. Baby Hortense and Dunham both rocked all day while she drove. Celia is a fine strong girl with good sense. She will need both for the long haul ahead.

We are Plagued with Tragedy. Little Patricia Sinnott wandered off this evening and can not be found. Paralee is crazy with fear that the Indians have stolen her. Frank Sinnott, James, and four other men have gone out looking for little Patty. I have my children near the fire where I can see them. Joshua is not pleased with staying here to watch out for us. He said he could ride after Kavanaugh. The scout would know what to do. I told him Kavanaugh and Ruckel Buckeye are hunting game and there is no telling in which direction they went.

Kavanaugh and Ruckel came back and went out with the men again. They looked for little Patty all day and found no trace of her. MacLeod said we can not stay another day. Paralee says she will not go on without her little girl. Franklin said it was her fault the child is lost. It was a harsh, cruel thing to say and not much different from what I said to James not long ago. I cringe thinking of it. Sinnott's son is from his first wife who died. Paralee is the second wife. She told me a few nights back Franklin has poured all the money she inherited into what he is carrying in those two wagons. Two of his oxen have died already from pulling the load. It appears to me Franklin

Sinnott is more worried about getting his goods to Oregon than he is about little Patty lost in the wilderness.

We made 20 miles today. Paralee did not come out of her wagon even for the nooning. Everyone thought she was grieving in quiet. They did not know until we camped that Franklin had her tied so she could not get free and gagged her so she could not cry out. MacLeod is fit to be tied himself now that he knows what the man did to his wife. Franklin insists he did it for her own good. He said she would have run off looking for little Patty otherwise. Kavanaugh told Franklin and Paralee yesterday the Cheyenne do not have their little girl. I sat inside our wagon and cried. It was what he did not say that grieved me so. Little Patricia Sinnott is dead. Everyone but Paralee knows. The nights are bitter cold and the days hot and dry. The child had no blanket or water. And there are coyotes and mountain lions and grizzlys and wolves. No three year old child could have survived one night out there.

Nellie asked me to pray with her that little Patty was taken home to heaven quickly and did not suffer long. I said I can not remember a time when God heard anything I said to him. The last time I tried was for Deborah and look what came of that. Nellie was shocked and said—God loves you, Mary Kathryn Farr, and you have got to believe that. I told her that God loves those he wants to love and I am not one of his chosen people. I told her that it was all right because I have no love for him either.

I did not mean to make her cry.

We are camped near a great rock that looks like a giant turtle. Almost everyone has carved their names upon it. Even me. Joshua and some of the others have climbed to the top.

Devils Gate is not far from here. Joshua is riding over

for a closer look. I can see it fine from where I sit writing in my journal. It looks like a giant ax cut through the stone mountain to let the Sweetwater River run through. And sweet water it is after the muddy Platte. It tastes so good. We will follow the river west.

James had to shoot one of our oxen yesterday it was suffering so. Beth is grieving over it. She asked why everything has to die. I had no good answer for her. Nellie was sitting with us and said death is just a door believers walk through to be with Jesus. Her words did not cheer Beth nor I. Why does she have to keep on talking about Jesus? Her words just raise a jumble of questions and heartache. Beth said Old Tom was just an ox and how could he know what to believe. Nellie knew she had raised trouble. Beth said it was not fair that people go to heaven and animals do not because animals are nicer than a lot of people. She is right about that but I could not let her go on with such thinking. A child needs a little hope in this world.

I told Beth Aunt Martha read to me about heaven once and I remember it said the lion would lie down with the calf. Nellie said that was right. She looked it up in her Bible right there on the spot. And I said I remember Aunt Martha reading that Jesus would ride down to earth on horseback. Nellie found that too. I told Beth there had to be animals in heaven for any of that to happen. Lions and lambs and horses maybe Beth said. She wanted to know if Werner Hoffman would see his dog again in heaven. I said likely so if Werner could get himself there.

We buried Dunham Banks today. Celia would not let him be buried in the road. The men dug as deep as they could but we are going over hard rocky ground. MacLeod said words over him. Celia gave baby Hortense to Beth to hold and started

gathering rocks to stack on top of poor Dunhams grave.
I helped her until the job was done. So did Nellie.

It is dark now and Celia is still sitting by the mound.

CHAPTER 17

SIERRA RECOGNIZED the highway patrolman even though he was dressed in a Sunday suit instead of a black uniform. He was waiting at the front steps just as he said he would be, and beside him was a young woman holding a baby. He grinned when he saw her.

"Be polite," Sierra said to her own children who stood glumly beside her, annoyed at being dragged off to church. Their father hadn't taken them to Mass more than three times in three years. In fact, the last time they had been inside a church was for their grandmother's memorial service.

"Welcome, Mrs. Madrid," the officer said, extending his hand. "I neglected to tell you my name. I'm Dennis O'Malley, and this is my wife, Noreen. The bundle she's holding is our son, Sean."

As people moved around them to enter the church, Sierra

introduced herself and her children. Rather than be annoyed at them for blocking a portion of the steps, people smiled warmly.

Over the last several days, since her experience on the freeway, she'd had a growing sense of . . . something. All the pain, all the crying out, had left her feeling empty. Drained. She had reached the end of her endurance, the end of her abilities to deal with the mess her life had become. And yet, much to her surprise, she wasn't depressed, or hopeless, or any of the things she'd expected to be. Instead, she felt . . . *directed*—as though a gentle hand rested on her shoulder and guided her. With love. She knew whose touch she felt. She'd heard her mother talk about the "presence of God" more times than she'd cared to listen. But now she understood better. She didn't know exactly what it all meant, but she was ready. She'd spent enough time trying to figure things out for herself, and look where that had gotten her. Now she wanted answers. Real answers.

And for some reason, she felt a certainty that this was the place where she'd find them.

The O'Malleys ushered them into the church and selected a pew near the back. Clanton sat on one side of Sierra, muttering, "What a bore," under his breath. Carolyn sat on her other side. Dennis sat nearest the aisle, while Noreen sat at the far end of the pew beside Carolyn and near the outside aisle.

"Just in case I have to leave," she said with a smile. "Sometimes Sean wakes up hungry. He's small but he makes a big noise." Her blue eyes were full of warmth. Seeing Carolyn's look, she smiled. "Would you like to hold him?"

"Could I?"

People turned around from the pew in front. Dennis made more introductions. Everyone was so friendly. They looked happy to see Sierra and her children, and she felt the oddest sense of connection, as though she'd finally come home. The feeling was even more poignant when the service began. Everything was so familiar, yet different. It wasn't that the pastor said anything she had never heard before. She had heard the gospel from her mother since she was old enough to remember. Yet now, inexplicably, it all made sense. It filled in the gaps of her life. *Oh!* her soul sighed. *Ohhhhh.*

The pastor spoke and the words pierced her. Her throat closed even as her heart opened wide. Parched from wandering in the wilderness, she drank in the living water of the Word.

"Why're you crying?" Clanton whispered, embarrassed and worried.

She shrugged, smiling at him. There was no time now to explain how she felt. *Connected.* A part of something tremendous and exhilarating. *Whole.* She tried to stop the tears, but they flowed like cleansing balm. Sorrow poured over and through her, filling her and bringing with it a deep hunger for the Lord. In its wake came hope and reassurance that everything would work out.

Forgive me, Father, for I have sinned mightily against Thee. Mea culpa, mea culpa. Oh, God! Oh, God!

How was it possible to feel so *alive* today, when only two days ago she had longed for death?

The congregation rose to sing, and she rose with them, fumbling through the hymnal and mouthing the words when emotion kept her silent. She couldn't read the words or even utter a sound, but it didn't matter. Her heart *sang.* Carolyn stood beside her, oblivious and enthralled with baby Sean in his mother's arms while Clanton, on her other side, fretted, convinced she was going nuts. She uttered a soft laugh and put her arm around him.

"I love you," she whispered.

"Let's *leave*," he hissed back.

"No, we're staying." Forever.

It was Dennis who served her Communion. She smiled up at him, remembering what she'd said to him as the traffic had streamed past them on the Hollywood Freeway. *"You know what I was doing when you pulled up beside me, Officer?* Praying. *So much for divine intervention."*

God had been intervening, all right. Mightily. He had brought her to a screeching halt on the dusty shoulder of a Los Angeles freeway rather than allow her to hurtle herself off the nearest cliff. And He did it because He loved her and would not let her go.

She almost laughed as realization came, bringing joy with it. She had been standing on sacred ground and hadn't even known it!

"'Bless the Lord, O my soul, and all that is within me, bless his holy name . . . ,'" the congregation sang, and she sang with them, unable to remember a time when she had felt so happy.

"Boy, am I glad that's over," Clanton said on the way home.

"You'd better set your mind to get used to it. We're going back."

"Oh, good!" Carolyn said.

She earned a glare from her brother. "You want Mom blubbering again?"

Sierra smiled at him. "I'll try to contain myself."

Lying in bed that night, Sierra knew she needed to make some changes in her life. Immediate changes. For one thing, she couldn't work for Ron anymore, not knowing how he felt about her. She realized her own feelings for him were confusing. She had always found him profoundly attractive. Several times, she'd thought how much better her life would be had she been married to Ron rather than Alex. That stopped her.

She was too vulnerable right now to think rationally. With Alex gone, she was needy. She was afraid of so many things. Ron was strong and confident. It would be too easy to turn to him for solace. Seeking solace could lead her into an affair.

She was still married. She needed to remember that, despite the present circumstances. For better or worse, Alex was her husband. Until death. Right now, she imagined Alex was wishing for hers. Not that she was feeling particularly fond of him, either. But feelings didn't make any difference.

She didn't want to think about Alex now. She couldn't and continue to feel the sense of comfort and rightness she had experienced this morning. "Do not be anxious for tomorrow," the pastor had read this morning, and here she was obsessing again. She couldn't do anything about Alex or her marriage. But she *could* do something about herself and her circumstances.

❦

Ron looked sick when he came in Monday morning. His eyes were shadowed.

"Can we talk?" she said before he went into his office. He paused and looked back at her bleakly. She didn't have to say a word. He knew.

"You've decided to quit."

She blushed. "I'm sorry. I'll stay until you can find a replacement."

"And feel uncomfortable every minute," he said, expression grim. How odd that this man, after only a few months, could know her better than Alex seemed to know her after thirteen years of marriage. Ron knew her better than anyone, except her mother.

"I knew when you left Friday this would happen. I talked

with Judy. She can stand in for you until I find a permanent replacement. What are you going to do?"

"I'm not sure yet. I think I'm going to sell the house." It hadn't even occurred to her until that instant.

"Are you going home to Healdsburg?"

"No," she said, surprising herself again. "I'm not sure what I'll do. I hadn't even thought about it until now."

"You never even guessed how I felt about you, did you?"

"Briefly, but I thought I was being foolish."

"I should've waited a little longer."

She met his gaze, her eyes compassionate. "It wouldn't have made any difference, Ron."

"It would've made all the difference in the world."

Looking into the blue depths of his eyes, she knew he was right. *Thank You, God,* her heart breathed. *Thank You that Ron waited as long as he did. Thank You for sparing me and Ron from what could have been a terrible mistake. And forgive me. All the while I was casting stones at Alex, I was tumbling into the abyss myself.* "I'm married, Ron."

"Until Alex can find a way out."

His words hurt, for she knew Alex was doing everything he could to gain that end. Every time he spoke with her, he felt the need to drive home two facts: he wasn't coming back, and he didn't love her anymore.

Regret washed over Ron's face. "I didn't say that to hurt you, Sierra."

"I know, but it does."

"I'll call you when it's over." He went into his office and closed the door.

Gathering her things, Sierra left. On her way out, she gave Arlene her ivy plant and a hug.

Instead of going home, she went to the mall. She bought a cappuccino, sat on a bench next to a big fern, and watched the hustle-bustle of people shopping. She supposed she had the qualifications to be a clerk, but was that what she wanted to do? Alex was sending a check once a month to cover expenses, and every time she opened the envelope, she wilted at the sight of his bold signature. Somehow, gut-level, she knew that check wrote her off.

Not once in her life had she supported herself. *Father, can I do this?* she prayed, feeling overwhelmed.

Ask and you shall receive, Daughter.

The assurance washed over her, and she settled back, sipping her cappuccino. She'd told Ron she was putting the house up for sale. She didn't know why she'd said that at the time, but it seemed a good idea now that she thought about it. If she remained where she was, it was certain she'd never be able to handle the finances herself. House payments were bad enough, but add to that the BMW payments and private school for the children and the sum was far beyond any expectations of earnings she might have.

Sierra could see herself living out her life at the mailbox, waiting for whatever money Alex doled out to her. She could imagine his resentment. He adored his children and wouldn't begrudge a dime to them, but every penny he sent for her support would be another matter.

She spent the day wandering in the mall, thinking. When she picked up the children, she took them to their favorite fast-food restaurant. "I've decided to sell the house," she told them, knowing her announcement was abrupt, but unable to think of any other way to break the news of her decision to them.

"Are we going home to Windsor?" Clanton said.

"No. We're going to look around San Fernando Valley and see what we can find near the church. We might even look at condominiums. There's a complex just down the street. I saw a swimming pool and tennis courts. We'll have to see what we can afford."

"Can we still go to the same school?" Carolyn said.

"No, honey. It's too expensive." She didn't want to ask Alex for any more money than she had to. "It makes more sense to go to a school in your own neighborhood."

"So I won't get to see Pamela?"

"You can see Pamela as often as we can arrange it, and you can call her whenever you want."

Sierra prayed that night, frightened by the speed with which her life was changing, but in the morning, she stepped out in faith and called Roberta Folse. She explained Alex had signed the house over to her before leaving her. Roberta was sympathetic but warned her not to expect a profit.

"You haven't been in the house long enough to build much equity, Sierra."

"We decorated. Maybe that'll help."

"You'll be lucky to break even. And then you're going to have to pay capital gains out of whatever you do get if you don't reinvest in something of equivalent or higher value in eighteen months. Is there any chance Alex will come back?"

"No."

"If he's keeping up the payments, you might do better staying where you are. I'd love a commission, Sierra, but not at the expense of your well-being. Why don't you take a few more days to think things over and give me a call in another week or two?"

Sierra did take a few more days. She prayed over it. She talked to Dennis and Noreen and got their opinion. The answer seemed clear. She needed to stand on her own two feet, trust the Lord, and stop depending on Alex. She called Roberta again.

Roberta came over the following afternoon.

"Oh, my word!" she said upon entering the house. "You didn't tell me Bruce Davies decorated your living room."

Roberta's remark absolved any doubts Sierra had ever had about Bruce Davies leaving his own stamp on everything he did. "Not just the living room, Roberta. The entire house."

"The *entire* house?"

"Yes."

"That must have cost you a bundle." Roberta sat down on the dark-brown leather couch and put her briefcase carefully on the thick glass-topped table.

Sierra grimaced, seeing how Roberta stared at the muraled wall with a perplexed expression. It was one of the reasons she usually avoided the living room. "It's one of Alex's video games," she said.

"I'd swear there's someone watching me."

"There is. Actually, if you look at it long enough, you'll see six men and one woman hiding in that jungle. It's called Camouflage. If I turn out the lights, their eyes glow red."

"How much did you put into decorating the house?"

Sierra told her.

"We'll add ten thousand to that and see what happens."

❧

Roberta called Saturday morning. "Be sure you take a look at the *Los Angeles Times* tomorrow morning."

Sierra forgot all about it until Carolyn came in the next morning while she was blow-drying her hair. "Daddy's on the phone," she said and held it out.

Surprised, Sierra shut off the dryer and took the phone, wondering why he was calling her so early on a Sunday. "Yes?"

"Is that our house on the cover of the real estate section?"

She could feel the heat of his anger through the receiver. It all but melted the telephone in her hand. Her defenses rose. She almost reminded him he'd signed the house over to her, so it wasn't *their* house anymore. It was *her* house. Instead, she managed a mild, "Yes, it is."

"What do you think you're doing?"

"I can't stay here, Alex. It's too—"

"You're not selling that house."

"I have to move, Alex. I've thought it all over and—"

"You have to move where?" he sneered. "To Healdsburg so I'll never see my children again! Over my dead body, Sierra! You hear me?" He swore at her in Spanish. He used a word so foul her face heated.

"I hear you, Alex, but I'm not—"

He didn't give her the chance to get further than that. Cursing again, he blistered her with the same accusations Audra had leveled at her a few weeks earlier, only adding personal and private faults on top. If Audra's words had shocked, Alex's battered and bruised. He meant to annihilate her, and he was doing a good job of it. He spoke in Spanish, which made it all the worse. He never spoke Spanish unless his emotions were out of control. Unfortunately, she understood every single word he said.

"I've called my attorney," he said, falling back into crisp English again. "I'm going to fight you, Sierra. No matter what it takes, I'm not letting you walk away with my children. I'm sick of this situation. I'm sick of *you!*" He told her she could hold her breath until Hades froze over before he'd send her another dime. "It's bad enough Clanton won't talk to me. Now you think you can put four hundred miles between me and my daughter!"

He took a breath, and into that brief space of time Sierra said with miraculous calm, "We aren't moving north, Alex."

"Where then? East? New York, maybe? That's three thousand miles instead of four hundred. Or Hawaii. Right! Hawaii. That's it. That'd put an ocean between us!"

The storm of his anger blew about her like a tornado around a bruised reed. "I'm hoping to buy a condo in Northridge."

Silence.

She looked in the mirror and wondered how much makeup it would take to put color back in that stranger's face. Looking away, she swallowed hard before she tried to say anything else. "I have to go," she said quietly, trying to keep her voice steady. "Church starts in less than an hour." She took a slow breath, squelching the desire to cry. She had cried enough over the past few years. Buckets of tears. Mostly for herself. "Alex, I promise you'll know everything as we do it. Clanton and Carolyn will never be out of your reach. I promise."

Pressing the button, she set the telephone on the bathroom counter. Nauseated, she thought about going back to bed and pulling the covers up over her head. But what good would that do?

"Three years I've watched you wallow in self-pity and keep up your temper tantrum. And it's been something to watch, Sierra. A real show!"

Shuddering, she turned her thoughts to Dennis and Noreen and a dozen others who welcomed her and the children every Sunday. She had a choice. She could stay home and do exactly what Audra and Alex would expect her to do, or she could finish getting ready and go to church. She could learn something and, with God's help, start putting her own life back in order.

The house sold the first week. Full price.

❖

When escrow closed thirty days later, the check Sierra received looked like an obscene amount of money. It dwindled fast when she sent half of it to Alex, made a 20 percent down payment on a modest three-bedroom condominium in Northridge, and paid her capital gains taxes out of what remained. If it weren't for her inheritance, she wouldn't have qualified for a loan in the first place. As it was, most of her assets were tied up in the Mathesen Street house in Healdsburg.

The telephone rang while Sierra was in the kitchen packing boxes. She avoided answering the telephone whenever possible. Alex had called several times during the past month. Luckily, Carolyn always flew to the phone when it rang, hoping it was her father. Clanton never picked it up, for the same reason. Carolyn spent two Saturdays a month with Alex, but she never said much about their day together. And Sierra didn't ask any questions.

"It's Daddy," Carolyn said now, holding the phone out to her. "He wants to talk to you." The hope in her eyes made Sierra want to weep.

"Thanks, honey." She took the phone, knowing exactly why he had called. She hadn't spoken with him since he'd read her the riot act over putting the house up for sale in the first place, and this conversation was destined to be no more pleasant.

"Why'd you send this check to me?" Alex said hotly.

Her heart gave a flip at the sound of his voice. "It's your half of the proceeds from the house."

"I signed the house over to you. Remember?" He sounded bitter about it.

"I remember, but I didn't feel right about keeping all the money."

"That's a big surprise. It never bothered you to keep my money before. Why change now? And while we're on the subject, why'd you send my check back last week?"

"Because you said you'd never send me another dime, and I thought I'd hold you to your word."

He spat a short, foul expletive. "So what are you going to do, Sierra? Make the kids eat at the local mission?"

"I have a job."

"Yeah, right. Working for Ron Peirozo at Los Angeles Outreach. I don't imagine it pays much."

"I don't work there anymore."

"Got fired, huh? Well, six months is something, I guess. That's longer than any other job you've held in your life."

Pushed to the limit by his scathing sarcasm and condescension, she almost blurted out the truth. *I left because Ron is in love with me and wants me to forget about you, to leave you in the dust like you've left me! He wants to be with me! He wants to marry me, Alex. He's a millionaire and he wants me! I left because it was the right thing to do, not that you care!*

But she didn't. He wouldn't believe her anyway. As much as he hated her, he'd find it impossible to think any other man would find her attractive or intriguing. And she wasn't about to humiliate herself by trying to convince him.

What does the Lord require of you?

She could hear the verse as clearly now as she'd heard it on Sunday, when the pastor had read it—and it brought her thoughts to an abrupt halt. What did the Lord require? Justice, kindness, humility . . . yet here she was, wandering down the familiar path of bitterness and self-pity again.

She drew a steadying breath. *Lord, I hurt him. I know I did. Please forgive me. I can't tell him I'm sorry right now because he won't listen, but You know how I feel. You know*

*what I did to start this war. I don't want to be part of it
anymore.*

"So, what are you going to do?" Alex demanded when she
made no response to his last insult.

"I'm going to be a secretary in an insurance agency."

"You'll last two weeks, tops."

"Is that an estimation of my abilities or of how boring
the industry is?" she said, trying to instill some lightness into
her tone.

"Take a wild guess."

His meaning couldn't be more clear.

"I'll send you another check, Sierra. You'd better hang on
to this one. You'll need it."

Hot, bitter anger swept over her, surpassing hurt and
obliterating wisdom. "I have a better idea, Alex. Don't send
the check. *Eat it!*" The words were out before she even knew
they were coming. They passed her lips, flying up from her
heart and roosting like vultures in the charged air, pecking at her head. She slammed the phone down, more angry
with her own lack of control than with Alex's contemptuous
laugh.

When a check did arrive in the mail two days later, it
came in an envelope with an embossed return address that
read Madrid/Longford. She tore up the envelope and check
and flushed both down the toilet. She'd stand out on a street
corner holding a sign that said Homeless and Hungry before
she'd take another nickel from Alejandro Luís Madrid.

Pride did have its place, didn't it? What had she just
heard at the last Bible study? *"Those who won't work, won't
eat."* Well, she'd work *and* eat. And so would her children.
Whatever money Alex sent for the children would go in their
college funds.

Dennis and several other men from the church helped

her move into the condominium. The complex was within walking distance of the church, and Dennis invited Clanton to play baseball when they finished unloading the pickup trucks. "We've got a team, but we're short some outfielders. Do you think you could help us out?"

"Sure. Easy!" Clanton looked more eager than Sierra had seen him in a long time.

"As soon as we get all this stuff lugged inside, we'll head on down to the field. Can he stay out until nine, Mom?" Dennis said, winking at her over one end of a couch he was carrying.

"I'll have to fix him some dinner first."

"We can get McDonald's."

"Great!" Clanton said, before she could respond. He dumped the box he was carrying onto the top of a coffee table and ran back for another.

"Mom!" Carolyn said, running up, her face flushed with excitement. "Susan lives here. Susan from church! She lives in the condo just down from us. See! Right over there. Can you believe it? Can I go play with her? *Please.*"

Susan's mother, Frances, came over an hour later. Clanton and the men had gone, leaving Sierra surrounded by boxes. Frances surveyed the chaos. "Why don't you join us for dinner?"

Removing the newspaper wrapping, Sierra set another plate into the dishwasher. She brushed damp tendrils back from her face and glanced around at the unpacked boxes, Mary Kathryn's trunk, the furniture dumped anywhere and nowhere in particular. It would take her all night to get half the unpacking done.

"Believe me," Frances laughed. "It'll still be here when you come back. Susan and I can help."

❖

By the time Sierra had finished her spaghetti, Frances had talked her into joining the choir. "It only makes sense," Frances said. "We meet on the same night as the youth group. We can walk down with the children, stay for practice, and walk back with them at nine."

"What if I can't carry a tune?" Sierra laughed.

"Then you'll just have to make a joyful noise!"

The telephone was ringing when she unlocked the front door and switched on the lights later that evening. Carolyn ran to the kitchen and answered it. Sierra could tell by the look on her daughter's face that it was Alex. She watched Carolyn hop up on a stool as she began telling her father everything that had happened that day. She sounded so happy and excited.

"Oh, and Mom's joined the choir. She's going to be practicing the same night Susan and I go to youth group. Susan? She's a friend from the church. She lives in a condo right down the path from us." She listened for a moment, her excitement dimming slightly. "He's not here, Daddy. He's playing baseball with Mr. O'Malley. Dennis is so neat! He leads the youth group, and he's a highway patrolman. He met Mom when he pulled her over on the freeway for speeding. You should see his baby. Sean is so cute, and Noreen lets me hold him in church."

Sierra went into Carolyn's bedroom. So much for keeping a few secrets, she thought, taking the sheets from a box. She made up Carolyn's bed, then went into Clanton's room and made up his bed. Carolyn was still talking when Sierra went into her own bedroom and began making up her own bed, the one she'd slept in all through her growing-up years in Healdsburg. She smoothed the comforter and plumped the pillows. Leaning against the bedpost, she looked around the room.

She'd had to get rid of the king-size bed she'd shared with Alex. After measuring the master bedroom, she'd realized it would fit but leave little room for anything else. Giving it up had been difficult. She'd mentioned it to Melissa during their last telephone conversation, and two days later her brother had called and said he was shipping her canopy bed from home.

She touched the lace covering that her mother had crocheted for her; it had taken her a year to complete it. Sierra remembered the joy she'd felt when she opened the big box on Christmas morning and found the lace folded in among sheets of lavender tissue paper. She'd been sixteen and madly in love with Alex.

Her eyes welled with tears. How many nights had she lain in this bed dreaming of what it would be like to be married to Alejandro Luís Madrid? He had been her Prince Charming. Ten years she'd known what it was like to be loved and fulfilled by a man of passion. Ten years of heaven, followed by three years of descending into hell.

God forgive her, she'd been the one to take the first step down.

The front doorbell rang. "Mom! Can you get it?" Carolyn called, unwilling to relinquish the phone.

When she opened the door, Sierra found Clanton covered with grass stains and dirt from head to foot and grinning from ear to ear. "I hit a home run, Mom! Man, you should've seen that ball fly!"

Dennis was behind him, looking pleased. "It wouldn't have been a home run if I hadn't tripped over my feet," he said in mock annoyance, "and you hadn't run like a rabbit."

"We're playing against the Baptist church on Saturday,"

Clanton said, entering the living room and tossing his dirty glove onto a pile of clean clothes that had yet to be put away. "I'm playing shortstop."

"You were supposed to ask your mother's permission," Dennis said, snatching Clanton's hat off. "Remember?"

"Mother may I?" Clanton grinned.

She laughed. "Yes, you *may*."

Carolyn slid off the kitchen stool. "Daddy wants to talk to you," she said, holding the telephone receiver out to Clanton.

Clanton's expression changed immediately. He stared at the telephone as though it were a cockroach he wanted to squash. "Tell him I'm taking a shower!" he said loud enough for Alex to hear and stalked down the hall. He went into the bathroom and slammed the door. Sierra heard the click as he locked it.

Dennis gave her a grim look as Carolyn relayed the message. "I can see we have some work to do," he said softly. He tossed Clanton's hat onto a stool.

"A lot of work."

"I'd better get home before Noreen sends out a search party."

Sierra walked with him to the door and thanked him for including Clanton in the adults' baseball practice.

"He's a great kid, Sierra," Dennis said.

"He's an angry kid."

"He's got reason. A lot of times it's not in our power to forgive someone who has hurt us. We have to ask God's help."

Words for her to think about as well, she thought as she closed the door.

❖

She tried to talk to Clanton when he got into his bed. "Would you please talk to your father the next time he calls?"

"Why should I?"

"Because it'd make things easier on me," she said, hoping that would make some difference. "He thinks I've turned you against him."

"I'll talk to him," Clanton said, eyes blazing with the same fierce anger she'd seen in Alex's the last time he'd spoken to her face-to-face before walking out. "I'll tell him he's full of—"

She put her hand lightly over his lips to stop the flow of angry words. Clanton clearly had some of her faults as well as Alex's. "Please," she whispered. "I'm not without fault in all this, Clanton. Try to understand." She bit her lip, trying to find words to explain. If she cried, that would only make matters worse. She stroked his cheek tenderly. "Your father loves you very much."

His mouth worked. "If he loved me, he wouldn't have left," he said and turned over on his side so she couldn't see his face. She didn't have to. Her heart felt like a hot ball of pain inside her.

"His leaving had nothing to do with you, honey. I was angry for so long about having to move, and I took it out on Daddy. He got tired of it."

Clanton turned his head slightly and looked at her. "Do you still love him?"

Tears did come then, but she smiled, combing his hair back from his forehead. Dark hair just like Alex's. "He's your father, honey. How could I not?" She took his hand. "What he's done isn't right, Clanton, but I wasn't right either. Looking back, I can see so many things I did wrong."

"You never did anything wrong."

"Yes, I did. I wanted things to be *my* way." She stroked his cheek, aching for the pain she saw in his eyes. Hate and love were so closely linked. "If you can't forgive him for your sake, honey, will you forgive him for mine?"

Clanton rolled over again. He had always been stubborn. Just like her. Just like Alex.

Heart aching, she stood and straightened the covers over his shoulders. "I love you, Clanton." Leaning down, she kissed his temple. "So does your father."

We are at the top of the Rocky Mountains!

We did not even know it until we saw the water was running west. The climb was so slow and gradual and then this great expanse before you so you know you are on top of a great range. It is cool and dry and windy right now. But it was a long hard day of travel.

Kavanaugh and Joshua shot three antelope. They are good eating. I am so proud of him!

We crossed the Big Sandy and laid by to rest our oxen. I did wash. Artemesia joined me at the riverbank. She was a robust woman when we started and is now so thin a breeze could blow her over. She says she feels much better. She does not look it.

The last week has been hard going through dark hills and deep ravines and narrow passes. We have crossed creeks and fixed broken wagons. One of the oxen died last night and the wolves kept up a constant howling. I did not sleep much. Tonight is not much better with the mosquitoes buzzing and Henry and Matthew fighting with each other. I have to sit a while and write something or I will crack their heads together.

Beth was feeling poorly again today. The fever comes and goes. I gave her some quinine and bedded her down for the night.

I am wearing new moccasins and pleased with the feel of them. My shoes were worn through and Henry is wearing my boots. Kavanaugh traded with a Cheyenne squaw and gave them to James to give to me. James offered him a dollar for them but he would not take it. He said it was payment for the suppers he has shared with us.

James has sent the boys to bed. The quiet is nice with the crickets chirping and the sky so starry. James is on first watch tonight.

Cal Chaffey is playing his mouth organ again. It is a mournful tune tonight. The wolves like it. They are joining in.

Paralee Sinnott has torn the sheets.

She was feeling poorly this morning, but Franklin made her drive the wagon just the same. She pulled out of line twice. By the end of the day she was at the back eating dust. We had made camp by the time she drove in. When she came in Franklin asked her where his son was and she said she shot him back in the road and left him for dead. Franklin Sinnott rode off fast as he could to go looking for him. As soon as he was out of sight, Paralee got down off her wagon calm as you please and set fire to his wagon full of goods to sell. It took flame so fast all we could do was pull the two wagons nearest out of the circle so they would not catch fire as well. Paralee just stood there with her arms crossed watching everything go up in smoke.

Franklin came back quick when he saw the smoke. When he saw what she had done, he come down off his horse like a wild man and hit her twice before MacLeod laid him out good and proper. Franklin lay there crying over his broken nose and dead son and calling her a crazy woman.

And right then young Frank rode in with a string of trout hanging off his saddle. He said Paralee sent him fishing.

We are laid by at Soda Springs and will stay over Sunday. Everyone has drunk from the springs. Some like it fine as it is. I did not like it much until I added sugar. Then it was tolerable good.

We are all in sore need of rest. It was hard pulling through mountains and crossing creeks. We have plenty of grass and wood here. Kavanaugh took Joshua hunting. James is annoyed. He needed Joshua to help him make repairs on the wagon but Joshua was off before we knew he was going. Joshua would rather ride point and hunt with Kavanaugh than drive our wagon or repair it. So Hank and Matthew are helping.

It is pretty here. I would be content to stop and sink in roots. James said I will like California better.

I am filled with sadness. When we pull out day after tomorrow, we will be taking the road to California. Most will be heading on to Oregon. I am thankful Wells and Nellie are going with us. Nellie is the closest thing I have to a sister and reminds me of Aunt Martha.

Oren McKenzie and Celia Banks have teamed up. Celia put the idea in Oren's head and he was agreeable. She has milk enough for baby David and her own little Hortense and she needs a man to help her work the land she is going to claim in Oregon. They will not marry until they have their allotments. Once they claim their 160 acres, they will tie the knot and have 320 acres together. She is a smart girl.

Winifred Holtz is grieving something awful. She loves little David as though he were her own. Celia wept with her and said she will not take him from her until all is settled in Oregon.

MacLeod led the wagons north toward the Snake River this morning. We and the Doanes, Stern Janssen, Ernst Holtz, and

Binger Siddons pulled out at the same time heading south. Nellie has cried the whole day. She is crying still as I sit and write in my journal. Wells keeps telling her the going will be easier to California but I can tell by Kavanaugh it will not. Robert and LeRoy are glad to not be separated from Henry and Matthew. Beth is mourning over not seeing baby Hortense again. I almost told her I would be having a baby in the spring but I thought it better not to. I am feeling poorly and may lose it. And I should tell James before anybody else.

Kavanaugh is going with us to California. I am glad of his company. He said he has not been over this land before but has heard much about it. He said the next eight hundred miles will be harder than anything we have traveled over before.

James says that means fewer people will come.

We crossed Raft River and have come as far as a City of Rocks. We will rest here a day before going on. Beth and I have made a game of seeing things in the rock formations. Some are hundreds of feet high. We have made out the shapes of turtles and rabbits. Henry pointed out a group of rocks that look like an eagle.

Joshua said he has no interest in childish games and rode off. Now I see he has climbed up on one section and is painting his name in axle grease high up for all to see.

It has been hard pulling since we left the City of Rocks. Kavanaugh said Humboldt Wells is still a day away.

I wish we had gone on to Oregon.

We are nooning three hours during the hottest time of day and then traveling on until the sunset. The dust has been bad. We fan out, but the winds keep us from escaping it. Nellie is sick from the alkali dust. I am so sunburned I look like an Indian.

The children keep asking how long it will take to get to California. James lost his temper and said we will get there when we get there and if they ask again he will take his belt to them. He has no patience with this Heat and the Hard Labor. The roads are heavy.

I think he is wishing we had gone on to Oregon.

We came over mountainous roads today and reached Thousand Spring Valley. We are camped by good water. Joshua has taken the horses to good grass. Henry has gone with him to cut and bundle grass to take with us. I am too tired to write more.

We are laid by at Humboldt Wells. We will stay an extra day here. The animals need rest. So do we all. Grass and water are plentiful. It is pretty and there is shade.

Kavanaugh does not say much about what is ahead. His silence fills me with disquiet. If the going was easy he would tell us so. Summer has its heavy hand upon us.

Joshua asked me who his father is. I said James but he said he means his Real father. I asked him why he wanted to know and he said he had wondered about it for a long time. He said Clovis told him I had him with me when I came to live with Aunt Martha. I told him James was the only father he ever had. He was not satisfied. He said a man has to know where he comes from. So I told him my brother Matthew McMurray married Sally Mae Grayson and he is her child. He wanted to know what happened to her and I told him she died giving birth to him. Then he wanted to know what happened to his father. I said he died too. He wanted to know how and I said what difference does it make. He is dead. Joshua got mad and wanted to know why it was so hard for me to tell the truth. I said I had never lied to him or anyone. I said it was hard talking about people I loved who were gone. I said the past did not matter anyway because he is as much my son as Henry and Matthew. He said he is not. I did not think words could hurt so much. I told him I have loved him from the moment I helped bring him into the world.

He did not ask more after that. He just looked at me like he knew there was more than what I was telling him.

Joshua rode on ahead. I am afraid for him. James said he has common sense and Kavanaugh will watch out for him. I am afraid for other reasons.

Stern Janssen lost a wheel today. The wood had gotten so dry the spokes fell out. James is helping him fix it. They have taken the wheels off and are soaking them overnight in the Humboldt.

Joshua is not back. Kavanaugh said he saw him and he is well but not ready to come back.

We have fallen into the practice of gathering and supping together. Nellie has been feeling poorly and I have been cooking. The men give me what I need of their supplies to stretch the meal for all of us. While I cook, Nellie reads from her Bible and the men make what repairs need doing on the wagons. The children are too tired and cranky to get into much trouble.

Joshua killed two rattlesnakes before the oxen were even unyoked. Kavanaugh said they are good eating. I told him he could fry and eat them both with my good wishes. He did just that and Joshua joined him.

The oxen were too tired to be frightened by the snakes but Beth is in the wagon and will probably stay there until California. I may join her. The boys are bedded down under the wagon with James.

We had trout for supper. Binger caught enough for all of us.
    Joshua is on guard tonight with Wells.

We passed more dead cattle today. We are using sage for fuel.

Kavanaugh said there is another company of wagons twelve or
so miles ahead of us. I am glad to know there are others ahead
and surviving.

Passed two dead oxen today.
    The sand is deep and very heavy on our teams.

Wells got stuck and we had to use our oxen to pull him free.
The grass is very poor but the water is plentiful. The skies are
clouding up. I can hear the rumble of thunder in the distance.
    It would be nice to have a break in the awful heat.

Our oxen scented water and went wild trying to get to it. We
turned all but one and it drank from alkaline water. James
and I doctored it. James held the animal while I poured grease
down its throat. Beth is watching over it now and praying it
will survive.

The milk cow has gone dry. We may have to use her to pull if
we lose another ox. I expect we will because we have passed a
dozen carcasses in the last four days.

We passed a grave today. Tobias Wentworth.
    Binger lost another ox.

Nellie said we are wandering like the Israelites in the desert.
The land is cruel and the heat unrelenting. We are pulling out
with first light and stopping when the sun is high. We wait

a couple of hours in whatever shade we can find and then go on until sunset. But even then the going is so hard I sometimes want to lay down and die and have done with it.

Maybe we are like the Israelites. God watched them die on the edge of the Promised Land.

The Humboldt has drained away into nothing. Kavanaugh just told us we got forty miles of desert ahead of us.

I do not think I can make it.

Stern Janssen's wagon was so deep mired in sand he had to unharness the oxen and leave it. We pulled three oxen out but the other just laid down and died.

Nellie is so sick from the heat she is riding inside their wagon. Wells is afraid she is going to die.

If this desert does not kill us all, the mountains I see ahead surely will.

CHAPTER 18

SIERRA SWUNG THE BAT and felt the hard impact of the ball. Dropping the bat, she ran for first base.

"Go! Go!" the base coach said, urging her on.

"Run, Sierra! *Run!*" others shouted from the stands as she crossed second.

"Come on, Mom!" Clanton hollered, jumping up and down near third and waving her on. "Go for it! Go for it!"

She rounded third and headed for home. The second baseman caught the ball from the center fielder and was turning to zing it toward home plate. She knew she'd never make it before the ball did. "Oh, Lord, help!" she said. Clanton would never forgive her if she made the last out. Giving it everything she had, she charged ahead, dropping at the last second just as the catcher caught the ball. She plowed right into him, knocking him off his feet. The ball bounced off her helmet as he came down in a heap on top of her.

"*Safe!*" the umpire shouted amid exuberant laughter.

"That's the way to do it!" Dennis was laughing as he ran over from his position as coach.

She and the catcher untangled themselves. "What do you think this is, Madrid? The World Series? Or professional wrestling, maybe?"

Rolling over, she made it to her hands and knees. "Sorry, Harry. You okay?"

"I will be in a minute," he said, flopping over onto his back, arms and legs splayed.

"Don't worry about Harry." Dennis grinned, giving her a hand up. "He's tougher than he looks. He just likes playing for sympathy."

Harry raised his head off the ground and scowled. "You taught her to slide, didn't you, O'Malley."

"My father taught me," Sierra informed him, laughing. She brushed herself off as her team surrounded her and began beating the dust off with their hats and pounding her back with congratulations.

Harry got up and pulled off his catcher's mask. "I tell you, there ought to be a regulation against plowing your elders down like bowling pins."

"Batter up!" the umpire shouted.

As Sierra headed for the bench with her teammates, she heard Carolyn calling her. "Mom! Mom!" Turning, she walked backward and waved. Her heart leaped as she saw Alex sitting in the grandstand next to Carolyn. Where had he come from?

The last inning of the game passed in a blur. She couldn't pay attention. She hadn't seen Alex in six months or talked to him in two. Her heart was hammering. Her palms were sweating.

Shame filled her. He couldn't stop by the condominium, could he? No. Of course not. He had to come to a baseball game looking as if he'd stepped out of *GQ* and see her wearing faded Levi's and covered in dirt and grass stains. No makeup. Her hair tumbling down. Dirt under her fingernails and in her teeth after sliding home. Perfect timing. She blew a strand of hair out of her eyes.

"You okay?" Dennis said, putting his hand over hers.

"Alex is here."

"I wondered who that guy was sitting beside Carolyn."

"Did you happen to notice when he arrived?"

"About two minutes before you went up to bat."

"Great," she muttered, thinking of how she must have looked plowing poor old Harry down at home plate.

Dennis glanced over at the stands. "Did Clanton know he was coming?"

"*I* didn't know he was coming." She took a deep breath, blowing it out through pursed lips, trying to slow her ricocheting pulse. "Kick me if I cry, Dennis. Kick me *hard*."

"You cry and I'll haul you off to the slammer."

She laughed.

The team gathered in a circle and gave a cheer for the Lutherans they'd been playing. "We only lost by two runs," Clanton said as Sierra put her arm around his shoulders. "We'll get them—" She knew the instant he spotted his father. His whole body went rigid.

"It's okay," she said softly.

Alex was holding Carolyn's hand as he walked toward them. He was looking straight at his son. He didn't even spare a glance at her.

Sierra noticed he'd lost weight, but then, so had she over the past six months. Fifteen pounds, to be exact. Thankfully in all the right places.

"I'm going to help Dennis put the gear away," Clanton said and started to turn away.

She gripped his shirtsleeve. "You will not."

"I don't have anything to say to him."

"Then you'll listen."

Alex looked between them as he came closer. It was hard to miss the fact that she and her son were having a slight difference of opinion. He did look at her then, his eyes narrowed and suspicious. What did he think she was doing? When he stopped in front of them, his eyes flicked over her mussed hair, dusty T-shirt and pants, right down to her scuffed tennis shoes. Her face filled with heat. One side of his mouth tipped. "Good hit."

"Thanks," she managed, feeling dismissed.

Courtesy dispensed with, he looked at his son. "You played well out there, Son." When Clanton didn't say anything, she saw a muscle tighten in Alex's cheek. But it wasn't anger. It was hurt. He looked more vulnerable than she'd ever seen him.

God, please, don't let Clanton say anything cruel. Please.

Clanton didn't say anything. He just stood beside her, rigid and silent, her champion.

"What do you say I take you out for a hamburger?" Alex said.

Clanton uttered a soft laugh, glaring up at his father. "The team's going out for pizza," he said coldly and looked away.

"Why don't you join us?" Sierra said impulsively.

Clanton shot a look at her that would have withered an oak. "He doesn't play baseball," Clanton said. He looked at Alex again. "He plays around with other women."

Alex's face went dark red.

Sierra didn't know if he was embarrassed or ready to explode with rage.

"You're such a jerk, Clanton!" Carolyn said, her mouth trembling.

"Shut up! What d'you know?"

"I know more than you do!" she said, her blue eyes filling with tears. "Elizabeth said—" She broke off, paling at the look on Clanton's face.

"You little Judas!"

Sierra could feel the blood draining out of her face. Was *that* where Alex took their daughter on Saturdays? On excursions with his mistress?

Clanton took a step toward his sister. "Why don't you move in with *them*, you little—"

"That's enough, Clanton," Alex said, steel in his voice. He barely spared a glance at Sierra, and she was glad of that. The last thing she wanted was for him to see how much it hurt to know Carolyn had been spending time with Elizabeth Longford. "You'd better learn to accept things as they are."

"I don't have to *accept* anything, least of all *you*. You're a cheat and a liar, and I wish you and your girlfriend were *dead*!" He took off across the baseball field toward Dennis and the other members of the team.

"Mom?" Carolyn said, tears running down her cheeks.

"I'll go after him," she said quietly, eager to escape before she made a fool of herself or said something she'd regret. She headed toward her teammates, swallowing the hot tears that were choking her.

"Mom!" Carolyn cried out. She made to follow Sierra, but Alex was holding her hand. "Let go!" she said, sobbing, and pulled free of her father to run to Sierra. "Are you mad at me, Mom?" Tears ran down her cheeks. "Do you hate me?"

"*No,*" Sierra said, kneeling and pulling her close. She stroked her hair and kissed the top of her head. "I just wish things were different, that's all."

"I didn't mean to hurt you. I only talked to her the one time. I—"

"Shhh . . . I love you very much, and nothing will ever change that." She tipped her daughter's chin and gave her a shaky smile. "You go have fun with your father while I talk to Clanton. I'll see you later at home." She kissed her.

"Clanton's so mean."

"No, honey. He's hurt. People say awful things when they're hurt." Just as she had. Just as Alex had. Poor Clanton. What chance did he have of being any better than they'd been? "You tell your father how much you love him. He needs to hear that. Now, go on."

"Sierra," Alex called. "Wait a minute." She recognized that tone and wished she could just keep walking. If not for what she'd just said to Carolyn, she'd run. She was reeling inside, her stomach quivering, her eyes hot with tears. She didn't need a lecture from Alex about what a lousy mother she was or what a lousy wife she'd been.

He looked at her, and she saw something flicker in his eyes. "Where's the team going? We'll meet you there."

No respite for the wicked. Not even privacy to have a good, long cry. "Three blocks down in the shopping center," she said, forcing herself to speak evenly. "I'll do what I can, Alex, but I can't promise . . ." She shook her head and turned away, resigning herself to a painful evening.

❖

Dennis did some long, hard talking to Clanton before they reached the pizza parlor. He knew how Clanton felt; his own father had left his family when he was in his teens.

"I saw him once after he left and told him I hated him. I never saw him again. He died when I was twenty-three."

Sierra saw how much that confession cost Dennis, as well as the impact it had on Clanton.

"He hurt my mother," Clanton said. "Every time he calls, he hurts her."

Sierra blinked back tears. "I hurt him, too, Clanton."

"Not like he did." Clanton struggled to contain his emotions, torn between love and loyalty to her and love for his father.

Dennis put his hand on Clanton's shoulder. "Your father's hurting himself most of all. He's cut off from you and your sister. Do you remember what we were talking about the other night at youth group? Everyone sins. No one is perfect. And no sin is greater than any other. When you believe in Jesus, you confess and repent, and He cleanses you. He puts you on the right track. What happens when you don't have that sustaining faith? You're cut off from love itself."

"He's not repentant," Clanton said.

"Are you?"

Clanton fought to hold his tears back. "He's still living with her!"

"And you're still hanging on to your anger against him. You just wished him dead."

Clanton hunched over and cried, muttering incoherent words. Dennis cupped the boy's head and pulled him against his chest. "Give it to the Lord, Clanton. Don't make the same mistake I did. It still haunts me." He looked at Sierra, and she saw the tears in his eyes. She also knew her son needed time alone with this man of God.

"I'll see you inside," she said, touching her son and then getting out of the van. She knew Clanton would open up more if she weren't present.

She spotted Alex as soon as she entered the pizza parlor; her instinctive homing device still worked. She could sense his presence anywhere. He was sitting with Carolyn in a booth back in the corner. She wanted to pretend she hadn't seen them and walk over to the others. The last thing she wanted to do was speak to Alex or think about Carolyn building a relationship with a future stepmother.

Alex was staring at her, and she knew she'd only gain his further ire if she left him to wonder where Clanton was.

Someone called her name. She glanced toward them, forced a smile, and waved. "Be there in a minute." First things first. She had to set Alex's mind at rest. She walked over to the table and smiled at Carolyn. "Did you order pizza yet?"

"Pepperoni!" She grinned and took a sip of her soda.

Sierra looked at Alex. "Dennis is talking with him. They'll be in soon." His eyes met hers, and she felt his pain. What a tangled mess they'd made of their lives—and dragged their children right into the quagmire with them. "If it doesn't happen tonight, Alex, we'll keep trying. All right? Don't give up on him. Please."

Again, that look she couldn't decipher. "I won't," he said bleakly.

Smiling tremulously, she left their table and joined the others.

When Clanton came in, Carolyn left the booth so her father could talk to him alone. She came straight to Sierra. "Daddy said he'll take us to the movies and then to dinner." She kept up a stream of chatter about her father while Sierra watched Dennis and Clanton sit down in the booth with Alex.

Dennis smiled and talked for a few minutes, undoubtedly trying to put his companions more at ease. Alex responded. She saw him smile. Odd how that hurt. When Dennis left them alone, Alex looked across at his son and started talking. He talked for a long time. Clanton just sat staring at Carolyn's empty soda glass. After a while, Alex didn't say anything more. He just sat looking at his son, grief and regret etched in the new lines around his eyes. He said a few more words. Clanton got up and left the booth. Alex raked a hand back through his hair and looked away.

For the first time since he'd left her, Sierra felt compassion for her husband.

❖

Carolyn left with her father. Clanton spent most of the evening talking with Dennis. Noreen came and sat with Sierra. "Children see things in black and white," Noreen said. "Right and wrong. Good and evil. They're so sensitive to those things. The older we are, the more shades of gray we see."

"I don't know what to do. So much of this is my fault. He wants a divorce."

Noreen put her hand over hers. "Are you still in love with him?"

Sierra gave a mirthless laugh. "I've been in love with Alex for as long as I can remember, and I'll probably love him until I die. But that doesn't change anything, does it? He said he's sick of me and in love with someone else. He's done everything possible to get me to agree to a divorce. In the beginning, I think I refused because I wanted to hurt him as much as he was hurting me. Then it was pure cussed stubbornness. But now? I don't know anymore. I just don't know."

Noreen squeezed her hand. "I don't know if this will help you or not, but my parents fought all the time when I was growing up. I used to cry myself to sleep hearing them scream at each other. They said they were staying together for us, my brother and me. I used to wish they'd get a divorce."

"Did they?"

"No. Never. They're still together and they're still fighting. They have other excuses now, and they still embarrass anyone who comes within ten feet of them. I don't go home very often."

Sierra remembered the fights she'd had with Alex. They hadn't screamed at one another, but the cold war had gone on for months at a time. At what cost to their children? She'd been so caught up in her own pain, she'd been blind to theirs. And Alex's.

Audra's words came back again, haunting her. *"Three years I've watched you wallow in self-pity and keep up your temper tantrum. And it's been something to watch, Sierra. A real show!"*

Sierra closed her eyes. *God, forgive me. She was right. I behaved so badly, Lord. What can I do to make things right again? How can I make amends?*

And the answer came, bringing with it a wave of pain.

Let him go.

Clanton said he had a stomachache, and they went home early. While he took a long, hot bath, she sat in the living room, praying. She knew what she had to do. When she tucked Clanton into bed, she stroked the black hair back from his forehead. "I love you so much, and I'm sorry I've made a mess of things."

"You didn't."

"Oh, Clanton, there's so much you don't understand. I pushed. I pushed so hard for so long for what *I* wanted. I never stopped to consider what your father needed. Please don't do the same thing. You'll end up losing him the same way I did. He *needs* you, Clanton. He needs to be able to love you."

"What about you, Mom?"

"I have you and Carolyn. I have Michael and his family. I have the Lord. What does your father have, Clanton? And I share the blame for it. I want to make things easier for all of us."

They talked for over an hour, and Clanton agreed he'd talk to his father the next time he called. Relieved, Sierra took a long shower and changed into black leggings and a long forest-green tunic. She was brushing her hair when the doorbell rang.

Alex stood under the porch light, their daughter sound asleep in his arms. "Where's her room?"

"Down the hall, second door on the right," she said and stepped back. She watched him carry Carolyn down the hall. She followed, switching on the light. She pulled the comforter back. Alex lay Carolyn down gently so she wouldn't awaken. Untying her tennis shoes, he slipped them off her feet. Sierra left the room as he drew the comforter up over his daughter and kissed her good night.

Her heart was hammering when Alex came into the living room. He looked around. "You didn't bring any of the new furniture with you."

She could tell nothing from his tone, but it occurred to her then he might have wanted some of the things Bruce Davies had brought into the house they'd shared together. She saw another glaring mistake, another selfish act on her part. "Roberta suggested I sell . . ." She shook her head, embarrassed. She couldn't pass the blame onto Roberta. It had been her own decision, another act of defiance. "I'm sorry, Alex. I never even considered asking if you wanted the furniture Bruce Davies—"

"I didn't say I did," he said abruptly. He looked away from her and around the living room. "Reminds me of the house in Windsor."

His words came back to haunt her: *There's a right way and a wrong way to decorate.* She looked around, trying to see things from his perspective. She'd kept the sofa they'd bought during their first year of marriage, though she'd recovered it last month with green corduroy. She'd found the brightly colored throw pillows on sale in an import shop. She still had the hatch-cover table. On it was a lead crystal platter with rocks the children had collected from a recent visit to the beach. The old brass lamps Alex had called ridiculous sat on modern end tables on each end of the sofa. She'd polished them to a golden glow and purchased new shades. In the corner, near the front window, was a tall, healthy fern.

It was as far from Bruce Davies's kind of decorating as you could get. Nothing went together, but somehow the mix made everyone who walked in feel comfortable. At least, they said so. Two had even asked her to help decorate their homes.

But how did it make Alex feel?

"Would you like me to make some coffee?" she said for want of anything else.

"It's a little late for coffee."

It was a little late for everything. Conceding, she nodded sadly. "I guess it is." She picked up the long white envelope from the kitchen counter. "I had a long talk with Clanton this evening after we got home. I think he understands things a little better now."

"Understands what?" Alex said, dark-eyed.

"That our marriage breaking up wasn't solely your fault. He'll talk with you the next time you call." Taking a breath, she took a few steps toward him and held out the envelope.

Eyes narrowed, he took it. "What's this?"

"The divorce papers you gave me. I signed them tonight. You can have your divorce, Alex. I won't fight you anymore." She hadn't realized the cost of those words, nor had she expected to see the look that came into his eyes. He wasn't relieved. As he searched her face intently, she used every ounce of her will to keep the tears back and to appear calm and accepting.

Oh, God, be with me. You are my hiding place. You are my shield, my ever-present help in times of trouble. And this hurts more than I ever thought possible.

"Why now?" Alex said roughly.

"Because it's time." A time for all things. A time to love. A time to let go. A time to move on with her life and allow Alex to move on with his. "It would've been easier on everyone if I'd done as you asked in the first place. I was hanging on to my anger. And false hopes. I know now it only made things worse. For everyone."

He looked at her for a long moment. "You've changed."

"I hope so."

He tucked the envelope inside his jacket pocket. She'd never seen him look so grim. He started to say something but shook his head. He walked to the door, opened it, and went out without a word. She closed the door quietly behind him and leaned her forehead against it.

I'll trust in You, Lord, no matter how much it hurts. I'll trust You.

When next Alex called, Clanton answered. Alex picked him up on Saturday and they spent the full day together, the first since Alex had left.

We are laid by in Ragtown with twenty other wagons.

There is water here and the animals have good grazing. James is letting me handle replenishing the supplies while he has the wagon refitted. And I am getting my wash done. The place is named for all the clothing hanging on bushes. Even unmentionables. It is a sight to see!

The Randolph party is heading out along the Truckee River tomorrow. They are eager to reach Sutter's Fort. They are answering Sutter's call for settlers. Several of the men here are Ohio farmers. The blacksmith with them fixed the rims on our wagon and sold us some spare bolts.

I was hoping we would be traveling on with the Randolph party. It seems to me the more people the less chance of trouble, but James thinks differently. He wants to wait and give the oxen time to fatten for the assault on the Sierras. The others agree. Kavanaugh gives no opinion one way or the other. I think he would speak up if it was a poor idea. So I am somewhat comforted. Joshua is angry. He is eager to see what is over the mountains. I suppose it is a good thing we are waiting another day or two. Nellie should be stronger by then. Another day in that desert and we would have been burying her. Nellie asked me to pray for her. All I could do was take her hand and say God help us. She seemed satisfied with that. She keeps on reminding me God has helped us this far. And I keep telling her we are not at the end of the trail yet.

Our oxen have good grazing here. James is cutting grass and bundling it for fodder. It was good he did that along the Humboldt or the animals never would have made the last forty miles.

I look up at the mountains and wonder if we can make it before winter hits. The wagon master of the Randolph party told us not to wait longer than a week. He said a party went through two years ago and got trapped in the winter snows. Most of them died and those that did not were reduced to eating their kin. After hearing that story, I was ready to pack up our gear and set out right then.

Kavanaugh rode ahead to find an easier route over the mountains.

Joshua went with him. They have been gone four days. I am afraid something has happened to them. James said we will follow the trail left by the Randolph party until we hear otherwise.

It is hard going. We crossed the Truckee four times and now have to dismantle the wagon and haul it up the mountain. Binger cracked two ribs when the windlass came loose, but we did not lose his wagon. Plenty of wood for a fire. The air is cold at night and the days are getting shorter. Joshua is keeping us in fresh food. He shot a deer. I have strips of meat drying on the wagon as we travel.

I heard the most fearsome noise last night. Kavanaugh said it was a puma. I asked him what a puma was and he said it is a mountain lion. James spotted a bear crossing the meadow this morning. I knew something was in the wind because the oxen were nervous. Kavanaugh put himself between the wagons and the bear and had his Sharps ready. That huge beast reared up on its back legs and scented the wind. I am thankful he knew better than to come closer.

Kavanaugh just told me to pack the drying meat away or the bear will come in for it. I have done so.

James is standing guard. Stern will take the watch in another two hours. The children are settled under the wagon and sound asleep. I can not sleep a wink for fear of that bear.

It has been so long since I have felt safe. The last time I can remember was when I was a child and my mama was still alive and well. I never knew the dangers that were around me while she lived. She was not even much afraid when the Sioux and Fox Indians were warring. She always said God was with us. I can remember hearing people talk about Black Hawk, but I was never afraid. I knew Mama and Papa would take care of me. And I knew God would too. I remember thinking Papa was the strongest man alive. All that changed so fast when Mama died. The McMurray family unraveled.

Sometimes I find myself wondering how Mama felt about being so far from Galena and her dear sister. She lost three children on that homestead. I was too young to remember how they died or when. But I remember the markers. Mama never talked about them other than to say I would meet two sisters and a brother in heaven someday. I remember Mama talking about Aunt Martha, too, but I can not remember a single time when she talked about the life she led in Galena. And it must have been a charmed life with church socials and quilting parties and afternoon teas. She never talked much about my grandmother and grandfather either except to tell me they both believed in Jesus and were in heaven and I would meet them someday, too. Aunt Martha told me my grandfather made his money as a smelter and Grandma was a Good Christian Woman. She died of consumption just like Mama did and my grandfather died of brain fever.

I never thought to ask more. I was so young and it never seemed to matter.

Now I have a hundred questions and will never know the answers to the least of them.

The weather is turning cold. Beth is down with fever again. I wish Doc was here to tell me what to do. I dont want to lose her like I lost my little Deborah.

Beth seems better. It snowed today. It did not stay on the ground around us but was still worrisome. We can see the mountains white above us. I have never seen anything so majestic and beautiful or terrifying. Kavanaugh said we have to push harder and make the foothills before the snows move down.

James is sick with mountain fever. Matthew and I are driving the wagon while Hank tends what few stock we have left and Beth sees after her father. Nellie is weak with dysentery.

Kavanaugh has sent Joshua ahead with Binger Siddons and Ernst Holtz. They can move faster without us and bring us help.

I could not help but cry when Joshua rode out of sight. He is slipping away from me a little more every day and I do not know how to hold him. James says I have to let go of the boy. My head knows it, but my heart says different.

I was his age when Sally Mae pushed him into the world. She died without ever looking at him. All his life I have loved him. In a strange way he is more part of me than my own babies. Maybe I love him so much because I had to fight so hard to keep him alive. I dream sometimes of him laying in his mother's blood crying. I took him to my heart then and will bear him there until my days end. He clung to life when his mama did not care and his father wanted him dead. Now he is hungry for more of life and I am afraid to let him go and find it. What I fear most is he will ride away and never come back. Just like Matthew did.

Kavanaugh touched me last night. It was just a brush of his hand over my hair as I was sitting near the fire worrying about James. I know he did not mean for me to know he touched me. But I felt it just the same. Feelings came up inside me I can't describe.

I did not look up at him afraid of what I would see in his eyes or he would see in mine.

I have wondered on occasion why he agreed to be scout for us and then why he said he decided to come along to California. Now I know. Maybe I knew the moment he looked at me in that mercantile back in Independence and I have just been fooling myself.

And James knows too or he would not have said if he dies I will be safe with Kavanaugh.

James is sleeping better since his fever broke and I am much relieved though still worried about him. He is slow in getting his strength back. Beth is doing better than her father. The mountain air seems to agree with her. She gathered flowers today and made a wreath for me. She is a dear thoughtful child who always wants to please everyone. She watched over Deborah. Now she seems to watch over me.

Matthew likes to tell stories. He is good at it. He will be happy when we get our land and I can dig through the trunk Aunt Martha bought me. His books are in it.

Nellie lets me read from her Bible in the evening. It is noisy getting started because everyone wants to hear their favorite. Beth likes the story of Ruth best. Nellie's favorite is Esther. The boys would rather hear the battles of King David. Wells likes the story of Gideon. He says it shows how God can take a cowardly farmer and turn him into a mighty warrior able to save an entire nation from destruction. James says he just likes hearing me read.

A great valley stretches out before us and the land looks rich and green from fall rain. Joshua has come back to us and says we are three days from Sutter's Fort.

We are all thankful the journey is almost over.

We had happy surprises when we arrived at Sutter's Fort. Virgil Boon and Ruckel Buckeye are here. They had a falling out with MacLeod and left the train at Fort Hall. They followed the Snake south and followed the Humboldt by the same route we did, but they took the Carson River route over the mountains. They said they passed one of the most beautiful lakes in God's creation.

They reached the fort two days ahead of us.

Wells and Nellie are going to take land north of Sutter's Fort. They take the ferry across the river tomorrow.

I am much aggrieved. I thought we would live near the Doanes who have become such wonderful friends. But James told me this morning he has decided we will go clear to the Pacific. Sutter bought Fort Ross from the Russians and says the land is rich there for farming.

If there is a ship waiting, my husband will want to board and sail until we reach China! And if he does, he will be going on alone.

We said good-bye to the Doanes this morning. I have been crying all day. James is not saying much. He is wise to keep his silence.

Joshua and Kavanaugh have gone ahead to see the lay of the land.

We saw Indians today. They are of the same kind we saw working at Sutter's Fort. They were gathering grain and roots in the marshes.

The wind and rain is bitter cold. We have crossed a range of hills and come into another valley. Mexicans came upon us and said the land is taken by Mariano Vallejo. They said we are welcome to come and winter at his rancho. James assured them we are only passing through and thanked them for their kind invitation. He told them we are heading north until we find the Russian River. He asked where is a good crossing and they told him. Sutter told us the river will be low enough to cross easily if we reach it before the heavy rainfall. Joshua has gone ahead to see if that is so.

The Russian River was wide but not too deep to ford. A day after we crossed, the skies opened up and it has been raining heavy upon us ever since. The river swelled so fast I could scarce believe it. Nellie would say God was with us and that's why we made it across.

Matthew is sick with fever. I have a touch of it myself.

Each day gets harder.

We are wintering in a valley northwest of the Russian River. The Russian Fort is still days away, but I can go no further. I was sick in the wagon the day the decision was made to stay here. The cramps were hard upon me and I was sure I was going to lose the baby. We stopped mid day to let me rest. When we started out in the morning, there was a crack and the wagon dropped. When it did, two wheels split.

Our axle is broken and two bolts are missing. James and the children have looked all day for them and can not find them and we have no spares.

I have not said so, but I am relieved we can go no further. If the axle had not broken, we would still be westering. It is like a fever in James. He thinks what is over the next mountain will be better than what is here. This is good land with timber for building and plenty of water. What more does he want?

Kavanaugh is gone. He and James had a falling out. It almost came to blows. It all started because James wants to go on to Fort Ross. He was all for leaving the wagon and packing the rest of the way but Kavanaugh would not let him. He said— Mary Kathryn has gone as far as she can go, man. Have you

no eyes in your head? And James got all red in the face and told
him I was none of his business. Kavanaugh said that might be
so, but it was time to build a shelter and wait out winter. James
accused him of tampering with the wagon. Kavanaugh said
nothing to that. James ordered him to leave. So he did. He got
on his horse and rode away without so much as a by your leave.

I wonder if he did do what James says. If so, I am grateful
to him. This child bears down upon me as the others never did.
Another day and I would have lost it and maybe died as well.

James is talking about building a cabin. It will be hard work,
but I am eager to have a roof over my head again. I do not want
this baby born in a covered wagon.

I am feeling much stronger. Staying in one place does wonders
for a body. James still talks of moving on after the baby comes.
I hope he will change his mind.

I keep telling him this is good rich, dark soil, with plenty of
earthworms and few rocks. We will not find better to build our
home.

James has started breaking the wagon down. He is going to
rebuild it into two carts like the Mormons use. He said we still
have two good wheels and not much left to carry. I guess I will
be walking again.

We ain't going anywhere. Looks like we are just going to die
right here. One by one.

James is dead.

I dont know what to do.

I can make no sense of anything. I can not even think.

God, why do you hate me so much?

CHAPTER 19

"I'M WAITING FOR SOMEONE," Sierra told the waitress. "A glass of water will be fine until she arrives." Providing Audra came at all.

It had taken the better part of two days for Sierra to gather enough nerve to call Audra and ask her to lunch. She'd expected Audra to refuse or say something painful. Instead, she had said simply, "Where?"

Sierra hadn't been prepared for that. "Wherever you'd like."

"The club. One o'clock on Thursday. Is that all right?"

"Eleven thirty would be better for me, Audra. I'll be on my lunch hour."

"Fine," she said in a clipped voice. "I'll be there."

Sierra arrived early and saw Meredith sitting alone in the

lounge. She joined her for a few minutes, reminiscing and catching up on news.

"That makes three of us," Meredith said when Sierra told her she and Alex were getting a divorce. "Eric dumped me for a younger, richer model, and Lorraine finally divorced Frank. Luckily, she got herself a first-cabin attorney. She's on a Caribbean cruise right now. And guess who's paying for it?"

"How's Ashley?" Sierra said, sorry to hear so many sad tidings.

"Bulimic. She collapsed a few weeks ago and is in counseling now. She looks like she's a survivor of the Holocaust."

A few minutes before Audra was due to arrive, Sierra wrote out her new address and telephone number. "Please call. I'd love to have you come for dinner. Mondays and Fridays are best for me. Pick a date and let me know."

Meredith looked at her with a bemused smile. "I might just surprise you and take up your invitation."

Sierra bent and kissed her cheek.

She was checking on her reservation when Audra arrived. Blushing, she extended her hand. "Hello, Audra."

After a brief hesitation, Audra took her hand. "It's good to see you again, Sierra."

"Your table is ready, Mrs. Madrid. Right this way."

They sat in a quiet alcove between some ferns. Sierra had asked for a private table and given the young man a healthy tip to ensure it. Audra didn't say anything after she ordered white wine. Sierra ordered a lemon-lime. Maybe it would settle her stomach.

Taking a breath, she blew it out slowly and lifted her head. "I've had a lot of time to think things over, Audra. You were right about everything. Not the least of which, you were right about the way I treated you. I wanted to apologize to you in person."

Audra stared at her for a long moment. "Well . . . ," she said slowly. "I came prepared to defend myself. I've gone over my side of our conversation a hundred times over the last few days. One word of condemnation and I could've nailed your ears to the wall. And here you go, taking the wind right out of my sails." She lifted her wineglass. "Congratulations."

Sierra didn't know what to make of her words. She'd known this meeting would be difficult. Clenching her hands together, she prepared herself for whatever Audra had to say. She'd keep silent and *listen* if it killed her.

Audra gave a soft mirthless laugh. "I *am* a snob, Sierra. I *am* a social climber. The one thing I've always wanted—and found absolutely impossible—is to fit in. The only person in this world who really loves me is Stephen. God knows why. From the time I was a child, I've had one great talent: alienating people."

She fumbled with her silverware and then, as though catching herself in a terrible faux pas, put her hands in her lap. She looked across the table, directly into Sierra's eyes, and tipped her chin. "Sometimes, I'd see a look on your face that made me cringe inside. That time on Rodeo Drive, for example, when I bought that ridiculously expensive dress and asked you why you didn't buy something, too. I don't even know why I did it. To put you in your place, I suppose. But you looked at me, and for just an instant I saw myself through your eyes. It wasn't pretty." Her hand shook slightly as she lifted the glass of white wine again. "So, for whatever it's worth to you, Sierra, I apologize, too. Truce?"

Sierra felt a sudden rush of warmth toward this woman she'd always seen as her enemy. She caught a glimpse of Audra's insecurities and loneliness and ached for her. Lifting her glass of lemon-lime, she smiled. "I think we can do better than that, Audra. We can be friends."

When Audra said Alex and Elizabeth didn't seem to be getting along, Sierra asked that Alex be considered a forbidden subject. "It's over, Audra. He's with someone else. It hurts to talk about him."

"It's not over until you're divorced."

"I signed the papers for him last week. It's only a matter of time."

An odd look crossed Audra's face. For a moment, she seemed desperate to offer some advice. Then, showing uncharacteristic sensitivity, she changed the subject.

They parted amicably. Audra said lunch would be on her next time. "I'll take you to La Serre."

"You will not," Sierra said with a laugh. "One of the things that used to bother me most was knowing I couldn't reciprocate. So you can treat me next time, if you like, but after that, we're going Dutch and someplace the average Joe can afford or we don't go anywhere at all."

"Oh, all right," Audra said, pretending to be annoyed.

Sierra returned to work feeling elated. She had gone to lunch expecting to face Audra's disdain and condemnation. Instead, she had come away with a new friend, one she might have had three years ago if she hadn't been so caught up in herself.

❖

When she arrived home, the children were already there, Clanton working on his math at the kitchen table while Carolyn talked on the telephone to Pamela. "Marcia says to say hi, Mom."

"Tell her hello back and remind her we're going shopping this Saturday." Alex was taking Clanton to Magic Mountain again. Friday afternoons, he always picked up Carolyn and spent the evening with her.

Dropping her purse on the counter, Sierra slid onto one of the kitchen stools and began opening the mail. In the pile was a course catalog from a local junior college. Scanning it, she saw several business courses that would help her at her job. While practical, they didn't look as interesting as one titled "Creative Decorating on a Limited Budget."

She chuckled. Now, there was a course that sounded right up her alley. But she'd already done all the decorating she could afford for the time being, and she had several projects that were yet to be completed. The old armoire that had belonged to Alex's parents was stripped and ready for staining, and she had the fabric she wanted to cover the wing chairs. She'd also bought the acrylics to start on the flower-and-leaf trim she'd drawn for Carolyn's bedroom.

Tossing the catalog aside, she picked up the bill for her car insurance. Since she had traded in the BMW for a Saturn, her rates had dropped drastically.

Carolyn hung up and slid off the stool, opening the refrigerator. "I'm hungry. What's for dinner?"

Sierra grinned. "How about hot dogs with macaroni and cheese for a change?"

"Aw, Mom. Can't we order Chinese tonight?"

"Not tonight, honey," she said, opening a letter from Alex's parents. She wrote to them once a week as she'd always done. They were inviting her and the children to spend Thanksgiving with them. María tactfully mentioned Alex had plans to go East this year. When she finished the letter, she left it out so the children could read it.

It was a long drive to Healdsburg, but it was time. She hadn't been home since her mother died.

The telephone rang again. "It's for you, Mom."

She took it. "Hello?"

"Marcia said you signed the divorce papers."

Her heart jumped at the sound of Ron's voice. "News travels fast," she said, keeping her tone light.

"I heard about it the day Marcia did. I waited this long so you'd have a chance to adjust."

Sliding off the stool, she put the kettle on. Audra claimed there was nothing like a cup of herbal tea to settle jumpy nerves. Ron asked about the children and her new home. She didn't have to ask where he'd gotten her telephone number. Marcia would have given it to him three weeks ago, along with the news of her divorce.

"Do you see Alex very often?"

"When he stops by to pick up one or both of the children," she said, sensing his caution with her. He was sensitive enough not to ask if Alex was planning to marry Elizabeth Longford.

Ron told her Judy's baby was crawling and Arlene had taken two weeks' vacation in Baja. "She came back tanned and sassy."

Sierra laughed. She'd forgotten how easy it was to talk to him. Relaxing, she asked about several of the teenagers she'd worked with while at Outreach. He told her one was back in high school and another had moved to Kansas to live with her grandmother. He filled her in about several others who had entered the program. They talked for over an hour before Ron said, "I'd like to take you to dinner Friday evening," and obliterated Sierra's sense of security and ease.

"I don't know, Ron. I'm not sure I'm ready."

"I'm asking you to dinner, Sierra. I'm not asking you to marry me."

"I know, but I have a feeling the one might lead to the other."

He gave a soft laugh. "That was frank. Am I that transparent?"

"You were open and honest, Ron. I was blind and stupid."

"You were trying to keep your life together."

"I'm still trying."

"Welcome to the human race," he said. "Look, what if I promise I won't even try to hold your hand for six months? Unless you give me permission to do so, of course."

She laughed. "It would be *such* a relief not to have to fight men off," she said dryly. He teased her for the next five minutes, making light of her concerns in order to alleviate them. "Give me some time to think about it," she said finally, noticing the way the children were looking at her. They knew it wasn't their father on the telephone.

"I'll call you Friday."

She had a feeling Ron knew Friday evenings and Saturdays were Alex's time with the children and her time alone to think. Marcia knew, and it seemed whatever she knew, Ron knew.

"Who was that?" Clanton said when she hung up the phone.

"Ron Peirozo."

"Hey! Are we going sailing again?"

She looked at her two children and saw the idea didn't seem to bother them in the slightest.

"Maybe."

I have been going over it again and again in my mind.

I want to figure out what could have happened. James said he was going down to the stream to try to catch some fish for supper. When he did not come back by dusk, I sent Hank to fetch him. Hank came running back screaming Papa was in the creek and would not get up. He was dead when I got to him.

It took the two of us to pull James up onto the bank. He was white and bloated and had a cut on his forehead. He must have slipped on a rock, fallen, and hit his head. He must have been knocked senseless. How else could he have drowned in less than a foot of water.

Events are plaguing me. I can not think of anything but the Horrible Thing I did to James.

I had to use the horse to drag James's body home. I washed and dressed him in clean clothes to prepare him for burial. I was so tired by the time I finished, I could do no more until morning.

Joshua dug the grave, but it took all of us working together to half carry, half drag James to his resting place. I knew it would be a fearsome thing to get him in it and did not want the children to see. Worst of all, I could not leave the blanket on James. We have none to spare and winter upon us. So I told Joshua to take them back to the wagon.

I unrolled James out of the blanket and he went down into the earth with a terrible thud. And then I cursed him. I was so mad at him that I had to do it. I cursed him for dying and leaving us. I cursed and wept and covered him over with dirt.

And now I can't stop thinking about him down there in the cold.

How could you leave me like this, James? How could you bring me and our babies two thousand miles and then die at the end of the trail? I should have listened to Aunt Martha and married Thomas Atwood Houghton. I would have been living in a nice warm house with plenty of food. My children would be warm, fed, and safe.

You never even thought of building us a cabin and now we are left here in the wilderness shivering in what is left of our wagon. You never thought about how few supplies we have left and winter on us. You just had to keep looking west, didn't you, James? You just had to keep on wondering what was over the hills. You never had a single thought what would happen to us if anything happened to you! And what will happen to our children if I die having this baby you put in me?

I hate you, James Addison Farr. I hope you rot in hell for what you have done to us.

I don't mean it. I'm so scared, James. What am I going to do without you? Where do I go to find help? How are we going to survive in this wild place?

There is this terrible silence without you, this ache inside that gets heavier every day.

Better had it been me who died. You would have known what to do to keep the rest alive.

I used the last of our salt pork and flour this morning. The rain is heavy upon us. The cold goes into my bones. Joshua says we should go on to the Fort. I am too sick to make it. I told him to take the children and go.

We ate the last of our beans tonight. Joshua leaves in the morning for Fort Ross. Hank, Matthew, and Beth will not leave me. Joshua said he will ride west as far as the ocean and then head north. He is riding James's horse and taking his own for packing. I gave him what money we had left for supplies. It was the last of what Aunt Martha give me.

God, please, help him find his way there and back to us.

Joshua has been gone four days. We have no food and no ammunition. The fish are not biting.

God, I won't ask You to help me. But please help my children.

You must be watching over us, God. I can think of no other reason for the Strange Occurrence.

A grizzly came into our meadow. I called a warning to the children. The boys made it to the wagon, but Beth froze. I told her to run, but she was too scared to move with that she-demon coming straight for her and making a roar from hell itself. I never even stopped to think. I just started running for her and praying. Oh, God, did I pray. Out loud. The words just came pouring out of me in Pure Terror. I have not prayed so hard since Mama was sick.

And You answered! You told me to sing to that beast from hell and I did. Oh, I did. I thought I must be going crazy with fear, but I did it anyway. I remember now MacLeod told the men guarding the stock once to sing to the animals during a storm. And we were in the midst of a storm, hard rain, thunder and lightning and that Terrible beast coming from the woods. I sang loud enough to wake James. I sang whatever came into my head, mostly hymns Aunt Martha used to play on the piano and Mama taught me. Hymns I had not sung in years. They come back. The bear was up on two hind legs and only twenty some feet from us. I thought we were dead for sure. That grizzly was eager to tear us limb from limb and there I stood with Beth tucked behind me singing like a crazy woman.

But that bear stopped! Oh, Lord, she did. She came down and cocked its head, and looked at me. I did not look it in the eyes but up at heaven, singing with all my might. The beast moved its head back and forth. I was afraid my voice would dry up, but it did not. The words kept coming back to me, one hymn after another. The bear stayed right there and listened for so long I thought my hair was turning white! And then she just lumbered off, calm and quiet as you please and disappeared into the woods.

I sank down on my knees and laughed and wept and held

Beth to me. She said—Mama, it was a Miracle. And all I could say was—Yes, A Blessed Miracle.

I feel changed inside myself. Something gave way or cracked open or something.

Oh, Jesus, You are there! Mama was right after all.

CHAPTER 20

SIERRA HAD ALWAYS LOVED walking along Mathesen Street in the fall. The trees were orange and gold, the light breeze crisp, the air clear. She'd taken the children down to the Plaza and bought them donuts from the deli while they wandered around, looking in shop windows.

Now, going up the steps of the old house, she felt the tug of grief again. When they drove up the drive last night, she'd expected to enter a cold, empty house. Instead, someone had turned on the furnace. A fire was going in the parlor, the screen in place and wood in the basket. In the kitchen was a Pyrex dish of warm enchiladas and a note from Alex's mother.

We look forward to seeing you and our grandchildren tomorrow. Dinner at three.

Love, María and Luís

She called them to let them know she and the children had arrived safely and to thank them for their thoughtfulness. "Your brother gave us the key," María said. "We left it under the mat on the back porch."

She called her brother to let him and Melissa know she'd arrived. "We'll come by tomorrow morning," Mike said. "There's something I need to talk over with you. It's important."

"What time?"

"Eleven. We're supposed to go to Melissa's parents for turkey dinner. We'll have to leave by one to get there on time."

"Eleven it is."

❧

She and the children had just shrugged out of their coats when Mike unlocked the door and his family poured in. For a few minutes, all Sierra could hear were the excited voices of reuniting cousins. She kissed her niece and nephews and announced she had brought back a bag of donuts from the deli.

Mike got right to the point. "A couple wants to buy the house and turn it into a bed-and-breakfast."

Sierra's stomach dropped. "Buy the house?"

"They've been looking for property in the area for over a year. They liked this house. Apparently they stopped by once, and Mom invited them in for coffee and cookies. She gave them the grand tour but said she wasn't interested in selling. She told them to check back in a year or two. They took her at her word and came by a week ago. When they found out Mom had passed away, they traced me through the church pastor."

"Did you tell them we don't want to sell?" Sierra said.

Mike exchanged a look with Melissa. He sat down and leaned forward, his hands clasped between his knees. "No, I didn't. I wanted to talk it over with you first."

"I thought you loved the house as much as I do."

"I do, Sis, but I've already got a home in Ukiah. My business is there. If I were to sell out and move, I'd want to go farther north to Garberville. Or Oregon. I haven't the money to hang on to this place for sentimental reasons."

Sierra got up and walked over to the fireplace. She ran her hand along the dusty mantel and looked at the old Seth Thomas mantel clock. It had run down months ago. Even with the furnace on, the house had a musty smell of disuse.

"The only other alternative is to rent the place out, and I don't want to do that either. I've heard nothing but horror stories from friends who've rented property and had their places destroyed. The law being what it is, someone can move in and wreck a place before you get them out."

Melissa rose. "I'll make some coffee," she said softly and left the room. Sierra knew her sister-in-law was making it clear to both of them that she had no say in their decision. It was up to them what they did about the house.

Her family had lived in Sonoma County for over a hundred years. Mary Kathryn McMurray had been the first one to put down roots in the fertile soil now covered by tract houses. Ah yes, Mary Kathryn McMurray, who had come with all the eagerness and joy that she herself had felt when Alex had moved her to Los Angeles!

"Do you want the house, Sis?"

Oh, God, do I have to give up my home? You know how much I love this old house. What do You want me to do?

Again, the answer was clear. *Let go.*

"Sierra?"

She leaned her head against the edge of the mantel. What

choice was there? "No matter how much I want it, it's beyond possible. I don't have enough left of my inheritance to buy out your share in it, and then there are the taxes." She lowered her hands and turned. "And I just bought my condo. I'd take a loss if I tried to sell it now with the market being what it is. That's why I got it for such a good price in the first place. And then, if it did sell, I'd be out of work up here."

"Do you want the house?" he said again.

She knew her brother would bend over backward to make things easier on her, even at cost to his own family finances. "I want what's best for all of us," she said quietly.

"So what do you think that means?"

She forced a smile for his sake. "What's this couple like?"

A look of relief filled her brother's face so that she knew exactly what he wanted. No more burdens to bear. And could she blame him? She was the one living in Los Angeles, too far away to pitch in and help with maintaining the house. He had been taking care of everything since their mother had died.

"They're nice people, in their midforties, financially set. They've been living in San José for the past twenty-two years. They have two children, a boy and girl. The boy's off at Bible college studying to be a pastor. The daughter's married with a baby on the way. Jack's hobby is woodcrafting, and Reka's into gardening."

Sierra thought of her mother's backyard going wild. It would be nice having someone pour love back into it and make it bloom again. Hadn't Mom invited these people in for coffee and cookies and given them a grand tour? Hadn't she been the one to say come back in a year or two? She'd known she'd be gone by then. Full realization struck her, tightening her throat with tears. "It's just like Mom to tie up all the loose ends, isn't it?" she said with a smile.

"Yeah," Mike said, his voice husky with emotion.

"So," she said more lightly. "Do you have their number?"

He nodded.

"Why don't you call and ask if they'd like to come up on Saturday and we'll talk turkey."

He laughed, his eyes moist. "Sure."

❦

She debated telling María and Luís the next day. They were upset enough over Alex's broken marriage, without adding to their worries of never seeing their grandchildren. One word about selling the Mathesen Street house and Thanksgiving would be ruined for María, who lived for her children and grandchildren.

There were a dozen running around when Sierra arrived. Clanton and Carolyn piled out of the Saturn and joined in the games. They remembered their Spanish, picking it up as though they'd been jabbering it nonstop at home.

Luís hugged her tightly when she came into the house and then kissed her on both cheeks. She hadn't seen him since Alex had left her, and his greeting brought a lump to her throat. María was right behind him, crying, and talking in rapid-fire Spanish.

Alex's brothers and sisters treated her with the warmth they always had. His older brother, Miguel, a vintner for one of the Sonoma wineries, even flirted outrageously with her. His sister, Alma, let it slip that Alex had brought Elizabeth Longford home for a few days to meet the family.

"Papa wouldn't let them stay here. He said Alex could take her to a motel room, but he wouldn't have them sleeping together under his roof. Alex rented a suite at the Doubletree. She refused to come back with him the next day. Alex and

Papa had words. He's called and talked to Mama, but I don't think he and Papa have talked since."

Grandfather. Father. Son.

Sierra changed the subject, but Alex's name kept coming up. And then he called. He talked to his mother. Then he talked to Clanton and Carolyn. Papa went outside for a walk. When he came back, Alex had long since hung up. For the rest of the evening, she could feel Luís watching her. María, too.

God, how much we hurt others without even thinking about it. We think we can make a decision without it tearing other people's hearts in two.

Sierra took Clanton and Carolyn aside when she found an opportunity. "How would you feel about coming and spending a few weeks with your grandparents next summer?" From their eager responses, she knew she could approach Luís and María about the idea. She found the chance while helping María wash and put away dishes.

"Would you and Luís like to have Clanton and Carolyn spend a few weeks with you next summer?"

María started to cry. *"Sí, sí,"* she said. "As often as possible. What about Christmas?"

Sierra hugged her. "We can't come Christmas, Mama. We're in a pageant at the church. Easter. We'll come for Easter, if that's all right with you."

"Sí. You come home Easter."

❖

Most of the relatives had already headed home to Santa Rosa or Cloverdale or the Bay Area where they lived. Clanton and Carolyn were the last of the younger generation lounging around in the small, neat country house on the edge of the vineyard.

"The family is scattering," María said, teary as each one left. "Alex off in Connecticut—"

"Mama!" Luís hissed and gave Sierra an apologetic look.

"It's all right, Papa," Sierra said, trying to ease their discomfort. "I know about it." The children reported everything, even when she wished they wouldn't.

Luís walked her to the car. "When are you and the *niños* leaving?"

"Sunday morning. Early. It's a long drive."

"I'm going to six o'clock Mass." He looked old—old and hurt—and she loved him unbearably.

She kissed his cheek. "We'll meet you there."

He cupped her cheek. "My son is a fool."

Sierra's eyes filled. "No, Papa. *I* was the fool."

Dear Lord, since that bear I have been thinking.

And I have been looking and seeing lots of things different from before. It is like something changed inside me. It seems to me everything around me now cries out You are here. You have put Your stamp on every created thing. I can hear Mama from so long ago pointing out flowers and trees and birds and animals and saying how they are all gifts from You. She said to me once that You decorated the world from the depths of the sea to the heavens just for us.

Maybe I am wrong, but I do not think You did all that purely for our pleasure. I think now You did it so we could see You.

I see things differently now, Lord, and spent a good part of my day choked up with grief over the hard things I have said about You.

It rained today and I kept thinking how it washes

everything clean and the earth drinks and becomes fertile. Aunt Martha used to talk so much about the Word being a double-edged sword revealing to us our sins so that we could confess and ask forgiveness and receive Your Mercy and Grace. The *so that* part always eluded me. Now it seems to ring in my ears day and night.

And I was thinking too about time. I suppose You do not have need of it, being God and all, but I am glad I have more of it.

The fog last night reminded me of how clouded my thinking has been where You are concerned, Jesus. I could feel the oppressing Fears that have been my companion for so long closing in again like that misty gray blanket. I was awake most of the night worrying over so many things. And then Dawn came pink and orange and took my breath away and the fear with it. How could I think of dying and my children starving before such Glory?

A good night's sleep is a precious thing, Lord. Sometimes I am so tired I ache for rest and sink into a cottony place where even hard ground feels like a feather bed. Maybe tonight will be like that now that I have told You what has been on my mind.

I guess if You heard my prayer over that bear, Lord, You can hear me about this. We are hungry, Jesus. We made do with two fish Hank caught today, and I am thankful to You for them. But it is not enough to keep us going. So, I am asking You again to save us from death. Please, Lord, help us again or we will starve just like those poor folks who did not make it through the mountains.

~~~

CHAPTER 21

"WHAT HAPPENED?" Sierra said when Clanton unlocked the door and walked in at three in the afternoon on Saturday instead of ten in the evening when Alex usually brought him home.

"He dropped me off," he said, slinging his backpack onto the wing chair she'd just finished recovering.

"Did you have a fight?"

"Not with him."

The look of defiance on his face and swelling across his left eye made her stomach drop. Had Alex hit him? "Did you say something to Elizabeth?"

"Yeah, you could say that, but she said something to me first."

"What?"

"She told me to take out the garbage." He gave a defiant

335

snort. "Yeah, right, like I'm the one living there all week. I told her she could take out her own trash. I'm not her personal servant. Then she launched into this lecture on how she had to give up every Saturday with *Alex* so he could be with his snarly, snot-nosed son."

She could feel the heat of anger rising and fought to remain calm. "Were those her exact words?" Elizabeth worked with Alex every day of the week. She spent every night in his bed. She had him all to herself on Sundays. And she was complaining about the *one* measly day a week he spent with his two children?

Didn't you?

"Close," Clanton said, giving her an odd look when she winced. "She called me a 'half-breed.' So I told her what she was."

"Oh, Lord," Sierra murmured and sat down on the couch. "What did you call her?"

"You know what I called her. I said it in Spanish, but I guess she got the point. What did you expect? She started in on *you*." His eyes glittered. "She said the reason Daddy left was because you were a dull housewife with no brains and no class. And it looked like I took after you. So I told her she wasn't any better than a common hooker, just a little more expensive on the upkeep. She slapped me across the face and called me a 'foul-mouthed, uncouth little wetback.'"

His eyes lost the heat of anger and glistened with hurt. "I didn't see Dad standing in the doorway. I've never seen him look so mad. He told me to get my things. He was taking me home. And she just stood there, smirking."

Sierra ached for him. She remembered the way Alex had looked at her the day he'd left. She'd never known a man whose eyes could be so hot and cold at the same time. "Did he say anything to you on the way home?"

"Nothing," he said softly. He turned away slightly, but she'd already seen his tears. "I'm going to my room."

Sierra wanted to call Alex and give him a piece of her mind about the fiasco. She wanted to take Elizabeth Longford into a ring and pulverize her.

A wetback?

A plague on her, Lord! Forgive my wrath, Father, but I'd like to rip her heart out!

If she didn't *do* something, she'd explode.

"Clanton? I'm going for a walk. I'll be back in a little while."

Her walk turned into a run, and by the time she returned, she was streaming sweat, her lungs heaving, her heart pounding like a kettledrum. She leaned over the kitchen sink, gasping for air, and splashed water on her hot face. She drank a few sips of water. The telephone rang.

Snatching the kitchen towel from the oven handle, she dried her hands. It rang again. If it was a telephone sales call, they were going to wish they'd picked another number. As it turned out, she barely said hello before Alex was making demands.

"Let me talk to Clanton."

God! Help! If You can cool me off, cool me off fast!

"Why?" she said tautly. She wasn't ready to hand her son over to Alex again. Not for a long, long time.

"Why're you breathing like that?"

"Because I went out for a run, okay? A hard run! It was either that or buy a shotgun and shoot *two* people!" She slammed the phone down.

It rang again. She gritted her teeth. Turning, she caught a glimpse of her face in the glass front of the cupboard-mounted microwave. Amazing! No steam coming out her ears, but she looked rabid enough to begin frothing at the mouth.

Clanton came out of his bedroom. "Aren't you going to answer it, Mom? It might be Dad."

"It *is* Dad. If you want to talk to him, you answer it, because if I do, I'm going to tell him what he can do with himself and that . . . that *broad* he's living with." She stalked off down the hallway and went into her bedroom.

The telephone stopped ringing. She could hear Clanton's voice, subdued, scared, his heart in Alex's hands. He didn't say much more than hello. Apparently, Alex wanted to do all the talking. She clenched her hands, wanting to pick up the extension and listen to the other end of the conversation. Instead, she sat on the bed and prayed through clenched teeth.

Strike them with lightning, Lord. Open the earth and swallow them.

Alex and Clanton didn't talk long.

Expecting to have to pick up the pieces, Sierra came out to find her son rummaging through the refrigerator. "What did he say?" she asked, surprised that he was hungry. She always lost her appetite after a big fight.

Clanton straightened, a carton of milk in one hand and a Tupperware container of cold homemade enchiladas in the other. "He said he wasn't mad at me, but it was going to be a week or two before he could see me again."

"And?"

"And, that's it." He shrugged, set the milk on the counter, and put the entire Tupperware container into the microwave.

❖

Sierra heard from Audra before Alex called again.

"He left her."

"Excuse me?" Sierra said, startled. Audra hadn't even identified herself before blurting out the news.

"Alex left Elizabeth," she said. "He packed everything and walked out on her last Saturday. They had a huge brou-haha over something, and this after Vesuvius erupted in Connecticut."

What had happened in Connecticut? She didn't have a chance to ask before Audra rushed on.

"Alex came in Monday morning looking like thunder and told Steve to assign someone else to his work. He doesn't want her within ten feet of him. She came in an hour later. Steve talked with her briefly. He wouldn't tell me what was said, other than that she gave notice and left."

"Where's Alex living?"

"In a hotel in Beverly Hills, I think. Do you want his number? I could get it for you."

Sierra thought about it for a moment. "No. He'll call when he's ready. He told Clanton he'd be in touch with him and Carolyn in a week or two."

"You don't want to talk to him?"

"I've said enough already." As usual.

❦

Alex didn't call. He came by. Not on a Friday evening, but on Saturday in the pouring rain. She heard the doorbell ring and Carolyn and Clanton talking to someone. They knew not to let strangers in, so she assumed it was one of their friends stopping by or her neighbor, Frances, with another delicious treat she'd concocted as an experiment for her gourmet cook-ing class.

"Nice."

Her heart jumped at the sound of his voice. Luckily, she was firmly planted on the ladder, where she was just dabbing the last touches of gold acrylic paint on the sunflower design she'd drawn along the wall of her bedroom. She'd completed half of it over the last two weeks.

She looked over her shoulder and saw Alex leaning against the doorjamb, watching her. "I wasn't expecting you." Amazing how calm she sounded.

"I know." His glance flickered over her.

Sighing inwardly, she looked away. The last thing she needed was his disdain. Why did he always have to catch her looking like someone who had crawled out of a bag of rummage sale rejects? She brushed a strand of hair back from her eyes, wondering how much paint she had smudged on her face. She had at least a dozen stains on her paint shirt, and her cutoff Levi's should have been trashed years ago. There was a hole under the right back pocket big enough that he'd be able to see the cotton flowered underpants she wore underneath.

"Are you taking the children out?" she said, feigning indifference. Maybe someday her heart wouldn't leap into her throat at the sight of him.

When he didn't say anything, she looked back at him and found him staring at her canopy bed. She felt the heat come up into her cheeks when he looked up at her again.

"What happened to ours?"

"I sold it."

Had he winced, or was she just imagining it? He looked around the room. "I guess it wouldn't've fit in here anyway." His glance halted abruptly on the old armoire she'd refinished. He'd moved it into the garage when Bruce Davies had redone the house, intending to take it to the dump. He'd left before he had the chance.

Something flickered across his face as he looked up at her again, his eyes barely grazing hers. "I need to talk to you," he said grimly and went out.

She shut her eyes for a minute and then gathered her brushes, balanced her easel, and went down the ladder. She put everything down on the drop cloth and went into the bathroom to wash her hands. Glancing up into the mirror, she saw tendrils of sandy-blonde hair curling in all directions. A smudge of green was across one cheek, some brown on her nose. Picking up the soap and washcloth, she scrubbed her face. That done, she debated changing into clean clothes and dismissed the idea. Raking her hands back through her hair, she French-braided it quickly.

When she came into the living room, she found Alex looking at Mary Kathryn's quilt, which she'd mounted on the wall. Audra had taken her to a museum a few weeks ago, and she'd seen a quilt mounted in the same way. Liking the effect, she'd promptly come home, purchased material to make a sleeve, and bought a wooden drapery rod. Audra had been impressed when she saw what Sierra had done. Even better, they'd spent the better part of an hour talking about the quilt.

"It belonged to Mary Kathryn McMurray," she said to Alex. "She was a relative of mine who came across the plains by wagon train. She settled in Sonoma County in 1848. That's her trunk at the end of the couch." It served as a side table. She winced, realizing the old brass lamps Alex hated so much sat on top of it. Naturally, she had to draw his attention to it.

He didn't say a word. The condo rang with silence. Frowning, she realized what was wrong. "Where are the children?"

"I asked them to make themselves scarce for a little while. Clanton said he'd play billiards at the clubhouse, and Carolyn said you wouldn't mind if she went to Susan's."

She was immediately filled with trepidation. Why would

he send the children off unless he was going to say something to her he knew she wouldn't like? What could he want?

Oh, God, *the children!*

"Don't look at me like that, Sierra."

"Like what?"

"Like a deer caught in headlights. I'm not planning to run over you."

She turned away and went into the kitchen. "Would you like some coffee?" Her mind was racing. She didn't even notice if he answered yes or no. She wished she had read the divorce papers over more carefully. What had they said about custody of the children?

"I'm not living with Elizabeth anymore."

"Audra told me." She fumbled in the cabinet for coffee and filters.

"Audra? I didn't think you even spoke to her anymore."

"We get together for lunch every few weeks."

"Since when?" he said in surprise.

She measured coffee. "Since I took her to lunch and apologized."

Alex came over and sat on a stool on the other side of the breakfast counter. She could feel him looking at her. Like a bug under glass. She poured water into the coffeemaker, refusing to look back at him.

"What do you and Audra talk about?" he said carefully.

"We don't talk about you, Alex. That was one of the first ground rules I laid down." She shrugged. "She broke it last week."

"Did she tell you what happened?"

"She said Elizabeth quit and went back East."

"I moved out after the little altercation with Clanton."

"Can we talk about something else, please?" she said, uncomfortable. She didn't want to hear about his love affair with Elizabeth Longford. She didn't want to hear about his broken heart. She didn't want to hear about how difficult things were for him. She wanted him to get to the point and leave so she could breathe normally again.

"I want to spend more time with my children."

Here it comes, she thought.

"You're shaking," he said softly.

"I'm not giving you custody, Alex. Whatever it said in those papers I signed and gave you, I'm not—"

He lifted his hands. "Relax. I'm not asking for that. I wouldn't. They're happy with you. I just want . . ." His voice trailed off, and he uttered a soft curse, dragging his hands back through his hair. He looked at her again, and she noticed the lines around his eyes and mouth, the unveiled pain in his eyes. "I just want a chance to be a part of their lives again. A couple of hours on Friday with Carolyn and a few on Saturday with Clanton isn't enough."

She almost reminded him that was more than he'd spent with them *before* he left her and moved in with Elizabeth.

Lord, keep me silent. Make my words sweet. Help me see his side of things more clearly and with more compassion than I have in the past. Give me Your eyes, Father.

Alex searched her face when she said nothing. Turning her back on him, she took two mugs down from the cupboard and filled them with coffee. She didn't invite him back into the living room. She liked having the breakfast bar between them.

"Thanks," he said flatly and put his hands around the mug as though to warm them. She couldn't remember ever seeing him nervous before.

"You can see the children whenever you want, Alex. As long as you don't prevent them from continuing what they're doing."

"Such as?" he said, eyes narrowed slightly.

"They both go to church youth group on Wednesday nights."

"Which church?"

The issue of religion had never been important to either of them. Now, it was of tantamount importance to her. "The church where we were playing baseball."

He thought about it for a minute, troubled. "Mama said you went to Mass with my father."

"The children went to catechism in Windsor."

"I know. Are they still going?"

O God, help me. I don't want to start a war with Alex, but I want my children to have a personal relationship with You. I don't want them to have to go through a priest or be bound by guilt or penitence.

"No," she said, clasping her own mug between both hands as he had done. "We're happy in this church, Alex."

"You don't think God's in a Catholic church?"

She felt the weight of Madrid family tradition behind his question. These were his children.

"I think God is wherever He chooses to be, Alex. Catholic or Protestant, it doesn't matter. When I sit with your father and mother, I know they love the Lord as much as I do. They've loved Him longer and harder. But this church is where I found my way home, Alex. It's where the children are learning the meaning of Christ's love. These people aren't just friends. They're like family. Dennis especially. I'd be dead and Clanton still wouldn't be speaking to you if not for him."

He frowned heavily, eyes fixed on her. "What do you mean, *dead*?"

She smiled, shaking her head at the memory. "Let's just say I was driving a little fast one day when Dennis pulled me over. He's a highway patrolman. He gave me my first and, I hope, *last* speeding ticket."

He looked at her, his eyes intent, searching. "I'm sorry, Sierra."

She knew he meant he was sorry about everything. "Don't be. It's the best thing that ever happened to me." If she hadn't hit rock bottom, would she have ever seen how much she needed the Lord? Would she ever have been soft fertile soil for the seeds that had been scattered throughout her life by a dozen different people? Would she have ever understood Jesus' love for her?

Alex got up and left the breakfast bar. She watched him move around the living room. He paused before the quilt again and rubbed the back of his neck. He had always done that when he was past exhaustion or depressed about something. In their earlier years, she'd rubbed his back and told him how she loved him. Often, they ended up in bed together, forgetting everything but the pleasure they found in one another.

Her skin grew warm, remembering.

It was better not to think about those times.

"How would you feel if I leased a condo in this complex?"

Her heart stopped. "I beg your pardon?" she said weakly.

Alex turned around and looked at her. "I said, how would you feel if I leased a condo in this complex?"

She recognized that look. Double-barreled, point-blank determination. "*You* want to live in a *condo*?" She couldn't believe he would even suggest it. He wouldn't even marry her until he had found them a small house to rent. "*I don't want to share walls with someone else,*" he'd declared. She would have lived in a shack as long as she could be with him.

His eyes never left her as he said, "There's a condo

available for lease. I wanted to talk it over with you before I signed the papers."

"You always swore you wouldn't live in an apartment or condo."

Alex looked around the living room. "It's bigger than I expected, and I haven't heard any noise while I've been in here today."

"My neighbors are working." Not that they made all that much noise when they were home.

"Then you object."

"I didn't say that. I—" She closed her mouth, deciding she'd better think before she went further. She felt a hint of panic stir. It hurt every time she saw him. Was she going to have to see him *every* day? And what if he found some other woman to move in with him? Or he started dating any one of a dozen attractive single women living in the complex? Or . . .

A hundred painful possibilities leaped into her mind, sending shards of pain through her. What if . . . what if . . . what if . . . ?

Alex sat down on the stool again and clasped his hands loosely on the breakfast counter. "I want to share the responsibility of the children with you again. I could keep them when you wanted to go out."

"Out?" As in dating? Was he hoping to marry her off? Ron would be delighted to know that.

"Clanton said you wanted to take a college class but didn't want to leave them home alone any more than you have to already with work. If I was living within a few doors of you, you could leave the children with me."

"It was an afternoon class, Alex. I was working."

"You don't have to work."

"Yes, I do."

His eyes darkened. "Not if you'd start accepting the money

I've been sending you, instead of doing whatever you've been doing with the checks."

"Live on alimony, you mean? No, thank you. Every time you send me a check like that, I'm going to tear it up and flush it down the toilet!"

"Why do you have to be so pigheaded stubborn?"

"Look who's talking." She tried to calm down. "Alex, I've seen what living on alimony does to other women. Some of them can't get along without it. Or they feel they deserve more and more. Cost-of-living increases. Petty vengeance. You want me hanging around your neck like a millstone for the rest of your life? Alimony is as bad as welfare, and I want some self-respect out of this whole mess. I may not be living in the fancy neighborhood we used to, but I'm making it on my own. I'm *happy* here, and I'm paying my *own* bills."

"I should be paying for your support. We've been married thirteen years."

"We *were* married, and you can consider the debt forgiven."

He started to say something and stopped. Letting out his breath, he raked his hand back through his hair. "Look, I know it's because of what I said to you that day I called after seeing the house in the real estate section. I hurt you. *Dios*, don't you think I know it?"

"Maybe it was that in the beginning," she said frankly, "but not anymore." Covering her face, she took a breath and released it slowly, trying to rein in her emotions. She lowered her hands to her lap and looked him in the eye. "You mention money, Alex, and I see red. It was one of the buttons you used to push all the time."

"I have a few buttons of my own," he said, eyes hot. "One of them is the fact you won't accept any kind of help from me. You used to lean on me, Sierra."

"Yes, I did. And look where that got us," she said, feeling the prick of tears. She swallowed and pressed her lips together, trying to think of words gentle enough, yet strong enough, to explain her position. "You've been very generous with the child support, Alex, and I'm thankful. Let's just leave it at that."

"Do you use any of it?" he said bitterly.

Heat filled her. Was he accusing her of misusing their money? "I put it in their savings accounts," she said, hurt and angry. "Some of it I use for clothes. I have records of every cent you've ever given them."

"No doubt, but what about that private school? Why aren't they going anymore?"

"Because they hated it! Because Clanton was suspended twice, and Carolyn was on the verge of ulcers trying to get straight A's."

"Why didn't you tell me what was going on?"

"And if I had? What would you have done?"

"Tried to help!"

She searched his eyes, wondering if he really would have.

"What did you think I'd do, Sierra?"

She bit her lip and said nothing. She'd been so convinced he would accuse her of being a rotten mother, the same way he'd accused her of being a rotten wife. She'd been afraid to tell him, ashamed she couldn't fix things on her own.

"Talk to me, Sierra."

"It doesn't matter now. You were busy at the time."

Color came into his face and a look of bleakness. "I'm not busy now. I'm going to be working a lot less at the office. I've already talked my plans over with Steve. He's putting up the money for the equipment. It's already ordered. All I need is a place to put it."

Why hadn't he made the same arrangements a year ago? It might have saved their marriage.

She caught the direction of her thinking and halted. If she condemned him, she'd have to condemn herself. Everybody has twenty-twenty hindsight. She could see her own mistakes with heart-wrenching clarity.

"I'll make it easy, Sierra. A simple yes or no. Yes: I sign the lease. No: I don't."

She wanted to say no. She wanted to avoid more pain. She wanted to avoid seeing him with other women. She wanted to avoid seeing him at all. She knew that was impossible. And if she said no, how would the children feel when they found out? Angry? Betrayed? They loved him. They wanted to see their father as often as possible. How could she be selfish and deny them that right? Besides, they *needed* him.

"I haven't said anything to the children," he said quietly, "and I won't if your answer is no."

She was touched by his sensitivity. It was one of the things that had made her fall in love with him in the first place, that and his male machismo, as her father once termed it.

"Go ahead and sign the lease."

His dark eyes took on a familiar glow before he looked away. "Can I use your telephone?"

She frowned slightly, uneasy. "It's over there."

Pulling a business card from his shirt pocket, he wasted no time punching the number. "Roberta Folse, please. Roberta? Alex Madrid. The answer is yes. How soon can you take care of the details? Good." He glanced at his watch. "I'll meet you there in about thirty minutes." He dropped the receiver lightly into its cradle.

Turning his head, he smiled at her. Her stomach dropped the same way it had the first time he'd looked at her. *"Gracias,"* he said. *"Las cosas serán más fáciles."*

She forced a smile in return, thinking how wrong he was. Things would not be easier. At least, not for her.

"I'll give the children a call later this evening. In the meantime, you can tell them I'll be moving into one-sixteen early Wednesday morning."

When he left, she groaned aloud and buried her head in her arms. "Oh, Lord, it's going to be a hundred times worse than I thought."

Alex would be only three doors away.

I never expected You to send a heathen to answer my prayer.

But I reckon You do things however You please.

An Indian came to the edge of our meadow today. Beth saw him first and thought he was a mighty strange looking deer. Well, I saw he was not a deer at all, but a man dressed up in skins and a deerhead mask. He had a bow and arrows and stood watching us intently. Hank was all for getting the gun, but I said we would wait to see what he would do. Besides, what good is a gun with no ammunition.

I remembered what Kavanaugh told us about the land belonging to the Indians and how we should give back something for the privilege of traveling through. Well, we are going nowhere, Lord. So I wondered what that Indian was thinking while he stood there looking at us. I wondered if he was angry that we settled in his pretty valley without asking first. So I told the children to stay by the wagon while I went to see if I could make peace with him. I know a few signs from having watched Kavanaugh.

I could not offer the Indian a bite of food to eat as we have no food for ourselves. The Indian was of small stature, muscular, and has dark eyes and hair. I could not guess his age.

He did not know what I was waving about, so I offered him the only thing of real value I own—the pretty cross necklace Aunt Martha gave me when I left Galena. He was well pleased by the gift but did not know how to work the clasp. I helped him. He disappeared into the woods and I thought that was the end of it. It was not.

He came back again later carrying a small deer, fresh killed. He laid it at my feet and made it clear it was a gift. I wept as I thanked him. Before he left us, he made his name known to me. Koxoenis. From his gestures and pantomime, I think it means Bringer of Meat.

I am weeping again. I am so undeserving and yet You have provided food for me and my family. We will not starve after all. The children are at this moment asleep with full stomachs for the first time in many, many days, and I have You to thank. You sent Koxoenis.

All hope was lost and is now revived in me again.

Joshua returned today with beans, salt pork, flour, coffee and powder, shot and lead. We are living with abundance. I told him about Koxoenis. He is very eager to meet him. I asked if he had seen Kavanaugh. Joshua said no. One of the men said Kavanaugh headed north to Oregon.

Koxoenis came back today. I was pleased to see him. He stood at the edge of the meadow until we waved an invitation for him to come to us. I think he is shy. Joshua made signs that he was welcome to share our supper. He ate sparingly of our bread and would not accept even a small portion of the venison he brought to us. When we finished, he motioned for us to follow him. He did not go more than a hundred feet from our fire when he used a digging stick he was carrying to pull up some plants. He gave them to me and made signs that the roots and leaves are good to eat. With a shy smile, he ran off into the woods again.

All this time we were so hungry and food was growing within reach.

Lord, I am having Terrible Trouble with Joshua. He is Intent on Doing Something! He keeps talking about looking for Koxoenis or going to Sutter's Fort or down to Monterey. He wants to go his own way whatever way that might be. He is not the boy I know him to be and he is not the man I think he can become. He is one huge pain in my heart and gut.

It has gotten me thinking how much Trouble I have been to You.

I am Truly Sorry, Lord.

I remember how full of Wrath You were at those Israelites You brought out of Egypt. They kept whining and fussing and complaining like Joshua does now. And like I was doing before the Day of the Bear. I remember too how You wanted to wipe all those Israelites off the face of the earth, but Moses begged You not to.

Well, Lord, I know just how You feel because I wanted to wipe Joshua off the face of the earth today. He made me so mad I was shaking with it. I said things I should not have said. But maybe that was better than what I wanted to do. Lord, if I had had a cane I would have beat him with it. He was none too happy with me either.

How can you love someone so much and still get so mad you want to kill them? I saved his life fourteen years ago. And today I was in the mood to take it.

Joshua is not much help to us, Jesus. He would rather be at Koxoenis village learning their ways than staying here and helping us in ours.

Would You please Do Something with him, Jesus?

I give him to You cause if I don't, I swear that boy won't live to spring.

Koxoenis came back today. He was curious about the wagon. I wonder what kind of house he lives in. I showed him inside our poor makeshift abode. Then I offered him fish stew, bread, and coffee. I said to the children it would be interesting seeing where and how he lived. Joshua said he will go with him and find out. I said if Koxoenis welcomed him, he was free to do so. Joshua made sign language with him and they went off together. They have been gone all day, but I have no fear my son will come to harm. You sent Koxoenis to us and he has proven to be a kind and generous friend. I think Joshua will have much of interest to tell us when he returns.

Joshua said Koxoenis lives in a village several miles southwest of us. He said the others were frightened when they got there and spoke harshly to Koxoenis for bringing him. I suppose there is good reason. When I think of the way the poor Indians were treated at Sutter's Fort, I shudder. Sutter fed them in troughs like animals and used them like slaves.

Joshua said Koxoenis has a wife and two small children who run naked wherever they please. He said his house is made of bark, bound tules, and mud and is weather tight and warm inside. His wife cooks a mush made of acorns in a basket by stirring hot stones! The chief has a great store of food stuffs and gives generously to the people.

Koxoenis showed Joshua other foods that grow around us. Joshua said he will teach Hank, Matthew, and Beth how to find these plants come daylight.

Joshua and Hank have been digging all day. Joshua said Koxoenis's people dig down two feet and build the dome house over the pit. He can build this house in a few days while it will take weeks of effort to build a cabin. Our duck cover is torn and leaking. We need shelter from the cold California rain.

Joshua has made a pole frame work over the pit and is covering it with tiers of bark and tules. He has the boys and Beth mixing mud. Thankfully, we have had two days of easier weather. The clouds lie over the ground like a blanket.

We are now living in a hut like Koxoenis and his people. I wonder what Aunt Martha would think of me living like a savage. I must admit living in this hut is far better than living in our wagon. We moved in as the rains started again, and we are dry and warm.

Thank You, Lord, for putting a roof over our heads again.

CHAPTER 22

THE CHILDREN REPORTED everything to Sierra whether she wanted to hear or not. "Dad rented some furniture," Clanton said after his first visit. "He's got a new couch and a couple of swivel rockers. He bought a whole wall setup with a big-screen television and stereo, and you should see his computers!"

Carolyn was more impressed with the white rats he'd purchased for her and kept at his place. "They're so cute, Mom. I call them Peaches and Cream. They're both males, so we won't have any babies."

"Well, that's nice."

"And he has an aquarium. Just a little one for some pretty goldfish."

Lures.

Clanton and Carolyn began spending more and more time with Alex. They'd come home from school, scarf down snacks, rattle off some news, whiz through their homework, and take off for *his* condo. She began wishing she'd said *no*. She missed the sound of their voices, even the strident ones when they were fighting. Sometimes she resented how eager they were to be with him, and then she was always struck with guilt afterward. Sometimes she found herself aching with loneliness.

Is it a sin, Lord? You're supposed to be enough. I love You. I do. Help me to accept these changes and not be so jealous and needy. Help me to know in my heart You are sufficient. Help me rest in You.

Choir helped. On those evenings, she and the children walked to church together and then went out to a family café afterward for a late dessert. Sunday was the one precious day a week, for she had the children all to herself. They went to church early and didn't get home until almost one in the afternoon. After a late lunch, she walked back to church with them so they could take part in the youth activities and she could attend the evening Bible study.

Gradually, she felt less alone. She used the time the children were away to study and finish all the little projects she'd laid out for herself but never had time to do. She turned on the radio and listened to a Christian station that played contemporary rock, free to sing along without anyone listening to her but the Lord.

Christmas drew closer. Rather than be elated, she was depressed. All her shopping was done, the packages wrapped and hidden in her bedroom closet and under the bed. The children knew better than to go poking around in her room after Thanksgiving. She'd begun addressing Christmas cards the first week of December and had started her letters. She always wrote to everyone. It was the one time a year when she could catch up on all the news from friends and family.

Ron called again. "You sound a little down."

"I'm writing Christmas letters, and I get a little depressed every time I have to write, 'Mom died of cancer, and Alex and I got a divorce' over and over again. Just the sort of glad tidings friends like to read at Christmastime."

"Would a proposition help cheer you up?"

Her mouth twitched. "That depends."

"Strictly honorable, I assure you. I'm having a Christmas fund-raiser at the Hyatt Regency, and I'm in desperate need of a pretty hostess."

"To serve drinks and appetizers?"

"No. To stand beside me and greet guests, the kind of guests who have lots and lots of money and love giving it to good causes like Los Angeles Outreach."

"Are any movie stars going to be there?" she said, teasing.

"A few."

"You're kidding!"

"I take it you might be interested."

She feigned hesitation. "Well, I don't know. Is Hugh Jackman attending?"

"No."

"Then I don't—"

"I'm begging."

She laughed. "I'd love to help out and you know it. How dressed up do I have to get?"

"Very. I'll be in a tux."

Ron gave her the details. He would pick her up early. The fund-raiser included a full-course dinner and dancing. "It'll go until the wee hours," he warned her.

Clanton was just going out the door when she hung up the telephone. "Honey, would you tell your dad I need to talk to him? It's important."

The telephone rang a few minutes later. "What's up?" Alex said.

"Can the children spend the night with you on December 21?"

"Spend the night? Where are you going to be?"

"At a fund-raiser with Ron. He said it'll be late before I get home."

"I haven't got any extra beds."

He sounded so cold. "Maybe I can borrow a couple of sleeping bags." Maybe he had made other plans, plans she didn't want to hear about. "Never mind, Alex. I should've thought it through before asking you. Carolyn's been wanting to spend the night with Susan, and Clanton can always go to—"

"I'll stay with them over there," he said firmly. "We'll do something fun for the evening, and I'll wait at your place until you get back."

"It's going to be very late, Alex."

"You've got a comfortable sofa."

"Are you sure?" He sounded less than pleased about the whole thing.

"Yeah, I'm sure."

Taking a deep breath, Sierra called Audra and told her she'd been invited to a formal fund-raiser and was going to be acting as hostess. "I need to find a dress."

"How much can you spend?"

"Don't even think about Rodeo Drive."

"What size are you?" When Sierra told her, she said, "Great. You can borrow one of my gowns. When can you come over?"

By the time Sierra got there, Audra had already picked out the dress she thought Sierra should wear. After seeing the others, Sierra had to admit she liked it the best. It was a deep-red velvet that fit her perfectly. "I bought it for a Christmas party four years ago and never wore it," Audra said, admiring it on Sierra. "My feet are a little bigger than yours, but I know just where you can get some satin pumps and have them dyed to match," she said while snapping on a gorgeous necklace that glittered like diamonds.

"These aren't real, are they?" Sierra said, fingering it.

"Zirconia. Stop sweating." She handed her matching pierced earrings and then helped her snap on the bracelet. Stepping back, she looked her over. "Perfect. It looks better on you than it did on me." She went back into her closet and came out with a fur coat.

"Not on your life!" Sierra said, backing up. "Absolutely not, Audra. If I damaged it or it got lost, I'd kill myself."

"I thought you were going to say something about all the little animals that lost their lives to make it."

"Well, that, too," Sierra said, making a quick calculation. It would take a lot of cute little minks to make that coat.

"That's what I told Steve, but men just don't think about those things when they're trying to show the world how successful they are." She carried it back into the closet. "I wear it to the opera once in a while just so he won't get upset about it. No one harangues me there. Oh, *good*! I knew I bought something to go with that dress." She came back out with a red velvet, satin-lined cape. She draped it over Sierra's shoulders and took a step back. "Take a look at yourself."

Sierra did, and her mouth dropped open. She looked like someone else, someone who'd stepped out of a fairy tale. "I remember feeling this delight as a little girl up in the attic dressing in grown-up clothes with my best friend." Laughing, she looked at Audra in the mirror. "What do you think?"

"I think you look fantastic. Does Alex know you're going to this affair with Ron Peirozo?"

"He's babysitting."

❧

Alex came early on the night of the fund-raiser. She'd told him Ron was picking her up at five, and he arrived an hour early.

"Mom, Daddy's here."

"Ask him if he'd like a soda, honey. I'll be out in a little while."

Nervous and excited, she had already bathed and was fixing her hair in a loose French braid. She put on a little makeup, then dabbed on Shalimar before she stepped into her dress. Slipping into the red satin shoes, she put on the jewelry. She was ready half an hour before Ron was expected.

"Mom, you look so *pretty!*" Carolyn said as she came into the living room.

Sierra smiled, gratified that at least one person in the room noticed the change in her. Alex just stared at her. He didn't say anything. What had she been hoping? That his mouth would fall open and his tongue loll out? She put the red cape carefully over the back of a chair.

"Where's Clanton?" she said as she laid her gloves and a red, beaded purse Audra had found on top of the cape.

"Brady's," Carolyn said. He was a friend Clanton had met at church who happened to live in the complex. "He said he'd be home in a few minutes. He's borrowing a video game. Are those diamonds, Mom?"

"No, honey. I wouldn't put my toe out the door if they were."

Carolyn looked at her father. "Don't you think she looks pretty, Daddy?"

Blushing, Sierra avoided Alex's eyes.

"*Sí, tu mamá es muy hermosa,*" he said softly.

Her heart tripped as she looked at him. She looked into his eyes and saw he meant every word.

Carolyn picked up her backpack and headed for her room. Sierra turned, tensing. "Where are you going, honey?"

Carolyn glanced at her dad. "I've got some homework to do."

"Tonight?"

"Just for a while. Daddy's taking Clanton and me to Magic Mountain. I guess I should take a bath, too."

Sierra looked back at Alex and saw the sad smile touch his mouth. "She was watching *The Parent Trap* a few days ago."

She put her hand over her stomach. "Great," she said dully.

He noticed the gesture. "Are you nervous?"

"A little." Less about going out with Ron than she was seeing that look in Alex's eyes. She let out her breath and came around the chair to sit down. The hatch-cover table was between them. She liked having something between them.

Alex's eyes narrowed slightly. "How well do you like this guy?"

This guy? "Ron's one of my best friends."

"How does he feel about you?"

She blushed. "Why are you asking?"

"You quit working for him. I'm curious why."

She almost told him it was none of his business. Considering his own behavior, he had a lot of nerve to ask *any* questions. Instead, she curbed her anger and decided to be honest. "I left because I knew if I stayed, I could end up in an affair with him."

Alex's eyes darkened, not with anger, but with pain. "The way I did."

"I don't want to talk about the whys and wherefores of you and Elizabeth, Alex."

"Neither do I. I want to talk about you."

"What about me?"

"You look . . . radiant," he said heavily. "Are you in love with this guy?"

There it was again, that tone. Was he baiting her? "I was *in love* with you, Alex," she said before she thought better of it. She paused, drawing in a steadying breath. This situation was impossible! "I don't think I'll ever feel like that again about anyone. And if I did, I think I'd run as fast as I could to get away from it."

"The way you ran from Peirozo."

She could feel the prick of tears and fought them. "Are you deliberately trying to spoil my evening, Alex? I *like* Ron. He's kind and fun. I'm looking forward to this evening. I've never been to anything like this. I just want to enjoy myself. Don't you think I have that right?"

"Don't cry," Alex said softly. "I wasn't asking to ruin your evening, Sierra."

"Why *are* you asking?"

"Because I don't want to see you hurt."

She gave a bleak laugh. She had never heard such a flimsy excuse in her life. Especially from him. "*You* hurt me, Alex. Ron doesn't have that kind of power over me."

He leaned toward her, eyes intent, searching. "Don't go out with him tonight."

Looking into those dark depths, she remembered everything from the past. She knew why he warned her. When they were young and deeply in love, when her emotions had crested over some crisis, real or imagined, Alex had been the one to catch the wave and ride the passion.

"I'm not your concern anymore, Alex. I haven't been for eight months." Why should those words bring that wounded worried look into his eyes? She felt compelled to set his mind at ease and gave him a tender smile. "Someone told me to grow up. I have."

The doorbell rang.

A muscle jerked in his cheek and he stood up. "I'll tell him you're not feeling well."

She stood as well. "No, you won't." Truth have it, she wasn't, but she had no intention of leaving Ron high and dry. This fund-raiser was far too important to him and his work. "I feel fine, Alex."

"You're pale." He turned his head sharply as the door was unlocked. "What'd you do? Give him a key?"

"Hey, Mom!" Clanton said, barging in. "Aren't you going to let Ron in?" He stared at her. *"Wow!"*

"You can say that again," Ron said from right behind him. He didn't even notice Alex. He couldn't have been more open in his admiration, which went a long way to bolstering her spirits. Clanton brushed past her in his hurry to dump his soccer gear in his bedroom.

"You take my breath away, Sierra," Ron said, leaning down to kiss her lightly on the cheek. She felt a touch of sadness that his compliment didn't have a fraction of the effect Alex's had. As Ron straightened, she saw his expression alter slightly and knew he had seen her ex-husband. She took his hand deliberately.

"Ron, this is Alex. Alex, I'd like you to meet Ron Peirozo, a dear friend of mine."

Ron held out his hand. Alex hesitated for a fraction of a second before taking it. Neither said anything. They were too busy measuring one another. Sierra knew under other circumstances they would get along very well. They might even be friends. Right now, she was the only common ground— and not one that would bring them together.

Letting go of Ron's hand, she picked up her purse and

gloves. He took the red cape and laid it over her shoulders. His hands gripped her arms gently, drawing her a few inches closer to him. "Ready to go?"

Alex understood the gesture and shoved his hands into his pockets. "Have a nice evening."

Sierra walked with Ron to the door. Ron gave Alex a nod as he opened it for her. "Nice meeting you, Alex."

"Yeah, likewise."

She didn't look back. She didn't dare.

❖

Ron didn't mention Alex, nor did she. He spent the drive to downtown Los Angeles filling her in on the programs at Los Angeles Outreach. "People are going to be asking you questions," he said and made sure she knew what was going on.

As she stood beside Ron and greeted guests as they arrived, she recognized numerous faces and names. Several lingered over her hand, making fulsome compliments. Ron teased her about it over a dinner of prime rib. "I should've brought a whip and chair to keep some of these animals back."

She was proud of Ron and impressed by him as he stood at the podium and gave a flawless and relaxed welcome and presentation. He was as at ease in front of this crowd of socially elite as he was with the children he found in the ghettos and beneath the freeways. She knew that those listening to him would be only too willing to support him and his work. He was sincere, zealous, and accomplishing a great deal. The young men and women serving were all "graduates" of the program. "Talk to them, and they'll tell you the difference Outreach has made in their lives. The Lord has blessed us that we might bless others. . . ."

When the band started playing, Ron led her out onto the

dance floor. "I've already had several pledges that'll cover the next few months' expenses," he said, holding her close. She felt the warmth of his hand at the small of her back and the brush of his thighs. He was a good dancer, smooth and graceful, guiding her expertly. She felt safe and protected in his arms.

After the first dance, she had other partners, all interested in hearing about Los Angeles Outreach and Ron Peirozo. A few asked her about her relationship to him. A few just wanted to get close enough to ask her out. She was flattered but not interested.

Ron danced with her again several times and needled her unmercifully. "I thought you'd succumb to that actor's charms for certain," he said, inclining his head toward a movie star who'd danced with her several times.

"Are you kidding?"

"I saw you swooning when he took your hand."

"That was before I spent five minutes with him. The guy's no better than a neighborhood masher. He asked me to spend a weekend in Hawaii with him. Can you believe it?"

"I believe it. I've had a few licentious thoughts of my own about you this evening. Want to go sailing with me?"

"Knock it off, Peirozo."

He laughed. "See the gentleman over there talking with Arlene? He was just asking me if you were taken."

"Tell him *yes*."

"I already did." Leaning down, he kissed the curve of her neck. Alex used to kiss her in the same place. With him, it had always sent melting heat all through her body and made her knees weak. With Ron, she didn't feel anything but the pleasing warmth of his lips.

She talked with so many people she lost count. She danced until her feet ached, and she relished every minute of it. On the drive back to Northridge, Ron talked about the pledges he'd received and what it would mean to ongoing programs. They'd made enough money in one evening to cover foundation expenses for the next year.

He pulled into the Haven's parking lot and shut off the engine of his Mercedes. Turning to her, he smiled. "Did you have a good time?"

"Wonderful," she said, drowsy. She never stayed up past eleven thirty, and it was almost two in the morning. She felt the light brush of his fingers and looked into his eyes. Warmth and desire were there, unhidden. For one brief moment, she wondered what it would be like to be loved by Ron. "I'd better go in," she said softly.

Sensitive to her feelings, Ron touched her cheek lightly and then got out of the car. He came around and opened her door, handing her out. They didn't say anything as they walked along the pathway to her condo. The porch light was on. She wondered if Alex was asleep on the couch.

Turning to Ron, she thanked him for the lovely evening. "Anytime," he said, leaning down to kiss her cheek. Thanking him again, she took her key from her beaded purse and opened the door. Glancing back, she smiled.

"Good night," Ron said and headed back along the pathway to his car.

Not looking into the living room, Sierra closed the door quietly.

"How was it?" Alex said, snapping Mary Kathryn's journal shut and tossing it heedlessly on the hatch-cover table.

The sound of his voice and thump of the book made her jump. "Wonderful," she said, turning to him. "How was your evening?"

"*Bueno.*" He stood up. He didn't even look vaguely tired. His eyes were clear and sharp. "We went out to eat and then rented a couple of movies."

"Sounds like fun." Her stomach knotted with tension at the look on his face. He was angry, though about what she didn't know. And she had no intention of asking. "Well, thank you for watching the children for me. I appreciate it."

"Sure."

"I'm sorry it's so late."

"You said it would be." He crossed the living room and stood in front of her. A small frown briefly puckered his brow as he studied her face. "I guess I'd better go."

"Yes," she said, having difficulty breathing, "I guess you should." She looked around. "Did you bring a jacket with you?"

"No." His mouth tipped in the sensual smile that had turned her heart over at sixteen. It still had that same effect. "Worried about me getting cold between here and my condo? I'm only three doors away."

"I think you're warm enough." She opened the door. "Good night, Alex."

He paused in the doorway and looked back at her. "Did he kiss you good night?"

She blushed. "Not that it's any of your business, but *no*, he did *not* kiss me good night."

Stepping back inside, he cupped the back of her head and abruptly pulled her forward. Before she could gather her wits, he leaned down and planted his mouth firmly over hers in a hard, hot kiss. He released her as suddenly as he'd held her, smiling sardonically. "You looked like you needed kissing," he said roughly.

Sierra stepped back from him, her heart pounding in her ears.

His eyes went dark as they stared into hers. He took another step toward her. "You still do."

"Don't," she whispered desperately.

He wasn't listening. Kicking the door shut with his foot, Alex caught hold of her and pulled her against his hard chest. His head came down and he kissed her again, with the same devastating effect she'd experienced the first time on the Mathesen Street porch so many years ago. He kissed her as though he never intended to let her go. . . .

For a moment she struggled against him. He dug his hands into her hair until it was tumbling about her shoulders and down her back. He kept on kissing her until her insides began to melt and quake.

Her love and the long months of celibacy and loneliness worked against her. Physical hunger swept through her. Sweet memories pulsed.

Oh, God! Oh, God, this is what You meant it to be between a husband and wife!

Husband.

Wife.

Not anymore.

In the midst of the storm of wonderful sensation came the army of doubts marching through her fevered brain, armed with devastation weapons.

Had he held Elizabeth Longford like this? Had he whispered incoherent words of Spanish as he touched and caressed her the way he was touching and caressing her now? Was she just a substitute? Available. Easy. A quick fix now that Elizabeth was gone.

So convenient, too. Only three doors away.

"Don't cry, Sierra," Alex said raggedly. "*Por favor*, don't cry."

But she couldn't help it. Her body pulsated with need for him while her mind tore her heart to shreds. She drew back as far as she could, her hands clenched. She felt him loosening his hold on her and wept harder. When he stepped back, she covered her face and turned away in complete humiliation.

If he hadn't known how much she still loved him, he could have little doubt now. It must give him a lot of satisfaction to know how easy it was to break down her walls and storm the citadel.

God, I'm such a fool!

"Sierra, I'm sorry . . . ," he said bleakly. "I didn't mean to . . ."

When he put his hands on her shoulders and tried to draw her back against him, she jerked away from his touch. "Just *go*, Alex," she said, hiccuping. "Get out of my life."

The door opened quietly and closed again.

She went to her room, crying, and removed the dress. She hung it up carefully, tears running down her cheeks. She removed the jewelry and put it back in the velvet box. She slipped out of the red satin shoes and stripped off her underwear, then turned on the shower and stepped in. She stood beneath the pounding stream of water and gave in to her grief.

❖

She was still crying when she went to bed. Curling on her side, she covered her head with her pillow. She'd just dozed off when the telephone rang. The clock glowed three forty-five. She wanted to ignore the intrusive ringing but was afraid it would awaken the children.

It was Alex, and he sounded strange. Had he been drinking?

"I don't want to talk to you," she said, starting to cry again.

He wasn't listening. He was talking in Spanish, making no sense at all. Usually she could understand Spanish well, but he was speaking so fast and she was so tired, the words were a blur. She did catch a couple of familiar words. One of which was *esposa*. Wife.

He had a lot of nerve.

"You divorced me, Alex. Remember? Leave me alone."

She hung up. When the phone rang again, she yanked the plug. Covering her head, she wept herself to sleep.

Joshua has been to the village six times in the past month.

Koxoenis makes him welcome. During his last visit, Joshua saw Koxoenis's preparations for another hunt. Koxoenis does not live with his wife or even look at her, but spends most of his time in a sweathouse where he rubbed deer marrow into his bow and arrows. Joshua said Koxoenis spoke to his weapons. He also drank a foul smelling concoction that made him very sick. Perhaps it is some kind of purification rite. After the sickness passed, he rubbed angelica and other herbs over his body and his spear.

Joshua followed Koxoenis to watch. He said Koxoenis mimics the movement of a deer so perfectly he was able to become a member of a herd grazing in a meadow at dusk. The animals were not even aware he was among them until he made his kill. Before dressing the animal, Koxoenis knelt beside it and stroked it tenderly, speaking to it. When the meat was prepared for the people, he did not partake of any of it.

Joshua has learned many valuable things from Koxoenis and his people. He has taught Hank how to make a fish trap and Matthew how to make snares for rabbits. He dammed our creek and threw a root into the water. It stunned the fish so that they floated to the surface. We smoked enough in one of our barrels to last us several weeks.

Joshua also taught Hank and Matthew how to make bolas using the side ribs of wild iris leaves and tying bones to each end. Joshua says the Indians use these simple weapons to catch quail, cottontails, and squirrels. The boys have been practicing diligently. Joshua said the Indians are not as fussy about what they eat as we are, but will dine on wood rats, snakes, lizards, and grubs. He has tried them all and said they taste good. I am not so adventurous.

Beth pulls up cattails and peels them. The stalks are good eating. Other edible greens are in abundance. Come spring, we will have berries. They grow in profusion near us.

Lord, You have made this earth as bountiful as Eden. We do not even have to put a plow to the soil to have food to sustain us. But we will come spring.

CHAPTER 23

"HE'S SICK, MOM," Carolyn said.

Hungover, more likely, Sierra thought, but she didn't say it aloud. Her own head was aching from lack of sleep.

"He didn't answer the doorbell, so I let myself in," Carolyn reported. "He's still in bed, Mom. Daddy's never in bed this late."

Clanton collaborated. "Couldn't you go check on him?"

"He was up late babysitting last night, remember? He just needs to sleep in."

"You're up," Clanton said.

"Couldn't you go see if he's all right, Mom?" Carolyn pleaded, worried.

"And do what?"

"Call a doctor or something," Clanton chimed in.

She'd like to *something* all right, but after last night, she was afraid to get within twenty feet of him.

"Please," Carolyn said.

She looked between her two children and realized if she didn't do something, they'd think she was a coldhearted, uncaring hypocrite of a Christian. Weren't you supposed to *love* your enemy? "I'll take him some chicken soup," she said and took a Tupperware container out of the refrigerator. Frances had given her a batch, swearing it could cure just about anything.

Maybe she should drink some and pray to be cured of Alejandro Luís Madrid.

Clanton gave her the key to Alex's condo. Her heart was in her throat as she unlocked the door and went inside. It was exactly the same layout as hers, but the decor was vastly different. The living room had a big black leather couch and glass coffee table. Modern lamps stood on each side of the room. The wall was solid with electronic equipment: a big-screen television, video player, radio, CD player, game systems, and a quartet of small, but undoubtedly powerful, mounted speakers. The kitchen was spartan, except for the coffeemaker near the sink and the rats in their cage on the end of the breakfast bar. There wasn't much in Alex's cabinets, and only a few pots and pans in the cupboards below. The stove and microwave were both so clean, Sierra knew Alex had never used them. Opening the Tupperware container of soup, she poured a portion of the contents into a big mug, added a little water, and put it in the microwave. Curious, she looked under the sink. The garbage bucket below was full of empty Mexican take-out food containers.

I am not *going to feel sorry for him!*

She went down the hall to the master bedroom and found Alex sprawled on his back, only partially covered by the vibrant Aztec-design comforter. All she saw was muscle, bronze skin, and dark hair. Heart flip-flopping, she looked away and spotted the pullover shirt he'd worn the night before. It was inside out on the floor. Nearby were his Levi's, also inside out, the belt still in the loops. His shoes were on the far side of the room, two dents in the wall above them.

Setting the mug of hot soup down on his side table, she picked up an empty pint of whiskey. In all the years she'd known Alex, she'd never seen him have more than one drink of anything intoxicating. He liked to be in control. She went into the bathroom and tossed the bottle into the trash basket.

When she came back out, she picked up his shirt and pulled it right side out, folded it, and put it on his chair. She did the same with his pants, removing the belt and curling it on the top of his dresser.

Steeling herself, she turned and looked at him. Her stomach tightened as she came over to the bed and looked down at him. He was so beautiful, so perfectly made. He was wearing the gold crucifix his mother had given him. Her heart squeezed tight with pity and tenderness. Frowning slightly, she noticed he'd added something to the gold chain, something she'd returned to him with the divorce papers he'd wanted her to sign.

Why was he wearing her wedding ring around his neck?

"Alex?"

He groaned. Shifting his body, he muttered something in Spanish and opened his bloodshot eyes. He stared up at her as though he couldn't believe she was really there.

"The children think you're dying," she said dryly, crushing the urge to brush the dark hair back from his forehead.

Wincing, he pushed himself up onto his elbows. "I feel like it," he said in a raspy voice. He looked at her again.

She avoided the intensity she saw in his eyes. "I brought

you some chicken soup," she said, nodding toward his side table as she moved away from his bed.

"I didn't mean to hurt you last night, Sierra. I swear—"

"I know. Let's just forget about it." He didn't need to do anything to hurt her. She hurt every time she looked at him. It came with loving someone, even after they'd betrayed you.

As she headed for the door, Alex shoved the comforter back. "Don't go." He groaned in pain as he sat up. Holding his head in his hands, he muttered softly in Spanish. "I've got to talk to you. Just give me a few minutes to take a shower."

"We can talk another time." She smiled faintly. "When you're feeling better."

Dropping his hands, he looked at her bleakly. "I'm not going to feel better, not until I talk things out with you."

She had thought she was finished with crying, but tears sprang to her eyes. "Maybe I don't want to hear what you have to say."

"Maybe you don't," he said, "but I'm asking you to listen anyway. *Por favor.*"

When he stood up, her stomach dropped. She'd forgotten he slept in his briefs. She'd forgotten a lot of things that came back with a rush. "All right." She would have agreed to anything at that moment just to get out of the bedroom and away from him and the feelings he could still arouse in her without even trying.

"Wait here."

"I'll wait in the kitchen."

She searched his cupboards until she found coffee. Her hands were shaking as she made it. She expected to have more time, but he came out a few minutes later, wearing sweats and raking his hand back through his wet hair. He looked handsome even with a hangover. Looking at him, she felt depressed. She was never going to get over him. Never.

"Gracias," he said when she slid a mug of hot coffee across the breakfast bar to him. She had to have something between them, something to fill his hands, something to fill hers. He took a sip. She had the feeling he was bracing himself. He finished the whole cup of coffee before he looked at her. "You're still my wife."

She felt the blood drain out of her face as she stared into his dark eyes. Panic set in. "No, I'm not. I did what you asked. I signed the papers. I gave them to you so your attorney could—"

"We're still married, Sierra."

"Maybe. For a few more months, until the divorce is final."

"Nothing's final, and it won't be. There's not going to be a divorce unless you file against me."

"I don't understand," she said, confused. Hadn't he told her over and over how much he wanted a divorce? "I did what you asked."

"Yeah, but I changed my mind. I didn't give the divorce papers to my attorney. I put them through the shredder at the office."

"You what?" she said faintly.

"I shredded the divorce papers."

"I heard you the first time, but why? Just so we'd have to go through all this misery again?"

"I don't know why I did it at the time, but it turned out to be a good idea."

"A—a good idea?" Did he think he could waltz back into her life and pick up where he left off? Or leave her dangling while he enjoyed himself? She wanted to throw the hot coffee at him. Instead, she slammed her cup on the counter and headed for the front door.

Alex caught hold of her halfway across the living room

and swung her around. "I never loved Elizabeth the way I love you, Sierra. I knew it'd lead to disaster the first time I touched her."

She hit him, a hard right hook square to his jaw, knocking him back two feet. Rage and hurt filled her. She lost control completely and attacked him again. Lunging at him, she pounded at his chest until she realized he was standing and taking it. With a sob, she gave him a hard shove over the back of his leather couch. Grabbing the back of her sweater, he dragged her along with him. They bounced, arms and legs tangling, and rolled onto the floor.

"You *jerk*!" She clambered to her feet, trying to get to the front door again. Alex was faster. He swung himself over the couch and planted himself in her path.

Spreading his hands, he presented himself. "Go ahead. Hit me again. I deserve it."

"Get out of my way!"

"I'm not finished."

"I *am*!"

"You're still in love with me, Sierra."

"I'll get over it!"

"No, you won't. And neither will I. Not ever."

She drew in another ragged sob. "Do you think it makes me feel better to have you say you didn't even love her? Do you think it *helps* to know you threw our marriage away for a fling?"

"It wasn't a fling."

"I don't want to hear about it, Alex. Don't give me the gruesome details. Just get out of my way!"

"Sierra—"

"*Let me out!*"

He caught hold of her shoulders. "My affair with Elizabeth had a lot to do with what you said. I wanted to feel I'd *made it*. Education hadn't done it for me. Neither had money. Daughter of the American Revolution, you said. Remember? A trophy I could hold up to the world to show them Alejandro Luís Madrid was more than a wetback's son!" His eyes were wet, tormented. "You knew me better than I knew myself, Sierra. Until Connecticut. I got a good look at myself there, and I wanted to vomit."

"Don't you *dare* call your father a wetback!"

His face softened. *"Te amo."* He cupped her face. *"Te amo muchísimo."*

She used her knee this time and caught him low and hard. Shoving him back, she made it to the door. "I'm not going to love you anymore, Alex," she said, sobbing. "It hurts too much!"

Yanking open the front door, she fled.

My lying in time is drawing near.

The weight of the baby presses down. I have made what preparations I can and have explained to Beth what she must do to help me. She is younger than I was when Joshua was born, but she is a calm and willing girl and a great comfort to me. I hope she will be strong for whatever happens.

Lord, I am afraid for all my children. Please bring this baby into the world without taking me from it.

I know you sent Kavanaugh to me, Lord, and I thank You that he was obedient and arrived in time. I am sure I would have died otherwise. Joshua had gone off to find Koxoenis and ask if his wife could help me. I was praying for deliverance when someone opened the tule mat cover over our doorway. I have never been so glad to see anyone as I was to see Kavanaugh.

He put his knife in the fire and then cut me. When that was done, he pulled me up so I was squatting. The baby came quick and easy after that. By the time Koxoenis, his wife, and Joshua arrived, my new daughter and I were asleep.

Kavanaugh told me today he will not leave again unless I tell him to go. He did not say more than that, but his meaning was clear. I think I have known he wanted me since the day he looked at me in the mercantile back in Independence.

I have named my baby daughter America Farr. Beth is taken with her and a great help to me. I am slow in mending and still weak. Kavanaugh is tender with me and firm in organizing the children. They do not mind. They have always held Kavanaugh in awe. Especially Joshua, though I sense tension between them now.

Kavanaugh is building us a cabin. He has set the boys to gathering stones for the foundation while he cuts timber. Joshua has not had much to say about anything lately. Something is eating at him and he will not say what. Hank and Matthew and Beth do all the talking.

The rains have been coming down steady for a week, but Kavanaugh and the boys continue to work. The rock foundation is complete and the sills set. Kavanaugh and Joshua work on notching the logs to build the walls.

This evening, we are all sitting around the pit fire. Hank, Matthew, and Beth are about their lessons while Kavanaugh whittles. He will teach the boys when they finish their reading and exercises. I am glad my boys do not fight learning like my brothers did. They must take after Mama. They can all read and write better than my father and brothers ever could, but they are far from Educated by Aunt Martha's standards. I wish

I had not been so foolish as to say I did not want to have a Bible in my possession.

Kavanaugh and Joshua have had a Falling Out. Joshua was swinging at Kavanaugh with all his might, but Kavanaugh blocked aside each blow. I kept screaming at them to stop, but Joshua would not listen. Kavanaugh unbalanced Joshua and took him down on the ground and held him there while trying to talk reason to him. Joshua was in no mood to be reasonable. When Kavanaugh released him, Joshua jumped up and spit on him. I could not believe he did such a thing and thought Kavanaugh would kill him sure. He did not have a chance to do anything because Joshua got on his horse and rode off. I ran after him and asked what had happened, but he would not say. He was crying and said he would not come back until Kavanaugh left.

Joshua has been gone for three days. My heart aches so I can not even eat. It did not take five minutes for me to find out what set Joshua on such a rampage. Kavanaugh wants to marry me. He asked Joshua for permission since he thought he was the firstborn son. Joshua said he saw the way of things and accused him of using him to get close to me.

Kavanaugh and I have had much time to talk about many things. I thought I would be with James all my life. I did not expect to lose him. Yet I know I can not manage on my own out here. A woman with small children can not build a homeplace and plant crops all by herself. And going back home to Illinois is impossible.

I know too that Joshua will not stay with us for long. His leaving us will have little to do with Kavanaugh and all to do with his own nature, though he may be contrary and stiff-necked enough to use Kavanaugh as an excuse. Each

time Joshua goes away, he stays away a little longer. He has
the same hunger to see the world that James had. I am afraid
it is the kind of hunger that will drive him before the wind
all his life unless he faces the Almighty and comes to himself.
I grieve knowing James never did. It must be in the Farr and
McMurray blood to contend with God and everything else.
We either see the light or die looking for it.

I have peace now I never thought to have and wonder often
why I fought so hard in receiving it. Coming to the light does
not mean it is easy watching Joshua wandering in darkness.
But telling him about You does not seem to get his Attention.
I guess I can not expect words to do it. Mama and Aunt Martha
talked to me plenty and I never saw the Truth in what they
were saying.

I have learned a little more about Kavanaugh over the past
days. His full name is Hamlet Bogan Kavanaugh. He is twenty-
eight years old and can read and write. He was born in Boston
to a blueblood father and an actress mother who thought
naming him after a Shakespearean character might lend him
some dignity. He did not think much of the name she gave
him. Despite the fact his mother never married, she made sure
his father paid for an Education. His father agreed to pay for
tutors if she promised to leave him alone. She kept her part of
the bargain. Kavanaugh is his mother's name. She died when
he was thirteen. He went to his father then, was given fifty
dollars and told to leave Boston and never darken his father's
threshold again. He did and has never been back.

I told Kavanaugh he did not have to tell me such Personal
Business, but he said I should know he was born on the wrong
side of the sheets before we get married and start bearing
children together. I became Flustered when he said that. He
seems to have things all worked out in his mind about the way
things will go between us. I asked him what he would have

done had James not died of a Thursday. He said he would have waited however long it took. I asked him how many children he expects to have and he laughed and said one at a time, Mary Kathryn, and gave me such a look I felt it down to my toes.

He is gone now and I can breathe freely without the wild drumming of my heart to get in the way of my head. I sent him away so I could think things through. I was surprised he did not try to talk me out of my solitude. He is a strong man, stronger than James in many ways. But there is not the hardness in him I expected. James ran roughshod over my heart. There was a wildness in him that could never be tamed. It seems so odd now I think about it. James, the farmer, the wild one, and Kavanaugh, the mountain man, so settled inside himself. For all his buckskins and long hair, Kavanaugh is a gentleman who will not take advantage.

I do not want him here when Joshua comes home. My son and I have things to settle between us before I say yes to Kavanaugh.

You do not make things easy, do You, Lord?

Joshua is gone and I sit here wondering if I will ever see him again. My heart aches so, and yet I knew this would come. I have been fighting against it for two thousand miles and it is no use fighting it anymore. He thinks he is a man and he has made up his mind to go his own way. At least he no longer believes Kavanaugh used him to get close to me. Kavanaugh likes Joshua for himself and understands the restlessness in him. Maybe knowing that will bring him back again someday. He made no promises.

He said he is going to ride back to Sutter's Fort and then head north to see what Oregon is like. After that, he does not know where he will go or what he will do.

I wept when he rode away. I kept thinking about those

Israelites wandering forty years in the wilderness and dying within sight of the Promised Land because they were so Contentious. If only they had trusted the Lord, they would have lived out their lives in a land of milk and honey.

I hope it will not take Joshua as long as it took me to find his way through the wilderness to You.

I have been thinking about Aunt Martha so much lately. Sometimes I wonder if our thoughts touch one another across the miles. I wrote her a long letter yesterday, but I do not know when I will have the opportunity to send it.

I think Kavanaugh has changed his mind about marrying a widow with four children. He has been gone twenty-three days.

I have begun the plowing. Hank and Matthew are helping me while Beth minds America. Together we will get a small crop in.

It is Terrible Hard Work, but I think I can manage with the children. We have enough to eat. We have a cabin to keep us safe and dry. We have good land and seed to plant. And we have You, Jesus. Aunt Martha told me anything is possible with God. So I am asking You to help us in this Great Enterprise. We are stuck here, Lord. Help us make the best of it.

CHAPTER 24

Sierra didn't see Alex the next day, and he didn't call the children. She thought it was because of what had happened between them until Carolyn said, "I told Daddy we were in the church pageant tonight. He said he was going Christmas shopping."

Then Clanton hit her with, "Can Dad spend Christmas with us?"

Sierra rebelled. "No, he cannot spend Christmas with us."

"He'll be all alone," Carolyn said, clearly distressed by the idea. "He'll be lonely. Couldn't we ask him? Please?"

"We'll talk about it later," she said, hoping in the interim Alex would be run over by a truck or kidnapped by terrorists. "Right now, we have to get to church and into costume."

During the next few hours, she relished being caught up in stage jitters and the excitement of getting ready to perform.

Once in costume, the choir members gathered together and prayed that their performance would do more than entertain. They prayed it would open the hearts of those listening to the music and the reenactment of the birth of the Messiah.

Once the program started, her nervousness cooled. She had practiced so much, her part all came back the moment she moved onto the platform some parishioners had built to extend the choir loft. She gave herself up to the music, singing from her heart, feeling the joy of the Christmas story and its meaning to the world.

Joseph traveled from the town of Nazareth in Galilee, on one side of the church, to Judea, the city of David called Bethlehem, on the platform, where he registered himself and his young wife, Mary, for the Roman census ordered by Quirinius, governor of Syria.

"And it came about that while they were there, the days were completed for her to give birth. And she gave birth to her firstborn son; and she wrapped Him in cloths, and laid Him in a manger, because there was no room for them in the inn."

Clanton was one of the young shepherds who knelt before the angel Gabriel as he sang his solo announcing the good news of great joy: "For today in the city of David there has been born for you a Savior, who is Christ the Lord." The adult choir joined as tiny pinpricks of light shone on the ceiling, and then the new, bright star appeared in the "heavens."

"Glory to God in the highest, and on earth peace among men."

Joining Gabriel was the heavenly host of children in white, complete with wings and halos, their voices blending in sweet harmony. Among them was Carolyn. The music expanded again as the adult choir joined the children's voices. Sierra's heart beat fast as the crescendo came, filling the church to the rafters with praise-glory sounds for the newborn King. Jubilation!

Oh, Jesus, Jesus, would that I could feel this joy every day of the year.

Her whole body felt alive and warm with the love and excitement of the Lord's birthday. She forgot everything else, especially what the Lord expected of her.

The pastor gave a prayer following the pageant, and refreshments were served in the social hall. The last person she expected to see was Alex. When she spotted him standing on the far side of the room, looking handsome in black slacks, a gray silk designer shirt, and black sports jacket, her heart dropped into the pit of her stomach and bounced up into her throat. He was talking with Dennis; it didn't look like a casual conversation.

"Hey! Dad's here," Clanton said, still holding his shepherd's staff.

"Yes, I see him." The rat. The creep.

Deserting her, Clanton set his staff before him and parted the sea of choir members and guests to get to his father. Carolyn spotted Alex soon afterward and fluttered over in her angel costume.

Little traitors.

Sierra was still reeling from what Alex had said to her in his condo. *"I never loved her the way I loved you."*

Yeah, right! If he loved her so much, why had he walked out? Why had he told her he despised her and couldn't wait for a divorce? Why had he looked at her as though he hated her?

The way you're looking at him right now, beloved?

She turned away, selecting a cookie from a large platter. Chocolate, her favorite. It tasted like dirt. All the joy she'd felt half an hour before while singing praises to the Lord evaporated, boiled away by resentment and anger.

He's ruining my Christmas, Lord. Couldn't You remove this ache I have when I see him? He cheated on me! The least You could do is give him some kind of awful disease.

"Daddy said he's flying to San Francisco tomorrow," Clanton said. "He's spending Christmas with *abuelo y abuela*."

Bitterness surged through Sierra. He didn't even have the sensitivity to stay at home alone for Christmas and suffer! No. He had to go to Healdsburg and enjoy a wonderful Christmas with Luís and María.

Of course, she completely disregarded the fact that they'd invited her to come, too.

Carolyn sighed expressively. "I wish we could go."

So did Sierra, but she wasn't about to admit it. "We'll go at Easter."

It was too expensive to fly three people north to San Francisco. Worse, she'd have to look at *him* over the dinner table and face the hopes of Luís and María on top of it.

Besides, she couldn't afford the time off work.

On top of that, it was too late to make reservations. All the flights would be booked solid over the holidays.

Excuses flooded her mind as she waited for Alex to come over and speak with her. Visions of him on his knees danced in her head, but he didn't come within twenty feet of her. Instead, he left quietly, unseen.

When she realized he was gone, she told herself she didn't care. But it galled her nevertheless.

❈

The telephone rang as soon as she walked through the door. "Cooled off yet?" Alex said.

"Why would I be hot?"

"You tell me."

She banged the receiver down, hoping she'd burst his eardrum. The telephone rang again. Snatching it up, she snarled, "I don't want to talk to you. I don't want to see you. I don't want to hear about you. I want to forget you live on the same planet I do."

"Merry Christmas to you, too!" Ron laughed.

Her face went hot. Covering it, she plunked down on a barstool. "I'm sorry. I thought . . ."

"I was Alex. I take it you two are talking again."

She gave an unladylike snort. "If that's what you call it." The doorbell rang. Carolyn *ran* to it. And guess who was standing under the porch light, his arms laden with Christmas packages, all professionally wrapped? He couldn't bother doing such menial labor himself. Wrapping had always been her job, along with the Christmas cards and shopping.

Sierra hissed when she inhaled. "I have to go, Ron. I need to find some Raid."

Alex didn't stay long, and after one brief glance at her face, he concentrated entirely on the children. "I'll be back December 28," he said, kissing Carolyn. "Want to see me out?" he said to Clanton.

"Sure."

When the door closed behind father and son, Carolyn turned and looked at her. "This is going to be the *worst* Christmas of my life!" Tears streaming down her face, she ran to her room.

Sierra had a strong feeling it wasn't going to be very joyful for her either.

And she was right.

In years past, Alex had fixed the turkey. Her father had taught him how. "It's a Clanton tradition. The men cook the bird on Thanksgiving and Christmas." She fixed the bird this year and it was dry as a bone. Gravy helped, but not much.

Clanton and Carolyn made no complaints, but she could tell they would have preferred Mickey D's to her festive efforts. The best thing about the turkey was the skin.

As soon as the dishes were in the dishwasher, presents were distributed. The children were clearly more excited about what Alex had given them than what she'd bought. Who could blame them? His gifts were frivolous, hers practical.

She played Christmas music on the radio, but it sounded flat and depressing. When she wasn't fuming, she ached with loneliness, thinking about Alex laughing and having fun with his father and mother, sisters and brothers, nephews and nieces, cousins, second cousins, *third* cousins. The neighbors would probably come to join in, for heaven's sake!

All through the evening, she kept remembering Christmases past. While the children played, she sat watching television. Dickens's *A Christmas Carol* was on. She identified with Scrooge. Then, to cheer her up even more, she watched *It's a Wonderful Life*. She made it all the way to George Bailey jumping off the bridge before she turned it off.

I'm a new Christian, Lord, and this is the worst Christmas of my life!

Who do you say that I am, beloved?

Lord. You are Lord.

Then obey Me.

"Do you have a headache, Mom?" Carolyn said, coming into the room and seeing her rubbing her temples.

Headache, heartache, soul ache.

❧

The last thing Sierra wanted to hear Sunday morning was a sermon on forgiveness. Peter's denial. Jesus had known his disciples' weaknesses. He had warned Peter. "The spirit is willing, but the flesh is weak." He had also known Peter would repent. "When you turn . . ."

Like Alex saying he was sorry, saying he loved her.

I can't, Lord. I can't forgive him and go through it again!

But the words from the pulpit kept hammering the wall around her heart. "If you love Me, you will keep My commandments . . . love does not take into account a wrong suffered . . . love bears all things, believes all things, hopes all things, endures all things."

Sierra kept remembering the look on Alex's face when she told him she didn't want to love him anymore. It hurt too much. It was true, but that didn't matter. She loved him whether she wanted to or not. Still, what kind of love tore people apart inside?

Nothing made sense to her anymore, least of all the war of emotions going on inside her. All the while she had thought there was no chance at all of reconciliation. She thought Alex hated her. She'd finally seen her part in the disintegration of her marriage. She had accepted blame.

Now, he wanted forgiveness . . . and she wanted revenge.

Unsettled, her conscience pricking at her, she shut her eyes tightly.

I'm not like You, Jesus.

"We can do all things through Christ who strengthens us," the pastor said.

I don't feel strong, Lord. The only solid things I feel are anger and hurt. How do I forget what he's done to me? How do I stop thinking about him with another woman? How do I ever trust him again?

". . . whatever is true, whatever is honorable, whatever is right, whatever is pure, whatever is lovely, whatever is of good repute, if there is any excellence and if anything worthy of praise, let your mind dwell on these things. . . ."

The way he *did, Lord?*

The way you're doing, beloved?

She wanted to leave the church. She didn't want to hear words that opened her eyes to her own sin; she wanted the finger pointed at Alex. She had come to be renewed, uplifted, enlightened. She hadn't come to be convicted.

If you love Me, you will keep My commandments. Love one another, just as I have loved you.

She wanted to cry out. *God, do You have to scrub an open wound? Do You have to pour salt on it?*

"Whatever you do, do your work heartily, as for the Lord," the pastor said, continuing his message.

She winced. What *was* she doing?

How could she hold a grudge against Alex and call herself a Christian? How could she expect to feel joy and peace in her life when she clung to past hurts and fears of future pain? The risk was what paralyzed her. Where were the guarantees of a happy ending?

I don't belong in Your kingdom, Lord. I'm not like any of these good people sitting around me.

What would they think of her if they knew she'd punched Alex not once, but half a dozen times with everything she had? And then kneed him where it hurt most. Never mind what *they* would think. God had seen!

Humiliation set in, her face heating up.

O Lord, I lost control. All I could think about was the fact he walked out on me. He said he was sick of me. He said he wanted out of our marriage. It was hard, but I let him go. I gave him the papers he said he wanted. I listened to what Dennis and the others said about allowing a nonbeliever to leave a marriage. And now he tells me he never loved her the way he loved me. How do I believe him? How can I trust him? I'm not strong enough to go through this heartache again. I'm not strong enough to go through it now.

I'm not going to give you more than you can bear.

Why don't I feel comforted by that, Jesus?

She walked home with the children and fixed them bologna sandwiches and tomato soup for lunch. Alex was coming home in a few days. Her mind whirred with conflicting thoughts. She wanted to forgive and forget, but she feared the cost of both.

"Maybe Daddy will call," Carolyn said.

"He never calls on Sundays," Clanton said between bites of sandwich.

Sierra knew he'd be at Mass with his parents today. But when he was here, what did he do?

And why was she allowing herself to think about that snake again?

She and the children walked back to church in the afternoon, and she was treated to another heart-wrenching lesson during the evening Bible study. The subject was self-righteousness. The Word was a double-edged sword, and she was sliding right down the blade of it.

Couldn't You ease up on me a little, Lord? Do You have to use a jackhammer?

She left the class before it was over and found solitude in a cry room built for mothers who were nursing their babies. She sat nursing her grievances in the rocking chair, locked in the silence until youth group was over and it was time to meet Clanton and Carolyn.

❖

Alex was walking down the path toward her condo when she and the children returned. She should have known.

"Daddy!" Carolyn cried and ran to him. Clanton wasn't far behind. The three talked briefly and walked toward her. She'd never felt so alone, so cut off.

"Have you eaten?" he said.

"Not yet," Clanton said. "I'm starved."

"Why don't I take all of you out to pizza?"

"Mom, too?" Carolyn said, excited about the idea.

"Mom, too," Alex said, looking at her.

She knew he would understand if she said no. He wouldn't argue or try to persuade. She knew the children would understand as well. That was the problem. She felt exposed and petty. They had such great hopes. Shouldn't she? "That would be nice," she said, lowering her gaze from his. She'd do it for the children.

He was still driving his Mercedes. He opened the door for her while Clanton and Carolyn piled in the back. When they reached the pizza parlor, Alex ordered a large combo and pitcher of soda while she and the children secured a booth. When Alex joined them, he handed the children a handful of quarters for the video games that lined the back wall. As they dashed off, he slid into the seat opposite her.

"Finally, we're alone together," he said, a rueful smile touching his lips. The place was packed with Sunday evening diners.

She smiled back, aching inside. Why was it so much easier to maintain her anger when there was distance between them? Now, sitting across the booth from him, she couldn't sustain it. It melted despite her determination, leaving behind a sense of vulnerability that frightened her more than anything else. "I thought you weren't coming back until the twenty-eighth."

"I couldn't wait."

She didn't ask for what. "Didn't things go well with your parents?"

"Papa's speaking to me again. We had a long talk. You paved the way for me." His eyes darkened. "I meant what I said the other day, Sierra. *Te amo.* I want us to get back together."

"Don't take my agreement for granted."

"I'm not. Don't you think I—"

"I don't want to talk here, Alex," she said, looking away, tears starting. "I can't."

"Yo comprendo," he said softly. "We'll eat and take the children home. Once they're settled for the night, we'll go back to my place."

"No way. I don't want to be alone with you."

"Don't you trust me?"

He meant the question to be light, seductive, but she looked him square in the eyes. "Should I?" She saw that the barb stuck and felt immediately ashamed. *Forgive,* the Lord said, and she had just stabbed Alex with a sharp blade. Looking down at her hands, she could almost see the blood on them and wanted to weep. The only way she could think to make amends was to be honest. "I know where we'd end up, Alex, and sex isn't going to help solve our problems."

"That cost you," he said huskily.

"It's true, isn't it?"

"It might ease the tension between us."

"And cloud the issues." She could see so clearly now how they'd often used sex to bypass issues that were causing fractures in their relationship rather than step back, look, listen, repair, and move on together. "If we're going to reconcile, we have to build a solid foundation this time."

"This time? Isn't love enough?"

"If it's the right kind."

Her words clearly hurt him but she couldn't weaken. When he searched her face, she felt he was looking for weakness.

Lord, help me stand firm. Show me what to do. I love him, but I don't want to give up my soul to him.

Alex frowned slightly, perplexed. "Okay," he said softly. "We stay at your place."

"No. We'll begin by talking on the telephone."

She needed space between them. She had made too many decisions based on her emotions, and look where that had gotten her!

The Lord said to renew your mind, and she intended to do that. With distance between them, she would be able to keep her mind clear to *think*.

One thing she already knew. It was going to take God to get them back together again and make their marriage work.

Kavanaugh has returned.

I was so relieved to see him riding across the field. He was gone so long I thought he had come to his senses. He said he has not changed his mind about anything, but figured I needed time to adjust to the idea of having another husband. He said he rode to Yerba Buena and then Monterey. He bought a wedding ring there from a Mexican jeweler. On the way north, he met other settlers. Five families have taken land east of us near the Russian River. While Kavanaugh was there getting to know everyone, a man returned from Sutter's Fort and said he heard a rumor gold was discovered in the trace at the mill on the American River. Two of the men have sons who are going back to find out if it is true.

Kavanaugh said one of the men at the new settlement said he could perform a marriage ceremony for us. He has a Book of Common Prayer and the wedding service is in it.

Kavanaugh and I are wed. Lester and Charlotte Burrell held a party for us after the ceremony. There were twenty-seven people there, all strangers who have quickly become friends. We had music! One man played a fiddle and another a mouth organ. I danced until my feet ached. They are good, hospitable people and were very happy to give us a proper wedding celebration. I feel at home in California for the first time since crossing the Sierra Nevada mountains.

I thought to make Kavanaugh and I a wedding quilt so that we would not have to share James's blanket. So I went to the trunk to take out the squares of fabric the ladies from the quilting club gave me. Beneath them I found a thin wooden tray and under it a Wonderful Surprise. Aunt Martha packed her pretty yellow dress and white lace shawl. When I took them out, I found her Bible in the folds.

I sat weeping over it for the longest time, just rubbing the black leather. The binding is worn from her loving hands, and just touching it makes me feel closer to her. I remember all the hours she spent reading it. When I opened it, I found her note.

I read from Aunt Martha's Bible for the first time this evening. We are starting at Genesis and will read straight through to the end. After I finished the story of creation, we all talked a long while.

The children are in bed now and Kavanaugh has gone out to check on the stock and take a bath in the creek before coming to bed. I have paged through Aunt Martha's Bible. I feel close to her with it in my hands. She has written prayers and notes in the margins. Favorite Scriptures are underlined. Pressed between the pages are other surprises that remind me of spring and Mama and days gone by in Galena—a golden Alexander, a pink-lavender shooting star, white Indian plantain, yellow-orange coreopsis, purple coneflower, black-eyed Susans, buttercups, blue aster, a rose-purple blazing star, and violet marsh phlox.

Lord, bless her and keep her always.

PART 4

THE RECONCILIATION

CHAPTER 25

ALEX CALLED EVERY EVENING at ten fifteen. Carolyn was always in bed by nine, while Clanton dragged his feet until ten. One conversation with his father made him cooperate.

Each night the telephone would ring, and Sierra's heart would jump. Taking a breath, she'd answer while sliding onto a stool in the kitchen. Alex did most of the talking, while she doodled on the notepad to keep from letting her nervousness come across the line.

As she contained her emotions, Alex opened up. The conversations became excruciating and confessional. The last thing she wanted to hear about was his relationship with Elizabeth, but he had a need to unburden himself.

"She left the East Coast in a bid for independence," he told her. "She was attracted to me because I was the opposite of the kind of man her father wanted her to marry. Not that she had marriage in mind."

Sierra could see how it had happened. Work had drawn them together. Elizabeth was assigned to work closely with Alex. Alex was a charismatic man, full of fire, brilliant and exciting. While Sierra was fighting with him at home, Elizabeth was waiting at the office, ready to console and sympathize, ready to build him up rather than tear him down. He'd spent progressively longer hours at the office. They started having lunch together, then dinner. A few drinks led to more. Then the guilt set in, and the only way to alleviate that was to cast blame. Sierra knew she'd become the perfect target. She had already set herself up for the fall by her own childish behavior months before Elizabeth Longford ever came on the scene. If it hadn't been Elizabeth, it would have been another woman.

"What happened when you went East with her?"

"What do you mean?"

"Audra said something about a fiasco in Connecticut."

"You could say that. Her father and I had words. The same kind your father and I had. You remember what happened?"

"Yes. You eventually became very good friends." It had taken a few years, but Alex and her dad had grown close. By the time her father passed away, he was Alex's champion, second only to herself and Luís.

"No," Alex said. "That's not what I mean. Do you remember what you did? You came down the stairs and stood beside me. You said you loved me. You made it a declaration, loud and clear. You were ready to fight for *us*, no matter what it cost you, even a break with your parents." He let out his breath derisively. "Elizabeth tossed me to the wolves and stood back to watch who'd win."

Rather than make her feel better, his words left her wondering if things might have turned out differently had Elizabeth been a little wiser or loved Alex a little more.

"Don't go quiet on me, Sierra. I'm trying to tell you I saw what she was. It took Connecticut for me to understand what she was doing. She didn't love me, and I didn't love her. We were using each other. She used me against her father. I used her against you."

"If you knew all that, why didn't you leave her sooner?"

He was quiet for a moment. "Pride."

"Be honest, Alex." She was tired of crucifying herself between two thieves: regret for yesterday and fear about tomorrow. She needed the truth from him, no matter how much it hurt. They couldn't build on anything less. "I promise I won't hang up on you, no matter what you say."

"All right," he said heavily, clearly not eager to impart what was coming. "I wasn't sure I wanted to come back to you."

Well, at least she knew he wasn't holding back anymore. Swallowing her hurt, she asked, "What changed your mind?"

"When you said you'd never take the children away from me, it stopped me cold. I'd expected you to fight dirty."

And why wouldn't he? She had been vindictive, carping and complaining over the move. After three years of that behavior, why should he have expected her to be fair when faced with divorce?

"Finally I realized *I* was the one playing dirty," he said. "And then there was the day I watched you play baseball." He gave a low laugh. "By the time the game was over, I was wondering why I'd ever left you in the first place."

"Because I hit a home run?" she said, smiling sadly as she made doodles on the notepad.

"No, because I hadn't seen you laugh in months. You looked young and happy again, the way you were when we first started out. You took my breath away. I sat there watching you and remembering the good times. I felt sick, wondering what happened to us."

And so it went. Alex called, she listened—and learned. As the days passed, she left the stool and sat on the sofa, feet propped up on the old hatch-cover table. "If we do get back together, what are you going to do with all that stereo and game equipment you have in your living room? And that horrible black couch," she said.

"What makes you think we'll be living in your condo?"

It got her to wondering. Where *would* they live? How would they meld their lifestyles? Sierra was beginning to realize how little they had in common.

Lord, how are we going to make this work?

She spent as much time as possible reading the Bible and thinking things over. Again, she learned: Be anxious about nothing. Be thankful. Work out the tangles of your life one by one before the Lord. She had to fix her eyes on Jesus constantly in order to live above it all with Christ, in Him, rather than get caught up in the old resentments, hurts, and fears.

Her feelings changed as Alex talked. The anger got lost somewhere and compassion slipped in, not just for Alex, but for Elizabeth Longford as well. She knew from Audra that Elizabeth had moved back to Connecticut. When Alex left, her life fell apart. Her bid for independence from her father had blown up in her face.

"She called to tell us she's getting married," Audra said.

Sierra told Alex, testing his reaction she supposed, but better to know now rather than later if he wanted to change his mind about the direction they were going.

"I heard." His response was quiet, neutral.

"From Audra?"

"No. Elizabeth called while I was in the office last week. She told me."

Sierra's heart dropped. She hadn't realized he was still in contact with her.

"It's the only time we've talked since she left," Alex said, seeming to read her mind. "I met the man she's marrying when I was in Connecticut," he went on. "She was engaged to him once before and backed out. He's a Harvard grad, a lawyer. Rich. Family connections back to the founding fathers. Her father's choice." He gave a soft self-deprecating laugh. "I *liked* him. When I put all that other stuff aside, he was a pretty decent guy."

Sierra gathered her courage. "Maybe Elizabeth called to tell you hoping you'd change her mind."

"That occurred to me," he said gently. "That's why I told her I'm doing everything in my power to reconcile with my wife."

Sierra closed her eyes, imagining how much it would have hurt her if she were in Elizabeth's position. "What did she say to that, Alex?"

"She said she was sorry."

Sierra pitied Elizabeth. She had taken Dennis's advice and spent a few minutes each day praying for Elizabeth Longford. Doing so had erased her animosity. She prayed now, during the lull in conversation with her estranged husband.

"Sierra? Talk to me. Scream at me. Say something."

"We never realize how many people we hurt with our actions, do we, Alex? It's like a chain reaction. I was so angry with you when we moved down here. I never listened to what you wanted or needed. I was only interested in what I wanted. I hurt you so much, and out of that I hurt Elizabeth, too."

"You had nothing to do with Elizabeth."

"Yes, I did. If I'd been the wife I should've been, you never would've turned to her. So I share the blame with you for her pain, too."

He said something in Spanish. "You remind me of your mother."

She teared up and swallowed them down. He couldn't have paid her a dearer compliment. "I still miss her. Sometimes I'll see something or read about something I know would make her laugh, and I pick up the phone to call. I'll be in the middle of dialing her number before I remember she isn't there anymore."

"I should've been with you," he said hoarsely.

He'd been with Elizabeth, instead. Blinking back tears, Sierra didn't say anything. Her throat ached. Would the hurt ever go away?

"I was trying to figure a way out . . . ," Alex said softly.

"Of our marriage."

"No. Out of what was happening between me and Elizabeth. The guilt was eating me alive. I knew you needed me, but I couldn't deal with it or face you. I couldn't face your mother. I was sure she'd know the minute she looked at me that something was wrong. Then Papa gave me that lecture on the telephone. I knew he was right, but I didn't like being told what to do. By the time I got there, I was uptight and ready for a fight. I had all kinds of excuses and reasons. Papa and I had words after the memorial service. He said he was ashamed of me for the way I treated you. Your mother's letter was the last straw. I had to get out of there."

"What did she say in the letter?"

"She wrote she knew the first time she saw us together that I was the right man for you." He didn't say anything for a moment, then added in a choked voice, "She said she loved me and was proud to have me as a son."

They talked past midnight, leaving Sierra bleary-eyed for work. After running errands, she came home, fixed dinner for the children, and stretched out on the sofa to read her Bible. The next thing she knew, Clanton and Carolyn woke her up at ten.

"We're going to bed, Mom," Clanton said.

Trying to focus through her exhaustion, Sierra pushed herself up. "I didn't mean to fall asleep. What time is it?"

"Daddy called earlier," Carolyn said. "He's going to call you at ten thirty." They each kissed her good night and went to their rooms.

As Sierra waited for the telephone to ring, she sat looking up at Mary Kathryn's quilt. It occurred to her that not only were her feelings changing, but so was the way she saw things. She thought about her first ecstatic months as a Christian. After having been told about Jesus from childhood, she'd finally understood for herself who Jesus was. Creator, Redeemer, almighty God, King of kings, Lord of lords. Realization had struck like an atomic blast. Hot white light blinded her for a little while. She'd been so caught up in the sudden opening of her mind and heart to Christ, she hadn't seen anything else clearly. She hadn't looked. She had known only one thing: Jesus loved her. Alex didn't, but the Lord did. After months of turmoil and grief, she'd felt happy. She'd felt hopeful. In the midst of everything, she had felt safe.

Then Alex pushed back into her life, rocking her foundations again. She'd finally adjusted to being without him; Ron stood by in the wings waiting to walk out onto center stage. She was working, carrying her own weight, being responsible. The children were settled in their new school, involved in the church. Clanton had stopped fighting. Carolyn had stopped obsessing about grades.

Why now, God? she had cried. Why couldn't things stay the way they were? Why couldn't Alex just stay out of her life the way he'd said he wanted?

But her vision had been adjusting to the light. It seemed each day she could see life—herself—more clearly, through Scripture, prayer, and her daily walk with Jesus. She could see right into the dusty, dirty, secret corners of her life. Christ brought everything to light.

Painfully, vividly, she saw her part in the passion play.

Anguish filled her as she recognized past sins and present ones she had fallen into out of habit, hidden ones she loathed to face. Alex wasn't the only guilty player. She stood stripped before a mirror, seeing herself as she had been: childish, self-centered, filled with self-pity, casting blame, complaining.

It is better to live in the corner of a roof than in a house shared with a contentious woman.

She was ashamed and grieved, yet oddly enough, a sense of peace followed her self-examination. She was reminded of her mother in the attic, the window open, the fresh air blowing in as she dusted, swept, and sorted out trash from the treasure.

Oh, Lord Jesus, do that for me. Please. You know me better than I know myself. Open my doors and windows and let the Holy Spirit move through me. You are welcome in my house. Come into me, into my foyer and my living room. Wander at will through my parlor and kitchen. Be with me in my bedroom and bathroom. Go through every closet and every drawer, from the basement to the attic of my life. I belong to You, Father. Stay with me forever. Jesus, please remove everything in me that doesn't glorify You. Make me Your vessel.

Oh, God, You are my God. I seek You. My soul hungers and thirsts for You. My body longs for You as dry land beneath a heavy rain. Your love is better than life.

"Are you falling in love again?" Alex said softly late that night after they had talked for two hours.

Eyes closed, her head resting against the back of the sofa, she smiled. "Yes." But not with Alex—she'd never stopped loving him.

She was falling in love with Jesus.

We found our dear Koxoenis shot dead near the banks of our stream today.

Lord, who would murder such a gentle man who did nothing but show kindness and hospitality to others? Kavanaugh thinks Koxoenis was badly wounded and tried to reach us for help. Thinking of him suffering fills me with anguish. Oh, God, that we had found him sooner. Kavanaugh said the wound was mortal and we could not have saved him, but we could have at least comforted him in his last hours upon this earth. We could have held him close and prayed for him.

Kavanaugh carried Koxoenis to our home. We washed him and wrapped him in a blanket and buried him beside James.

Lord, I am so grieved. Please do not hold it against Koxoenis that I failed to explain You to him. I tried so hard each time he has come to visit, but sign language leaves so much unsaid. He did not understand me, and I did not know how to explain. And now he is lost forever.

Father, please let me speak on his behalf. Koxoenis was kind and generous, and obedient to Your will. He heard Your voice that day we were so hungry. He came to us and gave us meat. He showed us the food You had planted all around us. He taught Joshua how to build us a shelter so that we were warm and dry through the cold winter months. He was our first and dearest friend, and though he did not know You, Lord, I believe in my heart he was Your child in spirit. I have never known a man more humble and loving.

Please, Lord, be merciful and bring Koxoenis into Your kingdom.

Beth and I gathered flowers today and took them to the small knoll where James and Koxoenis lie. But when we reached it, we found Koxoenis's grave empty. The cross we had made for him lay upon the mound of fresh earth and on it was a Pomo gift basket. It is the most beautiful thing I have ever seen with designs woven with red, yellow, and green feathers and small beads. Around the rim are tiny black topknot quail feathers.

I have placed the basket upon our mantel and will remember our beloved friend and his people each time I look at it.

Kavanaugh brought supplies back from the settlement near the river yesterday. Beth and I walked to Koxoenis's village today to bring apple pies to his wife and children, but when we reached it, everyone was gone. No fires were burning. No children were playing. No smoke came from the sweathouse. No women sat working with stone mortar and pestle crushing acorns. The village was deserted and desolate.

Kavanaugh said Indians move where the food is. He thinks this village site may be their winter home. Spring and summer must be spent elsewhere. The money beads the people wear are made of clamshells. So I suppose the people must spend time each year near the ocean. Perhaps they are there.

We learned from Joshua that Koxoenis's people ate fish, acorns, pepperwood nuts, buckeyes, and a mixture of toasted seeds and grains ground in a stone mortar and sifted in a basket. They called it pinole. Now that spring is here, everything is green and growing. There must be a hundred different things to eat that we have not yet discovered. And come summer, the berries and wild apples will be ripe. They will taste better than the dried ones I soaked to make the pies.

I hope we will see Koxoenis's people again come fall, but my heart tells me we will not be so fortunate.

Lord, please be with them and protect them from harm.

CHAPTER 26

"RED ROSES, MOM!" Carolyn called from the front door. "Come see!"

Sierra came into the living room and gasped as she saw the arrangement being brought in. "Living room table, ma'am?" the deliveryman said. He was young, sporting a T-shirt that said "God spoke and *BANG* it was," long black hair, and a single hoop earring.

"Yes, that'd be fine."

When he set the arrangement down, he gave her a saucy grin. "Someone's either smitten or in deeeep trouble."

She laughed. *Smitten* was such an antique word for such a modern young man. "Hang on a minute," she said and gave him a ten-dollar tip. She found the card tucked in among the baby's breath and ferns: *Happy Valentine's Day. I love you. Alex.* Twenty-four red roses in a crystal vase.

She called him. "Thank you for the roses."

"What do you say we take the children out tonight? Dinner and a movie."

She smiled. "I'd like that."

"How about letting them sit in the front row while we sit in a back corner and neck the way we used to?"

She laughed. "How about we all sit in the middle *together*?"

They had a wonderful evening together. As it turned out, Clanton and Carolyn pleaded to sit closer to the front, and she and Alex sat in the middle. At first Alex didn't touch her. They sat side by side, both staring up at the big screen with the animated Disney characters frolicking, both wound up like a couple of two-dollar clocks. Halfway through the movie, Alex took her hand. When she didn't try to withdraw, he finally relaxed.

"Aren't you going to invite him in?" Carolyn said when they reached the condo.

"I want to show him my new game," Clanton said as though on cue.

Sierra looked between them and knew what her children were hoping. How could she explain she wasn't ready?

"Another time," Alex said, coming to her rescue. He took a step back.

"Mom," Carolyn whined, her heart in her eyes.

"It's all right, Alex," she said. "Come on in. I'll fix us some hot cider while you take a look at Clanton's game."

She was in the kitchen putting cinnamon sticks in the cups of steaming cider when Alex came back. "Are the children coming?" she said, glancing toward the hallway.

"They're playing a video game."

"Carolyn?" She had never been interested before.

He shrugged. "You look nervous."

"I am a little," she said, giving a self-conscious laugh.

"Why don't we sit in the living room?" She gave him a mug of hot cider, took one for herself, and led the way to the couch she'd recovered. She sat at the far end, curling her feet up beneath her.

Neither knew what to say to break the tension. She remembered other nights on this couch. The silence stretched along with her nerves.

"It does get in the way, doesn't it?" Alex said heavily.

"What?"

"Wanting you this much. Knowing you want me, too." He looked at her, hiding nothing.

Sierra's heart began to drum hard. Alex set his mug of hot cider on the hatch-cover table and stood. She looked up at him, afraid he'd kiss her and start something she couldn't let him finish. Or worse, he would leave.

His expression softened. "As much as I'd like to, I'm not going to rush you."

"I'm not trying to be difficult, Alex."

"*Yo sé.* You've got to learn to trust me again."

She looked down into her cider. "So much has happened to me in the last year. I've changed in ways I don't think you understand." She looked at him again. "The Lord is the center of my life, now. I can't go back—"

"Dennis and I talked about it."

She was surprised. "You did?" She knew Dennis wouldn't hold back; he'd lay out salvation one, two, three.

"I go to Mass, Sierra. I have every Sunday since I moved here." He glanced away, rubbing the back of his neck. "I figured it was time I confessed and did penance. Dennis talks about grace, but there's justice, too."

She put her mug down and stood up. "I forgive you, Alex."

He looked at her, his eyes moist. "I knew that when you said you wanted to talk, but I can't let go of it. I said vows, *querida*. It doesn't matter that they were in Reno and not in a church. I could have been saying them in a parking lot and I still would've known I was speaking before God. The last thing I ever thought I'd do was commit adultery. And then I did. I never thought I'd be capable of hurting you. And then I did that, too. Deliberately. Every chance I got."

She wanted to put her arms around him, but he moved away slightly, putting distance between them. He was gripped with guilt. It was eating at him. She knew that look. She also knew he wanted to tell her something—something she wasn't going to like. The muscles in her stomach tightened.

No more, Lord. Please, no more.

"Father O'Shea asked if I'd had a blood test."

Sierra could feel the blood draining from her face. She blinked.

"Yeah, you look exactly the way I felt," he said bleakly. "That aspect never occurred to me, either. Not until a celibate priest brought it up. I called Elizabeth and asked some blunt questions. She wasn't very happy about them, but she was honest. I knew I wasn't her first. But I didn't know how many. Do you know what I'm saying, Sierra? Do you understand?"

"Yes."

"She's been with five other men, one in high school, two during college, one afterward, and the guy she's marrying. She said she didn't think there was a chance any of them were HIV-positive, but there's no way of knowing, is there?" His eyes were haunted. "I can't stop thinking about it." His eyes filled. "You came to me a virgin. You never even kissed another guy before me."

"Are you telling me you're—?" She couldn't finish the question.

"No. I've been tested four times over the past few months. All negative, but who knows? Are we hearing the truth about this thing?" He came to her and cupped her face. As he stroked her cheeks, his eyes welled with tears and torment. "How do I ever make love to you again without wondering if I'm killing you in the process?"

"Oh, Alex," she whispered, putting her hand against his chest. She felt his heart pick up speed; her own matched the rhythm.

He took her hand and removed it from him. "I almost didn't tell you," he said hoarsely, "but you've got a right to know. It's something else you're going to need to think about before you make any decisions, isn't it?" He moved away from her.

She knew he was heading for the door. "Alex . . ."

"I'll call you," he said hoarsely. Without looking back, he opened the door and went out.

It has been three years since I wrote anything in this journal.

We have spent our evenings reading Aunt Martha's Bible. I found out who killed our beloved Koxoenis and it near broke my heart. I might never have known had I not noticed the amethyst cross Charlotte Burrell wore to the Christmas gathering. My heart stopped when I saw it around her neck, and my throat closed so tight I did not think I could draw breath let alone speak. I was so full of anger I wanted to tear that necklace from her throat, but You held me from it. She asked me what was wrong. Soon as she did I knew I could speak.

I did not ask her about the cross. Instead, I did what You set in my mind. I told her about our first winter in California and how we would surely have starved to death had it not been for the kindness of a Pomo Indian named Koxoenis. Lester joined us as I told Charlotte about our dear friend. I told them how Koxoenis gave us meat and taught us how to find food. I told them how he welcomed Joshua into his own home and village and taught him how to make fish traps and build a shelter that kept us dry and warm through the cold, wet winter months. I said he was as near an example of God's love as I had ever seen in my life and a true answer to a prayer I had said in desperation. I told them the only gift I was ever able to give him was an amethyst cross on a gold chain exactly like the one Charlotte was wearing.

Lester looked sick. His face got all white and blotchy. I thought he was going to die right there on the spot. He said he was sorry. He said when he saw the Indian with his bow and arrows, he thought he was a threat and shot him. He took the cross because he thought Koxoenis must have killed a white settler and stolen it. Charlotte was too ashamed to say anything. She gave the necklace back to me and could not say a word.

I grieve now more for Lester and Charlotte than Koxoenis. They will live with this on their hearts for years to come. I told them I forgive them and You do, too. But I don't know that it made them feel any the better for taking an innocent man's life.

Oh, Lord, how many things I have done without thinking of the cost to others.

Ham has a son of his own now. I have never seen a man so taken with a child. He sits by the crib and watches Micah, sometimes for an hour or more. When Micah awakens at night, Ham brings him to bed and watches me nurse him. It is disconcerting at times. He said just last night how blessed a woman is. When I asked him why, he said a woman gets to feel a child grow inside her and, once the babe is born, she provides sustenance with her own body. No man can ever experience that.

James never in all his days talked this way.

What manner of man have You given me, Lord?

I never thought I would love a man so much my heart would break every time I looked at him. And it is so. I fell in love with James the first time I saw him, yet it is this fierce and rugged man who has grown to be a part of me. I have wondered about it much of late. I think it is because James withheld a part of himself. Kavanaugh gives everything. James yearned for more than I could give. Kavanaugh is so filled up with love, it pours out of him onto me and my children. James risked everything to reach his dream. Kavanaugh would die for us. James touched me and I burned. When Kavanaugh touches me, I see heaven.

Lord, may I be a proper wife for him. He deserves better.

The crops came in bountiful. As is everything. I told Ham I am in a family way again. He was distressed at first and asked if it was good for me to be having another baby this soon. I could not help but laugh. It is a little late to be worrying about such things.

Lord, I thank You. And if You do not mind me asking, I would like a girl this time.

Dear Lord, sometimes my heart swells so much with love for You it closes my throat up with pain. I am not much as children go, I know. I am not like Mama or Aunt Martha.

Mama used to pray thank You prayers in the meadows and sing to You. She said there are earth psalms all around us singing praises to You and it is nice to join in. Since I am not much good at singing, I hope You will understand I am grateful for so many things.

Tears, a balm, soothing and cleansing. Cups, of plenty and sorrow. Cold to make me appreciate warmth. Manure, though I do not know if You will like me saying so. But Lord, when spread over turned ground where new seeds have been planted, it brings forth growth. Like my troubles in my life, Lord. It was Affliction and Distress that made me come to You and now I do not ever want to leave.

I am thankful for the pieces of fabric the quilting club gave me—woven and designed like You wove and designed me in my mother's womb. Like You designed my children. I am grateful for our new fireplace that gives us warmth, light drawing each of us together.

Dust! The small particles dance on the light. Would that I could dance like that for You in broad daylight instead of going off in the woods because the last time I did it my children thought I was out of my head.

I am glad for the candles so I can see to write. You are my lamp, Lord, lighting my way out of darkness. I am thankful for the gold nuggets Kavanaugh brought home yesterday, pure and soft the way my heart should be. Lord, make me so.

Thank You for the Good Water we have. It quenches my body's thirst and reminds me that You are Living Water for my soul.

Even the Air I breathe, Jesus. I cannot see it, but it is there, moving and necessary to keep me alive. Like You. And the Flowers. I have never seen so many colors and kinds splashed across the hillsides. Even Gray Skies are a good thing from You because they make me yearn for sunlight. Seeds show me death and resurrection.

I do not know if You approve of me saying this, Lord, but I am grateful for the way I feel when Kavanaugh knows me. Even with James I never felt this explosion of fire and light inside me like a rain of stars.

Is all this but a hint of what it will be like to be in full communion with You, Jesus? Do You show us the part so that we yearn for the Whole? I remember Aunt Martha reading to me once that to look upon the face of God would bring death. Still, sometimes every bit of me yearns to be in Heaven with You all the while I still want to stay here and live to be an old dottering woman seeing her children and grandchildren around her. I do not understand all that is changing inside me.

Sierra held the worn journal tenderly, tears streaming down her face. Mary Kathryn's beautiful letter to God was the last entry in her journal. As she had turned the last page, she'd found an envelope carefully glued inside the back binder. Inside it was a single sheet of paper. She recognized her mother's clear, neat script.

Dear Sierra,

We have no other journals by Mary Kathryn McMurray in our possession. If there were others after it, I'm sorry to say they were lost or passed along to another branch of the family with whom we have no contact. We do know through family records that Mary Kathryn and Hamlet Bogan Kavanaugh had eight children together and lived to a healthy old age. What records we do have come down to us through your father's ancestor, America Farr, Mary Kathryn's last child by James Addison Farr. James was your great-great-great-grandfather.

Mike has all the family papers if you are interested in looking at the details.

I love you,
Mom

P.S. I went through everything carefully, but could find no further mention of Joshua.

CHAPTER 27

SIERRA SAT STARING at Mary Kathryn's quilt. Alex hadn't called in several days. She knew he was giving her time to digest what he'd told her. She *had* thought about it. She had taken a couple of days off work to be by herself in order to think things through. While the children had been in school, she had walked through the mall and sat at the coffee shop. Later, she sat in her breakfast nook, the sun streaming in through the window, and read her Bible and prayed. No solutions came.

I wish You would put answers in neon signs, Lord. What am I supposed to do?

When she'd crawled into bed earlier, she couldn't sleep, so now she sat on the couch and stared up at Mary Kathryn McMurray's quilt.

What would you do, Mary Kathryn? Shoot him? Forgive him and take him back?

Sierra's life had changed so much. She was happy with the changes, comfortable with them. Alex would only turn her life upside down again, not to mention the risks involved in trying to make their marriage work. She wasn't as worried about HIV as Alex was. She was more worried about the emotional risks, the fears inherent in loving him again the way she once did. Alex had been the center of her universe.

Jesus, You are my center now. Is Alex going to be happy with the changes in me?

They had barely brushed the subject of faith during their long evening discussions. Truly, she had been afraid to broach the subject with him. Church attendance had never been part of their routine other than to attend Mass with his parents on special occasions. Did Alex understand how important Jesus was to her now, that she needed the Lord more than she needed him? She *wanted* Alex. She wanted him to share her life completely. If she knew Christ had no place in his life, how could she reconcile with him without compromising her new faith?

I lived with him thirteen years, Lord, and I don't know what he believes. Truth to tell, I don't know much about the inner workings of his heart. It was always my own that mattered.

Oh, God, why are we so proud and foolish? We don't listen until we're faced with disaster, and then we come crying home to You, wanting You to fix us! I love him, Father, but is this kind of love enough to make our marriage work? We have so little in common. I never realized until now. We come from different cultures, different social backgrounds, different religions. He's brilliant and I'm average. He graduated from college with honors, and I managed to get out of high school and take a few business courses. He likes ultramodern, and I like antiques and sunflowers and lace. Lord, he likes seventies music, and I'm sick to death of it. When I think about all of this, my head reels. I wonder how we ever lasted as long as we did. Great sex. Was that it? Was it passion for one another that held us together, Lord?

A flush ran up her cheeks, and she caught her thoughts. Was it proper to talk with Jesus about such things? If not, she hoped He would forgive her, but there was no one else she could go to, no one who would understand her from the inside out. Who else could do that but the One who created her?

As she prayed and talked with God, she struggled with all the questions. Had she caused her own downfall by living in a fantasy world, never being willing to see who Alex really was? Was that why their marriage had worked as long as it had?

Was that it, Lord? I still ache when I see him. I'm a Christian now, and I still ache for him. I love You, Jesus. Everything's changed, not the least of which is me. And still I love him.

Lord, what do I do? What's Your will for me in all this?

She leaned her head back against the sofa and looked up at the quilt.

And then it dawned on her. A flash of insight from out of nowhere, from within her. And with it, God's quiet loving voice.

Be still, beloved. And know that I am God.

She blinked, amazed, overwhelmed. It was right there before her eyes, only she had been blind to it. The message her mother had said would come had finally arrived. Sitting forward slowly, Sierra studied the quilt—and understood.

"One day it will come to you like a star bursting in the heavens. And what a day that will be!"

Sierra stood and went to the quilt, smiling in wonder, her fingers tracing the scarlet thread that held all the pieces together and made them a whole incredibly beautiful work of art. "Oh, Lord . . . ," she whispered brokenly. How could she have been so blind?

Who am I, beloved?

"You are God. Almighty God."

Sierra wept with joy as enlightenment sang in her very blood.

Responding to an impulse, she called Alex.

"Sierra," he said hoarsely. "What's wrong, *querida?*"

She had awakened him. Glancing at the kitchen wall clock, she grimaced. She hadn't even thought about the time. "Nothing. The children are fine. I'm fine."

"Something's happened. What is it?"

Should she tell him to go back to sleep? Her heart was racing, her soul singing praises to the Lord. "Can you come over?"

"*Sí.*" He didn't even ask what time it was. After she hung up, she raked her hands through her hair. One fifteen in the morning! What must he be thinking? Embarrassed, she called him back to apologize and tell him her discovery could wait until morning.

Maybe it should wait until she'd had more time to think. Would he understand if she even tried to explain now in the feverish excitement of discovery? Doubts crept in. Maybe she was overreacting. Maybe she was getting overemotional. Maybe her imagination was running rampant.

O Lord. O Lord.

Alex didn't answer. Before she hung up, there was a tap on the door.

Taking a deep breath, Sierra opened it. Her heart turned over at the sight of her husband. He had pulled on his old sweats and stood barefoot, his dark hair disheveled. He looked worried.

"I'm sorry, Alex. I didn't even look to see what time it was."

"I'm awake now," he said coming inside.

"You'll think I'm crazy, but there's something I want to show you."

O God, let him see. Let him understand. Help us! Be the glue that holds us together this time.

Alex followed her into the living room, looking around for something out of place. No earthquake had happened. No ceiling falling in on her. Nothing unusual. He looked at her, bemused, questioning.

She looked up at the quilt. "The question's never been *whether*, but *when*," she said, more to herself than to him.

"When what?"

She smiled at him. "It says that every knee will bow and every tongue will confess that Jesus Christ is Lord. So the question is do we relinquish everything to the Lord, or do we make Him strip us bare before we understand *He's* in control."

Alex shook his head. "I don't know what you're talking about, *querida*."

"Sit down with me, please, Alex. I have something very important to ask you." She turned to face him as they sat together on the couch. "This is the most important question I'll ever ask you. Who is Jesus to you?"

Surprised, he searched her eyes. "God the Son, Creator, Father, Savior."

Her eyes welled with thankful tears. "So you do believe."

"*Sí, amor mío.* Since I was a little boy. I never wanted to make an issue of it with you. Your family . . . mine . . . *imposible . . . yo comprendo.* And then, when I walked away from you, I figured I'd walked away from Him as well. I didn't think He would forgive me, that He could—"

His voice broke, and Sierra felt her throat tighten with tears at the depth of his despair. He met her eyes. "But He has, *querida*. Dennis helped me see that. God has forgiven me—He has restored me to Himself. And that's why I won't give up on us. If He can forgive, He can help us to do the same."

Relief swept through her, and joy as well. She looked up at the quilt. "Almighty God, Creator, Master. He's the Alpha and Omega. Mary Kathryn McMurray came to understand. She made that quilt so others would see as well. I was just so blind."

Oh, the wonder of it all.

Alex touched her, a mere brush of his fingers, tentative, comforting. "Why are you crying?"

"Because He's *sovereign*, Alex. I guess I just didn't understand what it meant. I've been turning things over and around and inside out, trying to decide how to fix things, how to make them right, how to make sure everything would work the way it's supposed to work. And then tonight, as I was looking at the quilt, I realized I'm not in control at all. God is. He always has been. He is almighty God."

She looked up at Mary Kathryn's quilt. "She knew, Alex. It took heartache and tragedy for her eyes to be finally opened, but in the end, she knew. And she put it there in her quilt for all to see who had the eyes to do so."

I am so much like her, Lord. Stubborn, stiff-necked, and You have loved me through everything. Thank You for Your patience with me.

Alex looked at the quilt, frowning. When he looked back at her again, Sierra could see he wondered if she'd taken leave of her senses. She got up and went to the quilt.

"I noticed the scarlet thread the first time Mom and I took the quilt out of the old trunk in the attic. I just didn't understand until this evening why Mary Kathryn picked that color. Do you see how it stands out? Do you see how it holds all the pieces together, Alex? Mary Kathryn made each square separately over a period of years. Each shows something significant that happened to her: tragedies, births, changes in her life, upheavals. And here at the end, the stone wall with that red cord hanging from the window opening. I never understood that." She stood before the quilt, tracing a portion of embroidered grape leaves and grapes. Shaking her head, she turned and looked at him, her heart full of love.

"I read her journal, the whole thing, several times, and I never understood why she made that wall as her last square. There was never a mention of a wall in her journal. Tonight, I understood. It's Rahab's wall."

"Rahab?"

"Rahab, the prostitute who hid the Israelite spies who came to Jericho. Moses had died, and the Israelites entered Canaan to take possession of the Promised Land. Joshua sent spies to Jericho, and Rahab took them in. She was a prostitute who had lived a life of sin and disobedience, and yet, in that moment, she risked her life to protect those men and hide them from the ones looking for them because she believed in their God. She had faith, and she acted upon it. The spies told her to hang a scarlet cord in her window, and though everyone else in Jericho would be put to the sword, no one in her house would perish. And they kept their word. She married Salmon and is named in the lineage of Jesus Christ."

She looked up at the quilt again. "But it's more than that, too. Scarlet is for Jesus and His death on the cross. Scarlet is for the blood He shed for us so that we could be redeemed. He was there in the beginning of it all. Faith is the key."

"Scarlet for her faith, you mean?"

"No, not her faith. Mary Kathryn contended with God.

Early in her journal, she was angry and rejected Him. After that, she scarcely mentioned Him in a good light—not until much later. She wasn't faithful at all. In a sense, she was like Rahab, prostituting herself to other gods in a foreign land. Her home and land mattered more than anything. Then it was her husband and her children. And with each loss she suffered, God was there with her. She didn't understand that until the end. That's what the scarlet thread signifies. That's why the wall is her last block. The window is open, and the scarlet cord flowing out and upward, tying it all together. God was there with her throughout her life. He brought her through."

She laughed softly, filled with relief and joy. "Look at the stitches, Alex. Grape leaves and grapes, chains, doves, crosses, olive branches—so much skill and beauty. When she quilted this wall, she did it with a passionate love for her Savior. She realized everything that had happened to her was through God's will. She finally surrendered. She *believed*. And because she did, God opened her eyes so that she could look back and see how He had been intimately involved through everything. Death. Birth. Fire. Disinheritance. Love. Betrayal. Loss. God allowed her to go through all those things so that she would come to Him. Once she did, she saw the wonder of all of it."

She came back and sat down with Alex again. "The things that happen in our lives are allowed to happen because the Lord wants to draw us to Him. We make decisions and do things, thinking we're in control, but we never really are. God is. It's arrogance and pride to think we rule our lives. It's an illusion. We're never able to orchestrate a thing. God is in control."

She put her hand on his knee. "I thought you were in control of my life, Alex. When you moved me to Southern California, I felt powerless. I was angry and frightened. I rebelled. I didn't even think about turning to the Lord. I turned to friends, and their lives were in shambles. I turned to my mother, and then she was taken away from me. I wanted to turn back to you, but then you were gone, too. God finally got through to me on the Hollywood freeway." She laughed through her tears. "Sacred ground for me was a strip of macadam in Los Angeles County."

He brushed the tears lightly from her cheek, his eyes tender. She wanted more than anything for him to understand. "Oh, Alex, don't you see? I never would've needed Jesus if I'd had any control at all. Everything that's happened—all the pain—He's turned to *good*. It's served His purpose. It brought me to Him."

His dark eyes softened. "I saw the change in you." He cupped her cheek tenderly. "I was a fool to leave you."

She covered his hand with her own. "Had you not left me, Alex, the change would never have come. I thank God for all of it. I thank Him with every ounce of my being, Alex. All the pain was blessing. I didn't fall in love with you by chance. It was God's design. I know now He draws us to Him, all through our lives. If we let Him. Some of us are just so stubborn it takes a long time to see His will at work." *Some never do, do they, Lord?*

She held his hand between hers and searched his eyes. "Jesus is at the very heart of who I am now, Alex. I can't go back."

"I wouldn't ask you to give Him up, *querida*. I only ask you to allow me in."

Sierra's heart melted. God had given her this man for a purpose. She had married Alex as an untried girl, head over heels in love. She was still married to him, still in love with him. The difference now was that she was one with Christ, wed to almighty God. And with God all things were possible.

"We haven't anything in common really, have we?" she said softly. "Except Jesus. He's our common ground, Alex. He brought us together, and He'll hold us together if we make Him our foundation. I don't need to worry about the what-ifs anymore. I don't need to have an answer to everything. I don't have to have everything worked out perfectly in my mind before I can start over. Neither do you, beloved. We just need to draw closer to *Jesus*. We need to trust in His plan for us. We need to learn from Him. And we need to step out in faith and begin."

She touched his cheek tenderly, feeling the firm line of his jaw. "Oh, my love, if we make drawing closer to Jesus our goal in life, how can we not draw closer to one another at the same time?"

Covering her hand, Alex turned his head and kissed her palm. "*Mi querida, te amo muchísimo.* You are so beautiful to me, *mi amor*." His dark eyes were flooded with tears. "I am sorry for the pain I caused you."

"And I you, Alejandro."

Oh, God, forgive me for the pain I caused You with my stubbornness. I love You, Jesus.

She went into Alex's arms naturally, leaning her head against his chest. She could hear the steady, rapid beat of his heart. "We still have a lot to work out."

"I'll get rid of the black couch."

She laughed and breathed in the beloved scent of his body, familiar and heady.

Oh, my love. Be like a gazelle on the mountains of spices. I have awakened. Be with us, Lord. Make this a love triangle, a sacred one to last a lifetime and beyond.

Alex drew back slightly. "First things first." Releasing her, he pulled the gold chain with the crucifix his mother had given him and her wedding ring from beneath his sweatshirt.

Opening the clasp, he let the two slide into the palm of his hand. He looked at her then, the question clear in his eyes. He was taking nothing for granted this time.

Smiling, Sierra held out her left hand.

"Dios, te doy mi gracias y mi vida," he whispered in relief and thanksgiving. The tension fell away, and joy leaped into his dark eyes as he slipped the gold wedding band back on her finger. Taking her hand, he stood.

Fourteen years ago, they had faced one another as they did now, the future before them. Cupping her face, Alejandro Luís Madrid kissed Sierra Clanton Madrid reverently, before the Lord.

"May no man or woman put asunder what God has joined together," he murmured.

Sliding her arms around his neck, she kissed him back.

Oh, Father, we rejoice in You. We praise Your name!

Mold us and make us one with You.

Discussion Questions

Dear Reader,

We hope you have enjoyed this timeless story of family relationships and God's faithfulness. His faithfulness in our failures, His healing in our brokenness, and His timing in restoration.

Tattered and torn scraps of cloth may seem worthless to the onlooker, yet when sewn together by loving hands and embellished with shiny thread they become a treasured heirloom. So it is with our families and our lives. What we see as brokenness, failures, and hopelessness, God uses to refine us. He weaves the shiny *scarlet thread* of His love to develop our faith in Him. "For we are God's masterpiece. He has created us anew in Christ Jesus, so that we can do the good things he planned for us long ago" (Ephesians 2:10).

May the following discussion guide help you see the *scarlet thread* God is weaving into your life to make you fit for eternity.

Sincerely,
Peggy Lynch

1. In your opinion, what was the cause/causes for the family problems Sierra and Alex were having? How did Sierra and Alex contribute to their own problems? What efforts were made to resolve their differences?

2. Compare Sierra and Mary Kathryn. How are they similar? Different? How did their communication skills affect their relationships?

3. How do you rate your own communication skills? Read Proverbs 12:18 and 15:23. What do those verses say about communication? How can you apply them to your own life?

4. Contrast Alex with James. What self-perceived inadequacies did they operate under? How did this thinking affect their decisions and choices?

5. What perceived inadequacies motivate your decisions? How can you overcome those inadequacies? What solution does Proverbs 29:25 provide?

6. Proverbs 17:3 says, "Fire tests the purity of silver and gold, but the Lord tests the heart." What trials did Sierra and Mary Kathryn face? How well did they face those difficulties? What trials are you facing in your life?

7. In what ways are Ron Peirozo and Kavanaugh alike? How are they different from Alex and James? Why are they appealing? Read Proverbs 16:32 and Proverbs 29:23; how do those verses apply to the men in this story?

8. Who did God use to get Sierra's attention? How did she respond? Who did God use with Mary Kathryn and what was her response?

9. How has God used people in your life to draw you to Himself? What actions did you take in response? How can you be a loyal friend like the one mentioned in Proverbs 17:17?

10. Did Sierra do the right thing at the end of the story? If you were in her shoes, would you have made the same choice? Is there a time and a place where divorce is the right course of action? What does the Bible say?

11. Discuss God's faithfulness to Alex and Sierra. In what ways did God demonstrate His faithfulness to Mary Kathryn and Kavanaugh?

12. As you look back over your life, how has God been drawing you to Himself? In the midst of failures or brokenness, how has He been faithful to you? Can you see His scarlet thread of love making you fit for eternity? Read Psalm 25:6 and Romans 8:28-30.

About the Author

NEW YORK TIMES bestselling author Francine Rivers began her literary career at the University of Nevada, Reno, where she graduated with a bachelor of arts degree in English and journalism. From 1976 to 1985, she had a successful writing career in the general market, and her books were highly acclaimed by readers and reviewers. Although raised in a religious home, Francine did not truly encounter Christ until later in life, when she was already a wife, a mother of three, and an established romance novelist.

Shortly after becoming a born-again Christian in 1986, Francine wrote *Redeeming Love* as her statement of faith. First published by Bantam Books, and then rereleased by Multnomah Publishers in the mid-1990s, this retelling of the biblical story of Gomer and Hosea, set during the time of the California Gold Rush, is now considered by many to be a classic work of Christian fiction. *Redeeming Love* continues to be one of CBA's top-selling titles, and it has held a spot on the Christian bestseller list for nearly a decade.

Since *Redeeming Love*, Francine has published numerous novels with Christian themes—all bestsellers—and she has continued to win both industry acclaim and reader loyalty around the globe. Her Christian novels have been awarded or nominated for numerous honors, including the RITA Award, the Christy Award, the ECPA Gold Medallion, and the Holt Medallion in Honor of Outstanding Literary Talent. In 1997, after winning her third RITA Award for inspirational fiction, Francine was inducted into the Romance Writers of America Hall of Fame. Francine's novels have been translated into more than twenty different languages, and she enjoys bestseller status in many foreign countries, including Germany, the Netherlands, and South Africa.

Francine and her husband, Rick, live in northern California and enjoy time spent with their three grown children and taking every opportunity to spoil their grandchildren. Francine uses her writing to draw closer to the Lord, and she desires that through her work she might worship and praise Jesus for all He has done and is doing in her life.

Visit her website at www.francinerivers.com.

BOOKS BY BELOVED AUTHOR
FRANCINE RIVERS

The Mark of the Lion series
(available individually or as a boxed set)
- A Voice in the Wind
- An Echo in the Darkness
- As Sure as the Dawn

A Lineage of Grace series
(available individually or in an anthology)
- Unveiled
- Unashamed
- Unshaken
- Unspoken
- Unafraid

Sons of Encouragement series
(available individually or in an anthology)
- The Priest
- The Warrior
- The Prince
- The Prophet
- The Scribe

Marta's Legacy series
(available individually or as a boxed set)
- Her Mother's Hope
- Her Daughter's Dream

Children's Titles
- Bible Stories for Growing Kids
  (coauthored with Shannon
  Rivers Coibion)

Stand-alone Titles
- Redeeming Love
- The Atonement Child
- The Scarlet Thread
- The Last Sin Eater
- Leota's Garden
- And the Shofar Blew
- The Shoe Box (a Christmas novella)

www.francinerivers.com

CP0098